DENISE HAMILTON

"Engrossing."
— The Washington Post

LAST
LULLABY

"Gripping,
action-packed."
—Chicago Sun-Times

"Sexy and exciting

D0050136

AN EVE DI

$6.99 U.S.
$10.50 Can.

IF YOU WANT "MORE THAN A GOOD CRIME NOVEL"
(MICHAEL CONNOLLY), READ THE EXHILARATING
EVE DIAMOND SERIES FROM

DENISE HAMILTON

Uncovering murder on the Los Angeles streets leads
Eve Diamond into the mystery and foreboding
of the Mexican "Day of the Dead" in

SUGAR SKULL

"EXHILARATING."
— *Los Angeles Times*

"THRILLING."
— *Denver Rocky Mountain News*

Available from Pocket Star Books

ISBN 0-7434-8222-0

Don't miss Denise Hamilton's next
suspense-charged Eve Diamond novel

SAVAGE GARDEN

Coming soon in hardcover from Scribner

EAN

National bestselling author Denise Ham̲ 02/21
Diamond series "is the best thing to hit t̲ e
novel scene since Michael Connelly's H̲ $2.00
(Mystery Ink).

"Denise Hamilton and Eve Diamond are the real deal."
—*The Denver Post*

LAST LULLABY
Los Angeles Times bestseller
USA Today Summer Reading Pick

Nominated for the Southern California Booksellers
Association Award for Best Mystery

"Eve Diamond is sympathetic and believable. . . . She has
the right mix of street smarts, sass, and vulnerability. . . .
Hamilton is one of the brightest new talents to enter crime
fiction over the last few years."

—*Chicago Sun-Times*

"A well-plotted, unique mystery that cuts a wide swath
through Southern California's melting-pot landscape. . . .
Hamilton makes spending time with Eve worthwhile by
infusing in her humanity, vulnerability, and strength."

—*Sun-Sentinel* (Ft. Lauderdale, FL)

"A harried, varied, engrossing adventure. . . . Hamilton does
a beautiful job of describing L.A.'s neighborhoods and
unraveling its secrets."

—*The Washington Post*

"I wolfed down Hamilton's book in a single session—it's
that delicious a read."

—*Malibu Times*

"Hamilton [is] every bit as ambitious in tackling big-city corruption as Sara Paretsky. . . . Few readers will be able to resist her V. I. Warshawski with a tape recorder and a California tan."

—Kirkus Reviews

"So absorbing that you don't want to stop reading."

—Los Angeles Times

THE JASMINE TRADE
Los Angeles Times bestseller
Edgar Award finalist
A Booksense 76 Pick

"Gripping . . . intriguing . . . more than a good crime novel."
—Michael Connelly, author of *Lost Light*

"Hamilton['s] sharp eye, tough mind, and open heart give this novel its credibility, emotion, and compassion. . . . Revealing and unsettling."

—T. Jefferson Parker, author of *Cold Pursuit*

"The plot is a grabber and the book is a winner."
—The Washington Times

"An undeniably winning narrator: intelligent, impulsive Eve is sharp on the outside and vulnerable on the inside."
—Publishers Weekly

"Has all the plot twists and creepy characters one would expect from an L.A. noir thriller."
—Los Angeles Magazine

"An intricate story."

—USA Today

Books by Denise Hamilton

The Jasmine Trade
Sugar Skull
Last Lullaby

DENISE HAMILTON

LAST LULLABY

POCKET STAR BOOKS

New York   London   Toronto   Sydney

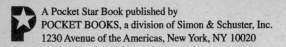

A Pocket Star Book published by
POCKET BOOKS, a division of Simon & Schuster, Inc.
1230 Avenue of the Americas, New York, NY 10020

Copyright © 2004 by Denise Hamilton

Originally published in hardcover in 2004 by Scribner

ISBN: 0-7434-8222-0

First Pocket Books printing April 2005

10 9 8 7 6 5 4 3 2 1

POCKET STAR BOOKS and colophon are registered
trademarks of Simon & Schuster, Inc.

Cover design by Jae Song

Manufactured in the United States of America

For information regarding special discounts for bulk purchases,
please contact Simon & Schuster Special Sales at 1-800-456-6798
or business@simonandschuster.com.

For Helene and Edward

CHAPTER 1

*L*ook lively, here comes Flight 1147."

We pressed our noses to the one-way glass and the parade began. A trickle at first, businessmen wheeling suitcases, cell phones already pressed to their ears. Then young couples in glitter platform shoes, bopping to Walkmans. Well-heeled families carrying duty-free bags, squinting into the fluorescent light to read the signs and line up in the right queue.

Then a pause in the traffic, empty spaces stretching out like ellipses. I scrutinized what the airplane's belly had disgorged, scanning for stains under silk armpits, restless eyes, hands clenching bags too tightly. They said even a preternatural calm was suspect, since it was normal to be frazzled after fourteen hours in the air, even if you had the patience of a Buddhist monk. Speaking of which, here came five of them, girded in saffron robes that ended in sandaled feet.

An elbow nudged my arm.

"Plenty a' room for contraband inside those layers," U.S. Customs Supervisor William Maxwell drawled lazily, watching the monks plod past.

I fingered my notepad, thinking that the monks looked more dazed than surreptitious.

"Don't you have dogs for that? Sniff out drugs and explosives and stuff?"

I realized as soon as the words left my mouth that bombs were a threat for those boarding, not getting off. If you were going to blow up an airplane, you'd do it in midair.

"One day they'll invent robo-dogs that sniff out jewels,

cash, and illegals, but for now we still rely on good instincts and bad paperwork," Maxwell said, scanning the crowd.

His eyes shifted to an Asian woman walking behind the monks, and I wondered if his interest was professional. She was tall, with a heart-shaped face and freshly applied lipstick. She wore a pantsuit of raw raspberry silk and carried a slumbering little girl over her shoulder. Behind her came the husband, pushing an elephantine cart heaped with luggage. Balancing precariously on top was a large bag that said, TOKYO-DISNEYLAND.

"You really think those monks are carrying?" I asked, more to make conversation than because I thought so.

"Prayer books, maybe," he said evenly. "But skepticism is a virtue. We caught some grief last week for pulling apart a Mexican grandma's wheelchair. She and the granddaughter got on their cells, jabbering to the consulate about their rights being violated. Had no idea what was packed inside those hollow metal tubes."

"Granny was a drug mule?"

Maxwell snorted. "My black homegirl was hitching a ride."

I thought I might be missing something because we were both staring out the window while trying to carry on a conversation.

"'My black homegirl'?"

Now some businessmen moved past in trench coats. Tall and blond, with glacier-blue eyes and the slanted cheekbones of the Russian steppes. Behind them sauntered two young Asian men, elaborately casual, their hair iced up. One had a camera around his neck. The other clutched a map of Hollywood. Props, I thought. Way too obvious. Here's a pair I would watch. I looked to see if Maxwell had noticed the same thing, but his gaze swept right past them.

"Heroin," Maxwell said. "Ten kilos of uncut tar. It's black and sticky and La Eme moves a lot of it across the border. Worth an easy five million on the street. They call it 'my black homegirl' to throw off the FBI phone intercepts."

La Eme was the Mexican Mafia. From the letter *M*. I knew that much from growing up in L.A. La Eme's tentacles snaked through the barrios and prisons of California and they laundered their money through juice bars and video stores.

"What about those guys?" I pointed to the Asian punks. "There's something off about them. Like, if they're so cool, why are they clutching all that tourist stuff?"

But he was watching three Asian women stroll past, big rocks on manicured fingers, strands of pearls, designer handbags. They were young but stout, in elegant, loose-fitting dresses and matching jackets.

"How much you wanna bet they're Korean and ready to pop?" Maxwell said.

I studied them. What crime slang was he lobbing at me now?

"Preggers," said Maxwell. "And loaded. They fly over here to give birth so their babies will be U.S. citizens. Big-time status. Shop and play tourist, stay at a fancy hotel till they drop the kid. Then skedaddle on back to Seoul. There's no law against it, but still . . ."

"You mean they don't want to stay?" For some reason, I was insulted on behalf of my country. Wasn't this the Promised Land?

Before he could answer, a large clot of tired humanity poured into the room on the other side of the glass and began to sort itself into lines. This was the last layer of the plane to be excavated, and it revealed the pitiless archaeology of overseas travel. First had come the rested countenances of first class, airplane royalty from both sides of the Pacific. Then the still-groomed, monogrammed, and pampered business class. And now the flying rabble, the pack I joined when I flew, we of the plasticine food and cramped leg space, the great unruly masses of economy—cranky, disoriented, and sleep-deprived.

My gaze lingered over a swarthy man with black hair. His clean-shaven face bore the unmistakable imprint of the Levant. The plane had originated in Beijing, with stops in Seoul and Tokyo with a final destination of LAX, where I stood now. Would he be pulled aside automatically? I wondered, getting an inkling, for the first time, how difficult it must be to look at people's papers and faces and make split-second decisions that could affect national security.

Not that I was here on anything quite so exalted. I was a reporter for the *L.A. Times,* and after the terrorist attacks of September 11, inquiring minds wanted to know how the government screened passengers. So U.S. Customs had set me up with a high-ranking official named Maxwell. I was shadowing him for a day before demystifying the process for *Times* readers. And there would be plenty of art. My star fotog, Ariel Delacorte, was out there among the disembarking passengers, shooting away. Weighed down by cameras and the shapeless khaki vests that all shutterbugs love, Ariel still managed a casual elegance, her posture erect as a ballet dancer's, her wavy black hair cut smartly to her sculpted jaw.

I turned to ask Maxwell about the Middle Easterner but he was halfway out the door, speaking into a crackling two-way radio.

"Yeah, that's them," he said. "Pinkie and the luggage coolie. Remember, it's hands-off. Send them through with a smile. I'll be right over."

I took two steps after him. "Stay here," he said. He pushed me back and I saw his hand go to his belt. "I won't be a minute."

The door closed behind him. By the time I recovered enough to run and yank it open, the hallway was empty.

I turned back to the one-way glass window. One of the

blond businessmen was gesticulating to a U.S. Customs inspector. He dug into his bags and pulled out some papers, which he threw down. The inspector shook her head.

The man looked around, as if enjoining his line-mates to commiserate. People were packed in tight, blocked by suitcases and carts, restrained into orderly lines by shiny black nylon ropes, children running around.

Then without warning, he pushed through the crowd, elbowing other passengers aside. At the same time, I saw lights flash and felt the glass rattle in sharp, staccato shivers. Someone out there was shooting.

As bodies crumpled to the floor, I wondered whether they had been shot or were just taking cover. The crowd surged and shoved as people tried to break loose of the Immigration holding area. On the other side of the glass, a jeweled hand rose up, vermilion nails clawing two inches from my face, before sinking back into the roiling mass. I saw a flash of raspberry as the smartly dressed Asian woman and her husband floated past, propelled by the mob. They slammed momentarily into the other blond businessman, then bounced apart. I noticed the woman no longer held her child.

On the other side of the glass, people were stampeding past the kiosks as security guards sought to push them back. One guard brandished a gun, then got down on one knee, sharpshooter style. Good Lord, they can't shoot into a crowd of people, it's going to be a massacre, I thought. The glass rattled again, and I ducked instinctively, hoping it was bulletproof as well as one-way.

Now here came one of the Asian punks, doing the Olympic high hurdles as he sailed over mounds of luggage and passengers who shielded their heads in 1950s duck-and-cover style.

The second Asian punk came into view, running for the exit. He had a gun and was yelling something. Nobody paid any attention. People pushed through the door, faces contorted in terror. After the July Fourth LAX massacre at the El Al counter, no one was taking any chances.

I realized I had been crouched at the window, peeking through my hands like a frightened toddler at the pandemonium on the other side of the glass. But I was a reporter, I needed to get in there. I ran to the door, threw it open, and stepped into a corridor, only to find a mass of people fleeing toward me, wild-eyed and disheveled.

"No," a man panted, grabbing my arm. "Go back. Terrorists. Shooting."

Ignoring him, I ran the way he had just come. Bursting through a set of double doors into the large room I had just been observing from the one-way glass, I saw a middle-aged man with blood on his face and a dazed expression. A teenaged girl sobbed and knelt on the dirty floor by a woman who looked unconscious. Sirens split the air, and a recorded voice calmly urged passengers to keep moving in an orderly manner.

On the other side of the room, I saw several crumpled bodies. I recognized the Slav man who had bolted. He lay on the ground with one arm outstretched, as if felled while playing tag. A morbid curiosity propelled me closer. Bright red blood matted his flaxen hair. One cheek was pressed against the linoleum, and I noticed grayish gunk splattered across the pale skin and clinging to his suit lapels. With a start, I realized it was the man's brains.

Five feet away, the second Slav businessman lay in a tangle of limbs and blood, entwined with the pretty Asian mother. It looked as though they had collided while trying to flee. The front of the woman's raspberry silk outfit was spotted with blood, fibers charred where the bullets had gone in. My eyes flickered over to the man. An explosion had detonated on his chest. I force myself to stare, to record every detail, ignoring the prickles of fear radiating outward from my spine. The "bolt" reflex was coming on strong.

More than anything, I wanted to flee, to run out of this terminal, back to my car, and out of the airport. What if at this very moment someone with a dirty bomb was preparing to detonate it? Part of me did run screaming out of that airport, shaking with fear and babbling incoherently. I let her go. Then I stepped forward. I had a job to do.

Where was the little girl this dead woman had been carrying just moments earlier as she stepped blithely toward Customs? I prayed she was still alive. There were more police and security now, their bodies beginning to block the carnage, but as they moved and space opened in odd geometric angles, I looked for a snub nose. A tiny arm. A head I could cup in one palm. And saw nothing.

My fingers hurt from gripping the pen so tightly. Unclenching them, I jotted down what I had seen. First impressions were important, even scattered and disjointed ones. Later, we'd unravel them for clues. Something teetered in the upper corner of my vision and I flinched. But it was just Ariel, who had climbed atop a pile of suitcases for a better shooting angle. As the machine-gun patter of her film advanced, people dove behind luggage and covered children with their bodies until they realized that the noise came from a camera.

On the other side of the room, Maxwell was screaming into his two-way. I walked over and saw that his men had the Asian punks on the ground, hands cuffed behind their backs. They writhed on their bellies, heads cranked sideways, jaws gaping as if they were some weird pupae begging to be fed. Seeing this, Ariel leapt off her luggage mountain and ran to photograph them. This seemed to enrage the men, who hollered at her to stop and averted their faces.

"Three dead," Maxwell was saying urgently into his radio, "Asian female and two Caucasian males. We're checking. Yeah."

There was a long pause. Part of me expected Maxwell to

blow his whistle any minute now and announce that the emergency preparedness drill was over. Then the "bodies" would get up, dust themselves off, strip off the shirts with the paintball blood, and go back to their usual business.

"Don't know about the males," Maxwell said into the radio, "but Interpol Tokyo alerted us about the family. I called INS but then all hell broke loose. And now Mom's dead and Crypto-Dad's MIA."

"Are you charging them with murder?" I asked, looking at the guys on the ground.

Maxwell ignored me.

He listened as a faint voice crackled on the other end of the two-way. His lips drew together into a thin line and he seemed to whiten under his L.A. tan.

"Son of a bitch," he said softly. He hooked the radio back onto his belt, turned slowly, and glared at the captives. Then he shook his head.

"Help these gentlemen up," he ordered, drawing the word out with a sneer.

"Are they terrorists or what?" I asked.

I knew al-Qaeda didn't just recruit Middle Easterners. The South Asian archipelagos were said to be awash with Muslim fundamentalists.

Maxwell focused on me. It looked as if he was trying to remember who I was. He scratched an ear.

"We are in the middle of a triple-murder investigation as well as two undercover-criminal operations. You'll have to leave. And you," he turned to Ariel, "will have to hand over that film."

Ariel Delacorte removed the camera from her face. Her eyes were a deep, translucent green. She slid the camera into her shoulder bag, tucked a strand of hair behind her ear, and said, "You'll get their names for the captions, won't you, Eve?" Then she turned on her booted heel and strode out the door without a backward glance.

"Fine," Maxwell yelled after her. "We'll let the lawyers duke it out."

He turned back and I nodded, eager to appear more sympathetic than frosty Ariel. I would *never* do such a thing.

"What happened back there?" I asked, shifting nervously as the Customs police roughly hauled up the two Asian men. They wore a look of angry vindication that confused me. Here I was, a reporter, an eyewitness, but I had no idea what had just gone down. All I knew was that suddenly the place had exploded into gunfire and chaos.

Maxwell regarded the men.

"Let 'em loose. Yeah, that's right," he told his startled colleagues. "You heard what I said."

One of the freed men brushed off his jacket, took a step forward, and jabbed the air with a forefinger.

"That was fucked-up, Customs," he said. "Real fucked-up. Your career is over. Starting tomorrow, you'll be lucky to find work as a six-dollar-an-hour rent-a-cop."

Maxwell jeered. "That's your future, G-boy, not mine. Bigfoot blew it bad.

"These guys," he said wearily, turning to me, "are not terrorists. They are not murderers. They are undercover agents for the FBI. Fucking feds were tailing two mobsters from Vladivostok who are now lying here dead, and they neglected to inform us. Little lack of interagency communication by Bigfoot. Who doesn't care who they stomp on so long as they get theirs. Meanwhile, we're doing our own tail, some nasty folks out of Bangkok traveling with a kid. Couple weeks more and we'd a'taken down the whole operation. But these cowboys," he hooked a thumb at the FBI men, "blew everything sky-high when their guys tried to run. And now one of my little chickens is dead and the other's flown the coop. Goddamn it!"

He swept his cap off his head and hurled it onto the linoleum floor with a slap that made me start.

A heavyset woman in a white uniform and a name tag walked toward us. She was holding the groggy toddler with the designer clothes who belonged to the dead raspberry lady and her missing husband. The child couldn't have been more than two. Her pale cheek lay against the woman's blouse and she observed us with slack eyes. Her breathing was thick and rheumy. When she coughed, her thin frame shook and her plastic diaper crackled. But that was the only sound. Separated from her beautiful and dead mama, witness to the massacre that had just erupted, held tight by a total stranger, the child didn't cry. She didn't wail. She didn't utter a word. One impossibly small hand curled around the woman's neck. In the other, she clutched a teddy bear.

"She'll have a Japanese passport, but my guess is she won't speak a word of Japanese," Maxwell said. "Her papers will show she's traveled widely in the last six months, but never stayed anywhere long. She jets around with loving parents who give her anything that money can buy, but she don't look too happy to me.

"Who are you, little girl?" he asked softly. "And why did they leave you behind?"

or a moment, nobody said anything.

I tried to lasso my galloping thoughts. Dead Russian mobsters. FBI. Glamorous Asian couple, mother dead, father missing. Abandoned child.

"What makes you think her father isn't searching for this child right now?" I said. "Maybe they got separated in the melee."

Maxwell eyed me with something approaching sympathy.

"You obviously haven't read the case file."

"Show it to me."

"I can't." He turned away.

"Yes, you can. You invited me here to watch you catch bad guys."

His face twisted as he watched the FBI men walk over to the airport police and pull out badges.

"Oh yeah. Bad to the bone. That's what today's catch was. Trouble was, they were our own bad guys. Goddamn bureaucracies are way too big. Nobody talks to each other, everyone's too busy protecting their little fiefdom."

And now a skirmish had broken out among the competing armies. Maybe I could use that to my advantage.

"Three people are dead, Maxwell. Tell me what just went down."

He just rubbed his face and blinked.

I gave him a minute, then stepped toward the uniformed woman holding the child. Her name tag read, CORVA LIPPMAN, AIRPORT SECURITY SERVICES, INC. She was plump and motherly, but her eyes were hard.

So I made mine soft. That wasn't difficult when I looked at the child.

"What's your name, wee one?" I said.

Tentatively, I reached out two fingers and stroked the rose-petal skin of her forearm. I thought she might recoil, but the child stared at me with lassitude. Her pigtails were tied with pink silk bows that matched her mother's outfit. Her legs, encased in pretty pink tights, dangled against the woman's bosom like a rag doll's.

"Get away from her, Diamond," Maxwell said. "You will not be conducting this interview."

"Can I sit in?"

"No."

He took out his wallet and extracted a card.

"Call my office tomorrow and we'll reschedule this visit when things calm down."

The tone of his voice brooked little dissent. I looked over at the FBI men, who were walking away. Should I run after them or stay here and work Maxwell? For a moment I despaired. A wrong move would cost me the story. And whisk me farther away from that child, whom I suddenly wanted to help. I closed my eyes and squeezed them tightly, coaxing forth somebody from deep inside, somebody I didn't like very much and usually kept under lock and key. But she had her uses.

"Calm won't cut it, Maxwell. The story's just morphed from soft feature into hard news. Two of them, actually."

I ticked them off on my fingers.

"Your banner headline is 'FBI Shootout at LAX Leaves Three Dead.' Underneath that you've got 'Russian Mobsters Killed in Firefight' and 'Mother Killed, Father Missing, Authorities Seek Identity of LAX Toddler.' Greedy guts that I am, I'd like to write both the suckers, but the other three are dead and she's here, so my money's riding on the pigtails. Who is she, Maxwell, and how does she fit into the big picture?"

He ignored me and motioned to several of his men, ready to give them instructions and move on. Leave me in his dust.

"C'mon, Maxwell. The wires are already warbling to every news outlet in the city. People are jittery. Everyone's on red alert and you just had a massacre in there. The public is going to want reassurance that it's not some new terrorist incident. And they're going to want details."

"They can get them at the press conference." He turned to go.

"I already have some of those details," I said slowly. "I don't know exactly who shot who and why, but I can describe that Asian couple pretty well. And the Russians too. I saw the firefight and how your agency and the FBI screwed up. I don't know what it adds up to, but I think the public would find it very interesting."

The skin around his eyes tightened.

"What were we supposed to do, open fire in a terminal filled with people? That would have been insanity."

"Obviously not everyone shared your squeamishness."

"It will take the LAX surveillance cameras and lots of legwork to reconstruct what happened," Maxwell said. "But the Feebs are claiming one of the Russians started it."

"Why?"

Maxwell shrugged. "Desperation. Thought the noose was tightening. But let Bigfoot tell you."

From the corner of my eye, I saw more uniformed guards. It was a little late for reinforcements. But instead of heading toward us, they marched on down the corridor, stone-faced, escorting a phalanx of dark-skinned, black-haired men who looked to be from the Indian subcontinent. Most kept their heads down as they passed, and I caught a whiff of humiliation and shame. Mouths set in anger and resignation, all of them tugging gigantic suitcases and card-box boxes lashed with rope. They kept coming, seventy or more, most of them youngish and skinny, all of them male.

"What the hell is that?" I asked Maxwell, who had also stopped to stare.

"INS action," he said.

"What?"

"Pakistanis. Overstayed their visas. After nine-eleven, government's been rounding them up."

"Fucking amazing," I said, wrinkling my nose as his words triggered something unpleasant. I thought of the Pakistanis I had met. Students, bellboys, graphic artists, taxi drivers, waiters, every last one of them sending paychecks home to extended families back in Karachi or wherever.

I studied their faces as they shuffled past, searching for something that would illuminate their innermost lives to me. That would reveal an ember of concealed fanaticism that might erupt in the conflagration we all feared. Were there terrorists among them? If not, there might well be in several years, as anger and shame at their treatment percolated back home.

"So they just stick them all on a plane and ship them back?"

Rounding them up, I thought. Words that smacked of cattle cars and deportation camps. Of hate-filled speeches. Of people singled out for one reason only.

"And good riddance," Maxwell said. "What should we do, offer 'em citizenship after they've broken our laws? They get treated humanely. Three in-flight movies and two meals. *Halal*, mind you. It's not like they put 'em in cargo with the pets."

I saw the hollow eyes in the dark faces, and felt queasy suddenly to be living in this black-and-white world where everyone had perfect moral clarity. Everyone except me.

"I hadn't heard about mass deportations," I said.

"INS didn't exactly send out a press release," Maxwell

said. "Get the human rights groups out, waving banners."

"Well, maybe they should have," I said darkly.

We fell silent then, out of some complicit unease at how the world had changed.

Any other day, the Pakistani roundup might land on Page One. But not today, with a slaughter at LAX. That was the crapshoot of journalism. Your disaster competed with everyone else's. I remembered how after 9/11, news unconnected to the attacks had ceased to exist. It had been the perfect time for military juntas to seize power. For energy companies to collapse. For evildoers the world over to act with impunity. The great journalistic eye was turned inward, weeping inky tears of sorrow.

"Are the dead people connected in any way?" I asked Maxwell.

His eyes glinted. "Too early to tell. You saw as much as I did, maybe more if you were still watching through the glass when it started," he said.

"It was chaos down there, I don't know what I saw. So help me piece it together."

"That's what our ballistics guys are doing right now."

"Fine. But the backstory, Maxwell. I need the backstory."

There was only silence.

"It sounds like neither the Russians nor the Asian couple knew you guys were tailing them," I finally said. "But their friends out in La-La Land will after they read my story. I have no choice except to write what I saw," I said cheerfully, "unless you deal me in."

He looked at me in disgust. "I'm trying to keep the borders safe so America can rest easy at night and you give me this shit?"

"You telling me they're all involved with terrorism?"

"Don't go jumping to conclusions."

"How can I do anything else when you won't talk to me? You know you can trust me, Maxwell."

"You're becoming a pain in the ass. Worrying me like a terrier worries a rat."

"You are not a rat," I said. "Not even a rodent, unless it's Mighty Mouse. Swooping in to save the day."

I looked off into the distance. We both knew I was shoveling it. But just because you know something doesn't mean it can't work. Besides, banter was the only way I knew right now to take the edge off the black reality that three people lay dead across the room.

"Give me an hour," he said finally. "Then come to my office. If I'm not there, the secretary will find me."

"Don't screw me," I said with an urgency that surprised me.

They were evacuating the terminal, and I had to show my press pass to jumpy officials about a dozen times before reaching a safe place. I found a neon sign that said BAR and sat down. Only then did I begin to shake.

Bluffer, bluffer, I told myself, putting my reporter's pad on the plastic table to review my notes. You've got nothing for a story and he knows it. He won't even show, he just said that to get rid of you. But his promise was a lifeline and I clung to it.

As I waited, I replayed the scene in my head, going over the key players, the shots, passengers hitting the floor, the jerky flow of people escaping, the utter pandemonium. But my thoughts kept getting rattled. I couldn't help staring at the people hunched over the bar, sleeping in seats, hurrying by, intent on catching flights. We were all casing each other, casting furtive glances, everyone trying to play cop and shrink and figure out if there was a monster among us.

I used to love airports, the freedom they conveyed, portals into other worlds, colorful crowds swirling in a babble of languages. But all that had irrevocably changed on September 11, 2001. Now you scanned the faces and the clothes around you and you judged. And what did my fellow travelers make of me, with my shaky limbs, darting eyes, perspiration curling tendrils along my forehead?

The cell phone jangled.

"Eve Diamond," I stuttered.

"What the hell is going on down there? Wires say three dead, the entire international terminal is being evacuated due to a possible terrorist massacre. Someone sprayed a waiting room with gunfire?"

It was Tom Thompson, my editor. I pictured him loosening his tie and squeaking his chair in the corner office thirty miles away in the San Gabriel Valley, his eyes wild and agitated. I didn't usually roam so far afield. But with the ever-expanding terrorism coverage, every bureau had been ordered to help out and my draft number had come up today.

"Three dead is right," I said, "but the shootings don't appear to be connected to terrorism."

I explained briefly about the FBI, Russian mobsters, the U.S. Customs investigation into the Asian family, and the abandoned little girl, saying I'd have more after Maxwell briefed me. "Ariel caught most of it. She's on her way in."

"Jesus, Eve, I could stick you in an empty intersection and within five minutes, there'd be a five-car pile-up. It's like you've got radar."

"I write good too."

"Don't go getting a swelled head," Thompson said. "Metro has three reporters on their way to LAX. And we'll get someone on the federal crime beat to track the Russky angle. You stay and see what you can find out on the kid. Might be nothing if the dad shows up to claim her. 'Big mistake. So sorry.'"

"Maxwell doesn't think that's going to happen."

Exactly one hour later, I found myself in Maxwell's empty office. It smelled as if someone had been dabbing eau de nicotine behind his ears and spilled the bottle. One wall was plastered with smudgy "Wanted" posters from Interpol, their corners yellowed and curling. Mounted against another wall were banks of video monitors, flickering with black-and-white images, a kaleidoscope of crowd shots—people walking down corridors, bent over laptops, standing in the numbingly tedious lines of LAX.

The chair behind the desk had one of those seats with large plastic beads that New York cabbies favor. The poor man's massage. I wondered if Maxwell had a bad back. I sure would have one from all the stress and pressure. The secretary assured me he'd be back in a moment, he was in a briefing down the hall. I hoped she was right. She had led me in and closed the door to the outer office, but the phone rang nonstop and I wished she had left it open so I could eavesdrop. Maxwell's desk was a mess of police reports, computer printouts, manila files, crumpled packages of chips and empty containers of vending machine candy.

It was twenty minutes before he came in, which gave me time to examine a fiberglass whiteboard on which someone had outlined the organizational flowchart of a criminal enterprise that looked exactly like that of a multinational corporation, down to the way it spread across five continents. In the bottom corner was a picture of a grinning Maxwell with his arm slung around Sylvester Stallone, who looked groggy and puffy-faced as he came off a plane.

Maxwell sat down heavily. "You've got five minutes," he said. "Now what can I do for you?"

"Who killed those people and why?"

"Internal FBI investigation's under way," he said. "Airport police too. Preliminary interviews indicate that one of the Russians fired first. LAX security may have taken him down, we're checking ballistics. Feds got off a few rounds. Nothing conclusive on anything until we get the tests back."

This was good. I wrote it all down.

"Got any names for me?"

"They're working on it," he said.

"What about an ID on the dead woman?"

He picked up a bag of Fritos and squinted into its shiny depths, then tossed it across his desk in disappointment.

"We're running everyone's names through the computers. Gotta cross-reference all the aliases."

"Were the Asians and the Russians connected? Did the woman get caught in the cross fire, or was it a takedown?"

"Good question. We'll need more time to answer that."

The flow of information was sputtering to a halt.

"Why was the FBI tailing the Russians?"

He gave me an inscrutable look. "You'll have to ask them."

I had figured as much. Well, Metro was working that end of it from downtown.

"Why were you following that family?"

"Next question," he said.

I sighed. "So where's the girl?"

"INS custody."

"Where? Does Department of Children's Services get involved?"

"You got me."

I dug my nails into my thigh, but casually, so he wouldn't see my frustration. I felt like screaming. Instead, when I spoke, my voice was low and modulated. It was an overcompensation thing I had.

"Look, Maxwell, I have exactly four hours to write a story saying what happened back there, who the dead people are, who the girl is, and why you were trailing her parents. I thought we had a deal. But I need more. You know I won't burn you."

He stared at me and flipped through some papers on his desk.

"Like they won't know exactly who leaked," he said. "You've only been with me all day. What I told you is all I'm authorized to give out right now."

Which meant there was more.

"The way I see it we've got INS, FBI, U.S. Customs, airport police, LAPD, and probably a passel of private security involved. It could be anyone. Just walk me through it."

He studied me for a moment, as if trying to decide something. Then he looked at the door, so I did too. It was closed.

"Not for attribution, or else I'm not saying another word."

"Then who do I hang it on?" I said.

He looked like he was wondering the same thing.

"How about 'a law enforcement source close to the investigation'?" I suggested.

He thought about it. "I guess that's sufficiently fuzzy."

"So, I take it the missing dad hasn't shown up."

"Correcto," Maxwell said.

"Were they her real parents? I heard you call him Crypto-Dad."

The eyes flickered back down to me, assessing and probing. "We're not sure."

"Okay, but what do you think?"

He examined a hangnail. "No."

"Then who are they? And why the false papers?"

"We're investigating everything."

"Have you found out the family's nationality? And what's the procedure when a kid just washes up on our shores?"

"I don't know. I'm not shitting you. It doesn't happen that often. Not with babies, at least. There's usually a parent or relative involved so INS keeps them together at Terminal Island Detention."

"But what about the Department of Children's Services? Couldn't they stick 'em in a foster home?"

The phone rang, shrilly and insistently. He picked up the receiver, listened, and said he was just finishing up.

"One minute left," Maxwell told me. "DCS would only get involved once the kid's in L.A. County. This kid's not technically in the United States yet. She's in Immigration limbo. The INS hasn't approved her tourist visa. That's what she came in on, by the way."

I wrote it down. *Limbo*, I thought, flashing to the Baltimore Catechism of my childhood. It was where unbaptized babies went when they died, sentenced to an eternity suspended in a netherland between heaven and earth. I imaged the tiny girl, floating with thousands of others of every race and nationality, all of them crying, tiny wings fluttering as they hurled themselves against the electrified borders of Limbo in search of a way out.

"And Japanese passport, you said?"

"Yeah, but our boys think it's a fake. A very good fake. INS has a Japanese-speaking clerk who tried to talk to her, but she's either deaf or she don't speakie Japanesie."

"So what's next?"

"We're going to trot out some more interpreters and let them take a whack at her."

"Thai, maybe? You said the family was out of Bangkok."

"Most recently. But it's a regional hub. Doesn't mean much."

"And in the meantime, where'd you stash her?"

"You've asked me that three times. And I'm getting tired of repeating myself. I'm just Customs. They don't tell me a blessed thing." His voice rose petulantly. "So take it up with INS and then you can enlighten us both."

"Why all the secrecy? They worried about her safety?"

He snorted. "It's a turf war. INS wants to keep her locked up and incommunicado until they can get her a one-way flight back across the Pacific. The Feebs want to debrief and use her. The L.A. bureau chief's got a lot to prove after that spying scandal. The girl could redeem things if she leads them to the folks responsible for today's carnage."

"And how would a toddler do that?"

Maxwell's upper lip curled.

"She wouldn't have to *do* anything. Just sit pretty. They'd come to her. To reclaim their property. Or at least neutralize it. And when they showed their ugly faces, the Bureau would pounce."

I was aghast. "They'd use a toddler as bait?"

"They wouldn't call it that. And they'd deny she was ever in danger. But don't worry, I have a feeling the INS is going to win this one. They've got possession, and that's ninety-nine percent of the law. They'll have her on a plane within two days."

"To where? They don't even know what country she's from."

"Makes no difference. Any one of our allies would take her. They can stick her in a relocation camp until they figure it out."

I thought of the rheumy-eyed child, her raspberry limbs dangling from the INS matron's arms, and felt the slow burn of outrage.

Maxwell was watching my reaction and I got a weird feeling he didn't approve either. He had already told me more than he should. Confused, I fingered my notepad and tried to keep him talking.

"I appreciate you meeting with me, when you're in the middle of a murder investigation and all. So what about this surveillance operation?"

"This is deep background. I don't want to see anything in the paper. Are we understood?"

I nodded.

"Our records indicate the kid's made five flights this year. All accompanied by two adults. She sleeps the whole way. Family claims they're here on vacation, the kid is crazy for Disneyland, Universal Studios. The beach. They flash jewelry and cash. Fancy toys. Nice clothes."

"Five times? A toddler?"

"Dad's a businessman."

"What do you think?"

Maxwell picked up a coffee mug. He lifted it and sniffed, his nose wrinkling in distaste at the white curds sloshing in brown liquid. "Do you know anyone who takes five vacations a year?"

I shrugged. "*Times* travel writers."

Maxwell leaned back in his chair. He picked up a pen and traced a staple mark on the corner of a legal document. "Well, there you go. We suspect this involves trafficking or contraband of some kind."

I threw his drug lingo back at him. "'My black home-girl'?"

His lip curled on one side like he was trying not to smile. "'S' only the Mexs call it that."

Whoops, there went the goofy reporter again, thinking she knew everything and getting it wrong. Such a person could not possibly pose a threat. You could lower your guard and relax a bit. And he did. He leaned back in his chair and launched into a lecture.

"Mexican heroin is brown 'cause it's less refined. Asian heroin is called China White on account of the color, and it's ninety percent pure. From the Burma–Chinese border. They stuff it in a condom, slather it with honey so it goes down smooth when you swallow it. Crap it out once they get here. It bursts inside them, they die."

My eyebrows went up. "They'd make a child swallow a condom of heroin? That's absolutely revolting. She did seem lethargic and sick."

What kind of people would do that to an infant? I wondered. And what kind of law enforcement types would watch a sick kid enter the U.S. with fake papers five times in a row, know she was being used for some unscrupulous end, and not do anything about it? That was equally revolting. And now to send her hurtling back into limbo? There was a sick equation at work here: a child's welfare versus shutting down a smuggling ring. In this algebra, the kid's value was nil. And I had just become part of the problem. I was privy to this too now. But I wanted a story and I didn't want my access shut down before I got it.

"Not that kind of sick," Maxwell said. "She'd be convulsing and frothing blood and dead in an hour."

"So maybe she's just sick from bad airplane air." I shrugged, knowing that wasn't the case. I had seen her clammy skin, heard the deep cough.

We surveyed each other across the messy desk.

"Can I get a copy of everyone's passport photos? Especially the kid's?"

"What for?"

"I want to stick them in my wallet, take 'em out and look at 'em from time to time. Why do you think?"

"Don't be a wiseacre."

"Well?"

"The deceased should be no problem. As for the kid, I don't know if we want her photo plastered on everything from newspapers to milk cartons. I'll think about it. Time's up," he said, getting out of his chair.

"Fair enough," I said. "Now, if you were a reporter, what would you do next?"

That's a favorite line of mine. It buys you time and flatters their ego and loosens them up. And almost always, it yields a nugget of intelligence that you didn't already know.

"I'd call INS. Talk to John Suggs. Just don't tell him who gave you the name. Good luck. I've got to get out of here. But first I want you to do something for me," Maxwell said. "I want you to yell and scream and call me all sorts of names and then stomp out of this office because I haven't told you anything."

"A bit late for that. We've been cloistered in here ten minutes."

He smiled. "But reporters are persistent. It's taken you that long to accept the word *no*. My supervisor, Scott Aiken, and his boss are in the conference room off of the reception area and I want them to hear you loud and clear. It will work better than any protestation I could make."

I opened the door, already raising my voice.

"I wait a goddamn hour for this? How the hell am I supposed to write a story when you won't tell me what went down? You can just kiss your Customs puff piece goodbye," I said, slamming the door behind me.

He opened it and followed me, watching me huff into the outer office. The conference-room door opened two inches and a crew-cut head poked out. He had steel in his eyes and "ex-military" tattooed all over his jaw.

"Scott Aiken," Maxwell said. "I'd like you to meet *L.A. Times* reporter Eve Diamond. She's having herself quite a tantrum because I won't play with her."

Scott Aiken flicked a pen. "You'll have to wait for the press conference, Ms. Diamond. Roger that?"

"That's what I told her." Maxwell turned to me. "The press briefing is at four P.M. and—"

I was gone before he finished.

CHAPTER 3

I went back to the airport bar and ordered a sandwich and lemonade.

Then I called Suggs, the INS man whose name Maxwell had given me. He demanded to know how I'd gotten his name, but I sidestepped his question with one of my own and eventually he confirmed that the INS had taken custody of the toddler. They were calling her Yasuko Sakamoto for now because that was the name on her passport. He wouldn't tell me where she was being kept. He said it was for her protection.

"How's her health?"

"Her health?" He sounded surprised.

"She looked sick when I saw her."

"No comment."

"What's your next step?"

"We are trying to ascertain who she is and what country she's from and who her next of kin are so we can reunite them without delay. We are already in touch with several consulates."

So Maxwell had been telling me the truth.

"Such as?"

"I cannot reveal that."

"And then what?"

"We'll let you know when it happens."

After it happens is more likely, I thought. "Well then, can you please explain what you do with unaccompanied minors?"

"We put them in the least restrictive environment."

"Can you be more specific?"

Suggs told me that the INS contracted with a variety of agencies and places. It might be foster care. It might be a hotel. It might be juvenile hall.

"She's a toddler, Suggs. Since when is wetting your diaper a crime?"

There was a long silence at the other end of the line.

"Ms. Diamond," he said finally, "twenty years ago, we didn't have kids showing up here illegally without parents or relatives. The law was silent on the issue. But now we get sixty thousand each year, and we're doing the best we can. The truth is that juvenile hall is usually full to bursting anyway. And it takes a couple of days to get the paperwork together for the Department of Children's Services."

"So then. Hotel, is it?"

There was a pause, then "No comment."

I took that to mean yes but I couldn't be sure, and he retreated behind his bureaucratic barricades and wouldn't tell me any more. Frustrated, I hung up. Since minors enjoyed a broader swath of protection and privacy under the law, anything involving kids was always incredibly difficult to track down. But ah, the glittering riches that awaited the reporter who succeeded.

If I couldn't wrangle myself onto the dead-Russian-mobster assignment, with its tantalizing FBI links to organized crime across two continents, this was the next best thing. Missing and abandoned kids made for hot stories. Sure they were tragic, but they were also media catnip. But I'd have to get to her before the INS deported her and my story disappeared into the contrails above the blue Pacific. If I could find her and publicize her plight, people would be outraged and the INS would be forced to keep her here until they learned whom she belonged to and whether it was safe to send her back. Meanwhile, the publicity I generated would quash any Bureau plans to use her as bait. There was an odd, counterintuitive logic at work here, in which she'd be safer in the public eye. Hiding in plain sight. I wanted to help this little girl. But even if I couldn't find her, anything I did to advance the story would keep it on the front page another day, and that would help my journalistic stock. By becoming her advocate, I'd also be acting as my own.

I sat there thinking of what to do next. Then I remembered May-li, a teenager I had once tried to rescue. I had lost that battle, thanks to a rabbity little INS officer at Terminal Island who I now recalled owed me a big favor.

I still had the INS officer's business card in my wallet. I wasn't even sure why I had kept it. Reporter pack-ratting, I guess. But now I called. She was on duty. She remembered me, she said, her voice vibrating with unspoken questions: What did I want?

"Mrs. Locksley, if the INS had a toddler in custody without a parent, where would they put her?" I asked, explaining that I was working on an overview story for Metro. It was a lie, but I absolved myself with a vow to propose exactly such a piece to Thompson when I got back. I was counting on the fact that Mrs. Locksley wouldn't yet have heard about the abandoned kid her agency had just taken into custody.

"Why, I don't quite know. Usually they're with a family member."

"What about illegals in protective custody who are going to testify against their smugglers?"

"Well, that's easy," Mrs. Locksley said, warming once it grew clear that I didn't want information about a specific case. "We contract with several hotels near Regional. They give us a weekly rate."

"Which ones?" I asked. The INS regional headquarters was downtown.

"I'm not sure. But the INS is on a limited budget." Her voice was prim.

"So probably not five-star hotels."

"I'm sorry I can't help you more."

"Are they in downtown proper?"

"Near Chinatown, I think."

"Heard any names?"

"I couldn't say."

I repressed a sigh. "And what, they just check them in and wish them good luck? Or are they accompanied by an INS person? Do they get a meal allowance?"

"They're under our care; they're supposed to be supervised at all times."

"Thanks, Mrs. Locksley."

"Did you ever find that nice Chinese girl? I felt ever so awfully bad about that."

May-li. I still had nightmares about her.

"No," I said grimly. "But I'm still looking."

I hung up and looked at my watch. Chinatown was on the northern fringe of downtown, and I thought there might be time to swing by before deadline. On my way back to the office, I called in what I had learned and got the green light from Thompson to check out a few hotels.

My first stop in Chinatown was a pay phone. They don't dot the streets of Los Angeles like they used to. Cell phones have taken their toll. So has the disintegration of the urban core. Whores and IV-drug users ply their trade in phone boxes and scavengers rip them apart for scrap metal. So pay phones are going the way of the trolley car, the full-service gas station, and the elevator doorman, all those quaint throwbacks to an earlier, more civilized era.

I stopped in front of a restaurant with a red neon lobster whose tentacles beckoned invitingly. But it wasn't food I was after. Stepping around a puddle of mustardy vomit, I heaved the phone book onto the metal tray and copied two pages of addresses and phone numbers. I've learned the

hard way to be neat and methodical, to write things down
and cross them off once I've checked them out. Unless I got
terribly lucky, this wasn't going to be a one-day job.

There were tons of fancy hotels in the business district—
the Bonaventure and the Sheraton, the Standard and the
Biltmore, and I put those aside for now, figuring that a cash-
strapped federal agency was not going to put up illegals in
luxury while it figured out how to deport them.

Still, I wasn't sure they'd stick people in dumps either.
And I knew Chinatown had grown moribund in recent years
as the overseas Chinese began bypassing the traditional port
of entry and settling directly in the suburbs. Places like San
Marino, if you had big bucks. Alhambra and Monterey Park
for the middle class. Only the poorest immigrants still landed
in Chinatown, and that usually meant Southeast Asians,
people whose spirits had been broken and their job skills
rendered obsolete from too many years in relocation camps.

But the community took care of its own, and in the meantime, a fresh wave of invaders had washed over Chinatown
as the empty storefronts, crooked alleys, and fanciful archi-
tecture began drawing artists in search of cheap loft space.
A nighttime music and gallery scene had coalesced around
them. And Chinatown had grown hip again in a way that
hadn't been seen since the late 1970s, when punk impresa-
rios had made unholy alliances with Chinese matriarchs at
Madame Wong's and the Hong Kong Café to showcase their
bands. And thus was a new playground born.

Now, list in hand, I wondered where to begin and found
my answer down the street, at the Royal Pagoda, a name
that mocked its crude, stucco box construction. When I
walked in, a stooped young man behind the counter looked
at me quizzically. He knew I wasn't after a room.

I asked my question and couldn't tell if he understood me
or was hiding behind lack of language when he shrugged and
threw up his hands. I put a question mark next to the name and

left. Up the street I found a similar hotel, the Golden Palace. There, I got the same reception. Frustrated, I went around the corner and spied a third.

It was a narrow shoe box of a place painted a Mississippi-mud brown. When I strolled in, the hotel proprietor clicked his tongue in a knowing way. My heart quickened. Had a little girl come in? I asked. It would have been only an hour or so ago. I described her.

"No," he said. "Why you want this girl so much?"

Something in his tone made me pause. I knew how to conceal my intentions better than that.

I smiled apologetically. "I'm not the only one looking for her," I said, turning the screaming question in my brain into a nonchalant statement.

"Why everybody want her?"

For a moment, I didn't trust myself to speak.

"You second person," the man behind the desk chided me.

I nodded, as if it made perfect sense. "That must have been my colleague," I said, trying for a conversational tone. "The *Times* is so big, sometimes one section doesn't know what the other is doing so they send several reporters on the same story. Man, right? What did he look like?"

The clerk shrugged. "Young. Not fat, not thin. Black hair."

"I think I know him. Asian dude."

"Caucasian."

The man leaned over and spat. Despite myself, I looked down. The phlegm glistened in the fluorescent light. In the sudden silence, I realized the light fixture was buzzing. No more so than my brain. A white guy was looking for the little girl, I thought, puzzling out this new information.

"Did he by chance leave his name?"

"Card," the man said.

"He left his *Times* card?" I said, perpetuating the fiction. "Could I see it?"

The man leaned over the counter and opened a drawer. He pushed things around in a desultory fashion, then shuffled to another drawer and continued his search. He pulled out a business card and handed it to me.

"He not work for *Times*. But he nosy like you."

I reddened but took the card before he could snatch it back.

FRANK, someone had scrawled in blue ink across the top. There was no last name or address, just a PO box in Los Angeles and a phone number that looked suspiciously like a business's: 583-7000. I memorized it.

"Guess I'm thinking of some other guy," I said, handing the card back. "He didn't, uh, leave his last name, by chance?" I asked, my cheeks prickly with heat.

The man pointed to the card as if it were self-explanatory. I gave up.

I could feel his eyes on my back as I walked away. I knew he hadn't been taken in for a minute and that furthermore, he thought I was a braying ass. Oh well. I had what I wanted. My face was throbbing. When I got back into the car, I jotted down the numbers and drove to the office. Who else was looking for the girl? I would have expected Crypto-Dad to show up, but a Caucasian man? And it couldn't be law enforcement, because the INS already had her. Was it FBI? And what was so valuable about her, anyway?

I recalled how the INS had drawn a web of secrecy around the girl's whereabouts, saying it was for her own protection. It was a stock phrase they tossed out, but this time, I thought they might be onto something.

In the bathroom, I ran into Ariel Delacorte.

"Hey, Ariel," I said. "I love the way you handled those guys back there who wanted your film."

I smiled at the memory, but suddenly could see only the sprawled, desecrated bodies. I knew those gobbets of gray matter would swarm over my subconscious tonight, giving me revolting nightmares. There was something utterly transgressive in seeing what only a brain surgeon should ever lay eyes on, and even then, only reverently cradled and pulsing inside a human cranium. The camera in my mind now panned to the spreading crimson stains on the delicate raspberry silk, filling me with inexplicable sadness that no one would ever wear that beautiful pantsuit again. And the toddler, she'd have to put her matching pink hair bows in a faraway drawer . . .

Embarrassed, I pushed the thought away and looked at Ariel.

"You were right in the middle of that shooting," I said. *Were you scared?* I wanted to ask. Instead, I said, "Did it, like, remind you of Bosnia or Chechnya?"

Ariel observed me in the mirror as she washed her hands. She was several years older than me and radiated the tragic mien that came from documenting man's beastliness to his fellow man. Several years back, she'd won a Pulitzer for a photo-essay about three generations of a drug-addicted family living in a crack house south of downtown. The story had taken two years and nearly gotten her killed, and since then, the paper had pretty much let her do what she wanted. She favored long projects and I often saw her striding down the hallway at odd hours, her bags trailing like obedient pets, off to Liberia or Iraq to cover the wars. Then suddenly she'd pop up on a daily, craving the adrenaline rush of breaking news close to home. Like the rush we had gotten today.

"No," she said. "It was over much too fast."

Was that a tinge of regret in her voice?

"But imagine," Ariel said, "them telling me what I can shoot. They've got some nerve."

"Censorship, pure and simple," I agreed. "Prior restraint. But they're going to call the *Times* about keeping the girl's picture out of the paper. Says it could put her in danger."

Ariel lifted one shoulder, then slowly rotated and lowered it. "Pity. She's awfully striking."

The kid had struck me as paralyzed by illness and fear. But unlike Ariel, I wasn't focused on the aesthetics.

"Well, I guess the editors will sort that out."

Ariel turned and angled one black jersey–clad hip against the porcelain sink. "Well, those FBI guys certainly don't need to worry about me blowing their cover. When I edited the film, I realized their faces are obscured in the best shots."

I was glad about that. If I was going to pursue this story, I needed to stay on Maxwell's good side.

"It's the torque of their bodies on the ground that's arresting, not their faces," Ariel continued. "Brings to mind those people buried in ash at Pompeii. Speaking of relics, Harry wants to have a drink sometime. You and me and him. He says we're his favorite dames in the news business."

Harry was Harry Jack, a cantankerous old fotog who remembered the golden age of L.A. newspapering and was quick to reel out his stories of all the celebrities, murderers, and politicos he had shot in more than a half century on the job.

"I'm around," I said, trying not to appear too eager. Ariel was so damn intimidating.

"He trained me, you know," she said. "More than ten years ago, when I landed a summer internship here. None of the other interns wanted to work with him. They thought he was washed-up. A hack. But I was too green to care. We'd cruise around on assignment and he'd point out places like the Ambassador Hotel, where Robert Kennedy got shot. The strip on Sunset, where the original Trocadero nightclub used to be. The motel in South L.A. where the SLA and Patty Hearst shot it out with the FBI. Harry had photographed them all, and he'd tell me about it, then take me into the archives to pull the photos. I felt like I was on a Disneyland ride into the city's past."

"With a cranky commentary piped in from the driver's seat," I said. "Each time I see Harry, I want to turn on a tape recorder and capture it for posterity."

"He's why I always keep an old Leica in my bag along with the digital cameras. There's a purity to film. But he taught me that taking the picture is the least of it," Ariel mused. "First you have to establish a rapport with your subject. I thought a lot about that when I was practically living at that crack house. Harry said I was crazy but I told him, 'It's your fault, you taught me.' The worst was the kids. Half-starved bitty things."

Her eyes took on a sad cast, her mouth drooped. "I used to bring them food. They were so little."

Her wistful tone jogged a memory. Of waiting for the elevator and overhearing two women whispering sympathetically, something about a lost baby. The conversation had stopped with abrupt warning looks as Ariel walked up. At the time, I hadn't paid it much thought, and I didn't know her well enough to ask. But now I wondered about her own private loss and whether suffering had made her a more impassioned photographer. Could someone who was happy and content turn out masterpieces?

Before I could answer, I heard myself paged. Saying I'd call her for that drink, I ran back down the hallway to write my story.

Metro had paired me with Josh Brandywine on a double byline for the main bar. He had been working the FBI-Russian mobster angle and taking feeds from four reporters out in the field who were interviewing airport security, eyewitnesses, and LAPD. A fifth would call in notes from the press conference. My job was the U.S. Customs end of it, describing the melee and the bodies I had seen. Now I played up the information Maxwell had lobbed me and threw in a few boilerplate quotes from Suggs.

But mainly I wrote about the little girl, explaining how she was in INS custody at some undisclosed location and might be connected to an ongoing Customs investigation, although authorities wouldn't give any details.

From time to time, I glanced at the newsroom TV, which stayed on around the clock. If Maxwell released the child's passport photo, it would beam out at me, all pixels and light waves, and she'd probably look ordinary and unremarkable, like a million other little kids. All over the Southland, people would absorb her image as they mixed a martini after work. Ladled out macaroni to their kids. Drank coffee in cafés that resounded with Tagalog and Mixtec and Armenian. Would they shudder for a moment and thank God that it wasn't their kid? "At least it isn't one of those serial killers," they'd say. "It's not like she's been kidnapped, like that other one on the news last week."

Soon it would be saturation exposure in every living room and bedroom and bar and boardroom in L.A. County, a stark, unsmiling image, until she was like your kid sister, or the neighborhood brat you couldn't escape, and yet she'd remain oddly impersonal. You'd be able to pick her out of a crowd, but you wouldn't have any idea about her life. And there would be no grieving parents in front of the cameras, begging for their daughter's release. This time it was the parents who had turned up dead and missing, and the kid who was the cipher.

At the next pod over, Josh was crowing into the phone. Muttering about show-offs, I tuned him out and wrote, my fingers flying across the keys, composing in that deadline vacuum where time slowed and stretched into impossibly long segments, the flow of words somehow synchronizing with the minute hand so that both reached the finish line together at five o'clock, that first and most exalted of deadline holies. Then, with silent thanks for the daily transubstantiation of my profession, I leaned back in my chair and hit SEND.

Blinking my way back to real time, I stood up and checked on Josh's progress. He was still bent over his keyboard, pecking furiously. "Brandywine," came a gruff voice from the city desk, "you sending that story today or what?"

I smiled. Josh was both my nemesis and my friend. We competed lustily for stories but once they were put to bed, we went out for drinks and dissected how we could have done it better. And he owed me one. I knew something about his secret life that I kept to myself. But he knew things about me too. There was a tacit understanding between us not to expose the other's soft, white underbelly.

Now a stab of hunger reminded me it was dinnertime. I ransacked my purse and pulled out some nori—dry, seasoned seaweed that I bought by the bushel at a Korean supermarket—and crammed a thin rectangle into my mouth, chewing pensively as I reread my lead.

It was both the blessing and the curse of my profession that we disengaged so easily from death, even when it happened right in front of us. There was no room for hysteria. Anguish had to be immediately alchemized into words. On that morning when the planes had slammed into the Twin Towers, the CNN announcers had recounted the news as it broke, speaking with those calm, newscasterly voices as the world they knew collapsed around them, the only perceptible difference a slight tightening of the mouth, a downward cast to the eyebrows, a charged urgency to certain words. I had wondered then if I would pass such a test if called upon, and whether doing so would rob me of some essential humanity. I saw how it could become addictive, to shut off that part of yourself, to channel your emotions into clipped, precise words, to grow ever calmer as events spun further out of control, if only to prove to yourself that you had no fear. How you might embrace this emotional anorexia, strive to refine and purify your detachment. And then how you could go on doing it, long after your shift had ended and you went home to the rest of your life.

"Don't you ever just crave a burger and fries like a real American?" Josh asked, peeking over the divider to see what all the rustling was about. He must have finally sent the sucker. Now that deadline was over, his voice was exuberant and flirtatious.

I pulled myself back into the present and kept chewing. "You should talk, Mr. I-Grew-Up-Eating-Street-Food-in-Delhi-and-Nairobi."

Josh smirked. "That's exactly why I like burgers," he said. "I used to dream of them."

I took my time swallowing. Then I gave him my full attention.

"After my father died when I was sixteen, I got a part-time job at McDonald's to pay my prep school tuition," I said. "If I don't see another burger and fries the rest of my life, it will be too soon."

A gulf had suddenly opened up between us. Josh's father had been a celebrated foreign correspondent for *The New York Times* and he had grown up in posh boarding schools and world capitals. My immigrant father had worked for the local school district and nursed his private sorrows in a suburban tract home behind drawn curtains.

"I'm sorry. I didn't know," Josh said, then did the graceful thing and disappeared. I peeled open another packet of nori and went back to rereading my story.

Josh wasn't at his desk when I got the all-clear, and I was glad for that. Gathering my things, I headed into the library to find the reverse directory. It was like a regular phone book, only backward. You looked up the phone number and it gave you the address.

I pulled out the scrap of paper on which I had scribbled

the contents of the business card the clerk had shown me in Chinatown. Frank. With a PO box and that phone number: 583-7000.

Now I flipped through the reverse directory for Los Angeles. My finger was scanning the long lines when I found it. 1527 S. Western Avenue. I put that in Koreatown, south of Wilshire Boulevard. Maybe one of those stately prewar apartment buildings that had fallen on hard times. There was no unit number, but I could wing that when I got there.

A shadow fell across the directory and I looked up, a guilty red stain spreading across my cheeks.

"Wanna get a drink?"

It was Josh, who with his infallible radar had tracked me down. His eyes danced but his words mocked.

"Oh, what's this? A little reverse directory detective work? Not ready to throw in the towel tonight? Who are you tracking, my friend? A lead on the wee girlie that you're selfishly keeping all to yourself?"

He leaned back and crossed his arms with studied nonchalance. I had seen something similar on the Discovery Channel, the feline elaborately grooming itself, feigning disinterest in the prey.

"Some other night. And yeah, I'm just following a lead."

"Hot one?" His smile grew wider.

"Just a hunch. I feel like talking about it would jinx it."

I should have told him more. Later, I would need his help.

CHAPTER 4

I was paranoid enough to check my rearview mirror to make sure he wasn't following. It would be just like Josh to do that as a lark.

Sailing west on Beverly, I passed families hanging out on stoops and street corners, the occasional scooter-riding kid, weary mothers trudging home from the *panadería*, lustrous hair swinging in thick Indian braids. I saw one lady wearing a *huipil*, the traditional embroidered Indian dress. A baby wrapped in a colorful blanket rode at her chest. In one hand, she clutched plastic grocery bags. The other held tight to a toddler, who in turn clutched the hand of a slightly older child. I wondered where little Yasuko was spending the night.

At Western, I turned left and was immediately in Koreatown. I passed the big thoroughfares of Wilshire, then Olympic. Finally, I hit Pico. Several blocks after that I stopped to let a fire truck pull screaming out of a station. Then I saw it: 1527 South Western. It was an old brick apartment house seven stories high, with some kind of nightclub off the lobby at street level. The streets were thronged, the parking nonexistent. Tempting fate, I pulled up to an unloading zone. Nobody would be making deliveries until morning, unless it was booze for the club.

I walked to the lobby of the building and looked at the tenant directory. There were no Franks. In fact, most of the people didn't list any first name at all. I marveled at the United Nations of names arrayed before me, the saga of twenty-first-century immigration writ large and melodic: Singh,

Garcia, Kang, Husseini, Hakami, Su, Mesrovian, Bangalore, Silva, Patathorn, Liongosari, Poot.

Almost everything except Anglo-Saxons, which surprised me, actually, since artists driven out of Silverlake by escalating rents were colonizing Koreatown. But when I looked at the bones of the building before me, I realized this would not be one of their haunts. It wouldn't have the classic grandeur, the high ceilings and arched entryways, the deco tile and carved moldings, that they wanted. This building had always been a brick tenement.

I climbed the stairs and started knocking. An hour later, I was exhausted. And pretty sure Frank didn't live there.

As I hiked back down to the lobby, my ear was drawn by a rhythmic *rat-tat-tat* and loud voices from inside the club. Flamenco lessons? On impulse, I decided to go in. Maybe they knew Frank.

When I pushed in the door, I realized it wasn't the type of club I had expected. The patrons were young and hip, but there was no bar, no alcohol, no "scene." Instead, there was a long, dim room filled with rows of computer terminals. In front of each computer sat a young man wearing a headset. Their eyes were glued to the screen, fingers skittering across the keys like tap-dancing mice. The room was bathed in an eerie green light, as if I had plunged into the deep end of a pool. But there was also an intensity to the stillness. The place was awash in distilled adrenaline and testosterone, an acrid, rubbery, male scent. I had seen a similar grim intensity in Vegas. But these were kids, and all of them were hunting down little figures on the screens, machine-gunning them, lobbing grenades and scaling tall buildings to avoid getting murdered. As they played, instant messages popped up at the top of their screens.

Intrigued, I looked at their faces and saw blacks, Latinos, Asians, and whites. It was the rainbow nation. Pierced, tattooed, hip-hopped, and clustered around the high-tech campfire. If the mantra of the sixties had been "drop out, tune in, turn on," the twenty-first-century motto was the opposite, an onanistic, narcissistic cocooning into a machine: plug in, check out, and die with your finger on the electronic trigger.

Behind the counter, a bulletin board ranked players with the top scores. They had handles like Space Dawg, Raygun, and Slim Shooter. In a corner of the room, I saw soda machines with caffeine-fueled drinks like Red Bull and Mountain Dew, canned espresso and ginseng tea. Another machine held chips and candy bars. Next to the dispensers, four youths slumbered on couches and easy chairs, oblivious to the noise, their skin a waxy pallor, their hair lank, as though this was the first sleep they had gotten in days. One young man twitched repeatedly.

A sign said the terminals rented for $2 an hour, but there was not an empty seat in the house. Some even had cheering sections, young men crowding around the screen and egging the player on.

"Kill him, kill him, or I'll do it for you," one young man with coffee skin exhorted his pal.

I pictured Frank here, tapping out death, drinking one of those violently colored tapioca boba drinks that were all the rage, and wondered how I would know him. Why was he after the little girl?

Just then a loud argument broke out by the counter. I turned to see a young Latino boy yelling at the manager. He looked about ten. The manager just shrugged and turned his back. The kid yelled one last obscenity, kicked the counter, and stomped out the door.

I went up to the nearest cluster of guys. They looked annoyed to be wrenched from their game. Frank, I said. White guy. Know anyone by that name? They looked at me with slack disinterest. It was hard to tell if they were lying or just bored. The usual rules about body language didn't apply here, where vacant, averted eyes and twitching limbs seemed the norm.

I gave up and decided to ask the manager. He was a young African-American man with a goatee, horn-rimmed glasses, and shaved head. He watched my approach, his eyes big question marks, both of us aware that I was a trespasser who had ventured across one of the city's many unmarked borders.

"I'm looking for a guy named Frank."

"Who wants to know?"

I didn't think I'd get a warm reception if I said I was with the *L.A. Times.* So I clutched my throat nervously, smoothed back my hair, and leaned across the counter.

"It's about . . ." I turned my head to make sure no one was listening, ". . . about a baby."

He looked at me with indifference and I thought I saw his nostrils flare.

"And you are?"

I bit my lip. "Eve Diamond. I'll write down my number for you. He does get messages here, doesn't he? That's what he told me."

"Look, lady, I don't know what he told you. If I see him, I'll pass the word on. Will there be anything else?"

The words quivered in the air. There were other things he could deliver, I just had to name them. The problem was, I didn't know the inventory.

He looked disappointed when I told him no and took his hands out from under the counter. I looked around one last time. As I left, he was chalking something new on the black-board.

Outside, I looked up at the entrance and saw a sign I had somehow missed on my way in: CYBERNATION. 24-HOUR NON-STOP INTERNET CAFE.

Intent on reading, I almost tripped over a small figure sitting at the curb. I put my hand out to steady myself and grabbed a shoulder, which immediately slid out from under me as the child jumped up.

"Hey, lady, watch it."

It was the high, clear voice of a boy who has not yet reached manhood and overcompensates by bristling like a porcupine. I studied him for a moment, then realized why he looked so familiar. It was the sore loser from the cyber-cafe. Now he crept closer, right into my face.

"Don't you got five dollars you can give me? I want to go back in there and play some more."

For a moment, we sized each other up, two con artists who recognized a kindred spirit.

"What's your name?" I asked.

"Lorenzo Valdez," he said. "But everyone calls me Lil' Fist."

He stood, jaw outthrust, hair spiked into discreet mountain ranges and bleached a reddish blond at the tips. His clothes were baggy and dragging-on-the-ground loose. Up close, he looked about eight.

"Is that because you're so tough?"

He smirked. "It's cuz I be smashing all the records."

"You pretty bad?"

He did some kind of whirling kickboxing step that made me step back. I hoped he didn't have a gun tucked inside that loose clothing.

"I'm like Jackie Chan. Move so fast I *destroy* them."

"You like playing those games?"

"'Mortal Killer' is the best." He pumped his fist in the air.

"How much do you play?" I looked at his oversize jeans. His sheer mesh top. His $150 sneakers.

"Every chance I get."

"How many hours?"

"Like tonight? Just six. Ran low." He shrugged.

"How about your friends?"

"John Boy, his record is fifty-four hours. That was Labor Day weekend."

"How old are you? Where are your parents?"

If my questions annoyed him, he didn't let it show.

"Ten," he said. "But I don't look it. There's just my mama. And she always works late."

"You live near here?"

He pointed to the apartment building I had just canvassed.

"Ever heard of a guy named Frank who lives there too?"

A look of caution appeared.

"Pretty common name."

"Not really." What an operator this kid was. "Well, I'm looking for him."

"There any money in it?"

I was taken aback.

"You mean if you help me find him? Well, no."

"You a cop?"

"A journalist."

He looked dubious. "Where's your cameras?"

"Not that kind. Newspapers."

"Oh." A visible waning of enthusiasm.

"I heard he lives there." I lifted my chin to the brick tenement.

"He doesn't live there. Though sometimes you could call it that."

A wave of understanding washed over me.

"You mean he hangs out at the cafe?"

"Oh, I don't know." The boy kicked a pebble with his foot.

I pulled out my wallet and he perked up again.

"Well, tell you what, if you ever see him, maybe you could give me a call, huh?" I took out a business card and his face sank. It wasn't the payoff he had been expecting.

"Have him call you?"

"No, you call me and tell me he's here. I'll come by."

Even as I said it, I realized what the more likely scenario would be. He would tell Frank a reporter was looking for him and the guy would toss him a few bills in gratitude before submerging, never to surface again. Still, it wasn't like I had a lot of other leads.

I pulled out a fiver. "Here," I said. "Go play for two hours. I'll be seeing you around."

He snatched it out of my hand and ran in without a backward glance. He was little. Unlike adults who beg, he hadn't yet learned to hide his need.

I went home, tired but still lit up from the day's reporting. At this hour, it was a pretty painless drive from Koreatown to Silverlake, where I lived, but the two neighborhoods were worlds apart in temperament. K-town was in the asphalt flats, crammed to overflowing with people and shops and bristling with a manic immigrant energy that rolled off the heavily congested boulevards like a heat wave on a summer day.

Silverlake was more diverse, a funky community of hills and dales northwest of downtown Los Angeles that drew artists, yuppies, gays, and families of every religion, income level, and ethnicity. The scale was more intimate here, the pace more laid-back. Maybe it was the trees and the lake, but our furniture and appliance stores tended to showcase sleek retro 1950s models rather than the newest, option-loaded Daewoo imports.

I let myself into my ramshackle California bungalow and saw that the light on my machine was blinking. It would have to wait. I walked to the fridge. I got out a beer, the beer I had denied myself at the airport, a cold Corona, opened it, and walked down the hall to the back porch. It was a warm May night.

A faint scent hung in the air, pricking my memory. I

stood at the back door, staring out at my million-dollar view, the Los Angeles skyline framed by sylvan hills, my very own Walden within sight of downtown.

Something moved on the far side of the porch where the shadows were deepest.

"Killer view, Eve. You always did have great taste."

I stood rooted to the floor, shocked at the familiar voice, clutching the neck of my beer so tightly I thought it might shatter. It had been years, but the sound print was etched onto my synapses.

"Tim. Oh my God, Tim."

I leaned against the doorjamb, not trusting my legs. It was Tim Waters. He had been a slim-hipped boy in black jeans when we had met, something craggy and unformed about him, an insolent sneer plastered on his lips. But I could see the vulnerability behind the swagger. And soon I couldn't live without the glow that suffused us when we made love.

How was I to know what a rare gift I held? I was young and hungry for sensation. I wanted to live a passion so large and cataclysmic, it threatened to engulf and destroy me. And so I burned my house down. I left Tim for another man, a suave and sophisticated reporter at the *Times*. My mistake had lasted all of three weeks, but Tim would not take me back. I had betrayed the most sacred of treaties between us.

They say you have to get over first love or it will kill you. Six years had passed, and I felt pretty confident I was over Tim. I had certainly worked at it, toughening up my emotions, carving out a career, dating other men, even fooling myself into thinking I loved them.

Then Silvio had come along, plunging me into that same free fall I remembered so well with Tim. We had met on a story when I profiled his family's music promotion dynasty. Things between us had gotten heated, and then they had gotten ugly when his brother and several others turned up dead. Now we both had to testify at the murder trial, and the *Times* lawyers felt strongly that I should stay away from him until it was all over.

With Silvio, I felt I had finally escaped my past. But hearing Tim's voice and seeing his silhouette just yards away, the sense-memory came flooding back with such intensity that I wondered.

The shadow on the chaise lounge threw its legs over the side and became flesh. And at that moment, I didn't want to see him any more clearly; I wanted him to stay in the safely buried past, where he belonged.

Tim said nothing. His eyes gleamed like a nocturnal animal's. I knew he could see me, lit up in the warmth of the kitchen lights. Suddenly self-conscious, I put a hand to my face.

Then I stepped into the penumbra of the porch. Two could play this game.

"Tim, what are you doing here? How did you know where I live?"

No longer hobbled by surprise, I could not stop the torrent of words stoppered up for so long.

"You never answered my letters. I thought you were still in Asia. Why didn't you call instead of showing up on my back porch in the middle of the night?"

He didn't respond. Just when I despaired that he ever would, he said, "I couldn't wait any longer."

My heart caught. I beat a retreat to the far side of the porch. I didn't trust him. Wanted to widen the distance between us. But in a secret chamber of my heart, a great elation swept through me. When a flame burns so brightly, can it ever be truly extinguished?

"I—is everything okay with you?" I said.

I thought it was interesting that after so long, neither of us made any attempt to move into the light. Conducted in this netherworld, our conversation didn't quite seem real. I thought it perfectly possible that I would wake up in the morning and realize I had summoned it out of my most haunted longings.

"It was, until about a year ago," Tim said. "Then I got swept up in the dot-com bust, ricocheted around Asia, and landed on a beach in Thailand, where I licked my wounds and regained my humanity. Watched the sun rise and ate grilled fish wrapped in banana leaves. Meditated. Slept like a dead man. And slowly came back to life. Your letters, Eve. They had a return address."

"You read them?" I made my voice as nonchalant as possible.

He exhaled loudly and noisily. "They were intense. Raw. Everything came rushing back."

I wanted to ask him why he had waited so long. Instead, I found myself addressing the green gloaming of the backyard, the feathery tops of trees outlined in silvery moonlight.

"So what brought you back?"

He knew I didn't mean the States. I hugged myself and shivered. We were separated by twenty feet of porch, two continents, and six years.

"I needed to see you again."

The disembodied words drifted over like wisps of fog. His face, I thought. If only I could see his face. But even shorn of context, the words seemed ethereal and strangely insubstantial. I tried to summon up Eve the reporter, with her cool, rational ways. She'd know what to say. But that Eve had fled, leaving a weak and heartsick fool.

"How did you know my boyfriend wouldn't shoot you for trespassing?" I asked lamely.

There was a pause.

"I looked at your mailbox. There's no other name. There's no other car in the driveway. And I felt it. I sat here in the dark and waited for you and I felt it."

A vein at my temple throbbed. Eve the reporter flooded back, filling me with outrage. I felt violated. What right did he have to come snooping around my mail, creeping up the back stairs, nosing at the windows, invading my privacy, my home, the refuge I had built so precariously in my efforts to get over him? And I realized that what one finds endearing in a lover can quickly turn to affront once intimacy has ebbed. I didn't like sitting here in the dark with a man I no longer knew, or quite trusted. Why now, after all these years? It only brought home that what I had wanted so fervently, for so long that I had built a shrine to it, had collapsed in the waiting, eaten away from the inside by the passage of time.

"What do you want from me?"

"Your voice," he said in wonderment. "It's cold all of a sudden."

The black form on the other end of the balcony shivered and threw its head back.

"Probably it's my fault," he said. "I've shocked you, landing like this on your porch. I don't want anything. I'll go away now if you want."

"Would you like to come in, have a beer or a cup of coffee in my kitchen, sit around and talk about old times like it was some romantic movie we once shared over popcorn? I don't know, Tim. I can't do that."

"You're a romantic," said my romantic ex-lover. "You'd rather worship the past than deal with reality. You're a big-shot reporter at the *L.A. Times* now, I hear."

His words, low and whispery at the beginning, had grown hot with resentment. They stung me because so many of them were true. But it was because of him that I had shut myself away. I decided to go for the easy denial.

"Not exactly. I'm a suburban reporter for a twice-a-week Metro section in the San Gabriel Valley. I only occasionally get to do big, citywide stories. But I like my job. It suits me. And I'm as flawed and fanciful as I ever was."

"You've done well. For someone who used to lie in bed and go into raptures reading Anna Akhmatova. You'd cry and laugh and pull me to you and kiss my eyelids so fiercely I saw stars."

"For God's sake, stop."

"And I became an Internet entrepreneur and you became a corporate journalist and I'll bet neither one of us has read any poetry in an elephant's lifetime."

He was right, that was the damn shame of it.

"You should go now," I whispered.

"Don't you even want to see me, Eve? You owe that to yourself, at least. Here's what I'll do. I'll walk down these stairs and into the yard and I'll stand in the moonlight, and you lean out over the railing, where the porch light gleams, and we'll look at each other once, and then I'll be on my way."

He didn't wait for my answer, but took his leave, picking his way down the old wooden steps so that his back twisted in some unspoken reproach. He stepped away from the house, straightened, and strode onto the grass. Then he turned and I would have known him anywhere, except his face was thinner and the shadows made lines I hadn't remembered. As if in a dream, I walked over to the railing and stood dutifully under the light. He watched me with a small, sad look on his face that I hadn't expected, because of his proud words, then turned and began hiking up the yard and out the gate. Against the deeper darkness, his receding silhouette was indistinct, though I could see the shoulders cant forward, as if to gather the night close to him.

I waited until I heard his car start up, then went inside, my beer now warm and somewhat flat. I took three sips and gave up. Instead I did my nightly rounds, checking that all the doors and windows were locked. My path took me past the answering machine and I remembered its red winking eye. I walked over and hit PLAY.

"Hey, Eve, long time no hablamos," said a man's voice, intimate and low. "And this machine just doesn't do it. Not when I remember . . ."

There was a wavering intake of breath. His voice trailed off.

"So anyway. They're close to setting a trial date. It's heavy, the pressure around here. And I, uh, got a second opinion. Lawyer says there's nothing wrong with us seeing each other as long as we don't talk about the case. Just wanted you to know that."

I knelt by the machine and played the message back, hoping to find some secret pattern in the words, some code I had overlooked. How did he know to call me on this of all nights?

Silvio. The tightrope walker. Balancing between two cultures, fully at home in neither. A formal man, from his posture to his language, whose elaborately scaffolded sentences echoed with the elegance of a Hanseatic cathedral. That was the public Silvio. But I knew another side of him. I had seen him bowed in grief as tragedy engulfed his family. I had traced his face as he slept, rosy in the dawn. I had felt the heat of an arm flung over my shoulder and been glad for its heft.

Something smoldered at the core of him that had barely begun to kindle when events outside our control had brought the romance to a screeching halt. Then I had retreated into pride and arrogance. I had yet to learn that being vulnerable could make me strong.

But I sensed that what lay between us had nothing to do with his family or my work. It was as elemental as breathing, as inevitable as spring. I had strong feelings for Silvio that I hadn't yet plumbed, but I was scared of where they might lead. The last time I had let myself go so completely was with Tim, which still left me knock-kneed in my own kitchen six years later, as I had discovered tonight. And that brought the circle neatly round again to my current predicament. Tim was back. What did he want? What did I feel for him? I had thought I knew. Now I wasn't so sure. And even worse, I had failed to ask him the basic reporter questions— the "Five *W*'s and an *H*"—who, what, where, when, why, and how. He was as much an enigma to me now as before.

I had been kneeling by the phone for so long that my knees were stiff, sending pain shooting up my legs as I straightened up. I missed Silvio terribly. But after what had happened tonight, I was also confused. It was probably good I hadn't been home to take his call.

As I got into bed, I wondered whether I would see Tim again. Probably, he would disappear for another span of years. For a moment, suspended between waking and sleep, I felt myself being pulled along a surging current, careening down a river, unable to stop or even steer.

I was asleep when the phone rang, and it seemed like a dream when I heard Silvio's voice.

"I know it's late, but I took a chance and called again. I couldn't stop thinking about you tonight."

Startled out of my slumber, my limbs heavy and languid and suddenly throbbing as I heard his voice, I made my decision.

"Why don't you come over," I said. "We don't have to talk."

After hanging up, I lay flat on my back, staring at the womblike curves of the coved ceiling. I wondered if I'd regret my impulsive invitation.

I was almost asleep again when I heard the knock, three intimate taps. I slipped out of bed, toes curling with the chill of the bare wood floor, threw an old kimono over my pajamas, and went to the front door. When I opened it, Silvio stood there, a studied casual expression on his face, as if we had seen each other yesterday. His wavy black hair was combed straight back. He hadn't shaved, and the stubble gave him a piratical air I hadn't remembered. But the jeans and the cowboy boots were the same. His lips were slightly pursed, as though he had just stopped whistling a song.

Behind him, I saw his old truck, the urban camouflage vehicle whose primer-splattered exterior gave no hint of the V-8 engine and audiophile stereo system concealed within.

"Eve, I—"

"Shhh." I grabbed his hand and pulled him in. The door shut behind us and he locked it and followed me into the darkened bedroom.

"I think it's okay if we—"

"Oh, Silvio," I said, and fell against him.

"It's all right." He stroked my hair, his hands moving, cupping, caressing, undoing.

I wanted him to perform an exorcism. I felt the thump of his heart against my chest, his warmth through the thin silk of my nightclothes. He smelled faintly of cloves and a hasty shower.

He lowered me onto the bed and I leaned back against the pillows, falling into puffs of down, then rising up to meet his lips. His hands, big and powerful and insistent, slid the silk off my shoulders. Now he fumbled with the pajama buttons down my front, but pulled so impatiently that one of them popped and flew through the air, landing on the floor and skittering like an errant marble.

He caught his breath. Lifting up my hips, he slid a pillow under me. He was still fully clothed, and I was almost naked, and the thought of that made my breath come faster. With one hand, he pulled aside the crotch of my panties, while the other slid up my thigh and between my legs, finding a soft expanse, which he explored, moving in slow glissades. Time fell away, and there was only this warm and steady pressure, slickness pooling as my senses awakened to his touch, memories unfurling like petals of a flower. Then I felt the bristle of his jaw moving down my body, chafing the skin so that I shivered, until he nestled against the insides of my thighs.

I pressed against his mouth, sliding and writhing, levitating, hands sinking into his hair, fingers twining fistfuls, desperate to hold on.

"Yes," I said, making my mind a blank, forcing Tim out. Tim sitting in the dark. Tim retreating from my backyard, stooped in sorrow. Tim's knowing, sarcastic voice. This was the only way to blot Tim out, to banish him back to the past where he belonged.

"Yes, Silvio," I said, my breath coming ragged. I felt myself hurtling through space, bursting through time back to the very beginning.

When I was still, he withdrew his head and clambered up the length of me until we were eye to eye. I felt him against me and realized he had shucked off his pants.

He held a small plastic packet that crackled as he tore it open. I pushed his hand away and tugged at his remaining clothes.

"It's okay," I said, fitting my hips against his. "I'm due tomorrow."

For a glimmer of a second, he hesitated, but I grabbed his

buttocks and guided him into me, and he reared and thrust, and I did not think about Tim anymore.

In the morning, I woke and felt remorse as I stared at him, slack-jawed in sleep. It wasn't that I didn't want him. Probably I even loved him. But I had used him to forget about another man. And I had broken a promise to myself. It couldn't happen again. I wanted to be able to testify in all honesty that I hadn't seen Silvio. Then, once the trial was over, we'd be free to pursue a relationship.

He sensed me watching him and opened one sleepy eye, reaching for me. It was the most fleeting of caresses, intimate and knowing. Face half-buried in the pillow, he smiled.

"How I've missed you, Eve," he said, stretching lazily.

"Yes," I said. "It's like I was in a howling wilderness, and now I'm home again."

I stopped, wanting only to feel him against me, radiating warmth, before I said what I had to.

"But if it's that good, it can wait. It has to. Then we can see each other openly again."

He arched like a cat. "Honestly, the lawyer said it's okay."

"Then let me run it by the *Times* guy. Either way, it's only a few more months." I glanced at the clock radio on my bedside table. "I've got to get to work, got a hot story I'm following."

"Aren't you always." He yawned. "What's it about?"

"That shoot-out at LAX yesterday with three dead? It also left a little abandoned girl with false papers. She's mixed up with some kind of illegal activity. I'm trying to sort it all out."

Silvio yawned again. "So what have you found out?"

For no discernible reason, a stab of caution went through me.

"Why do you want to know?"

"No reason, tough gal. Keep it to yourself."

"Maybe I will."

I stalked off to the shower, pleasantly sore, my body still tingling from Silvio's hands, his mouth, his entire body. When I got out, he was already dressed and pulling on his cowboy boots.

"We're having a birthday party for *abuelita* Sunday; she's turning seventy-five," Silvio said. "Will you come?"

I busied myself getting dressed.

"What's the matter, you want to keep your options open in case something better comes up?"

Despite myself, I thought of Tim and blushed.

"Well, think about it," he said. "I'll call you."

As we said good-bye on the doorstep, he pulled me to him and kissed me hard. For some reason I couldn't fathom, I pictured Tim staking out my house from farther up the hill, watching us, and my breath came faster as I moved against him.

"Whoa, whoa. You better get to work before we both change our minds," Silvio said, pulling away. With regret, he turned me by the shoulders and half pushed, half led me to my car.

But on the drive in, I wondered why Tim had come back into my life.

t the office, Thompson told me that Metro planned to follow the Russian-mobster story from downtown. But they wanted a daily on the Asian family— the dead woman in raspberry silk, the missing husband, and the now cloistered child.

"Maybe the dad's shown up to claim his kid," Thompson said quietly.

I looked at him and saw why he was hammering this angle. He had two young children and couldn't imagine a father abandoning his family.

"But Maxwell called him Crypto-Dad. They might have no blood ties whatsoever. I'll bet that by now he's disappeared into the Pacific Rim sprawl."

There were dozens of communities spread across Southern California, from Little Saigon to Koreatown, Thai Town, Little Phnom Penh, Little Tokyo, Chinatown, and the great pan-Asian valley that lapped all around us.

"He could be right here under our big Caucasian noses and we'd never find him," Thompson groused. "What about the girl?"

I told him more about my talk with Maxwell yesterday, recounting the tussle between the FBI and the INS over what to do with the girl and the INS's hope to deport her as soon as possible. When I got to the mystery man who was also looking for the girl, Thompson got very still and quiet.

"Do you think it's another reporter?"

His competitive instincts were aroused. I wondered

whether he'd be more likely to keep me on the story if I told him yes. Then I thought about the cybercafe.

"No," I said. "I think it's more sinister. There's something big swirling around this kid. If I can find her and describe how she's sick and terrified and the INS is holding her under armed guard at some squalid hotel while they get ready to deport her, it will crack the thing wide open. I'd like to spend the morning checking Chinatown hotels."

Thompson considered that for a few moments.

"There must be a hundred, and it would take days to visit them all," he said finally. "Look, I'd like to find this kid too. If what you're saying is true, it's shameful and should be exposed. But frankly, Eve, I can't spare you."

"That's exactly what they're counting on. That no one has time to look for one sick little girl in a county of ten million. And you're helping to ensure their plan works."

Something shifted in Thompson's eyes and worry lines spread across his brow. What if I was right? On the desk, the phone trilled and sang out urgently.

"Even if you find her, the INS will only slam the door in your face," Thompson said finally. An invitation to parry.

I shrugged. "They're not my only option. Maids and porters and desk clerks see things. And maybe they don't always like what they see."

Thompson rocked in his chair, throwing his back into it, chin bobbing, reviewing the chessboard I had just laid out for him, his mind already five moves ahead. He was a cunning and manipulative bastard and he knew I worked best when he cranked up the pressure. So now he did just that.

"You don't even know what language she speaks, but it sure as hell ain't one in your repertoire. And meanwhile you piss off INS so much they cut us right out of the loop, thin and pitiful though it is."

He wanted me to convince him. This was the way of it

with us, volleying the facts back and forth, repeating and reworking until we teased out the tendrils of a plan.

"Maybe they'll talk if we catch them by surprise. Maybe they figured out where she's from by now and are meeting with the consulate. Maybe she's been reunited with Dad, crypto or not, and they're holed up together and about to get deported and we'll never even learn about it unless I get on it."

Thompson scratched the back of his head, then seemed to remember his thinning crown and patted it back down.

"All right," he said. "But keep your sense of melodrama to yourself until we know more."

List in hand, I cruised down Hill Street.

The first hotel I came to had blue curvy tiles like ocean waves and a pitched, pagoda-style roof whose design evoked a Hollywood back lot more than Hong Kong. The clerk told me they had never rented to the INS, though the mere mention of these dreaded initials sent a flicker of fear through the otherwise impassive face behind the counter. As I turned to go, I realized the ratty phone book I had used the night before might be obsolete.

On inspiration, I asked the desk clerk about new hotels and he gave me several names. In this job, you have to be patient, even as your brain races ahead. Can you think of any more? I asked.

He inclined his head to indicate the next block.

"What's it called?"

"Hotel Variott," he said. "Dirty place, not clean like here."

I had seen the sign but it hadn't registered because half the letters were missing. Besides, it looked more like an office building than a hotel, two stories wrapped around a concrete courtyard. I decided to walk.

When I got there, I realized the clerk had merely been bad-mouthing the competition. The lobby of the Hotel Variott was neat and tidy. It was also abysmally depressing,

I thought, taking in the plywood coffee table, the vinyl sofa, the brown carpet shiny from wear.

But it was the smell that curdled my soul. Cleaning fluid mixed with bug killer, the high astringency of the ammonia giving way in the lower olfactory registers to a floral bouquet so sluttishly artificial that you could practically see the chemicals unfurl in the air.

I walked up to the counter, where a black-and-white TV blared, and explained my mission. The desk clerk shrugged, took a pull on his filterless cigarette, and kept his eyes on the screen. He was watching a Chinese game show that seemed to involve contestants performing humiliating stunts that were timed by a host with shiny white teeth and an unctuous smile. For a moment, both of us watched the contestants lap at bowls of soup with their hands tied behind their backs. One contestant began to choke.

As the TV host thumped the contestant across the back, the desk clerk grunted in sympathy, then cleared his own throat. Finally he turned in my direction. The fleshy pads of his thumb and forefinger were stained a deep nicotine yellow. I repeated my question.

"INS sometime bring people," the man said.

He looked to be in his sixties, but his eyes were that of a young man trapped in his grandfather's body. His white shirt was so threadbare it was almost transparent. The sleeves were too long, and he had rolled the cuffs over his bony wrists, revealing a pink Hello Kitty watch.

"Is the INS renting rooms today?" I asked, trying to repress excitement and a giggled snort at finding a grown man sporting "tween" girl gear. In the galleries and clubs of Hop Sing Way, such a timepiece on a fellow would have been admired as an ironic fashion statement. But several blocks of sorrow and a whole continent of pain away, my man behind the desk knew only that he had a new watch and it kept time pretty good.

"Checkout," he said, pointing at the clock.

"You mean they've already checked out? Gone?"

He nodded slowly, as though unsure of the question.

"Who was with them?"

He shrugged.

"Did you see who they came in with?" I repeated.

"Pass mid-a-night," he said, shaking his head.

At this, the door burst open and a small boy ran in, wearing dirty shorts and a T-shirt that said VENICE BEACH. He wore flip-flops and carried a silver tray bearing a pot of steaming tea and chipped cups. Laboriously, the boy slid his tray up onto the counter. The man took out some coins, placed them on the tray, then transferred the pot and one cup to the counter. He waved his hand, as though flicking away flies, and the boy said something. The man barked back, but dug into his pocket and pulled out another coin. With that, the boy snatched the tray and went flying out the door.

"So it was midnight," I said. "Were you here?"

"Always here," the man said loudly, as though I were hard of hearing. He kicked something out from under the counter and I saw that it was a gray cot, soiled by years of use.

Now his lips parted in a tortured attempt at a smile. I counted six teeth in all. Nothing like the slick TV host.

If we were in the movies, this would be the time when I'd slide a bill across the counter and he'd take it and spill all. Oh yeah, and suddenly he'd speak great English.

"Did you see a little girl with the INS?" I persisted. "This morning? She's about two years old," I said, holding up two fingers. "Little Asian girl."

He looked at me with boredom. "They pay for room, they business."

I gazed steadily into his eyes. Did that mean he had seen a little girl but it wasn't any of his business? Or he hadn't seen anything and wanted me to mind mine?

I decided it was the latter. And that if I wanted anything else, I'd have to find it for myself.

"Okay, thanks," I said. The clerk turned back to the TV. But the torque of his shoulders said he remained acutely aware of my presence.

"One more question," I said, trying for a double whammy. "What room was the INS and the little girl in last night?"

"Twenty-two," he said without blinking.

Finally, I thought, clenching my teeth to bite back triumph. I got the feeling that business wasn't too good and they might have been the only tenants bunking down at the Hotel Variott.

"Can I see the room?"

He shook his head vigorously.

"Maid clean," he said.

"That's what I was afraid of," I said. "All right. I'll be back in a few days to see if they've shown up again."

Outside on the sidewalk, I looked back through the window and saw the clerk roosting at his desk, eyes on the TV. I watched him until I was satisfied he wasn't planning to make his rounds anytime soon. His head sagged, as if our conversation had sapped his energy. I turned right and walked around the cheesily plastered walls of the poop-brown Hotel Variott and into the alley where I had seen a cleaning cart earlier. I stood there, scrutinizing the layout. The higher-number rooms were upstairs. That meant a quick trip up the concrete stairwell to reach my destination. I hoped the clerk was wrong and the maid hadn't cleaned Room 22 yet.

Just then the maid emerged from a downstairs room. She carried a tall stack of towels and sheets that obscured her face so I couldn't determine her nationality, though it was clear she was very pregnant. Then she bent over her tray and I saw her hair was black, which didn't narrow it down much.

I doubted she would speak much English. There were better menial jobs in Los Angeles for those with language skills. But I hoped she would be Latina, not Asian. Thanks to Silvio, I had been practicing my Spanish. I watched her a moment more. When she straightened up, I rejoiced to see the *india* features.

The pregnant maid looked up the stairwell and back down at her cart, as if calculating the distance. Then she lugged her woe-on-wheels to the bottom stair and began to jerk it up, step by bumpy step.

It was as good a cue as I was going to get. Running over, I grabbed hold of the bottom end and said, *"Por favor, señora, dejeme ayudarle."* Please, ma'am, let me help you with that. I added that she shouldn't lift such heavy things in her condition, and she looked at me like the apparition I was, stunned into silence. Then we pushed and pulled the damn thing, which seemed to weigh as much as a small elephant, up the stairs.

But if I expected effusive thanks, I was wrong. Mingled with her relief was suspicion, a wary once-over. And something else. Fear. As we reached the landing, her arms fell from the cart and dangled at her sides and her head dropped almost imperceptibly. A wave of comprehension flashed over me. She's illegal. No green card. She's afraid I'm with the government and I'm going to bust her.

I stashed this useful kernel away. But I knew I'd never use it. As soon as I'd seen her belly, I already knew I'd tell her the truth. She was about to become a mother. I'd appeal to her maternal instincts.

And I had to give her this much. Despite her fear, she listened. We stood there and she ran her finger along the laminated plastic press card and the gothic script that announced *Los Angeles Times*, as I whispered, *"Soy una periodista, señora."* I'm a reporter. Then I told her how urgent it was for us to track down the little girl, a mere baby, *señora*, who was in the custody of the INS, La Migra. And here I paused, letting the words sink in, knowing that the INS was widely loathed throughout the immigrant communities, but especially among Latinos for its brutality and coldheartedness in sending them back.

"La Migra has her?" the woman breathed.

"Yes. She came in yesterday on a plane from Asia."

The woman frowned and I realized my mistake. She had probably walked for days through the desert, almost dying of dehydration.

I needed this woman's sympathy back, and quickly.

"Her mother was killed yesterday in a shoot-out at LAX. Her father's disappeared. La Migra's trying to deport her."

"Oh, that one! I heard about it on the radio. Poor little thing," the woman commiserated.

"And all I would like," I continued, "is to take a quick look inside room twenty-two. She might have stayed here last night."

The maid appraised me. I sensed that she was compassionate but not stupid. She had gone through too much just getting here to blow it all in a moment's weakness.

"I can't afford to lose this job," the woman said, cradling her stomach. "I have a little boy at home. And the clinic says this one's a boy too, even though I prayed that God would send me a girl this time."

"You won't lose your job," I said. "If anyone comes in, I'll say I wanted to see the rooms because I need to rent one." I wondered how I would explain a night's lodging in Chinatown on my expense report. But I could justify that. I couldn't justify bribing this woman $50 to let me in.

"Think what could happen to this poor little baby if we don't find her," I said.

She stood there, unconvinced. I could see the argument raging across her face.

"A little girl, *señora*."

I clasped my hands together. "A baby in diapers," I whispered.

She bit her lip.

"Venga," she said, her mind made up.

Together we pushed the cart, inching our way, a caravan plodding through the Sahara. I angled my ears for footsteps behind us, concentrating so hard that it took me a while before other sounds seeped into my consciousness. Then I realized there were plenty of other tenants in this sad and dingy place.

Off in the recesses of the building, someone hacked, a tubercular rasp that ended with a wet gurgle, as if the afflicted had choked on a pink and glistening piece of his own lung. Through the thin walls, a radio blared tinny Asian pop, a female singer whose discordant *melisma* jangled my nerves. Across the courtyard, an American TV brayed, the dueling pop culture sounds joining in sonic embrace in the empty space above the concrete courtyard before dissipating into the sky. I'm big on omens and signs. And the raspy American laugh track seemed to mock the futility of my quest.

Finally, we stood before Room 22. The maid took a ring of keys from her pocket, selected one, and unlocked the door. Somewhere deep inside the bowels of the building, a generator rumbled on and we both jumped. I prayed the office clerk wouldn't come up, but didn't dare to walk closer to the balcony and check in case he saw me.

The woman divined my fear. It was hers too, after all. She sauntered over to the balcony with a towel, held it over the railing and flapped it. Then she stepped back.

"He's asleep in front of the TV. He never moves if he can help it. Something wrong with his joints."

She threw the door open. I stood at the threshold. It was a gray rectangle of a room. Stained yellow curtains hung from a tiny window, the lining frayed and bleached by the sun. There were two double beds. One was tangled with bedclothes. The other was neatly made, except for one corner, which had been folded back into a neat triangle, as though a doll had been tucked in to sleep there, only to be slid out in the morning. Someone had pulled a chair up near the bed. An adult who kept watch?

I stepped inside. Stale institutional air enveloped me. Sheets so old you couldn't wash out the sour smell anymore. A woman's perfume mingled with something I couldn't identify because I had little experience with it. The woman saw me sniffing the air.

"It smells of babies," she said.

Now I placed it. The chalky sweetness of talcum, the soiled diaper. I ran to the trash can to confirm my guess and saw a disposable diaper folded neatly into a small bundle.

So she had been here.

I dug to see what else was there. Dirty wipes. A fast food bag with a spreading grease stain. Kleenexes clotted with something yellowish-green and sticky. Two large soft drink containers, plum lipstick still decorating one straw. So there had been two INS agents and at least one of them was a woman. Who wore plum lipstick. Now I unearthed a white plastic spoon coated with a slick, greasy orange liquid. I sniffed. It smelled chemical, medicinal.

"*Aqui,*" the maid was saying. She came out of the bathroom, holding a bottle of medicine. The orange liquid inside matched the orange coating the spoon. I walked over.

"PediaCare," I read. You were supposed to give it to sick children; it helped bring down fever and stop coughs and runny noses. So the little girl was as sick as she looked.

From the bathroom came the swampy gas smell of a backed-up toilet. Water gurgled through the pipes in the walls.

I walked over and found myself inside a room the size of a closet. The maid had parked her cleaning cart alongside the shower and I had to push the plywood door nearly closed in order to see the cracked vanity mirror, the molded plastic sink masquerading as marble. The doorknob rattled in my hand, flecks of bronze paint sticking to my skin.

On a shelf above the sink, a clear plastic cup stood half-filled with water, bubbles of air clinging to its sides, the way it gets when it sits undisturbed. Next to it was a wet and neatly folded washcloth, the type of thing mothers lay across children's foreheads when they have fever.

I could hear the maid vacuuming in the main room. Then the noise stopped and I heard her humming to herself, an old ballad. I looked through the crack in the door and saw her, stripping the sheets, putting on new pillowcases and fluffing them, gathering up wet towels.

Hoping for more clues, I opened the bathroom cupboards. I could almost see the girl's afterimage here. She was sick. She had spent the night. She was with someone who wore plum lipstick and someone who didn't. There was a small trash can by the toilet and I bent over it. I'm not sure what I was looking for: a discarded prescription bottle with a name, a stray business card, a receipt. My eye was caught by a pair of yellow rubber gloves slung over the cleaning cart. That would be more sanitary. I slid them on, then lowered the toilet seat and settled myself on the lid to pick through the rubble.

The sound of splintering wood stopped me, mid-dig, as a booted foot slammed into a nearby door. I heard a small whimper. Something thudded in the outer room, like a body hitting the floor. Footsteps advanced.

"Where is she?"

From my toilet seat perch, I looked through the crack and saw a shadow darken the front door. The light was against me, shrouding his face in a beefy eclipse. My first thought was that the desk clerk must have followed us upstairs and had caught me snooping. I feared for the cleaning lady. I had endangered her job, exactly what I had sworn not to do, and now we were both busted. But the man's tone was too menacing, it didn't fit the crime.

"*No hablo inglés, señor,*" the maid squeaked.

A shadow moved on the other side of the room. A lamp crashed against the wall, the bulb splintering. The cloth shade rolled crazily across the room.

"Don't fuck with me," the voice said. "I said where is she?"

There were two of them. I saw the barrel of a gun prodding the air.

Fear shot through me, but I still had one tiny advantage. They didn't know anyone else was here. Looking around, I scanned the maid's cart. I found a cleaning smock and soundlessly slipped it over my silk shirt. I slid off my shoes and pulled off my socks, then rolled my pants up to midcalf. I found a soiled cleaning rag and tied it messily around my hair, then pulled out stray strands around my face to make myself more slovenly. I stripped off my watch, earrings, and an amber necklace and slid them into a pants pocket. My purse was one of those leather satchel jobs. I shoved it deep into a stack of folded sheets, then twisted my torso over the cart, craning to see in the cracked mirror. The lipstick was all wrong. I wiped it off with a square of toilet paper, then looked again. The silk top still showed through the smock. In the front room, the men were grilling the maid. At any moment they might burst through the bathroom door. I glanced around, saw two crumpled towels on the floor and bent to scoop them up, recoiling at their dampness. Underneath was a wadded green paper etched with faint writing, some kind of office form. I jammed it into my pocket, then straightened up and slung a towel over each shoulder.

I flushed the toilet, then reached for a scouring pad and the cleanser. The voices in the other room stopped abruptly.

"What the fuck is that? Who's there?"

As footsteps approached, I jerked the cleanser can up and down by the door, sending toxic white clouds billowing into the air. Quickly I retreated to the bathtub. I was scrubbing and humming loudly when the door was flung open. It banged once against the toilet, reverberated and shuddered. I forced myself to stay still.

"Julia?" I sang out, not lifting my head. *"Quién es?"* Who's there?

A short, heavyset man in a tight suit stood, pointing a gun at my chest. White dude. I glimpsed mingled relief and disappointment on his face. Then his features convulsed into a violent sneeze. Rubbing his eyes and cursing, he bent to cough, lungs filling with fine granules of cleanser that I hoped would trigger emphysema. It wouldn't be soon enough for my needs, but it bought me another thirty seconds.

"Jesus Christ, go easy on that shit," he sputtered. He blew his nose into two fingers, then wiped them on his suit, leaving a gooey white streak. He grimaced and swallowed hard and I hoped the postnasal drip was scorching his throat like bad crank.

I was glad he wasn't focused on me. If he thought I was just an ignorant maid who didn't know where the kid was, he might not kill me. I had realized, by now, whom they were after.

"Out," he screamed, waving the gun.

I lay down the scouring pad and put my hands up in the air. I couldn't move and he knew it; the room was too small, the cleaning cart blocked my way.

"Move it, move it," he said, spraying ropy strands of saliva.

"Sí, señor." I averted my eyes. Keeping my hands in the air, I climbed out of the tub and shoved at the cart with my hips, pushing it forward, toward him, through the door, my

bare feet inching after it, down the hall, and into the front room, as the man with the gun moved backward, step by step, like we were locked in some weird death tango, me *sí*, *señor*–ing him every couple of seconds, while the maid cowered in a corner, hands shielding her face.

"Shut the fuck up," he said, giving the cart a vicious shove so that it teetered, then fell on its side, spilling out cleaning supplies, towels, sheets, and another open can of cleanser, which immediately sent a second plume of smoke rising into the air.

"For fuck's sake," the man said, grabbing a towel and holding it over his face. Luckily, he was too occupied shielding himself to see the tip of my purse sticking out of the toppled sheets. I grabbed sheets and purse and retreated to the maid's corner, hugging them to my chest as if to protect myself. Still wearing my yellow cleaning gloves, I found the maid's hand and grabbed it, squeezing through the rubber.

The air-quality freak turned to his companion, who had stood so silent and motionless against a far wall this whole time that I had almost forgotten about him. Now he stepped farther into the room.

"Search the place," he said, the accent I had overheard falling into line with his Asian features.

I didn't dare look at him straight on. But from my peripheral vision, I could tell he had on a leather jacket and shades. The big gun he had trained on us made it hard to concentrate. But I thought I recognized him, and was dead glad he had never seen me, hidden behind that one-way airport glass. It was the beleaguered Asian man who had been pushing the mountain of luggage at the airport yesterday. The little girl's supposed father. The immigration ditch dog that INS and U.S. Customs were after. And that could mean only one thing. These two guys were on the trail of their missing dolly too, and they didn't know much more than I did.

Keeping my eyes down, I prayed the Asian guy didn't speak Spanish any better than the white one seemed to, or he'd soon realize I was no Latina maid.

Now the white guy strode into the bathroom and I heard him ripping off the shower curtain. He threw open the doors of the cupboard under the sink. Cursing, he came back out. He flung open the closet doors and pulled out the bureau drawers. He kicked brutally at the mounded covers where the maid had stripped the bed, cocking his head for the soft thud that would tell him he had connected with flesh. When that didn't come, he pulled up the knees of his trousers and lowered himself heavily to the floor, peering under each bed.

Nada.

He stayed on all fours, grunting and sniffing, trying to figure out where else in this bare, impersonal room someone might hide a toddler. Crypto-Dad held back, covering the room with his gun. I got the feeling he might be the boss.

Then the white guy lurched to his feet and walked toward us.

"Where's the little girl?" he screamed. "She was here with the INS. La Migra, you frigging wetbacks. Last night."

The woman beside me was trembling and cradling her stomach, and I wondered if she might go into labor right then and there.

"I only clean room, señor. I leetle English," she said, her head hanging like a dead flower on the stalk of her neck.

The barrel of the gun moved toward me.

"I suppose you leetle English too."

I stared at the carpet and made my face go as slack as possible.

"Disculpeme, señor. No comprendo inglés." I'm sorry, sir, I don't understand English.

"Fucking wetbacks," he snorted. The gun made a lazy arc. "Look at them. We got barefoot and we got pregnant. Like animals. Can't even afford to buy shoes."

I stared at the floor. Humble. Ignorant. Dumb as a beast. Anything except what I was. Please don't let them kill us, I thought.

Now the little man laughed, an unpleasant stutter, and took a step closer. The gun came up, rested against my temple. It was cold and impersonal. I felt a vein throb, a pounding and thudding against the metal, and I pictured my own death and suddenly my legs went liquid and I slid down. He grabbed my shoulder and shoved me back up, pinioning me against the wall, the gun nestling into position.

"You tell anyone about this and we'll come back and kill you. We know where you work. *Comprende?*"

The gun wobbled against the side of my head. I couldn't have spoken if I wanted to; I was paralyzed, frozen in a world somewhere between death and life.

"*Sí, señor,*" I heard someone say. The maid, whose existence I had completely forgotten, had piped up.

"*Comprende?*" the man said, rattling my shoulder.

Her voice had broken the spell. "*Sí, señor,*" I croaked.

"Maybe we should just kill them now and be done with it," my tormentor said.

I started to flinch, then froze and went slack again. I wasn't supposed to understand English.

I focused on the feet in front of me. The thug wore cheap black leather shoes and ribbed beige socks. I felt anticipation surge through him as he cocked his head, waiting for the green light.

"No," came a measured and indifferent voice from the other end of the room. It was the Asian thug. "It would bring the heat down and make our search more difficult. They won't go to the police. They're too fucking scared of getting deported."

A tremor passed through the maid. "No police," she begged, and shook her head vehemently.

"See," came the coiled, still voice.

I held my breath. The hothead seemed to be mulling it over. He exhaled noisily to show his displeasure at being thwarted. Then the hard metal was removed from my temple. I heard footsteps receding, then the door slamming. A hammering blackness was pulsing inside of me, lights dancing in my eyes. I fell to my knees, unable to stand. The maid crouched down beside me, her arm around my shoulders. I felt the surprisingly hard ball of her belly pushing into my side, her face against my neck. It was wet. We slumped there for a long time, too weak to move.

Slowly, the pounding stopped. I stirred. We looked at each other. We were strangers, but we had shared the most intimate moment imaginable—facing death together.

"What did they want?" the maid asked after a long time.

I cradled my head in my hands. I tried to make my mouth move, but my tongue was thick and lumpen and knotted, banging helplessly against my palate. I licked my lips and the maid must have understood, because she heaved herself up and brought me a glass of water. I took a sip and immediately choked. It was as if all my bodily functions had seized up.

"Remember I told you about that kid?" I said. "They're after her."

"But why?"

"I don't know," I said. "But I have to find her before they do." The water was slowly reviving me. "Don't worry. I'll tell the management what happened. But first we need to call the police."

"The police?" she said with fear. "No. You can't do that."

"Why not?"

She hesitated, and from her downcast eyes, I understood.

"I'm not legal," she finally murmured.

"But the police aren't supposed to call in La Migra."

She gave me a despairing look. "After September eleventh, everything has changed."

"But . . ."

"Please don't go to the police. Those men won't be back. They know we don't have her."

Perhaps she was right. Sighing, I reached for the jewelry I had hidden in my pocket and extracted a damp green paper. I stared at the crumpled form. It seemed a century ago that I had stuffed it in my pants. Now I pulled it open with care and smoothed it on the bed.

CLÍNICA LOS NIÑOS, it read. OPEN 24 HOURS. 435 BROADWAY. LOS ANGELES. SI ACEPTAMOS MEDICAL.

It was a carbon copy, one of those forms you sign in quadruplicate. But the damp had smudged the already faint writing. I had no way of knowing what the diagnosis and treatment had been.

But there was something else at the top. Under "patient name," someone had scratched in faint cursive. The writing was almost illegible, but I thought I could pick out the letters *s-e-r-e-y.*

"Did you find something useful?" the maid asked.

"Yes." I held up the form and she moved closer to examine it. Fatigue was etched into the muscles around her mouth, the ruddy circles under her eyes, the gray streaks at her temples.

I reached for my purse. If I gave her some money now, it wasn't a bribe, it was a thank-you.

"Here," I said, trying to stick a twenty-dollar bill into her pocket.

"No, señorita." She pushed the money away.

"*Para el bebé,*" I told her, closing her fingers around the bill.

She blushed, then slipped the money down her bra. I hunted for more but came up only with two guest passes to Arena La Puente, courtesy of Aguilar Entertainment. Silvio had given them to me months ago and I had forgotten all about them. I held up the tickets, asking if she could use them.

"*Mi amigo*," I told her. "My friend, his family runs Arena La Puente. Silvio Aguilar of Aguilar Entertainment. Please take them."

She did, then cleared her throat to speak, as if she owed me something more.

"I took my boy to Clínica Los Niños once," she said. "When he had pneumonia. We waited for hours. But the doctor was very nice. She apologized and made Pedro smile."

"I'm going to go there right now," I said.

She shook her head. "What if those men—"

"Those men have no idea. I picked this up off the bathroom floor before they barged in."

She told me to go with God, and as we said good-bye, I stepped forward and hugged her as best I could with that belly in the way and wished her well. Then I took off the smock and added it to the pile of laundry. I retrieved my shoes and walked the two blocks back to my car, losing myself in the noontime crowds of Chinatown, men in suits, mothers pulling tiny, solemn-eyed children, teenagers in school uniforms, all of us skirting puddles of oily black water and piles of shattered car window glass.

I was halfway to the clinic before I realized I didn't even know the maid's name. I should have given her my card, at least. But when I returned the following day with a stack of baby clothes a neighbor had given me, casting about fearfully to make sure the thugs hadn't come back, she was gone. The same sullen-eyed clerk at the front desk looked at me and his eyes glowed with hostility.

"She quit," he said. "Before boss fire her. Too much crash-bang in room twenty-two. Lotsa money fix. Maid say she know nothing but we not believe. Maybe you know what happen?"

"She didn't do it," I said dully. "Look, did she fill out an application when you hired her? Do you know where she lives?"

"A what?"

"You know, a personnel form."

"No forms," he said. "Only she work. We pay. Good workers hard to find. Nobody trusty." He gave an ugly sneer. "You like this place. Maybe you want job."

"I'm crash-bang too," I said, walking out.

CHAPTER 7

*A*s I drove toward the clinic, I tidied myself, brushed my hair, and strove to banish the terror that lingered in the corners of my eyes, the clench of my jaw. On Hill Street, I switched lanes to put plenty of space between me and a teenaged boy in a Hummer. He had a cell phone in one hand and a CD in the other and was using his elbows to steer the armor-plated behemoth. Hummers had been designed for patroling the war-cratered roads of Kabul and Kosovo, not running errands in L.A. The way things kept escalating, we'd all be driving tanks soon.

Soon I was on Broadway, the center of Latino downtown, where ranchera music blared and soapbox preachers with megaphones exhorted oblivious shoppers pawing through mountains of luggage, frilly children's dresses, purses, and cheap electronics. Clínica Los Niños was a storefront wedged between a stand advertising LÍQUADOS made of maguey, papaya, guanabana, and mango and a storefront Evangelical church with folding chairs lined up for the next service.

Once inside, I picked my way past children of all ages who played listlessly, watching TV and snuffling in their mothers' arms. Placing my precious paper on the counter sticky with lollipop juice and smudged little handprints, I asked to speak to the doctor who had examined the girl.

The young woman behind the counter picked up the paper and scrutinized it with a puzzled frown as though she had never seen anything like it before.

"Isn't this your stationery?" I asked, pointing to the "Clínica Los Niños" logo.

She put it down and smoothed it flat. "Yes, but this isn't the usual intake form."

"Oh? What is it then?"

"That's what I'm not sure of," she said. "Who did you say you were?"

I hadn't. "My name is Eve Diamond, and I'm with the *Times*," I said, feeling my heart flop and land somewhere by my toes. I feared what came next.

"Our records are confidential," she immediately said.

I leaned over the counter and scooped up my green form before she thought of confiscating it. "I understand. I just want to speak to the doctor who treated this patient."

A sullen look. "The doctor can't tell you anything more than I can."

I smiled, willing it to beam through my eyes as well as my mouth. "Still, I have a few questions."

The woman sighed. She was overworked and underpaid and no one had ever told her that shiny purple eye shadow did not go well with sallow skin.

"Have a seat," she said.

I waited a long time, noticing that no matter how many patients ebbed and flowed, the waiting room stayed full. Meanwhile, I reread the faint writing on my green form. There were some kind of initials in a box at the bottom. Finally the iridescent-lidded receptionist left and a chubby girl with a tight crushed-velvet top took her place. I counted to one hundred and then approached the desk again.

"Excuse me, please," I asked. "Could you tell me whose initials these are?"

The girl took the form and squinted at the bottom. "'BR,'" she read. "That's Berta Rodriguez. She's our new internist."

"That's right," I said. "Now I remember. Is she in?"

The girl looked at me, handing me back the form. "It took me a minute because that's not our usual form," she said conversationally.

"Yeah," I said. "It's that special one for when . . ."

I looked down the hallway, then pretended the effort had made me lose my train of thought.

"Actually," said the girl, "we have a number of in loco parentis patients. But I remember this one. Her lawyer sent it through the fax. He was very huffy about it. Dr. Rodriguez was wondering whether to get the police involved."

Her lawyer? I thought.

"Well, frankly, that's what I want to talk to Dr. Rodriguez about," I said, leaning one elbow on the counter in a confidential manner.

The girl's eyes widened. "Really? You're—"

"That's right," I said cheerily. "But ssshhh, I don't want to draw attention to myself."

"I totally understand," the girl said. "Some of our clients are very skittish if . . ." She paused delicately. ". . . their papers aren't in order. Not that you've come here for that," she added quickly.

"Of course not," I assured her. "Believe me, when it comes to those operations, there's no polite waiting and 'pretty please.'"

The girl smiled in relief. "Hold on, I'll ring her. Please have a seat."

I waited peacefully while she dialed and talked into the phone, wondering how far the cop ruse would take me. I knew I was being deceitful, but I just wanted a chance to plead my case before the good doctor.

"She's with a patient," the girl at the counter called out. "I'll squeeze you in next."

When a mother holding a tiny wrinkled baby wrapped in a blanket emerged from the inner sanctum, the receptionist directed me through the double doors and into the second door on the right. I felt the stares of tired parents and grandparents with sick children boring into my back as I walked, people who had waited even longer than I had and wondered why this *gringa* should get special treatment.

Halfway down a long hallway, I found the door and stepped inside. Berta Rodriguez was at the far end of the room, writing something on a clipboard. She was a young woman with black hair pulled back in a high ponytail, a brown smattering of freckles across her nose, and no make-up. She wore horn-rimmed glasses and surgical scrubs and seemed irritated by my presence.

"Yes, Officer, what can I do for you?"

"Actually, I'm a reporter, not a cop. There was a misunderstanding out there."

Dr. Rodriguez stepped back, regarding me with suspicion.

"Did you see that overflowing waiting room out there, miss?" she asked, her voice formal and cold. "I don't have time to talk to the press."

I told her I just wanted a minute of her time. She stood there, arms crossed in front of her chest. I decided not to wait for an invitation.

"I think you treated a little girl here yesterday afternoon," I began. "She was Asian. About two years old. With some kind of cold or flu. She was taking PediaCare."

"Yes," the doctor said slowly, almost in spite of herself. "I remember her. Most of our clientele is Latino, so she stuck out." The woman looked at me directly now. "That was one very sick little girl."

"What was wrong with her?"

"I can't release that information."

"But her name was Serey?"

The woman started. "I can't release that information," she repeated, unaware that her body already had. Flustered, she went on. "But I told them that under no condition can she get on—"

The woman bit off what she had been about to say. She

gave me a wary look, like I had slipped her some truth serum when she wasn't looking.

"Get on what?" I asked innocently. "A plane?"

"I'm not saying another word." She looked at her watch and her face tightened. "Please, Miss . . ."

"What's wrong with her?"

She strode across the room, opened the door, and held out one arm in an unmistakable gesture to usher me out.

"You'll have to talk to her guardian."

I took a step toward her so she'd see I was complying. "You mean the INS?"

"No. I said her guardian."

"Is that the same person as her lawyer?"

"Why don't you ask the INS?" Dr. Rodriguez motioned that I should go through the door first.

I considered her worn scrubs and rubber-soled shoes. She could easily have doubled her income in private practice on the West Side. But she chose to work here, within spitting distance of skid row, treating poor immigrant Latino families. That told me something about her sympathies.

I moved closer. "Have you ever tried to get anything out of the INS?" I asked. "It's not easy."

Dr. Rodriguez took her hand off the doorknob and I knew I had hit a nerve.

"I've heard stories," she said dryly.

"I'm here to tell you that most of them are true."

For a moment, we stared at each other.

"Is this little girl in some kind of trouble?" she finally asked. "Other than the usual, that is." She gave a short bark of a laugh. "Not enough food, nowhere to play, too many people crammed into poorly ventilated, mold-ridden, rodent-infested apartments."

"Yes," I said slowly. "She is in trouble. And that's why I'd appreciate if you give me her guardian's name. And her

lawyer's. Look, I'm very sorry to take up your valuable
time. And I understand that medical records are confidential. Just give me a referral and I'll be on my way."

She met my gaze silently.

"I'm not asking you to break any rules."

She made a small, capitulating movement with her hand.
"I suppose you're right," she said. "Hold on, let me get the
file. They made enough of a fuss about it." She went to a
cabinet and flipped through its contents. Finally she found
what she was looking for. She pulled out a manila folder, sat
at her stool, and opened it, careful to shield it from my line
of vision. She turned the papers over one by one, stopping
occasionally to scan them.

"You have an address and phone number handy?" I
asked, more to keep her talking with the file open on her
knees than anything else. Maybe there would be an earth-
quake and the papers would topple onto the floor and I'd
have to help pick them up, gleaning new and important
information.

She didn't answer. Her knee jiggled impatiently as she
flipped through the documents. After a long time, she
closed the file and stood up.

"I'm afraid it's not here. It must still be up at the front."

The intercom buzzed. "Dr. Rodriguez. Please call
Reception, Dr. Rodriguez."

She pressed a button by the phone. "I'll be there in a
minute, or do you need me sooner?" She listened to the
response, holding one hand to her eyes, as if to block any
more stimulus.

"I'm sorry," she said to me now. "I can't take any more
time right now. Can you call me this afternoon? After five?
I promise I'll look for it then."

This was bad news. By afternoon, she would have had
time to reconsider. To come to her senses. But there was
always that tantalizing possibility that she'd come through.

I smiled. "Couldn't we check with Reception on our way out?"

"I just can't."

"Yes, of course," I said. "This afternoon will be fine."

Just then Dr. Rodriguez swayed and put her arm on the metal examining table to steady herself. "You'll have to excuse me," she said. "I saw my first patient at seven-thirty this morning and I haven't stopped since. Or eaten breakfast, come to think of it. And there are twenty-five more sick kids in that waiting room. We're down a resident today." She walked to the door again, opened it.

"I admire what you're doing," I told her.

Her lips pressed together tightly. "That's where I'm from." She inclined her head to the waiting room.

"Still. A lot of people would have defected west. Gone into plastic surgery. Whatever."

She shook her head. "I wouldn't be happy. There's a purity, a beauty here."

Almost unconsciously, my glance went to the scuffed cabinets. The children's shelf lined with tattered board books, broken dolls, and a teddy bear with matted fur. The grimy window overlooking Broadway, where car exhaust and fried food vapors drifted up.

Dr. Rodriguez shook her head and adjusted the red ribbon around the bear's neck. "Beauty is not all astounding joy, you know. There is great sorrow and sadness in the world. But that doesn't mean it can't be beautiful. To feel a thing strongly, that is what's important."

She walked down the hallway and into the crowded waiting room, and I marveled at her serenity. She knew exactly where she wanted to be and what she wanted to do. I loved being a reporter too. But I was under no illusions that my inky touch healed people. Now she returned, leading a woman and a limping child. In her arms, Dr. Rodriguez held a toddler whose shaved head was encrusted with scabs. Watching her

speak to him in soft Spanish, her face animated in a way it had
not been with me, I felt a stab of envy.

I must seek beauty, strive for serenity, I thought. Instead, my
mind filled with fear and chaos as I drove the four short
blocks to the *Times*. I pictured calling up Thompson in the
bureau and saying, "Guess what? I almost got killed today."
But that would never fly. He'd insist I report it to the police,
regardless of what the maid had begged me. And he'd pull
me off the story, since there was no sense in losing a perfectly good reporter. Still, even without grisly details, I
could tell him plenty. I had proof positive that someone
unsavory was looking for the girl. And for the first time, I
had part of a name: Serey. She was sick enough to go to the
doctor. The INS was trying to put her on a plane. But to
where? And someone had hired her a lawyer. Meanwhile, I
was no closer to solving her mother's murder. The deeper I
probed, the more I felt a powerful but concealed hand jerking us all like marionettes in the execution of some complex
and far-reaching play. All that was missing was the script.

Thompson was at lunch, so I e-mailed him just enough
tantalizing details so that he'd salivate for more and keep
me on the story. I wanted to pin a nationality on this little
child so I could hit up the consulate. And who had hired her
a lawyer? It couldn't be the INS or FBI; they used the U.S.
Attorney's office when they needed help. Could this lawyer
be working for the people who had brought the girl into the
U.S.? If so, I'd best proceed very carefully.

What kind of name was Serey? I thought a few minutes,
then called one of my sources who worked Asian gangs. He
wasn't there so I left a message, spelling the name on his
voice mail. When I clicked the OFF button on my headset, I
heard a voice.

"Why do you need to know that?"

Josh's black head appeared above the partition wall.

"Because I do," I said, irritated that he had overheard me. "It would narrow things down quite a bit. Do you realize there are a hundred ninety-seven languages spoken in this city? That's more than on most continents. I think Los Angeles should adopt a universal language, like Esperanto, but something new and better. Everyone would have to learn it. It would be a lingua franca, like in the Roman Empire."

"We already have one," Josh said dryly. "It's called English."

"Oh," I said, deflated. I fancied the Roman Empire metaphor, wasn't ready to let it go. "We've got bread and circuses too. The *Times* covers plenty of those."

"This have something to do with that little LAX girl?" he asked, watching my face.

"Maybe."

"Let me hear it again and I'll tell you."

I rolled my eyes. "Oh, and you're such the linguist?"

I surveyed him. Posh Josh. An ingenue in rumpled khakis and a carelessly buttoned broadcloth shirt. Tie barely knotted. A warm gleam in his eyes. The princeling.

"I lived in that part of the world," Josh said.

"All right," I conceded. "But you stay away from this story."

"Scout's honor." He smirked.

"I only have part of it, and I don't know if it's a first or last name. Serey," I told him.

He pondered it. He repeated it, letting the syllables roll off his tongue. You could see him turning it around, examining it from all angles.

"It's not clear," he said. "Southeast Asian is my guess. Lao, maybe. Burmese. Also perhaps Cambodian. But it's tricky. There's a lot of borrowing from Chinese; everything's mixed up. Then there are all the ethnic minorities. Thailand, for instance, has dozens. Often you can't tell by the name. So," Josh said, his breath coming perceptibly faster. "Didja find her?"

"Not yet," I said, turning the tables. "Did you find out any more about those dead Russians?"

"Bureau says the bullets in their bodies didn't come from any FBI weapons. Or from the security cops' either. They've done ballistics tests."

"Then who?"

"Someone else in the crowd, someone who got clean away," Josh said. "Now the Asian woman, it was a Russky bullet that got her."

"Why?"

"All sorts of theories floating around. None of which I'm at liberty to discuss," Josh said.

"I'll bet you don't know any more than I do."

Josh leaned in. "That's where you're wrong," he said. "You know, I was thinking, it worked out perfectly that Metro gave me the Russians and you the kid. I know a lot about the rough-and-tumble world of organized crime, and, well, you're simpatico toward that little orphaned girl. I mean, you can relate, being a . . ."

He trailed off, seeing daggers flash in my eyes.

"Being a what?"

"Oh, you know, women and kids, there's a natural affinity. I've been watching you and I think it's great how this has become some kind of personal crusade. . . ."

"Josh?"

"Yeah?"

"I want to be perfectly clear on something. If Metro had assigned me the Russian mob story, I would have made that my personal crusade. I'd be reading Pushkin and dogging Bureau sources and slamming back vodkas at the Moskva Nights, where these mafiosos hang out. For me the professional is the personal. And vice versa. Do you understand? I don't know how to do things halfway; it's a failing of mine. The girl happens to be the object of my intense professional desire at this moment. Nothing more, nothing less. The fact that I have ovaries and produce estrogen is utterly beside the point."

I got up and walked over to the bookshelves against the wall, a bit taken aback at my own vehemence. I pulled down a phone book from the long row of fat directories that covered every community in Southern California. It would have been easier just to call directory information. But I was too embarrassed, recalling an old *Herald Examiner* story about how *Times* reporters cost the paper $250,000 a year on such calls because they were too lazy to look in the phone book.

I pulled the earphones over my head and began dialing consulates, figuring that the INS or this lawyer fellow might have been in touch with them. I tried the Burmese, Laotian, Vietnamese, Malaysian, and Chinese. At some I left messages. At others I explained what I needed and was told they knew nothing about such a child but would check. Then my luck changed.

At the Thai consulate, a young woman said she had been told to refer all inquiries to the vice consul, who was in a meeting. Carefully, I adjusted the foam rubber disk against my ear and asked to be put through to his assistant.

"Hold a minute, please," came the voice.

"Yes," I said, sensing a crack in the dam. Something was about to change.

"Mr. Lolivan Changyatuktik's office," came a crisp male voice.

I repeated my question, spelled out the name, and asked if the consulate had heard of her or was in touch with the authorities concerning her citizenship. The man at the other end of the line cleared his throat.

"This is a very unfortunate story indeed," he said. "We have made inquiries, and do not believe that this little girl is

Thai. Interpol is showing several aliases for her. And this name you have is just one of them."

My heart sank. If this man was telling the truth, then the name Serey was a dead end too, no more real than Yasuko. And Maxwell had said she wasn't Japanese.

"Any idea what her real name is and where she's from?" I asked.

"That has yet to be determined. All I can tell you is that she is not a citizen of Thailand."

I thought I detected a note of smug relief in his voice. Thailand had enough problems without adding some stateless, trafficked little girl to its list of headaches.

"What would you do if you were in my shoes?" I asked, throwing out my last line.

He paused. "If I were you, Ms. Diamond?" he said. "I would pose your questions to the Cambodians."

"Why?" It was not the most delicate of questions, but the word shot out of my mouth before I could catch it and stuff it back inside.

"As you know, Thailand is not a wealthy country. But compared to some of our neighbors, we are very rich indeed, and our nation is at peace. As a result, many refugees from our less fortunate neighbors have sought refuge in Thailand. The UN has many camps within our borders. Cambodia, because of its tragic history, has many such refugees." His voice lowered. "Sometimes children are born in those camps. But ethnically, you understand, they are not Thai."

I thanked him and hung up, then immediately called the Cambodian consulate and was told that no one would be in until 2 P.M. but that I could call back and make an appointment then.

Two o'clock found me in Chinatown again, pulling up to a squat building several blocks from the Hotel Variott.

I stifled my fear, took the elevator up, and found myself in an office, adorned only by several large paintings of

Buddhas and temples, including Angkor Wat, Cambodia's most spectacular calling card. The slim, suited receptionist behind the desk wore her long hair in a hennaed ponytail. She asked me to take a seat and seemed nonplussed by the fact that I didn't have an appointment.

I took out a novel and waited. I was good at waiting and never went anywhere without reading material. But in my head, I rehearsed the questions I meant to ask. Meanwhile, a stream of Cambodians and would-be visitors to Cambodia dropped in to apply for visas, fill out forms, and inquire about immigration issues.

A light caught my eye and I looked up in time to see the elevator moving. I had noticed while coming up here that the elevator had doors on either side. Now it stopped at the third floor, where I sat, but no one came out. I saw the young woman look up. She waited until the elevator began its descent, then picked up the phone. Someone must have gone out the other door. It must lead to a private office, I thought, wondering if my man had arrived.

The young woman pressed two buttons, then said something in fast Cambodian. Not that I would have understood slow Cambodian, mind you. She listened and nodded. Then she stood up, smoothed her skirt, and walked over to me.

"The consul is unavailable," she told me. My face must have dropped, because she added quickly that the vice consul would see me. She asked me to follow her and led me through an unmarked door and into another office, this one more richly appointed. A huge oil portrait of Prince Norodom Sihanouk was mounted on the wall. He wore an elaborate headdress and robe. Then there was another photo of Angkor Wat, mysterious and majestic amid the jungle greenery.

Behind a desk sat a small man with a wide face and bad skin. He looked vaguely ill at ease. He motioned to me to sit down and the receptionist left the room so quietly I didn't hear her go. I had the feeling that this was not the small man's office, that he had slipped into the leather seat behind the large desk and was now playing a role.

"What can I help you with today, Ms. . . . Diamond?" he said, taking a peek at the business card he had palmed from the receptionist.

"I'm so sorry to come here without an appointment, but it's rather urgent. We're trying to find out what happened to the little Cambodian girl named Serey," I bluffed. "Her mother was killed in that airport massacre and her father has apparently disappeared."

The man blinked twice. "But you know the INS is handling it. As soon as the paperwork is processed, she will be returned."

"To Phnom Penh, you mean?" I asked.

"That's right."

"Is Serey a Cambodian name?" I asked, playing dumb.

He gave me a probing look. "Her parents are Cambodian. She was born in a Thai refugee camp."

This tracked with what the supercilious Thai had told me.

"But wouldn't that make her Thai? Or stateless? Have you been able to locate her father?"

His eyes took on an opaque cast. "We're still looking. But this girl is Cambodian. Her mother returned to her village outside Phnom Penh after the baby was born. Her grandparents are there too. The family is eagerly awaiting her return."

I was still fixated on the beautiful dead woman in the raspberry pantsuit. "But I thought her mother was killed at LAX?"

"We are still trying to confirm the identities of all the relatives," he said. "But I want to assure you that she has family in Cambodia and she belongs there. It is misguided to try to keep her in the United States."

"Who wants to keep her in the States?"

"That is something you will have to ask your own officials," he said.

"But if her family are poor Cambodian villagers, how did she get here in the first place? And can you guarantee her safety if she goes back? I understand some unsavory people are looking for her."

He smiled at me. "The authorities are trying to unravel all these mysteries. There is undoubtedly a very logical explanation. And your INS would not send her back unless it was safe."

I averted my eyes to hide my skepticism.

His flickered away too. "Cambodia has a bad reputation abroad. But it is exaggerated. We take good care of our people. Unlike here in America, our, how do you say, 'extended families' in the villages help raise the child. She belongs with her people."

"But I understand she's too sick to fly."

He waved his hand. "That is ridiculous. Her family is waiting for her. We are working with the INS to see that she is repatriated quickly. Our relations with your government are excellent."

I sat there, ankles crossed demurely, watching him. I knew he didn't care one whit for this child. She was just a dirty piece of laundry to be removed from sight as quickly as possible.

The man frowned, as if he realized he wasn't winning points with me.

"We are the Cambodian consulate. We want what's in her best interest. And right now, that means getting her back in the arms of her loved ones, where she will be safe."

And where nosy American reporters will stop asking questions, I thought. I sensed that he wanted to say more so I kept silent.

"That's why this lawyer, who claims he represents human rights, has it all wrong. Who would persecute a child?"

"Oh, that guy," I said, waving my hand. "Yes, he pops up from time to time. My colleague has written about him. Oh, for goodness' sake, his name was on the tip of my tongue and now it's just flown out of my head."

I shook my head, smiling ruefully. There was a moment's silence. I forced the muscles of my face to stay relaxed and open.

"It was something like Hadley, wasn't it?"

"Brenner," he said.

"Those English names." I waved my hand in dismissal. "They all blur after a while."

"A highly unpleasant fellow," the vice consul said.

"I've heard that he's quite abrasive," I sympathized. "So where does his claim stand?"

"We don't know. But we hope to get her on a plane home in the next couple days. We are bringing in another doctor." There was a delicate pause. "One we work with on a regular basis who understands the pressures that face us."

I tried to stem the disgust creeping over my features.

"But the other doctor said she couldn't get on a plane."

"That's ridiculous. She's been on antibiotics for two days now. The ears will be fine."

His phone rang. He took the call and then turned back to me apologetically. "I have another appointment now. A long-standing one," he said, with a faint whiff of reproach. "So if there's nothing else . . ."

"Actually, there is," I said. "What's her full name?"

"I don't think I should tell you that. The INS has said it's for her own protection."

"But it's in all the legal documents on file at the court-house. In America, you know, we have what we call sunshine laws," I said, hoping to goad him with a nasty little lecture. "All court documents are open to the public." Unless they're sealed by a judge due to the sensitivity and danger of the case, I thought, as this little girl's case certainly is.

"I know about your press laws, Ms. Diamond," he said, every bit as insulted as I had hoped. "A lamentable tradition, in my opinion, that you certainly won't find if you come to my country."

"Then you know you're not revealing anything I can't find in the public record." I held my pen poised over my notepad. "So please, sir, just save me the legwork. What's her name?"

There was a pause. I held my breath and prayed.

"Her name is Serey Rath," he said.

CHAPTER 8

*B*ack in the car, I jotted all this down. Ears. Cambodia. Village. Brenner. Serey Rath. Finally I was getting somewhere. For now, the lawyer's name was more important than the girl's. In fact, I wasn't sure what good knowing the girl's real name would do me. But at least I had it.

Now I did call directory information. A bored voice on the other end of the line told me there were twelve attorneys with the last name of Brenner in Los Angeles alone. I sped back to the office. It was time to consult the Parker Directory.

Journalists have all sorts of tricks to help them find people. One is the Parker Directory, which lists the names and addresses and phone numbers of lawyers in our five-county area. I figured I could eliminate estate and intellectual property lawyers. I was after litigators who specialized in something softer and more ambiguous—human beings.

As I made my calls, I pulled the day's paper onto my lap and began skimming. At page 16, I stopped. There was a story out of Washington discussing a $165 million Cambodian aid package currently before the U.S. Senate to establish a health and social services infrastructure in the post–Khmer Rouge government. I thought back to my conversation with the third-string Cambodian envoy. No wonder the Cambodians were so eager to assist their American friends in repatriating Serey Rath.

With renewed zeal, I went back to my calls. About halfway through my list, I got a law firm called Wickam and Brenner in Los Angeles that did immigration law. The receptionist told

me I could leave a voice mail for Samson Brenner, but I told
her no thanks and hung up.

The name rang a vague bell and I leaned back in my
ergonomically correct chair and wondered why. I didn't
think I'd met him on a story. TV maybe? I closed my eyes
and an image came to mind of a large man speaking at a
press conference. Gesticulating with cuff-linked hands.
Face angry and angled toward the cameras. But I was hazy
on the particulars. Punching his name into the *L.A. Times*
database, I ordered up the clips on Samson Brenner and settled back to read as they came rolling into my in-box. Forty
minutes later, I could have written his obit.

Samson Brenner was an immigration attorney who specialized in filing lawsuits against the U.S. Government for
mistreating immigrants in detention and denying them asylum. Dozens of stories discussed class-action lawsuits he
had filed and most mentioned his colorful personality. One
reporter described him as an "imposing, charismatic man
with a booming voice given to oratorical flourishes, especially if the TV cameras are rolling."

The stories described a man who fought to fling open
borders with a zeal that approached the evangelical, and
alluded to immigration trouble several generations earlier in
Brenner's own family that had molded his convictions.
After 9/11, when America had been busy battening down its
borders, Brenner's views—which boiled down to keeping
out known criminals and letting in everyone else—had
begun to sound downright subversive.

As I read, I grew more sure that Samson Brenner was my
man. Now the only question was how to approach him. And
then with a clap of recognition, I realized why his name
sounded familiar. Hadn't he dated my friend Babette? Yes,
that was it. And if I was going to confront him about the little girl, I needed as much ammo as I could get. Including
pillow talk.

Babette was a childhood pal who had recently hit it big by writing a self-help guide to romance. Yet despite her outward success, it was a subject that sorely eluded her. Babette changed boyfriends more frequently than some editors I knew rewrote leads. Last year alone, she had dated a wildlife biologist, a Ferrari mechanic, a banker, and a nightclub promoter. And, for a brief time, Samson.

Now our conversations came flooding back. They had hooked up through a singles ad in *LA Weekly* and declared themselves soul-mates after exactly seventy-three minutes of impassioned conversation. In a county of ten million, such an aligning of the *étoiles* might be considered fate, but when you moved in certain circles, L.A. was really a village. This was especially true of the liberal lefties, a small and incestuous group whose members drank together, married one another, cheated with one another, and supported the same causes. So when Babette, a "fan of Goddard, Planned Parenthood, and *The Nation*," read a singles ad from a "SWM whose passions include Amnesty International, EarthFirst! and a free Tibet," well, it sent hopeful little bells of benison cascading through her heart. Their first date was an antiwar rally, and Babette should have known what lay ahead when he abandoned her to do a TV interview announcing that if America was going to bomb Afghanistan, then we had a moral imperative to let in every Afghani who applied for asylum. Instead, Babette was instantly and irrevocably smitten.

I hadn't seen much of her after that, but before she could gush properly about him, the relationship was over. She had resurfaced several months later, clinging shakily to the muscular arm of a horse trainer, and had thrown herself into Thoroughbred racing at the Santa Anita track in Arcadia, a leafy suburb at the foot of the San Gabriel Mountains. Oh, and she was now dodging her old PETA pals.

Since I worked nearby, I called her and we agreed to meet for an early dinner at the track clubhouse, whose windows offered a timeless vista onto the green grass, brown track, and purple mountains beyond. When I arrived, I was surprised to see Babette sitting opposite an elegant older lady, both of them bent over their rolls, wrestling with flat butter knives to spread the unyielding yellow squares.

As I got closer, I recognized Babette's grandmother Kissya, a glamorous old bird with a cigarette-ravaged voice and outsize cocktail jewelry who was a lifelong devotee of the track.

"Why hello, darling," Kissya said, her earrings bobbing in enthusiastic greeting. "Where have you been hiding yourself?" Without waiting for an answer, she turned to Babette. "I'm going to soften it up, it's too damn hard." She reached for a crocodile purse, undid the metal clasp, and rooted around until, with a pleased cry, she pulled out a gold lighter. Kissya flicked it on, sending a flame crackling into the air. With her free hand she took the butter tongs, seized a pat, then held tongs and butter to the flame.

"There," she said with satisfaction as the butter softened and began to drip. "Give me that roll." With a deft twirl of the wrist, Kissya placed the gooey square on the roll and handed it back to Babette.

"How about you, dear?" she asked.

"No thanks."

Kissya, who ate butter and cream with every meal and considered cholesterol a papist plot to deprive her of life's second greatest pleasure, applied her flame again. She spread the melted butter on a roll and was about to take a well-earned bite when she saw me examining the silver tongs, which had turned a smudgy charcoal from the flame.

"Oh balls," Kissya said. "It's not real silver, it'll wipe right off."

I wanted to ask how she was so sure, but held my tongue, knowing it would call forth a long and rambling monologue about silver dishes and caviar and no-account counts and barons from all over Europe. While I was a glutton for such fare, I wanted to spare Babette's ears. One of these days, I would invite Kissya to high tea at the Huntington Gardens, which put on a lavish service at the magnificent estate each weekend. With hundred-year-old oaks, mahogany-inlaid tables, and Corinthian pillars as a backdrop, the stories would flow from Kissya's powdered throat like wine from a Danubian cask. And what did it matter if I suspected, so deep down as to be unutterable, that Kissya was an old fraud, embroidering half-truths and tales gleaned from the historical novels she devoured nightly like bonbons? That only made me relish the storytelling even more.

I turned to Babette. "Well, this sure beats an oat feedbag. Speaking of which, where's the new beau?"

"Richard?" said Babette. "Oh, Kissya's thinking of buying a racehorse, so we sent him to have a look-see." Her eyes gleamed knowingly. "You said you wanted to talk about Samson Brenner. Richard doesn't need to hear about all that."

Kissya finished her roll and harrumphed in agreement. Then she fished in her purse for a compact, tsked at her reflection, and swiped on fresh crimson lipstick. Pursing her lips to admire the effect, Kissya snapped the compact shut and slid it back into her purse.

She had been thirty-eight when Babette had been born ("In those days, we got married and knocked up by seventeen, not always in that order," Kissya explained), still young, glamorous, and frisky enough to be appalled at the arrival of a grandchild. Rejecting the title of Grandma, she decreed that Babette was to call her Kissya, an affectionate nickname bestowed by a long-dead Hungarian count. Kissya liked an audience and especially enjoyed her frilly little granddaughter, and so Babette had grown up accompanying Kissya and her paramours to the track, to Ensenada cantinas, to the opera, always decked in velvet scarves and dripping with enormous sparkly jewels and glittery little-girl heels.

"So why did you and Samson Brenner break up?" I asked Babette. "Seems like a perfect match. You could fast for the Sandinistas together and march in the May Day parade."

Babette kissed her straw, sipping her iced tea in a magical way that left no lipstick traces.

"Babette, did you tell me about him?" demanded Kissya, ready to blame the breakup on sensible heels or lack of décolletage.

"You were in Madagascar on that lepidoptery cruise." Babette stared moodily into her ice cubes.

"Ah, the butterflies," Kissya said. "January in the southern hemisphere. I met the most fascinating Russian," she said. "White Russian, of course. Unlike my granddaughter, I wouldn't give the time of day to any other. He recited poetry on deck, and I thought I would swoon."

"You should watch all that swooning," Babette said. "You'll hurt yourself."

Kissya waved a jeweled hand, knuckles big and knobbed with arthritis. "Don't be silly, Alexei would have caught me." She turned to me. "As I was saying . . ." She stopped, a peeved expression filtering across her features as Babette's insolence sank in.

I reached over and speared a cocktail onion with a plastic sword. Kissya always ordered a martini with cocktail onions on the side; it was one of her little rituals. As I crunched the pearly globe between my molars, it collapsed against the enamel in a satisfying squirt of sour and salty juice.

Babette sighed and looked out at the mountains framed in the picture window.

"Samson's like the San Gabriels over there," she said. "He looks good if you don't get too close. Those mountains, it's only after you've hiked into them a ways that you realize they're parched and scrubby, infested with poison oak and rattlesnakes."

"So he's a venomous, cold-blooded reptile?"

"Maybe I'm exaggerating just a tad. I fell for him, didn't I?"

Over the rim of her glass, Babette studied me. Her black eyes tilted suggestively, legacy of some long-obscured Circassian or Tatar blood swimming through her veins. A woman of many veils, was Babette.

"You're not thinking about dating him, are you, Eve?"

"Yes, Eve," said Kissya, her great bosoms heaving like a bellows and sending warm gusts of Shalimar my way. "It would be a shame to let him slip away from both of you if he's such a catch."

I snorted, thinking of Tim and Silvio. "Got my hands full, actually."

Kissya clutched at the heavy necklaces around her neck in mock sorrow, her long nails clicking dramatically against the coral beads.

I remembered those necklaces. As a kid, I had loved accompanying Babette to Kissya's Encino cottage. The front yard was overgrown with banana trees and bougainvillea and rosebushes run amok, a real witch's retreat. We'd sit in the parlor and eat cucumber sandwiches with the crusts cut off, listening to her stories of ocean voyages and roadsters and narrow escapes. When she finally clapped her hands to dismiss us, we'd run to her bedroom, plunging our hands into chests filled with jewelry and trying on frothy scarves and gloves and negligees. They smelled sweet and fusty, of perfume and sea air and long-extinguished cigarettes. In her closets, we'd rummage for ball gowns and play dress-up and princess and make-believe, all the things that were frowned upon in my oh-so-rational home.

And as we reached adulthood, it sometimes seemed that

Kissya was not Babette's grandmother at all, but a solicitous older sister who instructed us both in the harem arts, though Babette took to them more avidly than me. After playing make-believe for several hours, I was ready to shuck it all off. I was learning that boys would look at me even if my hair wasn't meticulously curled and my face made up. But though my own nature shunned artifice, I couldn't imagine Babette and Kissya without their conspiratorial whispering, their feminine wiles. They would have seemed curiously naked, like bewildered butterflies suddenly stripped of their wings.

"What bearing does his love life have on anything, then?" Babette stirred her straw, making the ice cubes tinkle. "You said it was about a little girl."

"He's representing this little girl in INS custody. Everything is hush-hush and I need to learn as much as I can before hitting him up. Achilles' heel kind of stuff."

Babette's lips clamped down hard on the straw. She sucked fiercely, leaving a strawberry kiss on the pale stem.

"His weakness is he has no weakness. He won't admit human frailty."

"What do you mean?"

"You've seen him on TV, right? Those impassioned speeches about immigrant rights. Like he's marching in lockstep with God, avenging angels perched on each shoulder."

"Wait a minute, isn't there some funny story about him giving press conferences next to the Statue of Liberty?" There had been a reference to that in the clips.

"It's an office prop," Babette said. "One of his grateful clients made it. A Bosnian Muslim he rescued. Twelve-goddamn-foot-high replica, down to the flaming torch that lights up and flickers in the faux New York breeze when he gives those fiery speeches."

"But it's just a show for the cameras?"

Babette twirled her empty glass.

"Not exactly a show. Because that side of him is real. Plus oodles of charm. He just doesn't trot it out much unless he has an audience."

"And one's not a crowd."

"Exactly. But his publicity stunts are brilliant. Who can forget the dump truck?"

"Remind me."

Babette's eyes were beginning to dilate. "Samson learned that the INS was denying asylum petitions for all these Central American refugees and deporting them back to face death squads. So he filed a class-action suit on their behalf. He figured the liberal media would be all over it, but they ignored it."

"Sounds like a good story to me."

"It gets better. So Samson hires a truck from a construction site to dump ten tons of dirt on the sidewalk outside the regional INS office."

"No!"

"He gets arrested, of course, but he tips off the media ahead of time, and this time they do show up, so he gives a big speech with cameras whirring. Says that since the INS treats his clients like dirt, he's returning the favor. He has a grand time of it, scrambling up to the top of this huge mound of dirt to plant an American flag. Yelling about justice for all. And the clever bastard makes sure the load lands on the city sidewalk, not the feds' property. That's a much more serious offense."

"The guy's a performance artist."

Babette rolled her eyes. "That's exactly what his lawyer argued. In the great American agitprop guerrilla theater tradition, blah blah blah. The fine cost him a lot less than hiring a PR firm. But like many performers, Samson's oddly cold in real life. Maybe it's because of what happened."

"The clips alluded to that. A life marred by tragedy. From which he's never recovered."

"Most of his family was killed in the Holocaust. His grandfather made it out; he was a big industrialist. Fled the war in style, arriving in New York on the *Queen Mary*. They settled in Mobile, Alabama, of all places. He's from a long line of Red Diaper babies on his mother's side. It's part of the family mythology. A greater calling and all that. Mixed in with guilt about his wealth. It's been drilled into him from birth to fight on behalf of those with nothing. The way he sees it, he has to avenge the injustice of a whole people."

"Oh," I said, embarrassed that I had mocked him.

Babette flicked a crumb off her forearm. "It's like his life now is one long mea culpa for his grandfather's escape while millions died."

"That's a pretty heavy burden. What about his personal life?"

"Divorced three times. They keep getting younger and more exotic. No wonder he wants open borders." She tittered. "But I digress. One grown daughter. She was brilliant, they say, but turned to drugs and ended up on the street. They lost touch years ago."

"How sad. He's not even that old."

"He's fifty-four. And he's the first to tell you he wasn't a good dad. Always out slaying some dragon. Arguing before the Supreme Court. Gone for weeks on end."

"So he pours all his passion into his work, and there's none left when he gets home," I said. "Empty vessel syndrome."

"Lots of men are like that," Kissya said mildly, stirring crème fraîche into her lobster bisque. "So long as he's a good provider. Young women should develop their own interests, not be so dependent on men. That's what I did."

Babette blinked in rapid succession, as if she couldn't believe what she was hearing. "I think he's only capable of true passion when it's abstract, when he's fighting for three thousand penniless immigrants," she went on, ignoring

Kissya. "But give him one troubled kid, his own flesh and blood who acts out and whines and needs him home at night, and he can't handle it. For him it's all abstract. He, he . . ." Babette searched for the most damning fact she could dredge up. "He gave money to the Shining Path, for God's sake!"

Spoon halfway up to her mouth, Kissya stopped and cocked her head. "Shining Path, what a lovely image," she mused, oblivious to her granddaughter's distress. "So evocative. Like the title of a romance novel."

Babette groaned. "For God's sake, Kissya. They're Maoist rebels. In Peru. They'd string you up by your acrylic nails."

"I've met guys like him before," I said. "They litter the public landscape, great men and women doing courageous, important things. They need a large stage, the adulation of the public, that private love just can't provide."

"That was what was so frustrating about him," Babette said. "You could see exactly what needs fixing. Like the Tin Man, you know. If I only had a heart. So for once I took the advice in my book. I hightailed it out of there. But go and see for yourself." She looked at her watch. "It's Tuesday. The days are getting longer. At seven P.M., he'll be down at Plummer Park. With his dogs."

My heart beat faster. Was I ready to confront him?

"Doesn't sound like a dog person," I said.

She got a faraway look in her eyes. "Those dogs are more important to him than people. They're loyal. Adoring. And if he's traveling or has too much work or is tired, the dogs don't give him shit. Not these dogs."

CHAPTER 9

*T*ucked inside of greater Los Angeles, the kingdom of West Hollywood was an entity unto itself. Its dominant tribes were gays and immigrant Russians, two groups that distrusted one another, gave one another wide berths, and maintained separate eateries, retail shops, gyms, even social service agencies.

Plummer Park was their DMZ. A neutral green turf where everyone could meet and greet. But even here, there were minizones. In one quadrant lounged the bathing beauties, lithe young men on towels, wearing Speedos and reading *The New York Times* between sips of bottled water. They were almost completely ignored by the elderly immigrant men from the former Soviet Union who commandeered the picnic tables near the tennis courts. Dressed in dark suits and hats, they crowded onto the benches, playing cards and spitting out sunflower seed husks like so many roosting pigeons. The smell of their acrid smoke, the low hum of epistolary Russian, and the slap of cards onto the tables permeated the park. While the cops suspected they gambled for money, they could never prove it. Watching from under beaky noses, hawk-eyed and proprietary, the men had their runners, their patois, their furious hand signals, and somehow not one ruble was ever seen to slip from gnarled hand to pants pocket.

I stopped to ask members of both republics about a dog park and received only quizzical stares. Finally I found a city employee who was just locking up.

"Dog park?" The man looked me up and down suspiciously, as if I might be one of the park loonies. "Sorry, ma'am. I can't help you."

"Well, do you ever see a group of people with dogs? Doesn't seem like it would be something you'd miss."

Typically, whenever a dog park sprang up, rabid controversy followed. An L.A. councilwoman once told me that a dog park proposal in her district had received five times as many letters as a proposed halfway house for child molesters.

"No," he said decisively. "No dog park."

Dejected, I walked away.

"Wait," he called after I had gone thirty feet. "You don't mean the Aibos, do you?"

I turned back. "Aibos? Is that a breed? Sounds Japanese."

"You could say that. Tonight's Aibo night. Room 5E."

He pointed to the community center. I thanked him and headed off to the stucco building, wondering what kind of dog group met indoors. Wasn't that unsanitary?

Walking in, I went from room to room, passing classes in tai chi, ESL, watercolor painting, yoga, and other topics that remained obscured in the twenty seconds it took me to walk past. I halted in front of one room where a dozen men sat on mats, clad only in leotards or bikini briefs. They were affixing spiky collars and handcuffs and leashes to one another. Could this be what the parks-and-rec guy meant? I glanced at the sign on the door. BONDAGE 101, it read. I kept going.

Finally, I found 5E, a largish room tucked off to the side. I walked in and sure enough, there was a clot of people with dogs. The animals were uniformly small. They barked and skittered around the floor the way little nervous dogs tend to do. Owners were throwing balls for their pets and scolding them when they sniffed each other's behinds. One man got down on his hands and knees and called, "Here, Butch, here, Butch," and Butch, a pewter-colored puppy, gamboled toward him.

In addition to being small, the dogs were weirdly iridescent. Then I realized their movements were jerky, as though they were not quite real, but only robots approximating dogs.

And then I realized they *were* robot dogs.

"Your first time here?" a man asked pleasantly.

He smiled widely. Unable to face his jack-o'-lantern grin, I looked away.

"Are those . . . real?" I stuttered.

"They're almost as real as you or me. Here's some literature about Aibos. See for yourself."

He handed me a brochure. I scanned and saw that they were made by Sony, which I guess did make them Japanese. Prices started at $2,000. Now I realized why they didn't meet outdoors, on grass or dirt. At those prices, you didn't want to risk any rusting.

A ball rolled up. A dog scampered after it, metallic paws skidding on the linoleum. The dog was segmented, like an earthworm, its hard, metal exoskeleton doing nothing to diminish the perception that a large and shiny stink beetle had suddenly sprouted a few extra appendages and taken dog shape.

"Bring it back, Chester," a woman pleaded. The dog cocked its robotic head and barked, the sound emerging muffled from the ball clenched in its mouth. She walked up, admonishing him.

"Now, Chester. There are two parts to playing fetch, and you're just doing the first part. He's a puppy," she said, noticing me. "He's still learning."

"You can teach them?"

"Oh, yes, the more input they get, the more doglike they become. Chester here is developing quite a roguish personality. It's because I indulge him, don't I, sweetheart. Come to Mommy."

The dog ambled up, dropped the ball, and gave a playful *ruff*.

"They don't always respond in programmed ways," a voice said. I looked up and saw a big man calmly stroking a goatee. He was more stout than fat and carried himself well. Broad, powerful shoulders rippled beneath a white shirt of roughly woven cotton, but my eye was drawn lower. Instead of pants, he wore an indigo-print sarong knotted around his ample waist. It hung down to his calves. His feet were sheathed in leather sandals. Far from looking ridiculous, there was something majestic about him, a marble gladiator sprung to life. With his bulk, the sarong was probably a lot more comfortable than pants, anyway. His eyes were an intense, brilliant blue, and it took me a minute to place him, outside his usual attire, the understated and beautifully tailored suits he wore to court. But finally I recognized him from the newspaper photos I had called up earlier that day on the computer. It was Samson Brenner.

Now he called in a basso profundo that dripped with Southern honey, "Here, Huddled, here, Masses."

In response, two Aibos scuttled toward him. Brenner praised them, then turned back to me. "I play with them on 'DogLife V' at least once a day when I'm in town. That's why they respond so well."

"'DogLife V'?"

Brenner gave me a penetrating stare. "It's one of the software packages. Are you interested in Aibos?"

"I didn't even know what they were until a few minutes ago."

"You think we're pathetic, don't you?"

He held up a hand to forestall my denial. "I can see it in your body language. Bunch of computer dweebs. For us, you see, there's little distinction between organic and computer animals. I've programmed Huddled here to send and receive e-mail. I want to get inside his head. I also designed a program that lets me see the same images he does. I can gauge how he'll react, what emotions he feels. I know he's a machine, but still . . . Tell me, what kind of creatures are you close to?"

He had me there. No pets, no close family, and barely enough friends to flesh out a TV sitcom.

"Typical Angeleno," he said, scooping up Huddled and Masses. "Well, let me assure you that interacting with these guys is more real than having a TV relationship with Madonna or Tom Brokaw."

I threw my arms up in surrender. "Hey, you overestimate my media contacts. But I get what you're saying. It's a way for people to relate to something outside their solipsistic selves. And probably cheaper than therapy." I paused. "Or defending a Third World orphan just to have something to fill that aching void in your soul."

That caught his interest. "What would you know about Third World orphans?"

"I just know about one. I hear she's become a cause célèbre of yours. My name's Eve Diamond, by the way. *L.A. Times* reporter."

Sensing something tighten in the vast agglomeration of molecules that made up their master, the Aibos growled deep in their metallic throats and lunged at me.

"Hey," I yelled, stepping back. Did Aibos come equipped with lifelike teeth? "Call off your hounds. What are they, canine mood rings?"

"The great part about an Aibo," Brenner said, "is that you can turn them off." As the animals writhed and growled in his arms, he clicked a lever under one belly. Then he did the same for the other one. They froze in a half scrabble. He eased them onto the floor.

"I'm not exactly hard to reach," he said. "In fact, your paper has accused me of being a media whore. So why not come see me during business hours? Instead of here tonight, when I'm trying to unwind."

"Two words, Mr. Brenner: Serey Rath."

He had been smiling. Now he blinked, and retreated inside himself, and his eyes took on the opacity of a sated tiger's who lets the zebras come right up to the communal watering hole.

"Ah," he said. "So the media is hot on the trail of my latest project. I wasn't ready to go public with that one yet. Please keep me out of it for now."

"Sorry." I laughed. "You've just confirmed it."

"Still, I do wish you'd wait a few days," Brenner said. "She's going to be my poster child for political asylum, but it's tricky. She's an unaccompanied minor. The INS dens are full of them. Mostly Latino. This one happens to be from Asia. A trafficking case if I ever saw one."

"Why is everyone after her?"

He looked shrewdly at me. "Who's after her?"

I backpedaled, not ready to share my information and shivering at the memory of that gun against my temple in the bleak hotel room.

"Well, the media for one. And the INS says they're hiding the girl for her own safety. What's that supposed to mean?"

He gave a twisted laugh. "That means they want to keep her locked up until they can deport her without a lot of fanfare."

I thought of the Pakistanis being marched onto the waiting plane at LAX. To the INS, Serey Rath was just one more headache, one more undesirable to be shipped back COD ASAP.

"But she can't get on a plane because of her ears?"

He was thoughtful for a moment, puzzling out how I knew. Then his nature got the better of him. "It was a stroke of genius, getting that doctor's statement. We might be on risky ground legally, but you can't argue with medical necessity. She's too sick to fly. Ears so infected her eardrums would puncture from the pressure. We argued for and got a temporary stay."

"Fly where?"

"I'm not prepared to tell you that."

"Cambodia?"

His face reddened. "This is a very delicate negotiation. With these kinds of cases, all the papers are false. There are dozens of dialects, and war has mixed up the populations. The child has been so traumatized she barely speaks in any language."

"You mean she's mute?"

"Damn close to it."

"So why is the Cambodian consulate involved?"

"The thrust of your questions is highly emotional," he said, deflecting me. "Perhaps you feel personally involved with the case? Maternal impulses stirring for a sick, abandoned, trafficked child. Could this be the flickerings of advocacy journalism? Maybe we can use you."

"I'm only human. But I want to report the news, not become it."

"Of course you do."

"Any idea where they're keeping her?"

He smiled over my head at something I couldn't see. "As her lawyer, I am privy to all kinds of information that I am not allowed to disclose."

"Who hired you?"

Now his eyes shifted back to me. From his height he peered down, rolling forward onto the balls of his feet.

"I'm not prepared to discuss that here," he said. "But she's trafficked goods."

"Sez who?"

He smirked and caressed his Aibos in their binary slumber. "I've got my sources, just as you do."

He began to walk. I pranced alongside him, wanting to keep the conversation going. My fingers were itching for a pen. In my excitement, I had failed to bring one. Pretty pathetic, a reporter without a pen.

"It's just that . . ."

"That what, Ms. Diamond?"

"That's what I heard too," I said, thinking of what Maxwell had told me.

"Well then, that should satisfy your two-source rule. Isn't that what they teach you? If you can get two sources to confirm it, you can run with it." His lip twitched, as though he had tasted something rotten. "A much lower standard of proof than the law requires . . ."

We were in the parking lot now. He stopped his diatribe as a young girl approached. She stood ramrod straight, dressed in a fitted white suit, white leather shoes, and a white leather boating hat. It contrasted most becomingly with her toffee skin, almond eyes, and jet-black hair, which hung long and straight down her back. A band of gold around her slim finger matched Brenner's own.

I tried not to stare. Babette had told me that Samson liked them young, but this little chickie couldn't have been more than twenty. Was she a client he had rescued from the INS and helped gain asylum, perhaps? One grateful to have such a protector. She stood at attention, a slim splinter of a girl next to his bulk, as he strutted around in his sarong. I wondered if he wore underwear beneath the thin weave of batik, what games they played in bed . . .

"Talina," he boomed with a rapacious smile. "Here you are."

I waited for him to introduce us. When I realized no introduction was forthcoming, I asked him again how he had learned about the case. Certainly it hadn't been from the INS, since they wanted to keep this under wraps.

"Look," he said. "I'd be happy to sit down formally with you and explain what I'm doing. But not now. I mustn't keep Talina waiting. Shall we say dinner, Saturday, seven P.M. Tong?"

"That new place in Los Feliz?" I said, surprised at both

the dinner invitation and the place. Tong was hip. Exclusive. Celebrity-infested. Immigration law must pay better than I knew.

"Listen, Ms. Diamond. I work hard. I play hard. The owners of Tong just happen to be friends of mine. I know Alex from back home; we grew up together in Mobile. Ever been there? Postcard-perfect little antebellum town. As soon as I could, I got the hell out. I couldn't stand the extreme whiteness of where I was from. Oh sure, we had black people in Mobile, but not in my neighborhood. Except as maids and gardeners. L.A.'s much better. Here I sample it all. Isn't that right, Talina?"

She turned away. "As you say," she whispered.

"Our government, in its infinite wisdom, wanted to send Talina back to Burma, to the embrace of the military junta that killed her parents and older brother. Supporters of Aung San Suu Kyi. I argued her asylum petition. We lost and I appealed it to the federal immigration court. They're pretty much a rubber stamp for the INS; only three percent of cases get overturned. We're giving these immigrants a one-way ticket back to torture and death."

"Don't sound-bite me, Mr. Brenner. So Talina's one of the lucky three percent?"

"That's right. And over the course of that long battle, we grew close. And here we are."

He thrust out his chest and smiled at her. It was the grin of paternalism. Of neocolonialism. Of May-December lust.

He walked up to her, hands clasped behind his back, navigating a slow circle around her.

"I tell her she looks like Cher," Brenner said, stopping behind her. He grabbed her long, straight black hair and pulled down roughly. Talina's pale oval face tilted back, neck arched, and they locked eyes, gazing steadily at each other in some private ritual that I found abhorrent and yet strangely exciting at the same time.

Brenner snorted. "And what response do I get? Huh?" He shook the ropy black coils, then let go and walked back to me. "She asks me, 'Who's Cher?'"

Talina straightened her supple back, flipped her hair, and stood at silent attention, a lamplike glow receding from her eyes. I wondered if all his wives had been tongue-tied colonials. Maybe he just didn't want any competition at home. From pets or wives. We were different that way. And yet, I had seen something in Talina's eyes that was far from subservient.

"Until Saturday then," Brenner said.

He put the Aibos down, turned them on, and ordered them to the car. They trundled obediently off. They were beautiful in a sleek and chilly way, furless, like smoothly polished dog sculpture, modernistic, but somehow imbued with the essence of dog. Come to think of it, they made an appealing, guilt-free pet for a reporter who was rarely home.

Brenner and the girl followed the Aibos to a blue-gray Mercedes coupe whose metallic sleekness matched the polished gleam of the dogs. But then the script diverged. Talina slid behind the driver's seat. Brenner walked to the trunk and carefully placed the Aibos inside. Then he hiked up his sarong and clambered into the backseat. I saw him pick up a cell phone and dial. As they drove past, he must have seen the look of surprise on my face, because he leaned forward and told her to stop. The car slowed. Then, with a diesel whine, it backed up until it was directly before me.

Samson Brenner stuck his head out the window, cell phone still glued to one ear. "What's the matter, Ms. Diamond? You have a look of consternation on your face."

I blinked and tried to recover. "I'm just surprised to see your wife driving while you sit in the backseat like some Third World pasha, that's all."

He put the phone down. He ran his hand across his face.

And then Samson Brenner laughed. He threw back his head and had himself a good guffaw. In the driver's seat, Talina, looking rather jaunty in her captain's hat, regarded us impassively.

When Brenner recovered, he gave me a vulpine grin. "Talina's not my wife, Ms. Diamond. She's my driver."

"Your driver?" I said stupidly.

"Yes, my driver. Don't you know that all weird Southern people have drivers?"

He regarded me with bemusement, too well-bred and chivalrous to say what was on his mind. "Till Saturday, then."

He leaned forward and I heard him murmur, "Home, Talina." The big car leapt forward like a steel jaguar. And in the slit of the rearview mirror I saw Talina's cat eyes watching me as she drove away.

CHAPTER 10

*T*he next morning, I could hardly wait to get to the office and call Bill Maxwell. I wanted to tell the customs official about Brenner and recount everything that had happened, but Maxwell sounded weirdly stilted and said he'd have to call me back.

"Is that because you've got a break on the case?" I asked.

"I will call you back," he repeated, and hung up.

Puzzling over what it could mean, I walked to the lunchroom for a cup of coffee. On the way back, I noticed that the door to Tom Thompson's corner office was closed. Through the window, however, I saw the city editor, Jane Sims, standing over Thompson's desk. Both of them were peering intently at the computer screen.

What could have brought her to the hinterlands of the *Times'* San Gabriel Valley bureau, I wondered, butterflies fluttering to life in my stomach. Had they found out I had seen Silvio? What other laws might I have transgressed? With Jane Sims, everyone was guilty; it was just a matter of finding a punishment to fit the crime. We had declared an uneasy truce ever since I had found out something personal about her while investigating a murder. But I wasn't sure how long it would last.

I was dying to ask someone about the Jane Sims sighting, but everyone was out except for Trevor Fingerhaven, and he was conducting a loud telephone interview. So I sat at my desk, trying in vain to sort through my leads on the missing toddler. Finally I put on headphones to drone out Trevor's hyenalike laugh, which did not grow any more

palatable the longer I listened to it. Trevor had once won
some big investigative prize at an East Coast paper and the
Times, in its inimitable fashion, had hired him shortly there-
after, then stuck him in a suburban bureau to cool his heels
for a few years. Like all of us, he desperately wanted to go
downtown.

Lost in annoyed contemplation, I didn't see Thompson
and Jane Sims until they were looming over me, printouts in
hand.

"Meditation time?" Thompson asked with a grin.

"Medication time." I held up my coffee mug. Maybe with
some caffeine singing in my veins, I'd figure out the next
step to this increasingly complicated story. And if I slipped
away, they might give whatever boring assignment they
clutched in their hands to Trevor or someone else. I stood up.

"Not so fast," Jane Sims said, pulling up a chair to block
my path. She sat down and tried to prop an elbow on my
desk, but was stymied by a two-foot pile of files.
Undeterred, she seized them and lowered them onto the carpet. She inspected the dust patterns now visible on the desk,
then swept them with her paper printout into my trash can.
Satisfied, she allowed her arm, encased in a peach silk shirt,
to rest against my desk.

"What are you working on?" Jane asked without preamble.

"That missing kid story. I've just learned that—"

"It can wait," she cut me off. She drummed her French-
manicured nails on my desk and held up a photo. It showed a
car on fire in rush-hour freeway traffic, flames lapping the
metal greedily as firemen worked to douse the blaze. As far
back as you could see, lines of traffic had snaked to a stand-
still.

"Sandy Morse," the city editor said. "Burned to a crisp
inside her car on the way to work yesterday. Single mom.
Lived in Alhambra. Worked for the government."

"Horrifying," I said, wondering what would happen to the kids.

"Worked for the INS," Jane Sims continued, watching me.

Thompson pulled up a chair and dug his heels into the industrial carpet. I grew more alert.

"Wires are now saying she was scheduled to testify tomorrow before the grand jury," Thompson said. "They're looking into airport corruption."

"And since you're well sourced with them and Customs," Jane Sims continued, "we figure you can look into it."

"We want you to find out who she was, Ace," said Thompson. "Tell us her story."

Dear, earnest Tom Thompson. The bard of the poor, the downtrodden, the unfortunate. He felt their pain. But he was ignoring mine.

"But you promised I could pursue the little girl. Things are heating up."

"Now, Eve," he said, seeing my expression. "You know how people rubberneck at accidents. They'll read this story for the same reason. It's the 'there but for the grace of God' factor."

"I'm waiting for an important phone call."

"Call your source back, give 'em your cell, and get going. You won't miss a thing. And if you get a break on the little girl, we'll free you up. Promise."

Putting on my surliest face, I held my hand out for the printout.

"Attagirl," he said.

"Puleeze, Thompson. That sounds like I'm your dog."

"You are," he said. "You're my attack dog."

"Flattery will get you nowhere," I muttered to their receding backs.

I read the wire story, then called Maxwell and left my cell number on his machine. Then I called the Alhambra police to ask if they'd fax over the police report. They agreed and said

I should check with the L.A. County Fire Department, which had helped put out the blaze.

When the fax came in, I read that Sandy Morse, thirty-six, had been on her way to her civil service job when, according to witnesses, she lost control of her car and slammed into the center divider. The car had burst into flames and Sandy was trapped inside. She would have to be identified by dental records, but the license plate showed the car was registered to her, so unless someone else had been driving her car that morning, Sandy Morse was dead. She left four children, ages four through twelve. They would now be raised by Sandy's mother. The police report gave the address and I steeled myself to go out there and interview them.

When I pulled up to the house, I realized with a jolt that Maxwell hadn't called me back yet. Turning off the engine, I made sure the cell phone was on. The screen glowed, but there were no messages. I looked around. Sandy Morse had lived in a middle-class community of older homes. Giant California oaks arched their way gently over the street, forming a canopy that cooled the asphalt street all summer long.

Someone was sitting in an L.A. County Fire Department car parked in front of the house, writing on a clipboard. Wanting to postpone the inevitable confrontation with the grieving relatives, I approached, holding out my press pass. He put aside his work and watched me with a wary expression more common to police than firefighters. He had a brown handlebar mustache and lean features.

"How are they doing in there?" I asked. "I'm sure not looking forward to asking them more questions."

"Then don't." He inspected me with indifference.

I was trying to figure out an appropriate response when he cracked a grin. "Dennis Montblanc, L.A. County Fire Department arson investigator." His hand shot out.

I stuck mine out without thinking. My brain was chewing over the implications of his title.

"How can a car crash be arson?"

Dennis Montblanc shrugged. "Fire guys send us out, pretty regular, they think something's suspicious," he said. "That car went up awfully fast."

"But didn't it hit the center divider on the freeway?" I said, quoting from the police report. "Must have been going pretty fast."

Montblanc's eyes crinkled into a smile. He had tan skin, like he spent a lot of time outdoors, but the corners where the skin scrunched up were white.

"You ever go fast on Interstate Ten at morning rush hour?" he said.

"You mean she couldn't have been going fast enough for the car to explode on impact?"

"I'm not *saying* anything," Montblanc corrected. "Especially to the press. We're investigating."

I leaned into his car window so he had a good view down the front of my blouse. I was wearing a lacy black bra.

"Could some defect have made it blow? If the engine caught on fire, how long would it take to engulf the whole car?"

His eyes focused below my face.

"In car crashes, explosions are usually caused by gasoline leaking out of the tank and dripping down onto the engine. Typically, there's a lag."

"Witnesses say it went up, what did one guy call it, like a 'stunt show at Universal Studios.'"

"That's why I'm here." He sucked air through his teeth. "Poor lady in there didn't have a chance."

"So did you talk to her mother or the neighbors? Any enemies? A pissed-off ex-husband, say?"

"Former husband's been in Indiana for three years. No boyfriend in the picture, jealous or otherwise. Hasn't had any work done on the car recently."

"Could it be connected to her upcoming testimony?

Where exactly did she work?" I straightened up and pulled a notepad out of my purse.

"Like I said, we're just starting this investigation." Montblanc's hand moved to the ignition. "Good luck in there. It ain't pretty."

He pulled out and I stood there, collecting my thoughts. Then I steeled myself and walked up the driveway to a bungalow whose glory days had ended with the Great Depression. The ample front porch was supported by two pillars of river rock, the large granite stones buffed smooth in long-ago streams. It was crammed with rusting scooters and bicycles, their slack rubber tires an unspoken childhood reproach. I climbed up spongy wooden stairs that creaked under my weight as the termites held hands and moaned. In a more hopeful time, someone had painted the clapboard house a daring shade of green. But sun and rain had dimmed it to a dull moss, and now even that was going, slivers of latex curling up from the wooden slats like bits of apple peel left by a less-than-competent cook.

I banged on the black security door. The smell of pot roast wafted through the screen. There were shuffling footsteps, then a plump woman came to the door, breathing heavily, the labored wheeze of an asthmatic.

"Yes?"

I identified myself and asked if we might talk.

"We already take the *Times.*" Her voice was leaden as she moved away.

"Wait. I'm not a salesperson. I'm a reporter."

In the crepuscular light, the woman turned back. She cleared her throat and shifted her weight. "Please leave us alone," she said. From the background came the screech of an argument, high, clear voices raised in anger. Then a loud slap, a yowl of indignation, and running feet. "Nonni, Nonni," a child called, and a small figure attached itself to the woman's legs.

"Marcus took my favorite train and he hit me when I asked for it back," the child sobbed, then stopped. "Nonni, who's that?" he whispered, the slap forgotten. "Is she with the police?"

"Please, Mrs., uh, Morse—I hope that's the right name—we know your daughter had a hard life. Full-time job, kids, no husband. The cops gave us all the official stuff. What we're looking for now is the details. Anecdotes about her life. What struggles she faced each day. The *Times* is putting together a story on your daughter and it would honor her memory if you would talk to us."

Always frame it in present action—that was a basic tenet of journalism. It's going to happen whether you cooperate or not, so you might as well lay your soul bare. It might even be therapeutic for you, numbed survivor, and it will give you a much-needed feeling of control over how your loved one is depicted in the media, and we will do nothing to shatter that illusion.

There was a sharp intake of breath. "Who are you to tell me how to honor my daughter's memory? It's Mrs. Wainright, by the way. Dorothea Wainright. And I'd be very much obliged if you would please stop sending people here to try to talk to me. As you can see, I've my hands full. Four grandchildren who don't understand why their mama's not coming home anymore."

Then I was glad for the thick black metal grate that separated us. My shoulders drooped. If only I could get inside, sit on her couch, play checkers with one of her grandkids, maybe I could win her over.

"I'm so sorry, Mrs. Wainright. I totally understand, and I promise not to bother you. We'll just do the story without you. I was just wondering if I could—"

"Nonni," said a small but persistent voice. "Does that lady work with my mama? Maybe she knows where Mama went?"

Even through the darkness of the security door, I could feel Dorothea Wainright's righteous anger bubble up.

"No, honey," she said. "That woman's a journalist. She's not customary like your mama. And like I explained, honey, your mama has gone to heaven."

"What's a journalist, Nonni?"

Dorothea Wainright leaned forward so that her face almost touched the screen and I saw puffy cheeks, coarsely grained skin, and large, sorrowful eyes. Her gray hair was pulled back in a neat bun.

"I don't want to slam the door on you, miss, because that would teach my grandson bad manners. But for God's sakes, will you please leave us in peace?"

"Yes, ma'am," I said and hightailed it off the porch, almost tripping on a pair of Rollerblades in my scrambling shame.

I feared she or the grandchildren might be looking out the window, watching me, so I quickly put the car in gear and drove two blocks, where I parked and pulled out my notepad to write everything down.

Something that Dorothea Wainright had said was echoing around in my brain. Something about being customary. Me not being customary, like the boy's mom. I thought about the story that had been occupying all my time lately, that had started with William Maxwell, a supervisor with U.S. . . . Customs. Customs, not customary. Now I needed to talk to Maxwell more than ever. Could it be that Dorothea Wainright's daughter, whose fatal car crash was being investigated as a possible arson crime, worked not for the INS but for U.S. Customs?

*I*t was lunchtime when I got back and the office was empty, except for Trevor, who always ate at his desk, messy as a parrot, so he wouldn't miss any calls. He kept instant noodles and cookies and jerky and chips stashed throughout his desk drawers. It was a righteous larder and I figured that if Armageddon came, he could keep us fed for weeks.

Now he looked around the desk to see what the wind had blown in.

"Want one?" he said, offering me a six-pack of cookies.

I thanked him but declined, thinking of hydrogenated oils, a new enemy against which I must stay vigilant. Then I put on my headphones, slapped the ON button, and punched in Bill Maxwell's number. He didn't answer. I was leaving another message when I heard a bloodcurdling shriek behind me. It sounded like someone was being killed. I threw off the headphones, leaping out of my chair and jerking around so fast that my neck hurt for a week.

"Aaarggh," said Trevor. He shoved his chair against the wall and writhed like he had been hit by an electric current. Bits of half-chewed cookie and crumbs trickled down his shirtfront.

"Jesus, Trevor, what's wrong?"

"Eeeeee," gurgled Trevor, lunging for his ankle. He pulled the sock down and shucked off his shoe, exposing sluglike toes with yellowed nails.

"Have you gone mad? I was making an important call."

"Aaaaah," he panted, plucking at his pants leg. "There's something . . . aaah, Christ, it's going up my leg."

Trevor raised his leg high in the air and shook it violently like a lunatic kickboxer. He screamed again, thin and pitiful. Something small and furry and brown flew from inside his trouser leg, landed with a thud on the desk, and scurried away, tiny feet scrabbling on the slick surface of the plastic.

"M-m-mouse," screamed Trevor. "Filthy little paws. Ahh, disgusting."

I ran to look, doubling over so he wouldn't see me laughing.

"Where'd it go?" I said, crawling under the desk to look for a flash of fur.

From my mouse's-eye view, I could see crumbs salting the carpet under Trevor's desk. No wonder there were mice. He might as well put out a sign: FREE FOOD FOR RODENTS.

Trevor stalked angrily to the window and looked out. For weeks we had watched workers cutting down trees in the neighboring lot and leveling the ground for construction. That's how I knew the local economy was healthy again: all the empty lots got filled in. Soon, there would be no green space left. The mouse must have been flushed out of its longtime home and found a new one by following Trevor's trail of crumbs to his desk.

"This is an outrage," said Trevor, his voice quivering. "I'm going to contact the building superintendent."

"If you didn't leave so many crumbs lying around, this wouldn't be a problem in the first place," I said. "Imagine, a big investigative reporter terrified of a mouse."

"You would have screamed too if it crawled up your dress," Trevor said, his indignation blooming into a leer as he contemplated what such a mouse might find.

Before I could summon a sufficiently acid response, the phone rang. I dived for the headphones, checking quickly under my desk to make sure that Trevor's mouse didn't have any accomplices.

It was Maxwell.

"Thanks for calling me back so fast," I said, trying to suppress my excitement.

"I've been busy," Maxwell said. His voice was far away.

"So I'm wondering, what can you tell me about Sandy Morse? Does she work for—"

"Ms. Diamond, I, uh—"

"Either on or off the record," I said, wondering why he had gone all formal on me.

"That's exactly what I want to talk to you about . . ."

But then he trailed off. His voice was all wrong. Stiff, as if he had pinned it to a board and shellacked it.

"Spit it out, Maxwell."

"You know I can't disclose anything about pending investigations, don't you, Ms. Diamond?" His voice was wheedling now, cajoling.

"Yeah, yeah, Maxwell, come off it. Did you have too much to drink at lunch today? And what's with the—"

"Ms. Diamond!" He cut me off, his voice finally shaking itself awake. "We are still on exactly the same footing as we were earlier this week when you asked about another investigation. Do you understand?"

His voice boomed like a drill sergeant's, and his breath came hurriedly on the other end of the phone.

Some long-dormant instinct inside of me sluggishly raised up on its haunches and looked around. I fell silent. The tension between us practically crackled over the phone line. And then my senses were awake, my heartbeat pounding in my ears, and I knew that I had come very, very close to making a terrible mistake. It was as if he were flooding my brain with a powerful message. I heard the barely perceptible intake of breath again, and I knew it wasn't him. There was a third person listening on the line. Someone who had forced Maxwell to call me and now stood by, waiting for me to damn us both.

And then relief flooded through me, because finally I understood my role.

"Officer Maxwell, are you suggesting that I would ask you to do anything improper such as leak information?" I said, outrage swelling my voice. "I called you because Media Relations keeps giving me the runaround."

"Miss Diamond, I'm not trying to impugn your reputation. I just want it clear that I can't comment on an open investigation. The spokesperson will get back to you." His voice sagged with relief.

"Can you even confirm whether she worked for you or not?"

"I've just finished telling you that all requests have to go through Media Relations." A cocky tone had crept into his voice.

"All right, Officer Maxwell. Well, if you'll excuse me now, I've got a daily to write. Without your help, as usual," I added.

I hung up and sat there, wondering if I were imagining things. No, the dread I felt was real. Had I let anything slip? What if I had blown it?

Trevor came sauntering over. "What's the matter?" he said. "Did that mouse crawl up your leg now?"

"More like a rat," I said. "A big, fat, dirty rat."

I looked at the shelf above my desk, staring but not really seeing all the reference books. *Roget's Thesaurus.* Webster's dictionary. A directory of L.A. Unified schools. I lowered my eyes to the paper stacked neatly on my desk, tried to read it for a while, but couldn't focus on that either.

The phone rang. I glanced at the clock. Ten minutes had passed.

"Eve," a by-now-familiar voice whispered.

"Yes," I said, playing dumb.

"It's me. Maxwell. That was great. You caught on almost immediately. You saved my ass. My supervisor, Scott Aiken, was on the line, listening in. He made me call you. He thought it had been me, leaking you all that information. He wanted to catch you incriminating both of us."

Now my paranoia kicked into high gear. What if the supe was still listening in? A double feint.

"Maxwell, it sounds like you need a vacation."

"Wha—? Oh, I see, very clever. Just in case this is also a setup, huh? Well . . ." I heard an intake of breath and then a gurgled snort. He tried to speak but choked and sputtered, and I had an image of someone sneaking up behind him and strangling him.

"Can you please tell me what is going on?" I said, wondering if I should call 911.

But the noises went on, growing progressively more alarming. I heard Maxwell gasping for breath. "Oh God, I can't . . . It's too . . ." and then a spasm of coughing and whoops again. I heard him panting, clearing his throat. Slowly, the threat seemed to recede.

"Okay, I'm getting myself under control. I was gargling my own adrenaline there for a minute. But everything's fine. I'm calling you from a pay phone at LAX. Listen, you were fabulous. What a pro. And now I have a present for you. Can you meet me at four in front of the Griffith Park golf course?"

"I'm not sure if this is a prank call, but I'm going to hang up now," I said, replacing the receiver.

I sat there, head in my hands, then let go, cackling like one of Macbeth's witches. Relief mingling with fear and apprehension. The cackle dipped to a moan. The world had gone crazy and I was supposed to play along, skipping nonchalantly with my basket through the forest as if big, salivating, fanged wolves weren't waiting behind the trees for my slightest misstep. A sharp realization stabbed through me: I couldn't trust anybody anymore. Even Maxwell. I'd meet with him, see what he had to say. Eventually, we might even have a genuine laugh over all this. But I could still feel the fear oozing through the phone line. Maxwell's constricted voice. And then, all of a sudden, I thought I knew what Maxwell was going to tell me.

I got to Griffith Park early and found the golf course. Then I sat in my car, waiting for him, wondering if this could be yet another setup. I twirled the radio dials for a while, hunting for *rock en español* songs. That was Silvio's influence. I thought of the last time we had been together. I wanted to linger there, in that memory, but I had work to do.

It was warm in the car so I got out, intending to stroll around, when I saw a herd of animals on the golf course. They moved slowly, heads bent to nip the tender green shoots of grass, grazing in a familiar bovine way, and I froze, afraid to startle them, stifling the cry that rose in my throat. Ten feet away, white-clad golfers moved across the greensward while the brown herd drifted, placidly munching, each group oblivious to the other.

But domestic herds didn't have antlers. Neither were they as graceful as these hooved creatures, whose hides shone a burnished pewter. Bucks, does, and fawns. How did they survive here, so primeval and pure, on a diet of chemically treated grass irrigated with reclaimed sewage?

"Don't kid yourself, they're filthy with Lyme disease."

I turned and saw Maxwell. Legs apart. The stance of a hunter.

"They're breathtaking."

"As a reporter, you, of all people, should know to look beyond the surface of a thing. C'mon, let's go sit in my car."

I followed him to a white Camry. He pressed a square pad on his key ring. It yelped and the locks chirped in cheerful welcome. I thought about how I hadn't heard him pull up, so enchanted that I had let down my guard.

The car smelled like one of those artificial air fresheners. I sniffed, and he chuckled and leaned over me, popping open the glove compartment to expose a bar of soap.

"Little trick my last girlfriend taught me," he said. "Keeps the car smelling nice. She couldn't stand the smoking. I finally gave it up but figured I'd leave the soap."

He turned the radio on and shoved in a tape. It was Ry Cooder doing the *Paris, Texas* soundtrack, a steel guitar twanging, and it made me think of dusty borders and cactus-dotted deserts and uniformed men patrolling in jeeps with guns slung around their shoulders. Men like William Maxwell.

He pulled a red leather briefcase onto his lap, unzipped it, and I waited eagerly. He thumbed through some papers and, to my great disappointment, handed me only one slender sheet. It was a smudged photocopy of a Japanese passport with a little girl's face plastered across it. Serey Rath.

"This what you had in mind?"

"Frankly, I'd prefer an eight-and-a-half-by-eleven glossy color I can give to the photo desk. This won't reproduce well."

"That was the idea. It's for your eyes only. Whoever lost her undoubtedly has feelers out, people looking for her. No sense in making it easy for them."

"Then why give it to me at all?"

He shrugged. "So you don't forget what she looks like. Maybe I want you to find her at some fleabag hotel, crying under armed guard. Maybe you'll write it up and people will read it and cause a stink and the INS will be forced to put her in foster care or somewhere more humane."

I studied him, remembering his earlier concern for the girl. Here it was again. Was this genuine? On some level, it didn't matter.

"What else you got for me?" I said, looking at the fat bunch of papers. But he just said, "Man, oh man, I was praying back there, on the phone. And you came through."

"I'm still not sure what that was all about. Why don't you enlighten me?"

"My boss," he whispered. "Aiken. I have a feeling he's mixed up in this somehow. And he's trying to use me as a fall guy. Remember I had you pretend to be pissed the other day that you didn't get a thing from me? He didn't buy it. So he set me up."

"How?"

"He comes marching in and says, 'Call her. Call that *L.A. Times* reporter right now. I'm going to listen in. And we're going to settle this thing once and for all. Someone's leaking to the press and I aim to plug that hole.'"

"So you called," I said dryly.

"I couldn't refuse, could I? That would make it look like we're in cahoots. Which we're not." His lips pressed tight. "I just think all this secrecy stinks. Ever since nine-eleven, they're trying to curtail information, even on stuff that's got zip to do with terrorism."

I didn't believe for a minute that Maxwell was so upset about government censorship. More likely he got a kick out of playing Deep Throat, seeing his leaks in the paper, and maybe needling a boss he didn't like. But whatever flipped his skirt. The shadows were lengthening and I was getting tired of circling around the meat.

"So as I said on the phone, I'm doing a story about a lady killed in a suspicious car crash yesterday. Sandy Morse. Did she work for you?"

There was a pause.

"Maxwell?"

He sighed. "A fine woman. Honest as the day is long, loved her job, had fought hard to move up the ranks, went to school at night while her mother watched the kids. She had four and her husband left her. She will be missed terribly."

A passel of clichés, strung together like railroad cars. "So she did work for you. Then why all the secrecy? What did she do?"

He shot me a sideways look.

"Off the record, right?"

"Yes, although I fail to see what you've told me so far that's so top-secret."

"She was internal affairs."

"Why hasn't this come out? And why did they say she was with the INS?"

"Now don't go getting all paranoid. It's in the latest press release the cops are sending out. They just didn't know this morning when you went out there."

"You're the second person in twenty-four hours to tell me not to get paranoid. Did you know that Arson is investigating? Seems like the car went up awfully quickly."

"Eve?"

"Yes."

"I've got a meeting tomorrow morning at nine A.M. with an L.A. County Fire Department arson investigator named Dennis Montblanc. And I'm going to tell him the same thing I'm about to tell you. This is deep background and I don't want to see my name in the paper. But listen carefully now.

"Two weeks ago, Sandy Morse received a subpoena from the L.A. County Grand Jury. They are investigating a case of official corruption at LAX that may have allowed as many as two hundred aliens to enter the United States. Those proceedings are done in secret and not made public until an indictment is handed down. Sandy was supposed to testify on May seventh."

"That's in two days."

"Someone didn't want Sandy Morse to get on that witness stand."

"What did she know?"

Maxwell looked at the clock on his dash. "And now I've really got to get home. I've already told you more than I should have."

"Maxwell," I wailed. "Don't do this to me, just when it's getting good."

"I can't tell you any more." He leaned over and opened my car door. "Good-bye, Eve." His eyes held rue and something more.

"She meant something to you," I said.

"What?" He looked at me, and the emotions of a moment ago were gone.

"You were seeing each other."

"Now what in the . . ." He sat there a moment longer, then let his head fall forward on the steering wheel until he was resting his brow on the wheel.

"I saw it, in your eyes."

He sighed. "She was a good woman, trying to keep it together."

"Tell me." I was the mother confessor.

"This has nothing to do with a story, or anything. Just two middle-aged people trying to squeeze a little joy out of life."

"Were you in love with her?"

He shook his head. "It hadn't gotten that far. Couple of dates. She was circumspect. Private. Didn't want to introduce me to her kids, her mother. Unless it got serious. She told me that up front."

"But you had serious feelings?"

"It doesn't matter." His cheek twitched. "She's gone."

"Who was she going to testify against?" A horrible thought ran through me. Was it him?

"Nobody knew."

"But you must have a theory."

"There were some drugs missing, that's all I know. Aiken told me."

Scott Aiken again.

"But you told me that he . . ." I started. "You think Scott Aiken is . . ."

Maxwell turned to me. "I don't have any proof. All I know is he just bought a house on the Palos Verdes peninsula and his living room window looks out onto the Pacific. You can't touch those views on a U.S. Customs salary."

"Maybe a wealthy aunt died and left him some money."

"He ain't been to any funerals lately."

We looked at each other.

"Don't call me anymore at work, okay? But do me a favor and call up Media Relations and harangue them every couple of days. That'll make it look like you're getting frustrated because I'm keeping my mouth shut."

"What else have you learned about the little girl?" I asked, hoping he'd keep talking.

"INS is still holding her. They're saying now her mama's some hype whore in Phnom Penh who sold the kid in exchange for some dope. So now we're looking into kiddie porn. A lot of that going on over there."

The story had just gotten much uglier.

"But why bring her here?"

"Why not, if they can charge more?"

The thought made me sick. I flashed to something else. "The Cambodian embassy told me they want to send her back to her wonderful family in a village outside of Phnom Penh. They and the INS are cooking up a plan to get her on a plane."

"It's like I told you," he said. "They don't give a shit about the kid. None of them."

"But there's a new wrinkle. She's got a lawyer now."

"I heard." Maxwell's eyes appraised me. "Maybe he can help her. It's enough to turn your stomach, these stories. Interpol says the girl's mom was sold into prostitution herself at age twelve by her junkie uncle. Just when you think you've heard the most vile thing one human can do to another, it gets worse."

I was torn between commiserating and pumping him for more.

"Can you get me those docs, Maxwell? Telexes, reports, anything I can quote from?"

He stared at the golf course. "Maybe," he said. "But not yet. Let the investigation widen a bit. In a couple of days, twenty people will have access to those documents. Then you can run with it."

"What did the LAX video monitors show, by the way?"

Maxwell looked disgusted. "You spend millions on a security system, and it still can't catch everything in a crowd that size."

"So it was a bust?"

"The techs are examining each frame."

"But you've nailed down that the raspberry lady wasn't the girl's mom?"

"She was Thai. Interpol's checking her out. Got a long record back in Bangkok. I'll get it for you, but you have to be patient."

"Thanks, Maxwell. But tell me something."

"What?"

"Why?"

"Why what?"

"Why are you leaking to me? Not that I'm complaining, but you're putting yourself at risk. And for more than losing your job, if you think Aiken's in on it somehow."

"Don't you see? Once the press gets ahold of this, it will flush him out. He'll get nervous and make a crucial mistake, and he'll go down. Little kids shouldn't get bought and sold like bolts of cloth."

"I know," I said, wondering if Maxwell would be in line for Aiken's job if his boss went down.

"It doesn't just happen in the Third World," I said.

"You know how many stories I've done about American parents who beat their kid to death for soiling their pants? For spitting up? For crying too much? You do enough of those, you start thinking they should distribute birth control to girls when they hit puberty. Put it in the birthday cake. Keep 'em on it through high school. Make sure they get a diploma, a GED, some job skills. Then we'll see."

Maxwell looked at me. "Well, I'll be hogswalloped, Eve. You sound just like a conservative redneck."

But it was one of my pet peeves and I couldn't shut up.

"You know how people claim a woman has civil rights to reproduction? Well, what about the babies' rights? They don't ask to be born. But then they are, twitching from the meth or alcohol or slammed around by Mom's boyfriend until they have brain damage. Or shuffled among fifty foster homes till they're eighteen and then put back on the street to start the cycle all over. Having a baby shouldn't be an unalienable right. It should be a privilege. You should have to get a license, just like you do for a dog. A baby has the right to get born into a family that can love it and take care of it."

"So who gets to decide?"

"Hell if I know. I'm no social worker. All I know is I could have had ten babies by now. But I didn't. And I have two degrees and a good job. I make enough to take care of them."

"You'd probably be one of those career moms put 'em in full-time day care."

Something stabbed at me inside. That he would assume such a thing.

"Maybe that's why I haven't had any," I said. "I'm not even responsible enough to have a pet. I lack the ma-toor-ity. But at least I know it."

"You're young, Eve. You'll change your mind."

"I don't know. I lose enough sleep worrying about other

people's kids. Like our little friend here." I touched the photo he had given me. "Speaking of which, why didn't you tell me you were tailing her parents the other day at LAX?" I asked, channeling my anger into something closer at hand. Something that had me miffed, I now realized.

"Now why would I have done a silly thing like that?" he said jovially. I was glad he had let the other topic slide. Despite my rant, I had no idea what the answer was. I just knew that what we had now wasn't working.

"To give me a heads-up," I said.

"The whole city got a heads-up."

"Indeed."

We said good-bye and I climbed out of his car, ashamed at my outburst. I had been getting emotionally worked up lately, and didn't know why.

CHAPTER 12

*A*t work the next day, I tried to advance the story for the paper, but no one would tell me anything more about the little girl. Brenner's secretary said he was tied up in court but confirmed dinner on Saturday. The INS was silent. The Chinatown hotels had no idea what I was talking about. The Cambodian consulate, after their initial chattiness, must have been warned against talking to a reporter. Frustrated, I finally went home.

Daylight saving had begun and the days dawdled and took their time drawing to a close, stretching out twilight into a blue gauze so thin you could peer into tomorrow.

I changed into workout gear and ran through the quiet streets as jacaranda blossoms detached themselves from the trees and drifted down, transforming the cracked asphalt into a plush lavender carpet. It wasn't true that we had no seasons here. When the jacaranda bloomed, it was late spring. Summer was when everything grew still and parched and brown, the deer and coyotes creeping down from the mountains to drink from profligate, misfiring sprinklers that sent fountains of water crashing onto indifferent sidewalks. Fall was the season of the flame, when the Santa Anas whipped up arson fires, and by November the maples and sycamores were ablaze with their own flames, as staid, older neighborhoods took on the fleeting hues of a New England sunset. Winter was bright and often warm, with a clear, pellucid light that you never saw during the long smoggy summers.

As I ran, I cataloged not only nature's beauties but its poisons. Castor plants, oleander, and morning glory, growing wild on the side of the road. For anyone familiar with the city's floral arsenal, there was no need to resort to crude weapons like guns and knives. Each year brought tragic news of toddlers dying after they pulled castor plants apart and chewed them for a lark. Of campers in the Angeles National Forest who had broken off sticks from the pretty red, pink, and white flowering bushes to roast marshmallows, then keeled over dead. We might live in paradise, but we weren't immune to the ravages of hell.

After my shower, I thought of Silvio, and how I had run into his arms the other night to inoculate myself from Tim. I walked over to the phone and picked it up. I ached for Silvio. My body felt ripe. Swollen. Tender in that premenstrual way that heightens every touch. I put the phone down. I had to get a grip on myself before I saw him again.

Work always helped. I realized that Lorenzo, the boy from the cybercafe, had never called. Still, there was some connection between that place and the little girl. Frank had been looking for the child and his name was known there. Should I try again? But after almost getting killed in the Hotel Variott, I was leery. With different hair, clothes, and demeanor, would my tormentors even recognize me as the cowering Chinatown maid? Besides, what could happen in a roomful of people?

I brewed some coffee and went onto the back porch. I had been so tired this week. I turned on the light and took out the folded piece of paper that Maxwell had given me. I smoothed it on the table and studied it. A little girl in pigtails, with a moon face. Mouth a horizontal slash. Something shy in her eyes, unwilling to meet the camera. Features blurry from the photocopying.

As I watched twilight come on, something caught my eye. I had excellent peripheral vision, and Tim's unexpected appearance had put my nerves on high alert. It was a quick, furtive movement, but by the time I looked up, it was gone. I bent back to my photo. There it came again. I looked up. A silhouette appeared. A rat. Crawling along the power lines strung across my backyard. Then another. Then a trail of them, silent and focused as a train. Creatures of the night on their own mysterious pilgrimage.

I dithered. This was an omen. If I went, I'd need someone at my back. On impulse, I called Maxwell. He had given me his home number. He answered on the first ring and listened while I explained my plan.

"Where'd you hear about this place?" he asked, suspicious.

"A source," I told him primly, wanting him to know that I had my secrets too.

"Why don't you let me come with you? It could be dangerous."

"A middle-aged guy would stick out like a cat at a dog show. Just take down this address and if you don't hear back in ninety minutes, I want you to call the police."

"You should stay away from that place."

"Just please do me this favor. I'll be careful. And remember: after an hour and a half, call the coppers."

"I *am* a kind of copper."

"You know what I mean."

I hung up and and dressed in what I hoped was a very unmaidlike outfit: black Iggy Pop T-shirt, orange jeans, boots, and a motorcycle jacket. For good measure, I topped it off with a baseball cap. I looked in the mirror, added lipstick, scowled, and squared my shoulders. Humming "Lust for Life," I drove down to Koreatown.

I parked in an underground structure two blocks away and asked for a receipt. At the elevator, I fidgeted to the Korean techno, a weird hybrid of traditional female singing set to a thumping trance beat. Lit up by the fluorescent lighting, my movements tracked by a video camera screwed into the ceiling, I felt exposed and vulnerable. I thought about taking the stairs, and even opened the heavy door to peer inside, but the iron stairwell with its empty, tomblike space made me feel too claustrophobic. At least with the elevator I could make sure I got in alone.

Wrong. I found myself sharing a ride with a young Asian couple, she in a leather minidress and four-inch heels, he in designer glasses and black jeans. I got out at street level. As the elevator doors closed, the girl moved closer to her date and he smiled and inclined his hennaed head toward her glossy black one.

I stood on the sidewalk, feeling a void in my heart that the cool air and buzzing street life couldn't fill because it was too small and intimate, the exquisite melancholy of a warm spring night that would end alone.

Then I rubbed my face, wiping away all trace of longing, and headed for the cybercafe. But before I could grasp the rough metal bar of the frosted glass door, it flew open and a tall figure emerged, hauling a smaller one. I recognized the manager of my earlier visit, but it took me a minute more to identify the howling bundle locked in his arms, shrieking curses in two languages. With a loud grunt, the manager heaved the whirling windmill of arms and legs onto the sidewalk and I saw it was Lorenzo, the smart-alecky kid from my last visit to whom I had given $5 for computer games, the one who claimed to know all about Frank.

The manager stood in the doorway, arms crossed over his chest, feet planted apart as if ready for another assault. He looked us over, his eyes flickering with a bare suggestion of remembrance. Then he uncrossed his arms and pointed his middle finger at the kid.

"I don't want to see your ugly, motherfucking face in here again. Or you're gonna wish you had never been born."

He gave one last snort of disdain at the sniveling heap sprawled on the sidewalk and turned and walked back in slowly, making a point of leaving his back undefended. As soon as he was gone, Lorenzo raised his cheek off the gum-spattered sidewalk to survey the door, then laid it back down and redoubled his sobs.

Appalled, I ran up.

"Are you okay? Please sit up. Here."

I wrestled him into a seated position and he leaned against my shoulder, his cries enraged and impotent. One side of his face had begun to swell.

"What happened?"

"That bastard Roger. He thinks he's so tough. I'm gonna destroy his ass. I'll show him."

"Why did he throw you out?"

The kid shrugged and wiped his nose on his forearm, leaving a gummy snail trail that flattened the fine hairs against his skin.

"I told him I'd pay him when the AFDC check came in." His voice rose defensively. "That's just one more week, man."

AFDC was money the government doled out to poor single mothers with dependent children. I wasn't sure what kind of tab the boy had run up in there, but you could be sure a cybercafe wasn't what AFDC officials had in mind for its money.

"Hey," he said with a sly twist of his mouth. "Aren't you the lady who was here the other night, looking for my man Frank?"

"That's right," I said. "He been around?"

"Naw." He frowned and bent his head in concentration, picking at a black and flattened circle of gum, a Rorschach blot for a streetwise IQ test. I knew he was lying.

The boy clenched his fists and his mouth hardened into a pout again. "I'll show him. Who does he think he is, dissing me like that."

"How much do you owe him?"

"It's chump change."

"Well?"

"One thousand two hundred and four."

For a moment, we just stared at each other.

"You spent one thousand two hundred and four dollars playing computer games?"

"Aw, man, you're just like him. I told you, I'm good for it. But he doesn't believe me. He better watch it." The boy stuck his little sparrow chest out, fluffed himself up. "I'm gonna fuck him up bad."

He stood up and cast his eyes about. Seeing a trash can several feet away, he ran to it and rummaged around until he found a piece of metal. It was jagged, about eight inches long and two inches thick, detritus, maybe, from a nearby construction site. He ran to the glass door of the cybercafe and drew his arm back.

"Don't," I yelled, scared now for both of us. But the projectile was already sailing out of his hand. It hit the door and I heard the ugly two-A.M.-in-a-sordid-alley sound of breaking glass.

The boy hopped in place, exhilarated by his success. His arm pumped up and down. "Yes," he said. "I'll show you, asshole."

Then he stopped, as if realizing the implications of his actions. With a quick look around, he sprinted off. By the time the door opened and the murderous-looking manager ran out, he was not even a shadow at the corner anymore.

"Why, that no-good little punk, I'm gonna wring his neck."

He whirled, as if expecting to find the boy hiding behind the lamppost or the trash can, then saw me standing off to the side.

"It was him, wasn't it? The kid I threw out?"

I wanted to staunch the malevolence of his anger. I also didn't want to get involved. But I nodded slightly.

"I knew it," the man said. "Little shit. He owes me.

Softening me up all the time. 'Oh, Roger, you're the best. Oh, Roger, just one more hour on "Mortal Killer."' It comes out of my paycheck if we're short. The boss don't care."

Roger shrugged his shoulders, trim in an orange and brown T-shirt with a map of Senegal. He wore a large gold loop in one ear that set off the white of his teeth.

Now he picked his way through the slivers of glass and back into the cafe and I followed him, glancing nervously around for the men who had attacked me and the maid in the hotel room. At the banks of computers, the teen zombies played on, oblivious to the mayhem around them.

Roger went to the back room and bellowed, "Manuel," and a small man came out and Roger pointed to the door and made a sweeping motion with his hands. Manuel wiped his hands on a rag and went back for a broom.

"You could shoot someone in here and no one would notice," he said contemptuously.

"Has there ever been any violence?"

"Nah, not here. But right outside, someone got stabbed to death once. Players from competing crews who squared off to avenge some honor after they lost. Not only were the kids oblivious, but they kept playing after the cops came in and asked what had led up to the brawl. These games rewire your nervous system in a serious way."

Roger moved back behind the counter and started wiping it down. I counted six rings on his fingers.

I perched on a stool near the cash register and put my purse on the counter.

"So you let the kid run a tab, huh?"

His head swung up and he glared at me with barely contained disdain.

"What do you want?"

"Seems like a really lost little kid."

Roger grunted and didn't say anything.

"It was nice of you to let him play on credit," I said.

"Probably other places wouldn't have given him a break."

Roger threw his towel into a corner.

"What the hell am I supposed to do when he comes in here offering me food stamps to let him play?"

"Um, don't take the food stamps?"

"Look, I know his mom, okay? She's a hardworking lady. Trying to get by. Works two jobs. Problem is, she ain't got no money for a sitter. So he's running the street half the night."

"And he ends up here?"

"At first he just sat around, watching the players. Pestering everybody, asking a million questions. Then one day he shows up with some cash. I set him up on a machine and he's, like, a natural. Killer hand-eye coordination. But he's got a jones for it. Sitting here, fourteen, sixteen hours a day on weekends. The cash runs out, he starts bringing me cartons of hamburger buns. Boom boxes. Ties. Claims it fell offa trucks and he wants to trade it for game time. I'm like, you pay me legal tender like everyone else or you're out of here. That's when the trouble started. But what's it to you, Mother Teresa?"

I had found myself warming up to ole Roger. I had to remember why I was there.

"What it is to me, Rog, is that the kid claims to know a guy by the name of Frank who I've been trying to reach. I was here a few days back, remember? I thought the kid might be able to lead me to him."

Roger's agitation about the boy receded. So did his anger. His face zipped up. His eyes went flat and glassy. From his nose dangled a sign that said AUTHORIZED PERSONNEL ONLY.

"So," I continued, "you said when I was in here that you'd pass on the message if you saw him."

"I seem to recall saying that."

"So have you?"

"Have I what?"

"Have you seen him and passed on the message?"

There was a long silence, punctuated only by the occasional whoop from the back of the room as someone scored. "Kill him, kill him, kill him," an agitated male voice said.

"You want my advice, stay away from him. Go back to the Valley where you belong."

Roger pulled out a DVD and polished it with a chamois cloth. I stared at him, trying to get behind the mask. We eyeball wrestled for a while, and he was the first to look away.

"I don't live in the Valley," I said. "I live two miles from here."

"Then congratulations, intrepid pioneer. Do you get a little rush each time you step out of your tastefully renovated Spanish bungalow and drive past the graffiti to one of those hipster-infested nightclubs of lower Sunset?"

I couldn't help but laugh. "For the record, it's an unrenovated California bungalow. Not too tasteful, according to my gay friends. And this little cybercafe," I waved my hand around, "is about as cutting edge as I get."

He adjusted the arm of his expensive glasses in a fussy gesture that told me I was wasting his time. This time, I definitely saw his nostrils flare. In disdain.

"Still, I'm surprised you ventured into the flats without your flak jacket."

The more he talked, the more I realized his vocabulary hadn't come off the street.

"Who do you think you're kidding? You probably grew up middle class in Houston or Orlando and came here with your head shots and your demo tapes to get discovered."

He lit a cigarette and exhaled luxuriantly, ignoring the NO SMOKING sign against the back wall.

"Try Inglewood."

"Some nice parts there."

"Some not-so-nice parts too."

"But you got out."

"Catholic school. Saved many a poor boy before me. Rode that Jesuit train straight to Loyola Marymount University."

"Good school, that. Gave a talk to their journalism students once. They asked smart questions."

He offered me a cigarette. I demurred but took it as a peace offering.

"So what can you tell me about Frank?" I asked.

But his eyes were heavy-lidded again, wreathed in smoke.

"I really can't help you there."

What a shame, I thought. Just when we were getting so cozy.

I dug into my purse and pulled out a business card. He took it and turned it around.

"I knew last time you came round that you didn't want to see him about no baby," he scoffed.

He stalked off and disappeared into the back. I followed him and found myself in a small room stacked with extra computers and cardboard boxes. The floor was made of thick black interlocking slabs of toxic-smelling rubber. I stood there, waiting for him to come out of a storage closet. He emerged with a bottle of Windex.

"That's where you're wrong, my friend," I said. "It *is* about a baby. We're all looking for her. And I've got some information he might find useful. Tell him that, wouldja?"

I hesitated before I said it, figuring that if I ever did hear from Frank, I wouldn't meet him alone. I'd get myself wired for sound and bring Maxwell or another reporter or a passel of cops.

"If I see him around," Roger said.

We walked back to the front together and he saw me out. I think he wanted to make sure I was really gone.

I was halfway home when my watch alarm beeped. I

knew I had forgotten something. I pictured Maxwell waiting anxiously by the phone, ready to call in a Darryl Gates–style SWAT team with a battering ram. Boy, wouldn't that surprise all those gamer kids.

"Everything's fine," I said into my cell phone when I reached him. "You can go to sleep now."

"So what'd you get?" His voice was thick with anticipation.

"Nothing but a bad attitude."

CHAPTER 13

Early the next day, I drove back to Koreatown instead of going in to work. The boy was on my mind. He was the weakest link, not Roger. If I wanted to find Frank, he was my ticket.

In the morning, with the sun shining and the sidewalks empty, the midcity looked as if redemption was still possible. I saw merchants rolling up the metal grates in front of their stores, hosing down their patch of sidewalk. Inside, wives with glasses perched on the tips of their noses peered at the cash register tape and counted out bills.

The Koreans had been the biggest boon to hit the struggling mid-Wilshire area in decades, although Gaylord Wilshire, one of the city's founding fathers, would probably have blanched at the thought.

The industrious newcomers had revitalized a slumbering, decaying area of former grandeur, putting in three-story malls, spas, and luxury condos. It wasn't all good development—the area had more bars and nightclubs per square foot than almost anywhere in the city due to a slimy councilman who seemed to sprout a new Rolex each time a liquor license was up for approval. But there were lots of hardworking people too, and it was because of them that the boxy Hangul alphabet marched from Western Avenue in every direction. Of course, the Koreans were no different than anyone else: as soon as they made some money, they moved to nice suburbs with good school scores. But new immigrants quickly took their place.

I parked and walked over to Lorenzo's apartment build-

ing. He had told me his last name so I trudged up four
flights of stairs, mentally preparing what I would say if his
mother answered. I knocked and heard the sound of scuffling feet behind the door.

"Who's there?" came a theatrically husky voice.

"Hi, Lorenzo. It's Eve Diamond. The reporter. We never
got to finish our talk last night."

A pause, then the boy's natural voice, high and clear and
brimming with disappointment.

"How did you know it was me?"

The door cracked open. He stood, wearing ratty sweatpants, tennies, and a T-shirt, a scowl plastered across his
face.

"You told me it was just you and your mom, and that
wasn't a woman's voice I just heard."

I watched a cowlick rise and quiver, erect and electrified
atop his head, as though he had just gotten out of bed. "But
it did sound like an older boy," I allowed. "You had me
going there for a moment."

The scowl ebbed. He opened the door wider.

"What's up. Hey, you want to give me a ride to school?
I'm late."

"Why not," I said.

He yawned and scratched his head. "Okay then. Be right
back. Gotta brush the fangs."

He took a step and suddenly he was gliding across the
living room, disappearing into the hallway. Maybe I was the
one who wasn't quite awake yet. The living room was spar-
tan. A TV. An old faux-leather couch that looked like a
Salvation Army special. A wicker rocker. Plastic flowers
sprouting out of a dime-store vase. Where a dining room
table would sit, I saw a twin mattress and box spring, faded
cartoon sheets, and a sleeping bag for a blanket. Sprawled
on the floor was a Walkman and some schoolbooks.

The boy reappeared, and damn if it wasn't that peculiar

moonwalk all over again. One minute he was twenty feet away, stepping toward me, and the next he was doing this weird little toe pirouette right in front of me. I looked down. His tennies were flat as far as I could tell. I examined the rest of him. His hair slicked and wet, the cowlick gone. He had changed, but his school clothes looked worse than his makeshift pj's. Low-hanging, baggy cargo shorts. A T-shirt splattered with paint or dirt, it was hard to tell.

"Okay, I'm ready. We have to hurry."

He did that little step-glide thing and was at the door, spinning around. It was disorienting; he seemed almost to be two places at the same time.

He waited, soles flat on the ground, noticing my puzzlement.

"Haven't you ever seen these before?" he asked, holding up one foot to reveal a little set of wheels. "Got 'em for Christmas," he said offhandedly. "Lets you get around a lot faster."

I grabbed the shoe and he hopped on the other foot to keep his balance. With those tiny wheels, I was surprised it didn't slip right out from under him. I spun the roller thoughtfully with one finger: so that was how it worked. Then I let go and his leg dropped to the ground.

"They're not as big a deal as last year," he said, turning toward the door in a fluid, roller-enhanced motion. "Now everybody's got them."

"I think they're pretty cool," I said as we walked out of the apartment. I imagined myself wheeling around a press conference, chasing after politicos for a sound bite. Maybe I would have even gotten to the little girl before she disappeared in the airport crowd.

The boy looked at me as if that was exactly the problem. Once grown-ups caught on, it was all over. He locked the door and dropped the key into his pocket.

I wondered how he had roped me into this. What if I hadn't been here to drive him? And what about breakfast?

Or lunch, for that matter. I hadn't seen a brown paper sack. Or was there a cafeteria?

Lorenzo fumbled for something in his ratty backpack and I caught a glimpse of a textbook before it disappeared in the general chaos within. Algebra II.

"That's your math book?"

He looked embarrassed. "Teacher gave it to me."

"What grade are you in? I didn't study Algebra Two until I was sixteen."

"Fifth," he muttered. "Next year I start middle school."

Dutifully impressed, I asked if he went to a magnet school.

"What's that?"

"You know, for smart kids. They have magnets for math, science, art. Lots of subjects."

He dug his toe into a chipped tile in the lobby, rotating it back and forth, trying to pry out another fragment. The tiles were yellow and blue, the prettiest thing about this run-down building.

"Don't," I said.

He withdrew his foot. "I read about magnets. They're pretty cool. Ancient Egyptians used to navigate by them, but they called them lodestones."

Get him away from those damn computer games and this kid was bright as Polaris.

"You're awfully smart," I said.

He looked up. "That's what my teacher says. He sent a note home to my mom about transferring to another school. But I lost it on the bus."

"Get him to write you another one. And he should pin it to your shirt this time."

"My mom's usually so tired, we don't talk much. Besides, I have to translate everything for her."

I bent my head forward, getting in his face. "This is worth the effort."

I looked at my watch: eight-thirty. "Yikes, we'd better go or you'll be late. What time does school start?"

"Seven-fifty."

"Well then, you're already—"

"I'm just missing math," he said. "It's a big snore. That's why I've got this book, so I can work at my own speed."

"A magnet school will challenge you."

He opened the car door, then looked over his shoulder.

"I've got plenty of challenges in my life already."

Then he gave a cocky smile and I knew he was only a ten-year-old boy.

"Math and 'Mortal Killer.' Those are my two favorite things," Lorenzo said, looking out the window while I drove. "When I was a kid, I'd see big numbers in my head, multiplying themselves, spiraling into infinity. I'd daydream about them. The teachers got mad that I wouldn't sort the blocks by colors and sing along. Then a man came and asked me a bunch of questions and we played some games. He sent a paper home saying I had ADD. It was supposed to be confidential, just for my mom, but who do you think translated it for her? She signed a form so they could give me drugs, but it whacked me out."

"What, like Ritalin?" I said, wondering what effect it had on developing minds. Couldn't it make them psychotic?

He shook his head, as if he hadn't heard me. "Whack City," he said. "That's why I'm not sure about this new school. She's got to sign another form. What if they give me that stuff again?"

"They're not going to give you Ritalin at a magnet school, Lorenzo. These are two very different things."

He looked at me, suspicion darkening his brow.

"Finally my mom took me to the *curandera*. This old lady, she had skin like a lizard and smelled like smoke. It was way down on Pico somewhere. She lit candles and burned herbs and told my mom to throw the pills away."

He put his head in his hands. "Then the cybercafe opened. Since I started playing, I haven't thought that much about the numbers. Maybe it's a good thing. Sometimes they're scary. They come to me at night, and I can't get to sleep."

"Your mom should really talk to your teacher."

He kicked the underside of the car, right below the glove compartment.

"She feels uncomfortable. On account of her English. She says I should respect my teachers and do what they say."

"But they can't do anything until your mom signs. You don't know what an opportunity this is. There are huge waiting lists."

Yes, indeed, I thought. Huge waiting lists of savvy yuppie parents who knew how to play the public school system and pressure administrators, demanding the best for their kids.

"I don't care that much about school anymore, I just want to play 'Mortal Killer.' It's the coolest. Hey, Eve, do you think you could give me ten dollars so I can play after school? There's another cybercafe in Thai Town."

"No, but I'll give you five dollars for lunch. You have a cafeteria?"

"Yes!" He pumped his hand in the air. His eyes shone, huge orbs in his head. He looked more animated than he had all morning, and my gut told me the money would not go toward sloppy joes or whatever they were serving in the beleaguered cafeteria that day.

I thought of the photo that was burning a hole in my wallet. You didn't have to be an abandoned little Asian girl to be in trouble, I thought, seeing the bundle of energy bouncing on the seat next to me.

"So does Frank live in your building too?" I asked cautiously.

He shot me a wary look. "No."

"Is he the guy who owns the cybercafe?"

Lorenzo observed a sports motorcycle weaving in and out of traffic.

"He does some work for one of the owners. I owe him money too," he added self-importantly.

"For letting you play?"

He nodded.

"Why didn't you want to tell me this earlier?"

He shrugged. "I didn't know you."

Oh, and now you do? I mused. Now that I've admired your roller-tennies and driven you to school and lectured you about magnet schools and poked and prodded around that rattling little brain of yours? But I just nodded sagely, as if that made all the sense in the world.

"Tell me something. Have you ever seen Frank with a little girl? Or do you have any idea why he might be interested in a little girl? I'm talking like two years old."

Lorenzo laid his head back against the headrest and closed his eyes, thinking.

"Once he came in with a kid."

"How long ago?" I tried to keep the excitement out of my voice.

"Last year."

Now that's interesting, I thought. Serey Rath wasn't the only little girl; there had been others. What did that mean?

"And, um, Frank's a white guy, right?"

Lorenzo's eyes opened and looked uncertain.

"I mean, he's not black or Latino or Asian?"

Lorenzo looked at my arm. "I'd say he's about your color."

"And what about the little girl, was she white too?"

"Korean."

"You mean specifically Korean, or just Asian?" I asked, wondering how he could know, when Asians themselves often said they couldn't tell just by looking.

"Yeah, that's it."

"What's it?"

"Asian."

"And, um, did she look scared?"

"I don't remember. I was playing. Winning that night too. Yes!"

"Then how do you even remember?"

"Because he came over and poked me in the ribs and said I'd better pay up. Roger told him I was getting in deep."

"And where was the little girl?"

"On his shoulder. Okay, yeah, now I remember. She was sleeping."

"And did you know who she was? Like, his niece or something?"

"I didn't ask. I just kept playing. Until Roger Dodger kicked me out at two A.M."

He looked at me and saw the expression on my face.

"Don't worry, it wasn't a school night."

"Your mother lets you roam around at those hours?"

He jiggled his leg. "I sneak out after she's asleep."

CHAPTER 14

Brenner was already at the bar when I drove to Tong to meet him on Saturday. He had left his sarong at home, although it would have been entirely appropriate here. The decor evoked a colonial tea plantation that had been bombed by the Viet Cong.

I ordered a Singapore sling. He asked for another pekoe-infused vodka, straight up.

"I'm surprised you wanted to meet here," I said as we watched the bartender bring the drinks. "I would have pictured you at some proletariat cafeteria, munching grimly on kasha."

He looked elegant in an Italian suit, his hair swept back in a barely controlled leonine wave that must have been all the rage on the Serengeti.

"Don't confuse me with my politics," he said. "I told you the owners are old friends of mine."

"But aren't you afraid it will look bad, if people learn that you, who rail against big government and cultural appropriation and wretched excess, eat here? This is kind of the epicenter of wretched excess, don't you think?"

He took in the ceiling fans, the wicker chairs, the crashed plane debris painted in army camouflage, half-obscured by tropical plants. The unseen water trickling through sculptural bamboo.

"I happen to be a big fan of Foucault," he said. "And this deconstruction is brilliant, brimming with irony and whimsy." He leaned in closer, drifts of pekoe following in his wake. "Look, I work hard for my money. And a man's got to eat. Doing it well is my one vice."

Or perhaps the only one you'll admit to in public, I thought, flashing on Talina.

Soon our table was ready. As we sat down, a woman glided over, arms extended in greeting. Brenner jumped up and enveloped her in a bear hug. No air kisses for him. Then he pulled out a chair and hovered attentively until she sat down. Finally he introduced me to Alexandra Dubrovna, one half of the swashbuckling restaurateur duo behind Tong.

I recognized her from magazines, where her strong features glowered imperiously in photo spreads. In person she seemed softer somehow, or perhaps it was merely the embroidered Indian tunic she wore over flowing pants, a *salwar kameez* that might have been made for the daughter of a maharaja. It was hard to believe she had ever lived in Mobile, and easy to see why she had left.

Alexandra was tall, with lustrous red hair draping in coils across her forehead, then sweeping down and off her nape in an elegant French twist that exposed a long neck and swanlike shoulders. Her thick, auburn brows presided over deep-set eyes and prominent cheekbones, the skin smooth and powdered with a sprinkling of pale freckles. But something in her facial geometry didn't track. With her strong features, I would have expected a noble beak of a nose, proud and defiant as the rest of her. But Alexandra's nose was an upturned button that seemed to have been transplanted from a perky blonde woman.

Trying not to stare, I congratulated her on the restaurant, then with relief transferred my gaze to a waiter who arrived with a chilled bottle wrapped in linen cloth. Somehow, without any discernible signal, Alexandra had summoned him. Soon our large and elegant glasses were filled halfway with a pale yellow Semillon, beer having been all but banished at Asian fusion places since foodies had discovered that California vintages paired well with Eastern spices.

"How did you come up with the name?" I asked.

Alexandra Dubrovna raised her glass to her cheek, as if the chilled wine might cool her on such a busy evening. But I noticed the goblet never actually touched her flesh, which would have smeared the carefully matted powder.

"It's rather provocative, don't you think?"

I had been under her piercing scrutiny ever since Brenner had introduced me as an *L.A. Times* reporter. He seemed to relish not specifying what kind, thus suggesting the tantalizing possibility that I might be there to review the food. Of course, Alexandra knew that I wasn't Sofia Bordalino, the *Times'* notoriously mercurial restaurant critic. Still, there were other reviewers, and in the gulf of what remained unsaid, I was suddenly the most interesting person in the house.

"Even a bit unsavory," I said. "Isn't *tong* the Chinese word for an organized crime syndicate?"

"It's also the word for a Chinese benevolent association," said Brenner, turning a bemused eye upon me. "They have roots going back centuries."

As he spoke, Alexandra's eyes scanned the front door, where the maître d' was effusively greeting three middle-aged men in collarless Armani shirts, their cheeks smooth and pink as a baby's bottom. Each was talking on a cell phone, ignoring the leggy young dates who clustered, fawn-like, at their sides.

Raising a jeweled hand, Alexandra signaled the maître d'. She extended a long, manicured nail toward an empty table in the center of the restaurant, where diners would be able to see and be seen by anyone who came in. The man nodded almost imperceptibly, then led the party to their thrones.

"DreamWorks," Alexandra muttered, more to herself than to us. As a waiter scurried past, her arm shot out like a python, seizing his wrist. He bent his head and I saw a faint beading of dew on his upper lip.

"The party that just sat down." Alexandra inclined her chin. "Bring them the green papaya salad immediately. The

Szechuan foie gras. And a bottle of Cristal. On the house."

With a military nod, he disappeared into the kitchen. She turned her attention back to me. For some reason, the mere thought of Szechuan foie gras made me queasy. Hoping it would calm my stomach, I sipped at my wine.

"Now where were we?" she said, patting at her French twist. "The name. Yes. We think it's got just the right frisson for today."

"Eve apparently fears it might offend some of our Pacific Rim brethren," Brenner said.

"Not at all, darling. It's edgy and ethnic," Alexandra reassured me, hand touching my arm for emphasis. "Angelenos are ready for that."

So what's next, I thought, a rustic Sicilian *osteria* named La Cosa Nostra?

A plump man in a toque emerged from the kitchen, bearing aloft two platters. He strode to the DreamWorks table and put down the appetizers with a flourish. He shook hands with the men, exchanging pleasantries while the young women bent to sample each dish. But when they were done, the food had only been pulled apart and pushed around the plate in an illusion of eating.

Alexandra called to him, "Lothar, over here for one second, there's someone I want you to meet."

Lothar was the famous Lothar Klimt, who had practically invented nouvelle cuisine in California a generation earlier. Strange accomplishment for a refugee from Mitteleuropa, where pork fat was the emollient of choice. Guess that's what they meant about getting as far away from your origins as possible.

I recognized him, of course. I had seen him on cable TV, hawking everything from braising pans to frozen dinners. His was an open, pleasant face, and he was as beloved by his staff as his dragon-lady wife, Alexandra, was feared and reviled. Profiles described him as a sort of idiot savant, who

couldn't balance a checkbook, remember to pay his rent, or
even navigate the L.A. freeways. But when it came to cooking, his genius was unmatched.

Still, it was agreed that Lothar Klimt would still be slav-
ing away in obscurity if not for Alexandra. She was the
management brains of the outfit, the one who negotiated
leases, costed out new ventures, and dragged him out of the
kitchen and into the salons of wealthy patrons upon whom
every successful restaurant relies. It was Alexandra who had
thought of playing up her husband's connection to the Art
Nouveau painter Gustav Klimt, a distant relation and a century removed across the Austrian *Schlosses*. She had appro-
priated Klimt's shimmering, jeweled canvasses for a more
modern but equally gilded age. Tong's logo featured a stun-
ning Eurasian model clad in a glittering robe of gold thread
and jewels. But instead of straight black Asian hair, the
model's long, curly, Klimtian hair created a brilliant melding
of East and West, of the Viennese Mitteleuropa past and the
Blade Runner–esque Pacific Rim future.

Now Lothar walked toward us and leaned to kiss his wife.

"Isn't she looking good?" he said to Brenner.

Alexandra looked around to make sure no other diners
were listening.

"I've lost five pounds. I stopped eating my breads and
pastas."

"Those fabulous, fabulous foods!" Brenner cried out.

"A woman in Los Angeles cannot be seen eating bread,"
Alexandra said.

"Why ever not?"

"It's ridiculous, I know, but that's how it is. People look
at you weird."

I pulled my hand hastily back from the breadbasket, where
it was already curled around one of her fennel-millet brioches.

"I guess that means you've given up pork fat too,"
Brenner said.

"Oh, don't remind me. What *were* we thinking, Lothar?"

"Do tell," I said, smelling a story.

"Well," said Brenner, leaning back in his chair, "it seemed that Lothar and Alexandra once smuggled a five-kilo slab of smoked pork fat into the United States from Italy that had been hewn from a pig fed solely on black truffles."

"Don't exaggerate," said Lothar. "You know it was chestnuts and favas."

Brenner tilted farther back, hands cradling his belly. "At any rate, it was an unspeakable delicacy, but it's also illegal to bring in meat products."

"So you smuggled it?" I asked. "Those poor drug-sniffing dogs, you must have driven them berserk."

"We decided to decoy U.S. Customs," Alexandra said.

"My wife bought the largest and garlickiest salami she could find and hand-carried it onto the plane," Lothar said.

"Once we arrived at LAX, I marched into U.S. Customs, brandishing it like a missile," Alexandra said.

"And they didn't bother to declare it, so sure enough, Customs pounced," Brenner said.

Alexandra laughed. "And they impounded the salami with much tsking."

"She was practically waving it under their noses, weren't you, darling?" Lothar said.

"And they missed the real contraband, the slowly melting slab of fat hidden inside Alexandra's lingerie," Brenner said triumphantly.

"Was that my idea?" Alexandra asked. "How brilliant."

"So they got it home, and invited me over. It was extraordinary. Melted like butter on the tongue. But our smug smugglers soon grew so overwhelmed at the treasure in their refrigerator that they would only eat tiny slivers, savoring them guiltily when friends came," Brenner said.

"Sometimes we opened the fridge door and just gazed at it," Lothar said.

"And so time passed," Brenner said. "One day they noticed a new smell. Their precious block of fat had grown rancid. Eventually . . ."

A groan went up from Alexandra and Lothar.

"We threw it out, can you believe that? Such a waste. But by then it was inedible."

"What an extraordinary story. A fable, really," I said, sipping my wine and noticing that it was almost gone. Alexandra's mention of U.S. Customs had rung faint bells of alarm in my head. I was here to talk to Samson Brenner about the little girl. But right now, all I wanted was to enjoy this extravagant performance and get someone to fill my glass.

"Yes," agreed Alexandra. "So many stories." She turned to her husband. "I was just telling this *Times* reporter here," she paused ever so slightly, "about how we picked the name Tong."

I caught the italics in her speech. She was starting to suspect that I wasn't a food critic. But even if I didn't know my rillettes from my ganaches, I was still a bona fide member of the chattering classes—and she could do worse than to cultivate me. But something like rancid pork fat was seeping into the back of my throat as I listened to her. The girl, I told myself. You must turn the conversation to the girl.

"A lot of our West Side customers find it very adventurous to come east of La Brea," Alexandra was saying. "It's terra incognita, and not without a little simulated danger. We play that up with our name."

"I can probably find you some gangbangers who could enhance your atmosphere," I said, thinking of a Chinese restaurant scam I had written about in the San Gabriel Valley. "Nothing too fancy, just a little barging in, guns waving, tie up the patrons and strip them of their jewelry and wallets. No one would get hurt, of course."

Alexandra's eyes goggled as though I'd made a rude bodily noise.

"That would probably be a little too surreal for our crowd," she murmured, as Lothar said his farewells and returned to his natural habitat.

Watching his receding back, Alexandra gushed about how she was getting the nursery ready, and I wondered if she and Lothar were now growing their own organic produce. Certainly the plants in the restaurant were exquisite—banana palms and frangipani and whispery ferns.

"How lovely for the baby," Samson Brenner said, and I realized my mistake. She didn't look pregnant, though with those flowing robes, it was hard to tell.

"I'll be right back," she told Brenner. "My doctor's just arrived. Time for my B-twelve shot."

I raised an eyebrow at Brenner but he was watching Alexandra disappear into the back after an absurdly young man with long, wavy hair and round spectacles.

"Gosh," I said, "I hate to break up the party, especially now that Dr. Feelgood's arrived, but didn't we come here to talk about a two-year-old girl?"

He turned his attention back to me. "I suppose we did. What would you like to know?"

"Why don't you start at the beginning and tell me how you became her lawyer."

But Alexandra returned just then in her swishing silks, rubbing her backside and complaining. I wanted to throttle her.

"Why it has to hurt so much, I'll never know," she said, flinging herself down and taking a sip of mineral water.

"All the best things in life require sacrifice," Brenner said, smiling at me. He picked up a set of chopsticks and ran them along the linen tablecloth. "Isn't that right?"

I sipped my Semillon and resigned myself to the spectacle. Brenner would lay this egg when he was ready, and there was nothing I could do to hurry him along.

As the room filled, Alexandra was like a ruby-throated

hummingbird, darting up to greet patrons by name, praising the latest play they had directed at the Geffen, the works of art they had loaned for the LACMA exhibit. But underneath the flattery, a one-note symphony played in her proud, disdainful eyes—*me, me, me, me, me*.

Now she jumped out of her chair once more. "Oh, look," she said. "There's Jonathan. L.A. Phil. I *must* have a word."

Brenner turned to me with a wicked gleam in his eye.

"One of Alexandra and Lothar's pet charities is the Los Angeles Philharmonic," he said, "and it just so happens that Alexandra's name has been drawn out of a hat for an unprecedented opportunity. In two weeks she will raise her baton and conduct the entire Los Angeles Philharmonic in 'Ride of the Valkyries' from Richard Wagner's *The Ring of the Nibelung*. She's been practicing every day."

"No!" I said.

"It will be a private performance, for only her closest friends and family," Brenner murmured.

"I should hope so," I said, then changed the subject. "So when's the baby due?"

"Due?" he grunted. "They've been trying for years with no luck. They're adopting."

"Oh."

Alexandra came sweeping back. "Now where were we? Oh yes, the baby. They've told us it will be sometime this month. Thank goodness we were able to get Tong launched first. Lothar plans to wean her directly onto salmon mousse. Would you like to see a picture?"

"That's o—" I began.

"Of course," said Brenner, kicking me under the table.

"I'm one of those people who was so busy working throughout my thirties that I forgot to have children," Alexandra said. "Then when the restaurants took off and we began trying, well, all the money in China couldn't get us pregnant. We thought about donor eggs. But in the end, we

decided that would be selfish and egotistical, especially
when there are so many babies out there already who need
homes. It's not what we are *about*. We are about doing good.
Sustainable consumption. And with branching into Asian
cuisine, well, Lothar was able to research Southeast Asian
spices while I researched babies."

I gazed at her, amazed by how color- and theme-coordi-
nated her life was. But underneath, I sensed a deep yearn-
ing. She seemed to divine my thoughts.

"I longed for a baby," Alexandra said, regarding me with
her big, liquid eyes. "I dreamed of this child. My ovaries
ached." She dabbed at the corners of her eyes with a napkin.
"I never thought it would be so difficult. All that prodding
and poking, injecting hormones. When I think of all those
years we worked so hard *not* to have a child, I could just
weep. But now, our life will be complete."

She pulled out a photo and passed it to Brenner and he
commented on how lovely she was. I waited for the photo
to come around so I could dutifully praise the baby. As I
reached for it, I upset my drink and the big bubble glass
bounced onto the linen tablecloth with a resounding spring
before crashing onto the floor.

Standing up, I brushed shards of glass off my shoes. The
wine was staining my shirt. Saying I'd be right back, I headed for the rest room, where I could scrub away the stain.
Thank God it was white wine, not red.

Wending my way through the room, I looked at the mir-
rored bar and saw the diners reflected in its light. Then a
familiar figure walked into Tong and headed for the bar. What
was he doing here? Was it possible he was following me?

CHAPTER 15

*I*t was Tim Waters. Or at least I thought it was. Frozen in place, I wondered why in the hell I hadn't seen him for six years and then whammo slammo, he pops up twice in one week. Why couldn't he have stayed on the other side of the Pacific?

A couple walked by, blocking my view, and I thought for a moment that I had lost him. There were so many fashionably dressed men here, all exuding the same sinuous strength, but no, there he was, his wavy hair combed up into that modified pompadour I remembered so well. If only he would turn around.

Then he crossed his legs and jiggled one foot impatiently, leaning forward to shout some instruction at the bartender, and I was sure. He'd always had the nervous energy of a jungle cat.

There was a murmur of voices from the tables but I paid no attention. A ringing in my ears drowned out all other noise. I didn't know how long I stood there, but feeling self-conscious now, I took two steps and stopped. What was I going to say to him? He seemed oblivious to my presence. What if he was here to meet a date?

Tant pis, I decided. It seemed to take forever to cross the room, but then I was standing behind him, watching him sip his martini, absorbing the intimacy of the moment with a voyeuristic thrill. Unaware of my scrutiny, he moved naturally. But then my presence registered across his extra-sensory line of vision. His shoulders tensed. He cranked himself around in his chair and saw me.

"How long were you going to stand there, spooking me out?"

The restaurant noises flew around us, creating a swirling vortex. Everything was spinning. The wine coursed through my system. The other night, I hadn't seen him well or up close. Now I did. He was considerably thinner, his cheekbones more pronounced, the skin taut against his skull. Bouts with malaria, perhaps. Feverish tossing on tropical nights as his body adjusted to the monsoon air. I saw golden hairs curling on his nape, the azure of his eyes. It was like going from black-and-white to Technicolor, dazzling my receptors into overload.

"Now you know what it feels like," I said.

He was absorbed in his drink, pushing it around the counter like a kid playing with a toy car.

"I worked with Alexandra's sister in Hong Kong and she told me to look up this place when I got into town," he said, though I hadn't asked. "She bragged that her sister and Lothar had become celebrities. But she barely recognized Alexandra anymore, what with all the Botox and lipo and collagen. Said her sister had to keep up appearances so she wouldn't get left behind."

It occurred to me that Tim was rambling. A breach of his usual sangfroid. He sipped his drink. Up close, I saw it wasn't a martini after all, but apparently some kind of dark tequila, set off by a curl of orange peel and jalapeño.

"Lothar's not going to leave her behind," I said. "They're about to adopt a baby."

Tim regarded me with a slightly mocking look. "So long as he keeps his dalliances discreet, Alexandra shouldn't care. Where would she be without him, anyway? Another Mercedes Lady."

My feminist fur bristled. "What would he be without her? Just another Teuton in a toque. This town's lousy with them."

He stretched his long frame lazily. "There are two words a well-brought-up young lady should never say," Tim chided. Our old banter, stolen from *I Love Lucy* reruns.

"Swell, let's hear them."

"One of them is *swell*."

"Well, of all the lousy—"

"And the other one is *lousy*."

I stared at the bottles behind the bar, deciphering the labels, not daring to look at him. He spoke first.

"Oh, Eve, it's been a long time. And you're not even wearing that new hat I bought you."

I felt a light touch on my hair and stepped out of his reach. I couldn't believe that I had built a life without him, painstakingly, over time, and now he was back. And not only that, he was hanging out in my neighborhood, insinuating himself into my emotions and reawakening memories I had banished years ago.

"Just how long have you been back, Tim?"

"But Alexandra's wearing her hat. Look."

I turned and saw Alexandra examining herself in a compact mirror while Samson Brenner beamed with approval. She had put on some some sort of straw cloche that predated Lucy Ricardo by several decades, in pastel tones, extending the European-royalty-on-the-Asian-plantation metaphor.

"Yes," said Tim. "Lothar has definitely put her in the show. Whatever they've got going, it's a team effort. They've created a buzz on both sides of the Pacific. So I figured, when in Rome . . . I've been back a few months. What about you, Lois Lane? What brings you here tonight?"

He cocked his head to one side, then lifted his tequila jauntily to his lips.

"Dinner with a source. I don't usually eat at places like this but—"

"Too chichi for your blood? You prefer some dilapidated

storefront on Normandy that's been closed down by the Health Department for rodent infestation?"

I blushed that he knew me so well.

"What are you atoning for? Live it up a little. You don't have to feel guilty. You're a pleasure Stalinist. Remember we used to fight about that?"

I noticed that his hand shook when he put down his drink. There was a faint beading of sweat on his upper lip. His martini glass was almost empty.

A cell phone went off and it took me a minute to realize it was his. In the years of absence, Tim had turned into another cell-phone-wearing, cocktail-swigging dot-com hipster. In my private fantasy world, none of that existed. We inhabited some exalted plane, shopping at thrift stores, attending art openings, hanging out in punk clubs, and quoting Verlaine and Auden to each other in bed. A time before money was so important and careers meant everything. I caught myself leaning toward him and felt his body exerting a magnetic pull. If I got too close, it would burn me. I stepped back and he looked at my feet, and it flashed over me that he felt the electric current too. And that we were having two conversations. One was this superficial, verbal one, the other was a dance of our bodies, straining together, then apart.

He pulled out his phone and said, "Yeah." He listened for a moment, then said, "How much?" He licked his lips and said he'd pass on the message. Hanging up, he shoved the phone into his pants. Then he picked up his martini glass, brought it to his mouth, tipped it, and swallowed the last drops.

"It's been nice seeing you, Eve, but I've got to run. My, uh, date is running late and wants to meet farther west."

My world crashed around me. Wingless, I looked up at him. Why had he told me that? And why did I care? He was a complete enigma to me. And now there was no casual way to pry any more information out of him. He was on his way out. As I stood there thinking, something else washed over me. And then I knew that he was lying. I could smell it, just as I could smell his essence wafting up from the hollow where his shoulder met his neck.

He reddened, then tried to backpedal. "Aw, Eve, it's not that kind of date."

Had I been so unable to hide my disappointment? I, who prided myself on my poker face, my ability to put my emotions on ice?

"You won't see me here again, Tim," I said, unable to let him go, unable to say anything more profound.

"Give me your card, I'll call you," he said, and the banality of his words made my eyes sting. I fumbled in my purse, threw down a card, and stumbled back to the table, practicing what I would say. "I'm sorry, that was an old friend I haven't seen in ages." I said it ten times as I wound my way back to our table. As I sat down, I realized my shirt was still stained with wine.

Alexandra was just putting the photo away. The table was filled with dishes that I didn't realize we had ordered— clear, fragrant broth; sweet shrimp; shredded green papaya salad; flat noodles studded with tiny vegetables. A whole fish redolent of ginger and lemongrass. My stomach growled.

"Sorry," I stammered, going into my speech. It was halting and forced, but no one seemed to notice.

"That's exactly what we want our restaurant to be," Alexandra said with enthusiasm. "A serendipitous place where old friends can meet and catch up. Where romance and intrigue can be born."

She craned her neck and I wondered if she was looking for Tim. I turned, but his seat had been taken by a young woman in low-cut pants with a large tattoo on her lower back.

"Eve didn't get to see the photo," Brenner said. "And I know she loves children." He flashed me an evil smile.

"My apologies," said Alexandra, opening her purse. "Now where's that photo? We've already named her. Star Saffron. Star because she brings light and warmth into our lives. Saffron, well, Lothar's crazy for that spice. Nectar of the gods. Did you know that King Darius of Persia ordered his court poets to compose odes to saffron? Commoners were forbidden to taste it, on pain of death. It's hand-harvested from the stigma of the crocus flower, then toasted, and it takes a hundred and sixty thousand flowers to produce a kilogram. Ounce for ounce, saffron is more expensive than gold. But all you need is a pinch."

"I've never cooked with it," I confessed.

"Well, it looks like bits of ragged thread, crimson in your palm. You grind it with a mortar and pestle. Lothar likes the streaky effect on his sauces. And the taste? Like the extracted essence of gold. Some kind of alchemy. Only thing that comes close for Lothar is garlic, but we couldn't exactly call her Garlic Clove, now could we?"

She found the photo, pulled it out, and handed it to me. When I saw the image, I almost dropped it. The child that Alexandra and Lothar were about to adopt bore a striking resemblance to the little girl known as Serey Rath.

I scanned Samson Brenner's face for signs of complicity, but saw only the beaming glow brought on by a fine California wine as he served us and handed plates round. He didn't know. He might have filed reams of legal paper on her, but he had never seen the missing child's photo. Or perhaps only a photocopy of her passport. He hadn't seen her in the flesh the way I had, being carried by a pretty woman who wasn't her mama. But could I trust my own adrenaline-shot memories of that day?

Staring at the photo in my hand, I stammered stupidly but nothing came out.

They were all looking at me. "Isn't she a doll," Alexandra prompted. It wasn't a question.

I tried to give the photo back, but my hand shook so much I feared I would drop it into the cumin-dusted olives. "Just one more minute," I said, putting the photo back in front of me and cradling it in my hands. Suddenly I wasn't hungry anymore.

As Alexandra jumped up to greet a new party of diners, I leaned across the table.

"Mr. Brenner, am I crazy or does that look like that little girl you're representing?"

He took the photo from me and scrutinized it, then handed it back.

"Yes, that's a little Asian girl, all right." He looked at me evenly.

"But don't you see the resemblance?"

"Not really. I don't. This girl has short hair. Her face is thin."

"The photo was probably taken a long time ago. Hair grows. Cheeks fill out."

"I see only a general resemblance." He shook his head. "And I hope you're not going to get Alexandra upset by even suggesting that—"

He stopped as she walked back. I had to distract them to hide my shock.

"She's lovely," I murmured. "But are you concerned about naming an Asian baby Saffron? Some people might think it insensitive."

Alexandra looked at me blankly. Then her nostrils flared magnificently.

"Anyone who would dare to criticize our choice of name is beneath my contempt. We're giving this baby a chance at life. Let *them* go adopt a poor little abandoned Third World orphan." Alexandra drew herself up in her chair as if she were doing Pilates. "And for your information and that of any other gastronomically challenged people out there, saffron isn't always yellow. The stamen is red. A flaming sunset red. It turns yellow when you add it to food."

"I think it's a fabulous name," Brenner said. "The alliteration practically trips off your tongue. Now do tell us when she's coming."

"It was supposed to be last week but there's been a slight delay, and I almost can't bear it. I want to hold her in my arms all night. To watch her face light up as she plays with her toys. To read her books in my lap and kiss her good night. I so want a child. I've already told Lothar not to expect me at work for the first few weeks."

"Where is she from?" I asked. While Alexandra had been lecturing us on the properties of fine spices, I had been figuring out my next move.

"Cambodia. There are so many abandoned little babies there, and you can get boys too. You can't get those from China."

I shot a meaningful look at Brenner.

"What agency?"

She looked at me.

"Are you thinking of adopting? Lots of single women are doing it. Gay couples too; why, we know—"

"She looks familiar," I muttered darkly.

They both looked at me, taken aback by my intensity. I had broken the First Commandment of small talk. I had made it big.

"So, what's the name of the agency?"

Alexandra waved her arm. "Some long, unpronounceable Cambodian name. Offices in Phnom Penh." She gave me a piercing look. "I could dig it out. We usually just called them by their acronym. HAW."

"Is there an English translation?"

"Why, yes, I believe there is." She wrinkled her nose. "I don't remember it offhand. My brain's so full of useless things, and here I've forgotten this very important one. I'll look it up and call you. But I can tell you all the money gets plowed back into the orphanage. That was one of our initial concerns."

Pushing back my chair, I murmured something about the bathroom, ignoring their puzzled looks, since I had supposedly just gone. My brain was going round and round, and I needed a few moments to get a grip on myself. Sometimes a coincidence is just a coincidence, I told myself.

I walked through the restaurant and into a corridor that opened onto the kitchen. In hot, cramped spaces, line chefs were busy sautéing garlic with ginger and plunging pakora fritters into sizzling oil. It smelled like Asia.

Taped to the door of a stainless-steel walk-in freezer, I saw a color Xerox of a frumpy-looking woman with frizzy black hair and glasses. The camera had caught her with a forkful of pasta halfway to her mouth, and she wore a look of anticipation tempered with annoyance, lips parted, eyes red as a demon's in the flash.

URGENT!!!! it said. *This is Sofia Bordalino, the ALL IMPORTANT restaurant critic of the* Los Angeles Times. *If ANYONE spots a woman who looks even REMOTELY like her in the dining room, the maître d' and chef must be alerted IMMEDIATELY and the kitchen is to go on RED ALERT. Failure to do so will result in termination.*

A man in a chef's hat saw me angling my head to read and walked over.

"Can I help you?" he asked in a mellifluous European accent, taking my elbow and leading me out of the kitchen.

"I'm looking for the rest room, sorry."

He looked around to see how I could possibly have mistaken a kitchen for the bathroom, then pointed and waited until I was halfway down the hall before returning to his post.

Shamed at being caught snooping, I found the next door

and walked in. But this was not a rest room either. It was an office with a large desk and neatly stacked files. As my eyes took in the room, a door opened from the other end and a head peered out, revealing none other than Lothar Klimt. His toque was askew. He stepped into the office, followed by a statuesque young woman with severely cropped hair wearing a smock and clogs. Her skin was tawny and flushed, her eyes the same glittering color as the tiny obsidian earrings that dangled from her pearly lobes.

For one comical moment, we stared at one another. Busted all around. Klimt recovered first.

"Yes?" he said, his eyes dancing with unasked questions. "Can I help you?"

"Sorry," I said, stepping backward. "I was looking for the rest room."

I don't think he believed it any more than the first guy did, but his face was suffused with relief.

"Well then, you've gone too far. Larissa's just heading that way. She'll be happy to show you."

He sat down at the desk and picked up the phone, humming a Viennese waltz as we disappeared into the hall.

"You passed it on your way down," Larissa said, stopping before a door emblazoned with the silhouette of a woman in a high-collared cheongsam, the traditional Chinese dress.

She stood attentively, hands clasped, as I entered. Was it only my imagination, or did I see them tremble?

In the bathroom, I put down the toilet lid and sat for a moment, thinking about what I had just seen. While Alexandra was greeting guests in the front room, her genius-chef husband was helping himself to a side dish in the back. Things were moving too fast. Tim. The little girl. The mysterious adoption agency. Now this. All the subterranean currents of life, churning and bubbling up to the surface. I had to compose myself.

Brenner was just finishing dessert when I walked out and

Alexandra was chatting animatedly at a corner table with an important-looking older couple.

"Sorry to leave you sitting here by yourself," I said.

"That's fine. I have been concentrating on these exquisite flavors. Lemongrass." He gestured to a celadon bowl filled with sorbet. "You, my dear, look as though you've seen a ghost."

"I'm still in shock. Those little girls could be sisters."

"Let's hope not," Brenner said. "I've got my hands full with one."

I gulped from a fresh glass of Semillon as Brenner raised his eyebrows. Now we could finally talk business.

"So Alexandra. She's quite a character."

"Alexandra is prey to impulses," Brenner said. "Not all of them good."

"You mean her impulse to have a baby?"

"They're both workaholics. I know because I'm one too." He gave a disparaging laugh. "Ah, well. I suppose there are good nannies."

"But it sounds like she's going to cut back," I said, feeling an inexplicable impulse to defend Alexandra. "The maternal impulse can kick in quite unexpectedly. Or the paternal one," I said, thinking about Lothar.

His face darkened, and I feared I had said something insensitive.

"Love can only get you so far," he said quietly, and I wondered whether he was thinking of Star Saffron or his own child, grown up and estranged from him. "Sometimes situations arise that are beyond everyone's control."

"I know," I said, thinking about Tim. But he hadn't heard me.

"You return from a business trip to find the training wheels have come off the bike. A couple more trips, and there's makeup in the bathroom drawers. You embarrass her in front of her friends with your talk about Nigerian political prisoners. But you've got an amicus brief to file for the Supreme Court so you peel off a few bills, tell her to order in dinner, and lock yourself in your office. And slowly, you lose her. Lemme tell you, arguing before the U.S. Ninth District Court of Appeals is a piece of cake compared to arguing with Rachel."

"That's your daughter," I said softly.

He nodded. "Not everyone is cut out to be a parent. The shrinks told me to be firm, that tough love was the answer. I learned differently. Jeez, I don't know why I'm talking about this."

That gave me a perfect segue into the little girl.

"Does the little INS girl remind you of your daughter somehow?"

"Yeah," he said slowly. "I deal with kids all the time. But this one, I have a chance here to do the purest kind of good. To redeem myself."

He pushed away the sorbet that lay pooling in the bowl. "The cars, the fancy food, the clothes, it's all just to distract me. I can win all the lawsuits in the world and it's meaningless. But with this little girl, I can make something right in the world."

I considered that Babette had gotten him all wrong. He had a huge, raw heart and it had broken in two for his daughter, and now he was trying to sublimate that loss in the battle for the little girl. But then I wondered whether it was all an act to gain my sympathy and manipulate me to his side.

"So yes, let's talk about that girl. Where is she?"

A moment ago, his face had been suffused with grief. Now a look of cunning moved across it.

"That is about the only thing I cannot tell you. Ask me anything else."

"Why can't you tell me?"

"I hate to throw the INS's own words back at you, but for her own safety, that's why. We know where they're keeping her. They've had to disclose that in the court documents. But they're sealed. For the girl's own protection. They're moving around every few days, just to be safe."

"Then who's paying you?"

"This is pro bono."

I made an exasperated noise. "I might have figured that. But who sicced you on this?"

He leaned back in his chair. His eyes twinkled. He took a sip of wine, then set the glass back down. It was clear he was enjoying this.

"It's a coalition of interests."

"You want to elaborate?"

"There's a Southeast Asian Community Services Agency that helps immigrants get on their feet. Their director called me in the middle of the night, explaining the situation. We had to move quickly. We've gotten some immigrant rights groups on board. Plus human rights wonks and antitrafficking wonks. We're asking for political asylum. She should get placed in a nice adoptive home here, not shipped back to the hellhole she came from."

"You mean Cambodia?"

"Perhaps," he said, playing coy.

"But how did the director who called you in the middle of the night learn about the little girl?"

He paused. "The consulate called her in the middle of the night."

"How did they find out?"

"INS called them. The consulate basically wanted the director to help get the kid back on a plane as soon as possible. But she broke ranks and called me."

He was practically clapping his hands with glee. "You see, it's very delicate. We've banded together to fight for human rights, as personified by this little twenty-five-pound baby girl. And we got temporary guardianship. But the law is up for interpretation. When it was drafted, we simply didn't have kids coming here without their parents. Now it happens every day, although this one is by far the youngest we've seen. These kids need access to medical care and school and should live with foster families until their status is resolved. It's inhumane to put them with armed guards in a hotel."

"So you confirm she's in a hotel?"

He hesitated. "Yes, near downtown."

"I hope you have time to grab some dim sum when you visit her in Chinatown."

He gazed into my eyes and I felt him probing and assessing. But he didn't rise to the bait. "Now why do you say that?"

I shrugged. "I've got other sources besides you, Mr. Brenner."

"Well, I can't comment," he said, his eyes commenting anyway.

"I want to re-create this story for the newspaper. There will be a public outcry when people learn about this. It's an outrage."

Instead of growing animated or dismissive or anything else that would reveal what he really thought, Brenner's face took on a sleepy, heavy-lidded cast. I thought he might have drawn the shutters to hide his gloating.

"Give me a couple of days to think about how we can make this work," he said. "I can't have the federal judge pissed off at me, thinking I'm trying this case in the press."

"Even though, of course, you are," I said. He was playing me like a master. But never mind. Each of us had something the other wanted.

"I know what you need, Ms. Diamond. I can give you access."

He spoke with total confidence, his voice at once lush and intimate, like a lover making a promise. And I shivered with something not altogether unlike lust.

"Wait for my call," he said, looking deep into my eyes,

and I whispered to him that I would. I said good-bye to Alexandra, then sailed out the door, congratulating myself that I hadn't thought about Tim for at least fifteen minutes. Flush with the wine and the promise of a good story, I didn't notice until it was too late to turn away. On the sidewalk, talking on his cell phone under the restaurant awning, was Tim Waters.

CHAPTER 16

I shook my head in disbelief.

"Are you following me?"

Shoving down the antenna of his cell phone, he turned it off and slipped it into his pocket.

"No," he said decisively. "I'm not."

"I thought you had to meet someone on the West Side."

"I do, but now that's not happening until later."

He glanced at my hand to see if I held a valet parking stub, then smiled, remembering, probably, that I didn't like handing over my keys to strangers. We hadn't had money for valets back then anyway.

"Walk you to your car?"

"I'll be fine," I said stiffly. "I'm four blocks away. Near the Vista." It was a theater we had once frequented for foreign films and midnight cult movies.

"Do the gams good. Come on." He loped off, then turned and inclined his head. "I'm not going to bite," he said.

I had to go that way anyway. "All right," I said.

We walked several blocks down Vermont, where the sidewalks were thick with people getting out of cars, heading for the clubs, sitting over late-night espressos, and digging into dinner.

"Just like old times, eh, Eve?"

In the old times, this neighborhood had not yet gentrified. In the old times, there had been only a couple of vintage clothing stores, an independent bookstore, a few restaurants, and a scruffy coffeehouse called The Onyx run by a cheerful Beat poet who served burned espresso in chipped Fiestaware. In the old times, we had been together.

Soon we neared the Vista Theater. It had always felt so safe to me, my old hood. That was the problem. It felt safe until suddenly, it wasn't. And then it was too late.

Tim walked fast, his black shirt billowing in the night breeze, and I scrambled to keep up with his long, lanky stride. At the same time, I kept my eyes on the old sidewalks, scanning for protruding tree roots and buckled concrete that could trip me, make me fall. I didn't want to fall.

"What are you working on these days?" Tim asked, looking at me sideways.

I told him a bit about the melee at the airport, and he said he remembered seeing it on the news.

"So anyway, I'm trying to track down that little girl," I said.

He slowed down to let me catch up. "Any luck?"

I looked up from root patrol, remembering how I had snapped at Silvio when he asked me the same question. Tim was staring ahead, and I caught only his ragged profile, the nose that jutted from his face and gave him his rough, appealing character.

"I was at a hotel the other day where the sheets were still warm, but she was gone. Then I traced her to a medical clinic where they had treated her."

"Oh yeah? Where was that?"

I stopped, struck by a surge of anxiety, some warning flare going up inside me. He kept walking. Strider, I had called him a long time ago. When we hiked, he'd bring along a worn walking stick with a carved wooden handle that had come down from his grandfather in Donegal. The Irish, they had wandering in their veins.

He noticed I was no longer beside him and stopped. "The moon, Eve." He raised his head to bask in its glow. It was high in the sky already, a merciless white orb surrounded by a pale ring of cold stars.

"It's like she's wearing a halo," he said.

I followed the arc of his arm and saw the moon, really gazed deep. That was what he did for me. With his skewed way of talking. His connoisseur's eye for severe beauty. His reverence for transitory joy snatched from deep, odd places. It came back to me how I had missed that about him.

But he had lived under foreign skies and become a stranger. One who asked pointed questions that made me uneasy. I waited to see if he would bring it up again, but he didn't. Soon I had talked myself into believing I had imagined it. At the corner, he grabbed my hand and I relaxed and let him pull me along, until we were children playing Crack the Whip and I was soaring through the air at the end of his arm.

"So, you think you're closing in on where the INS stashed her?" Tim asked when I landed, breathless and exhilarated.

I slid my hand from his. It was suddenly slick with moisture. I watched the back of his head, walking and bobbing.

"Did I say anything about the INS?" The accusation flew out of my mouth before I could snatch it back.

He turned, shoes scuffling on the old sidewalk.

"I told you I saw it on the news."

He stopped before an old Karmann Ghia. It had been fixed up and painted cherry-bomb red. But we were still a block away from my car. Tim reached into his pants pocket, pulled out a key, and unlocked the passenger door with a flourish.

"Have a seat in my parlor," he said. "You're not in any hurry, are you?" He looked up anxiously. "I want to play you this trance music I discovered in Goa. It's killer."

"Well, actually, I . . ."

"Then I'll drive you to your car."

"It's only that . . ."

I stopped. Only what? That I didn't like the questions he asked? That I didn't know him anymore? That things were moving too fast?

"If there's one thing you learn in Asia," said Tim, "it's that life is fleeting, and you have to seize the moment, live it to its fullest."

"Don't give me those New Age platitudes."

"Oh, I dunno," he said, leaning against a streetlight. His eyes danced with concealed mirth. "I was thinking more of Robert Herrick, seventeenth century: 'Gather ye rosebuds while ye may.'"

At that I laughed. And for one incandescent moment, it worked again. He and I. It wasn't due to any rare magic, but rather to the accretion of hours we had spent rubbing each other's edges smooth. The braiding of time and shared experience that came back to me now in discrete motes of memory. How the frames of his glasses had tangled in my hair. How he'd woken me up once to watch lightning dance across the sky. How we'd spooned rice pudding out of a pot, our mingled breath warm with cardamom and rose water. Timothy the beguiler. And so instead of running away, I slid into the seat he offered, catching my pants on the cracked leather.

Tim pulled out a CD decorated with curvy Urdu script. He fitted it into the slot and pushed a button. Immediately, the car was swirling with sound. I leaned back and let it wash over me.

"I can see why they call it trance music."

We listened wordlessly, the music shimmering and looping back on itself, the bass resounding in the close quarters. As the first cut slid into oblivion and the second one started up, sinuous and slow, Tim pulled out a joint and lit it up and the familiar paranoia of a decade ago flickered over me. *What if we get busted?* He lit it, the paper crackling, and took a long toke before handing it to me. I stared at it, fat and familiar, then remembered to lower it below window level. So no one could see.

Blame the music, the company, the shock and intoxication of the evening, for what happened next. Holding the blunt between my fingers, I inhaled deeply, held it in, feeling my lungs expand. It had been years. Smoke curled around my lungs, moving into the dark, fleshy, throbbing corners, the cilia dancing and swaying in time to the music, and immediately I choked on the acrid smoke, a series of stuttery snorts that ended with me doubled over in the seat.

"Christ, Eve," said Tim, taking it from me. "You never did learn how to inhale."

"You say that like it's something to be ashamed of."

Then I laughed, a sibilant, Wile E. Coyote laugh. I listened to the hoots and hollers of pedestrians wafting up from the boulevard. I watched the neon flicker on the Vista Theater marquee. I read the titles: *Drunken Master* and *Enter the Dragon*. Bruce Lee and Jackie Chan facing off on the large Silverlake screen. How many times had Tim and I headed out languidly to an art film, then to eat at some cheap ethnic place, then home to make love? The slow pace of our scattered lives.

Perhaps that's why I didn't flinch when I felt his eyes on me, staring in a curiously intense way. If I closed my eyes, the car would levitate, spin around a couple of times, and land with a bounce of its crappy suspension back into the past.

Tim leaned over the gearbox, his slim torso twisting into an apostrophe, and reached a tentative hand to touch my hair. I closed my eyes, felt his fingers, soft moth wings beating against my temple.

We were embarking on something that had once been so natural that time's passage had made it alien. I leaned back and lowered the seat and saw the torn cloth roof and Tim's hollowed face on the seat next to me, all planes and angles. The headlights of a passing car illuminated him and a red glow seemed to come off his hair. I reached out to touch his face and we were like two blind people refamiliarizing ourselves with a Braille classic we didn't realize until this very moment that we had forgotten.

I could only focus on a tiny bit of him at one time, and noticed it was the same for him. If we looked straight into each other's eyes, we'd glance away, unable to bear the nakedness that had nothing to do with clothes. It was in our brains. Paths blazed, synapses rewiring to accommodate each other's smells, touch, taste. When you've spent years tamping down memories, it's almost unbearable to have them rise up again. The stakes are too high.

This is ludicrous, I told myself. We are acting like two teenagers on a Saturday night. And even as I looked at Tim, I imagined Silvio, his nose pushed up against the glass window of the car, his mouth an oval scream of protest. I felt myself watching from the curb with pained regret.

Supporting himself with one arm, Tim leaned close and I thought he might kiss me. I closed my eyes and felt his breath, alcohol tinged with mint and pepper, vaguely spicy and not unpleasant.

Then an animal sound rose from his chest and was lost in the air. I opened my eyes as he wrenched himself away. He bounced against his seat and faced the car door, hunching into himself.

"I can't," he said.

I froze. Embarrassment came driving home with the next set of headlights. I had never meant to let this happen. But stronger than my embarrassment was my shame. I had seen his face in that moment when he had torn himself away. Something about me had revolted him.

I stared at the tear in the ceiling and waited, confusion rippling through me in expanding circles.

"I can't, Eve," said the huddled mass on the other side of the car.

"Something I said?"

"It's not you, it's me."

What a fool I had been to imagine we could recapture what we had once shared. I had been seduced by the past, not by the Tim who sat slumped before me.

"I shouldn't have touched you. It was a mistake. I'm sorry."

"Why?"

"Because . . ."

I realized suddenly where his revulsion came from.

"You have a girlfriend, don't you?"

He shook his head no. He turned back to me and his face looked red and splotchy, a bumpy canvas illuminated by the light of passing cars.

The truth came to me now, and it was so simple that I initially failed to grasp it. He just wasn't attracted to me anymore. Some vestigial feeling from the past had both propelled him toward me and prevented him from following through.

My hand found the door handle, yanked it open. I tumbled out and had to steady myself, one foot in the gutter.

"Eve." He leaned out, his face contorted with pain and a nameless need that shot past me into the night.

"What?"

"Don't go."

I looked at him. He was sweating and wouldn't meet my eyes.

I felt dirty. Nauseated. Humiliated. Suddenly, I could stand it no longer. I ran, not exactly sure what I was escaping from but desperate to be gone.

*A*t home, I lay in bed, wondering what had come over me. Ever since Tim had reappeared, my life had been careening out of control. I wasn't thinking straight. I'd almost been killed in that hotel. I was jittery from too much coffee, and yet so tired I was losing touch with reality. Sometimes while doing interviews, I saw sparks coming from people's mouths, their hands moving in liquid traces of energy. At night, I collapsed into thick, dreamless sleep. Even tonight, thoughts of Tim couldn't keep away slumber.

When I awoke on Sunday, the fear that I could barely articulate gnawed at me again. I chugged some OJ and fingered my mental worry beads. A tiny scene kept repeating itself in my head: Silvio holding up the condom and me pushing his hand away.

I had been desperate to blot out Tim. So I had slept with Silvio. And now I was late. That just never happened. I was regular as oranges and lemons, the bells of St. Clement's.

A flock of crows flew past outside my bedroom window, raucous and clamoring, and I rolled to the other side of the bed so I wouldn't have to see them. A small and tentative croak came from a nearby branch. The bird seemed to be calling me, so I rolled back over to have a look. He was thin and small for his species, more like an overgrown blackbird, and he perched on the branch and regarded me.

Then a second, much bigger crow alighted. Using his claws, he bobbed closer to the little one, and I feared a fight and prepared to lift up the window and shoo him away if he tried to take advantage of the small one's weakened condition.

The big crow leaned forward to peck, and I put my hands on the pane, then let them fall to my sides when I saw that he held some kind of insect in his beak, several gangly legs protruding. The little one opened his mouth and the big one pushed the insect inside, their beaks touching.

I pulled the covers over my head and burst into tears.

Sunday afternoon, I showered and dressed with special care for Silvio's party.

"Please come," he had said on the phone earlier that week. "There will be a hundred chaperones. I promise we won't talk about the case."

"The *Times* lawyers . . ." I had said.

"They're afraid of their own miserable shadows. After the trial, they'll tell you to stay away from me because one side might appeal. It could take years."

I saw time stretching out before us. "But, c'mon, Silvio, we saw each other just last week."

"That's too long ago for me, Eve. Life is in session."

He had a point. Why should I let these intrusive lawyers meddle in my love life? Whenever people laid down the law, I itched to do the opposite. I knew it was immature and knee-jerk, with roots stretching back to childhood and the authoritarian bonds of a rigid private school. As an adult, I fought it, but the impulse was never far away.

I realized I really did want to see Silvio. He, at least, still found me desirable. I thought I might even tell him about my gnawing dread, but wondered what I could say that wouldn't unnecessarily alarm him. Probably it was just the stress of this story, the shock of being threatened with a gun. My body had shut down.

Soon I was pulling up to his *abuelita*'s house in Alhambra. It was a town six miles northeast of Los Angeles, dotted with Spanish stucco houses built in the 1920s boom and still imbued with that era's hopeful pride by longtime white residents and new immigrant homeowners. Everyone kept their lawns mowed and their houses cheerfully painted, here a teal blue, there a mint green, each with its own unique architectural flourish. One man had added a home-made turret to his stucco box, another had designed security doors of baroque, curling metal. There were aluminum awnings shaped like the petals of giant flowers and hedges clipped into fantastic desert iguanas, as if, on these little plots of *tierra* they called home, a concerted attempt was being made to reclaim their individuality and so defy the larger culture that sought to lump them together under one census classification.

As I turned onto Silvio's *abuelita*'s street, I saw his father on the front lawn, spinning like a colorful pinwheel on a rickety old exercise bike. Felipe Aguilar was a self-made millionaire/music promoter who specialized in bringing Mexican acts to Los Angeles, to the delight of homesick immigrants, who regularly packed his Arena La Puente. I had met him only once before, at the wake for his dead son, and then he had been in full patriarchal regalia, somber and regal as a judge. So his attire and relaxed demeanor today amid the potted plants, succulents, and cactuses of the garden took me aback.

Felipe wore sweatpants and a T-shirt that said HOMEBOY TORTILLAS and pedaled furiously as he entered the home stretch of his workout, mopping his brow with a white cotton towel slung around his neck.

"*Buenas tardes,*" he bellowed. "You're Silvio's friend. Come in, come in. I'm the welcoming committee. This way I don't miss anything. Everyone's out back." He lowered his dripping face to mine. "Level six, pretty good for an old man, eh?"

"You've got more energy than the rest of us put together,"

I told him, amazed at his public display of sweat, something you'd never see in my more decorous part of town. Looking around the yard, I saw bougainvillea sprouting out of a hot pink toilet that Silvio's grandmother had salvaged from God knows where. It sat next to plastic tubs from Home Depot and chipped orange and blue Bauer pots she must have picked up for a song in the hood, where people didn't yet know from California pottery.

"Pasa, pasa." He waved me in, and I took my leave.

In the formal living room, there were family photos everywhere, of kids getting diplomas, smiling gap-toothed at the camera in second grade, making their Confirmation, receiving First Holy Communion in frilly white outfits. In a family portrait, Silvio and his brother, Ruben, composed themselves stiffly around Felipe and their mother and beamed grimly at the camera. There was a black-and-white photo of a stern and wrinkled man in a cowboy hat who must have been Silvio's great-grandfather and a plump lady in a long, high-collar pleated dress who looked like his great-grandmother, the bearer of eight sons and three daughters back on the ancestral ranch in Mexico.

In the kitchen, women I didn't know were working, pounding chiles and seeds with a mortar and pestle. I smiled at them and made my way into the backyard, looking for Silvio.

The last time I had been here, I hadn't gone outside. Now I realized the yard was one of those deep lots that went back a quarter acre. There were tables piled with food, and beer kegs sitting in icy tubs. More people were arriving, probably second and third cousins once removed, embracing and opening beers and piling plates high with *carne asada*, frijoles and tortillas and potato salad, while they watched the afternoon wane.

Normally I would have filled my own plate with gusto, but now the food didn't seem appetizing. I looked in vain for

Silvio. The guest of honor was nowhere to be seen either. I walked through the partygoers and deeper into the yard, wondering what I would tell Silvio. His *abuelita*'s property looked out onto an arroyo, and as the afternoon shadows lengthened, a small breeze had kicked up. It was a green haven, planted with fruit trees and tall grasses, and I went all the way to the end of the property line and peered over the cinder-block wall and into the arroyo, where I half expected to see coyotes prowling or a deer looking up with startled eyes. But I saw only detritus—rusted coils of box springs, old mattresses long ago overtaken by vermin, empty beer cans, and dead cactuses. How the hell did you kill a cactus? Over on the other side of the arroyo, I could see into another backyard, where an old wooden shed leaned perilously to one side.

By the time I wandered back up to the party, Felipe had showered and changed and was setting out white plastic chairs in a half-moon on the grass. He was in a good mood, pushing drinks and food upon everyone, greeting friends who trickled in late with their families. Now I finally saw Silvio's *abuelita*—perhaps she had been taking her afternoon siesta. She sat enthroned on a dais, swathed in shawls, her white hair held back by silver combs, her hands laden with rings and bracelets, and received her audience one by one.

I wondered if she would remember me. Where was Silvio? Now the *músicos* were arriving, wearing the large-brimmed white hats of the Mexican cowboy, hauling their gear, setting up. I wanted to ask Felipe where Silvio was, but was suddenly paralyzed by shyness.

Then I felt the pressure of a hand on my shoulder. I turned and saw Silvio. He was smiling.

"You came!"

"Yes." Abashed at the emotion in his eyes, I looked down.

"My father told me, and I've been looking for you. But I didn't see you. How long have you been here?"

"Oh. Awhile. I didn't see you, either, so I hiked to the back of the property and sat there a spell. It's enchanting. So peaceful."

So unlike my own heart, I wanted to add.

"I'm sorry. *Abuelita* sent me out for more ice. It's so warm today."

"That's fine." I waved my hand in dismissal. The band was clambering onto the stage and tuning their instruments.

"No, it's not. I invited you here. You don't know anyone. It was rude."

"Journalists aren't shy. We know how to make our way among strangers."

Far away, I saw Silvio's father working the crowd like a small-time politician, pressing the flesh, slapping backs, bringing beers, making sure everyone was having a good time.

But we journalists also hold ourselves apart, I thought. We are the world's designated observers, forbidden to participate. It was a job requirement that suited me all too well, and only reinforced my innate solitary nature. I had been here close to an hour and hadn't spoken a word to anyone other than to exchange greetings with Felipe.

"Did you eat?" Silvio asked.

"I'm not hungry right now."

The band had launched into its first song, an old *ranchera* tune from Felipe's youth.

"Later, then," he said, and grabbed my arm. "C'mon, let's dance."

He pulled me onto the grass for a Mexican polka, that unholy mix of Teutonic accordion and Mexican *ranchera* that coalesced a century ago when German immigrants settled in the Southwest.

"I don't know how to do this," I whispered.

"Stop trying to lead and you'll be fine."

I relaxed into his arms. It felt good to be gripped and turned and flung and always caught before I careened out of control. As we clomped along, I saw the backyard moving like a kaleidoscope, boys playing soccer, people eating and drinking, older ladies sitting primly in chairs, knees together and feet tucked beneath them. Then Silvio's dad appeared out of nowhere, gave a hearty yell and swept up the nearest lady, dancing her around until she grabbed his shoulder and squealed and he put her down and they commenced a sloppy polka, he charging happily to and fro while the lady, who wore heels, sashayed properly.

Just then the band launched into a traditional crowd-pleaser called "Margarita." It was a *norteña* ode to a young maiden, in which the singer implores her to seize the day and stop being so haughty, because "the leaves on the trees don't last forever." I thought of Tim quoting from Robert Herrick the night before, and where that had led, and I buried my face in Silvio's shoulder to hide my blushing shame. Taking it for a gesture of affection, Silvio gathered me tighter against him.

People poured onto the dance floor now. Young couples clomped and children held aloft by parents squealed with glee and dizziness, waving to their relatives as they twirled. The band thumped on and a cool breeze blew down the arroyo, filling the air with the malty smell of beer, sweat, and drugstore perfume. I felt transported.

Ay, que lástima, que lástima, que lástima me da. The words were sad and playful, sung by an old Mexican with a pencil-thin mustache *en el estilo antiguo*, who didn't even have a good voice, really—it was whiny and nasal—but the imperfections made it all the more appealing.

As the moon rose, and Silvio and I dipped and twirled next to each other, I forgot about everything for a while, and I knew that the world was a good place and that things didn't get much better anywhere than a warm spring night in the *barrio*.

Then suddenly it was late, and I had to leave, like Cinderella, before the truth was exposed. I stumbled off the dance floor and Silvio followed.

"What's wrong?"

"I've got to go. It's perfect, right now, the way it is, and I want to remember it this way for always."

He caught my hand. "I thought we might—"

"Silvio, I—"

"I promise I won't even bring up the trial in my sleep."

He swayed in the lights.

"I can't," I said.

How could I say anything? I had waited too long and there was no longer an opening. Whatever I said would ruin the warm glow that now enveloped us. I had to tell him that I was late. I couldn't. He deserved to know. But this was not the right time.

"What's the matter with you?"

"I'm not sure," I said unhappily. Was it irrational to be so worried?

"Talk to me."

But I couldn't tell him what weighed so heavily on my mind. So instead, I told him about Tim. Perhaps it was blunt and cruel, but I can be that way sometimes. More so than is necessary, I've been told. As I spoke, his expression changed from concern to something colder and steelier.

He turned to watch the musicians, his face a calm and studied mask, the face he must have perfected with the little neighborhood gangbangers who had confronted him as a kid. Avoid fights. Don't engage. Slip inside and lock the door and crack the books, there's a more worthy battle ahead, the spoils more lucrative. It was how good kids in his neighborhood survived into adulthood. Some of them, anyway.

I couldn't stand his silence.

"So that's why I wasn't thinking straight. When you came over . . ."

He didn't seem to understand. He shook his head and rubbed his eyes, then asked, "Who is this guy again?"

"I told you," I said. "He's a very serious boyfriend I had in my early twenties, and he has popped back into my life in an unsettling way that has confused me. I thought I was over him. I still think I am. But he has dredged up feelings that scare me. And that's why I wanted so much to be with you that night."

His mouth set in a grim line. "And here I was trying to give you your 'space,'" he said. "And meanwhile this old boyfriend has returned and now you're going to go off with him, have his babies, live happily ever after."

Maybe I'm already having your *baby. How's that thought for you?*

He shook his head in disgust and I knew I wouldn't tell him. Not tonight.

"You did the right thing," I said, unable to meet his eyes. "You couldn't have pushed any harder. You still can't."

"You tell me you have confused feelings for an ex-boyfriend and you don't expect me to get angry? You're involved with *me* now."

He pulled out a chair and straddled it.

"*Ay que lástima, que lástima, que lástima me da,*" sang the band. What sorrow you bring me. And on the floor, people danced, looser and jerkier as it got later, as if it were their last chance and dawn would bring the end of the world.

"Am I?" I said.

His face closed in bewilderment. "I thought you were. I thought we had an agreement. You said you wanted to see me. And now this guy blows into town and I'm history?"

"Silvio," I said. "It never really ended properly between

me and him. So much was left unresolved. I'm trying to do that now. I care about you. I care a lot. But it's going to take time."

"Maybe I'm the one who needs time. Maybe I'm being foolish, hooking up with you. What are you, some kind of dog in heat? He touches you and you melt. You have no restraint, Eve."

A dog. So that's what he thought of me. But I didn't hate him for it because I knew where it came from. Silvio had spent his life battling the spontaneous side of his nature.

"I know," I said steadily. "That's why I'm trying to show some now. I'm trying to change." For you, I wanted to add, but didn't. Because it would sound condescending, even though I meant it.

"I don't even want to think of you being with this person."

"Then don't. Because I'm not with him. I just need to find some clarity."

"Clarity this, then. You want to risk losing me, then go. Just remember: I won't wait around."

Funny, I thought. Those were the same words Tim had uttered to me six years ago. Forcing me to choose. And it seemed I never could. I wasn't strong enough.

"If I didn't miss you so much, I would have stayed home tonight. But I needed to talk to you."

"So I should thank you for tormenting me?"

You should ask me why I need to talk to you.

He lifted my hand and I felt his lips brush my fingertips, their pressure soft and warm.

"Good-bye, Eve. Go fulfill your quest. *Que te vaya bien.*"

I almost gave in then. I almost threw myself at him. But I held my body still. He'd never know the restraint I was capable of. And when he walked away, I turned and didn't look back.

Chapter 18

*I*n the morning, I decided not to torture myself any
longer.

It was only five-twenty, but there was a twenty-four-
hour pharmacy down the street where I could buy a home
pregnancy kit. That's funny, I thought, walking out and seeing
my car door hanging open on the driver's side. I could have
sworn I had locked it.

My steps slowed to a crawl. There was something on my
windshield, tall black slashes. I looked around the deserted
street but saw no one. Birdsong filled the air. Far away, a
dog barked. A breeze rustled through the trees.

The car was empty, the door hanging open in beckoning
invitation. Come inside, it seemed to say. Look what we
have for you. A door slammed, making me jump, and
Violetta, my landlady, who lived downstairs, shuffled out in
her furry slippers to get the paper. Now it was safe. Now I
had a witness. Stealthily, I crept to the car and looked inside.

The first thing that hit me was the smell. It took me a
minute to focus on what lay in the car seat. It was a very
large, very rotten fish, its flesh mottled brown, its innards
slowly seeping out and puddling in the vinyl seat as the
warmth of the early morning hastened its decomposition. But
what was truly surreal was what lay in the fish's open, smiling mouth. Clenched between tiny rows of razor-sharp teeth
was a single red rose.

My gorge rose and I staggered back, doubled over, and
vomited into the hydrangeas. It was mainly dry heaving and
bile. I hadn't eaten much last night. Still bent over, I stole

another look at the bucket seat, the gruesome sight both repelling and compelling, and my eyes connected with something else, nestled by the fish's tail, that I had over-looked. It was a very large bullet casing.

In the driveway, Violetta was bending down to scoop up the paper. She lifted the bundled pages to her nose to read the headlines. Without her glasses, Violetta was almost blind. Now she finally saw me and walked over. How was I going to explain this to her? To anyone?

I glanced at the front windshield again and slowly made out the letters that someone had slashed in black spray paint across the glass. Reading them backward took me a minute, and then my brain balked, unwilling to believe it.

STOP, the letters said.

Violetta was beside me. She wrinkled her nose.

"Good gracious, Eve, you should clean your car more often, it really stinks," she said. "But never mind that, how are you, sweetheart?"

She smiled and pushed the hair back from her eyes. Unable to speak, I pointed to the bucket seat.

"Vot in the vorld?" Violetta said in a much different tone of voice, and I knew she was shaken because she had lost her ability to pronounce *w*, the dreaded bane of nonnative speakers everywhere.

Newspaper clutched to her chest, she leaned forward and made out the letters spray-painted across my windshield. "*Stop?*" Violetta said. "Did some jilted boyfriend do this to you, darling? What a filthy trick."

"I think," I said grimly, "that this may have something to do with a story I'm working on."

Violetta looked at me quizzically. "But this is getting quite personal."

"Yes," I said.

With that, I turned and retched into Violetta's hydrangeas again.

* * *

An hour later, after laying a cold compress against my head and tucking me into bed, Violetta went back to her apartment downstairs. She had been adamant about wanting to tell the police, so we had made a call and now a dubious desk officer took down the information.

"Have you recently broken up with a boyfriend or husband?" a bored male voice asked me, and after thinking about Silvio and Tim, then dismissing the possibility, I told him no.

"Any neighborhood spats, recent arguments over retaining walls or views?" he droned on.

Again, I told him no. I brought up the fact that I was a reporter, but he seemed unimpressed. I didn't tell him about the little girl, and the *malditos* at the Hotel Variott. I had promised the maid. And I didn't want to get pulled off the story. But I have to admit I wavered for a moment. I cleared my throat and was about to say something when he offered to send someone out that evening to interview me and photograph the evidence, intimating with his tone of voice that the Hollywood division of the LAPD had more important things to worry about.

"Never mind," I said, imagining how the dead fish would stink up my car if left to fester on a warm spring day.

Then I dragged my carcass out of bed, got an old newspaper, and gingerly picked up and heaved the decaying fish into the trash can, along with the rose. I stuck a pencil inside the bullet casing and carried it to my bedroom bureau. One day, I might need it for evidence. Then I went back outside, rolled down all the windows in my car, and attacked the seat with disinfectant and paper towels. Violetta emerged and together we used scrapers to chip off the thick black paint.

I went inside and made myself some scrambled eggs and coffee. Someone was trying to warn me off the little girl's trail. They knew where I lived. I'd have to lie low for a while. To lull them into complacency. And then make my move.

As I pondered all this, staring out the picture window toward downtown, I realized I had never gone to the pharmacy. It was only seven, though I felt half the day had passed. Now I got into my car, careful to lay a towel over the driver's seat, and bought myself a home pregnancy kit. As I drove, I breathed through my mouth to avoid the oily, fishy stink.

Back home, I went into the bathroom and locked the door. Against whom, I wasn't sure. I lived alone.

I unwrapped the plastic package and read the instructions. The test gave 95 percent accurate results within twenty-four hours of conceiving. But in the end, I couldn't go through with it. I needed a witness or something. I called Babette and she agreed to come over on her way to work.

"I can't believe that you, of all people . . ." she said, putting down her beaded handbag as she clip-clopped into the room forty-five minutes later.

I closed the front door behind her and stood there, uncertain of the formalities surrounding such a thing. She appraised me critically.

"You look pretty shaky, like you've been on a bender. Your face is green. What's gotten into you? How did this happen?"

I told her about what I had found in my car this morning, and how I thought it might be connected to a story I was working on. I explained what I had told the police and what I had left out.

"Good God," Babette said. "And is this all connected somehow with your pre—with taking this test?"

I opened my mouth, but only one word came out.

"Tim," I said.

Babette looked at me with disbelief, concern brimming in her voice.

"You think you're pregnant by Tim? You haven't seen him in years. Eve, are you sure you're okay?"

I sighed impatiently. "He came by last week. He was waiting for me out on the back porch."

"And you slept with him? Oh, Eve, how could you? After all this time. Do you think he left those horrid things in your car?"

"No. And no, I didn't sleep with him. But I slept with Silvio."

"What? You're not making any sense."

"Yes, I am. I was so shaken by seeing Tim that when Silvio called me later that night, I told him to come over. And now I'm late."

I looked miserably at her, huddling against the wall.

"Now I get it," she said. "Why didn't you just say so in the beginning?"

She threw open the bathroom door. Soundlessly, she handed me the stick and I followed the instructions and waited for the stick to change color.

"Two lines means you're knocked up. One, you're home free," I said.

"Yes, I know. I've had a few scares myself," Babette said.

I watched the first line form, wondering how this flimsy three-inch plastic stick could hold my fate and decide my future. The moisture kept rising up the stick and I let out a breath. I was safe. Then a faint second line began to form.

"Do you see that?" I asked.

Babette's blond head bent over the stick. "Let's just stay calm and see if it keeps developing," she said.

I watched. It was just the moisture reacting with the chemicals. It was some kind of optical illusion. Too much time had already elapsed. It wasn't fair. I sat on the toilet and watched my life change as a second line formed parallel to the first. I blinked and rubbed my eyes, then looked again. It was still there. The tile felt cold against my bare feet. I shivered in my cotton shirt. There it was. Two lines. Pregnant.

"Maybe the test is wrong," Babette said. Her voice was brave, but her eyes were wide with panic.

"Maybe I'll miscarry."

"Maybe you'll terminate."

"I could give it up for adoption."

"You could marry Silvio and have five more," Babette said. For some reason, that made us double up with hysterical laughter. It was too crazy even to contemplate.

"Aw, Babette, you know me better than that. I've never been gaga over babies."

Even as a child, I had preferred my stable of stuffed animals to dolls. If I had a biological clock, I couldn't hear it ticking. I thought that was all foolish nonsense. Perhaps that meant I didn't have a maternal instinct. Or did it kick in once you stared at their wrinkly little faces?

"Here's what we do," Babette said. "We wait. In two days, we take another test. Then we see what we've got."

For a long time, we sat on the couch, looking out at a heartbreakingly blue sky, unable to bear the light but too shocked to flinch from it.

"Lots of people give up babies for adoption," Babette said finally.

I looked at her. "But I couldn't carry it inside me for nine months, give birth, and then not ache to hold it, to keep it."

"Then you'd be a good mother if you wanted it that badly."

I shook my head. "What about work? I love my job. I work long hours. How could I raise a baby when I don't even have pets because it wouldn't be fair to them? How do single moms do it, anyway? And Silvio? Does he even want kids? Would that be a good way to start a life together?"

I thought back with scarlet shame to how I had ranted to Maxwell in Griffith Park. Perhaps I should have gotten

myself fitted out with Norplant before I went off on that
holier-than-thou tirade. Why, I was no better than a twelve-
year-old girl who thinks she can't get pregnant if she only
does it once.

*"A baby has the right to get born into a family that can
love it and take care of it. . . . I could have had ten babies by
now. But I didn't. . . . I lack the ma-toor-ity. But at least I
know it."*

Now my own words echoed in my brain. What gave me
the right to dictate what poor teenagers should do while
allowing myself to flout the same advice?

Finally Babette sighed and said she had to go to work.

"Maybe this is all a mistake," she said at the door.
"Please don't freak out yet. And Eve? This fish thing has me
worried. Promise me you'll be careful?"

I mumbled something to satisfy her and she left. It was
still only eight-thirty, but I couldn't bear the thought of going
to work yet. Whether I wanted a baby or not, there was
something hallowed about the whole idea. But the more I
tried to think about this new reality, the more it eluded me.

I sat cross-legged on the bed, opened my wallet, and got
out the by-now-familiar photo of Serey Rath. I unfolded it
and studied it. There was that blank toddler face, the photocopy making it look slightly out of focus. A child that no one
had stepped forward to claim. Surely she had a mother, a
father, a family somewhere. Were they missing her at this
very moment? I touched her hair, her nose, her lips, and for
the first time, the reality of the girl's plight reverberated
somewhere deep inside, far away from Eve the journalist.
Ears, throat, chin. At what stage do they form? Once this
child too had floated in a warm salt sea. Did she miss the lapping of the tides, the metronome of a familiar heart? I felt my
own, pounding through my chest, and rested my head against
the pillow, trying to steady my breathing. Then I sat back up
and folded my paper into neat squares. The corners were

beginning to fray, a slight silkiness to the edges. I slid it back into my wallet.

I walked outside, my bare legs brushing against the lavender that grew along the flagstone path, the oil from the crushed petals lingering in the air, so redolent and heavy that I would probably still smell it this afternoon.

It was spring. All around me the earth was bursting with fertility, animals and insects chasing each other, pollen drifting through the air, flowers open and inviting. At work, women talked about hormone shots and in vitro, ovulation cycles and child care. So many women I knew were trying desperately to get pregnant. As usual, I was out of synch with my age group, floundering somewhere in deep water.

I went back inside, got dressed, and drove to the San Gabriel Valley with the windows rolled down. Finally the rotten fish smell was beginning to ebb. I didn't want to think about the bullet casing and what that meant.

CHAPTER 19

*S*itting down at my desk, I sifted through my messages and found one from Alexandra Dubrovna, giving me the name of the Cambodian adoption agency. *Hands Across the Water*, the receptionist had written in her neat cursive. Followed by a number with too many digits to be in the U.S. I called the international operator and recited the number. In a few minutes, it rang and a groggy-sounding woman came on.

I had forgotten the time distance. In Cambodia, it was the middle of the night. I apologized, told her who I was, and asked if I had reached an adoption agency. She responded in a singsongy language I took to be Cambodian.

"English," I said. "Is there anyone there who speaks English?"

The woman said something and I heard the phone being put down on a hard surface. From far off, I heard a muffled discussion in the same language, then another voice came on, male this time.

"Hallo? Hallo?" he said.

I repeated my question.

"Yes," the man said. "You call back tomorrow. No speak English."

I hung up in frustration, then looked them up online. Typing in www.handsacrossthewater.com, I came up empty. I called Tong to confirm the name and number with Alexandra, but she wasn't there so I left a message. Next, I tried variations on the name and domain but got no matches for adoption agencies. Perhaps the receptionist had written it down wrong. Googleing them brought up 857 hits, and the thought of scrolling through all those entries sent a wave of weariness rolling over me. I decided I'd better eat something first.

In the lunchroom, I got my fruit salad out of the fridge and went to sit at a table with Harry Jack. Seeing the veteran photographer triggered a memory.

"I was out with Ariel Delacorte on a story the other day," I told him. "She's a big fan of yours. Wants the three of us to get together for a drink."

Harry looked at me dubiously over his sack lunch. "I haven't seen much of her in the last year. Don't know as anyone has. She keeps to herself."

"Did she have a baby or something and it died?"

He gave me a level look. "That what she told you?"

I hesitated. "No. But I'm curious. Do you know what happened with that baby?"

Harry hunkered over his lunch bag. He pulled out a package wrapped in butcher paper, unfolding it with a delicacy born of great anticipation.

"She had it on her own, didn't she?" I persisted. "Got tired of waiting around for Mr. Right?"

Unveiling a bulging pastrami sandwich, Harry reached back into the bag and pulled out a cardboard container with an aluminum handle. Potato salad.

I waited. Harry was usually so straightforward that the evasive food maneuver immediately betrayed him. For such a raconteur, he was a terrible liar.

Now he pulled out a long cylinder of butcher paper and unwrapped a dill pickle. He picked it up and waggled it at me. "I guess a lot of you gals have that problem today."

"Put that thing down," I said. "But, Harry, you used to be tight with her. So tell me about this baby. Did she go to a sperm bank or what?"

I paused for a whisker of a moment, amazed that I was

even uttering the word *sperm* to a seventy-seven-year-old man who could be my grandfather.

He bit down on the briny dill, and green juice squirted across my arm. The lunchroom filled with the sounds of bovine crunching. I waited until I saw his Adam's apple bob, then raised an eyebrow.

"Well?"

"She decided sperm banks were too elitist," Harry said.

"Mmmm," I said. "That's something, coming from her. Miss Upper Crust."

"Well, I don't know, Eve. I mean, a broad can walk into a bar any night of the week and get knocked up by closing, but ya gotta consider the gene pool."

"Surely those aren't the only two options. So what did she do?"

"Never told me," Harry said. "But next thing I knew, she had a baby."

"Next thing?"

"Well, it might have been nine months or so."

"Men!" I said, laughing.

"Actually she adopted. It just took a while for the baby to come," Harry said. "Cute little thing. Pigtails and slanty eyes. One a' them Chinese babies."

"Almond, Harry."

"What?"

"Say *almond* eyes, not *slanty*. I know you're old-school, but still."

"I got no preference, Eve. You know that."

"I'm just telling you."

"I got some Mexican neighbors just moved in. They're very nice. Polite, but mind their own business. Not sneaky, mind you, like they're in one of them drug cartels. I'm working on the husband to join Kiwanis."

"Oh, Harry, you're hopeless."

Affronted, he surveyed me. "Why do you say that?"

"Oh, never mind. So what happened to Ariel's adopted baby?"

"It was squirrelly from the beginning."

"The baby?"

"The adoption. She was always complaining. 'Harry, they're missing a document and it's going to cost me five grand. Harry, they can speed it up for another five. Harry, the kid is sick and medicine's expensive over there.'"

"How do you know all that?" I asked, invoking the first commandment of journalism: If your mother says she loves you, get attribution.

Harry looked out the window. His jaw twitched. "Who do you think loaned her the extra twelve grand?"

"Well, that was awfully nice. I hope she paid you back."

Harry nodded sagely, rocking back in his chair. "Every cent. Once she got her credit cards under control. That gal spends too much on clothes. Do you know she once paid seven hundred and fifty bucks for a pair of shoes?"

I did know. Ariel had even written a column about it. It was shortly after September 11 and she was jittery. The frivolous purchase had helped soothe her nerves. Besides, the president was telling everyone to show their patriotism by going out and stimulating the economy, so she had done her share. Never mind that the shoes had probably been stitched in Mexico from raw materials shipped out of China, so that it wasn't our economy Ariel was stimulating.

"So she finally got the baby?"

"Yeah, but it turned out the birth mother hadn't agreed to give up the baby. For months it was up in the air. Finally she had to give the kid back. Nearly broke her heart."

So that explained Ariel's distracted air, the veil of sorrow she had drawn around herself some time back. Her obsessive traveling. The puffy eyes and pitying looks from editors who cut her uncharacteristic slack. The shaking hands in the cafeteria as she reached for the tuna plate. But something was gnawing at me.

"You sure the baby was from China?"

Harry waved his arm. "Somewhere in Asia."

"Did she ever say China?"

"Aren't most of 'em from China? What difference does it make, anyway? Why are you so interested in Ariel's lost baby?"

His eyes flickered to my belly, then back up to my eyes, and I knew what he was thinking. Why did everyone think this was personal? Was my body giving off some sort of chemical clue that I was pregnant or wanted a baby?

Harry's chair came back down with a thump.

"Why don't you ask her yourself? She likes you, you know."

"She doesn't even know me," I said, surprised. "We've never said more than two words outside of assignments."

"You think all photographers do is take pictures? We listen too. She's been out with you on stories. She says you can always count on something edgy and unusual with an Eve Diamond assignment."

It's always a shock to see yourself reflected through the prism of another's eyes.

"Well, all right," I said. "I will."

Belly full, I scrolled through my 857 Google citations but found nothing resembling an adoption agency until the last page, when I found one called BeautifulCambodianBaby.org. Could that be it? With trembling hands, I typed in the name, only to slam my palms down with disgust when I got a notice saying the site was down and couldn't be accessed. Even the Internet couldn't work miracles.

By that time it was 3 P.M. and I had to go downtown for a meeting. In the newspaper lobby, I ran into Ariel. When I asked if she'd like to have a drink that evening, she looked startled and said she had plans. But as I walked down Spring Street to the employee lot after the meeting, I heard someone calling my name.

"I thought that was you," Ariel said breathlessly as she caught up with me in front of the security booth. "Are you still up for that drink? My plans fell through."

So we turned around and walked up Second Street to the Redwood, the old booze-hound bar where the drinks are as stiff as the waitresses' hairdos. After we ordered, she opened her briefcase and pulled out some proof sheets.

"Take a look at this," she said.

I peered through the loupe she handed me and saw a young pregnant girl wearing a gym bra and bicycle shorts washing herself at a park fountain, oblivious to the children playing nearby. Behind her stood a heavyset youth with a buzz cut, holding a can of beer. Several frames later, he was yelling at her, face contorted in anger. In successive shots, the girl's hands were on her hips, her mouth twisted and jeering. There was an arc of flying suds as he threw his beer on her. She splashed him with water and as the proofs marched into a second, third, and fourth page, the boy wound up and hit her in the stomach. The last shot showed them embracing, and the expression on the girl's tear-streaked face was so haunted and forlorn that I felt it radiating off the proofs and into my own heart.

"Who are they?"

"Emancipated foster kids," Ariel said. "Once they turn eighteen, the county sets them loose. I've been following these two. County helped them get an apartment, but they partied too hard and lost their jobs, fell behind on the rent. Now they're living on the street."

I studied the photos some more. There was a raw, naked quality to them, as if the subjects had been unaware of the camera lens clicking on their ugly domestic squabble. Ariel had captured the shifting emotions of boredom, rage, fear, humiliation, love, and ultimately resignation that moved across their features in the span of minutes. The photos seemed to suggest that these two had been plunked into adulthood without an owner's manual and were struggling in vain to forge a path.

I considered how Ariel was drawn time and again to children. It was her eternal theme, replicated the world over, whether it was child soldiers in Africa, child prostitutes in Nepal, or child drug runners in American crack houses. They were the locus of her art, giving voice to something inside her that had had no other way to emerge.

I heard her soft breath and saw spots of color high on her cheeks. She knew the power of the saga she had captured in five rolls of film. The photos were brutish, tender, violent, and sorrowful, all at once.

"These are extraordinary," I said. "Harry was right, you're a natural."

Her face softened. "He's a treasure," she said, sipping her vodka and grapefruit juice. "He helped me out of a jam once, and I've never forgotten it."

My ears burned. I felt like she knew Harry and I had just been talking about her.

"With the baby?" I asked cautiously.

Beside me, her body tensed.

"Yes," she finally said, staring at her tumbler, and I got that warm reporterly feeling that she might want to talk about it.

I picked up my own glass, ready to take a sip, then put it down with a thud. Poison for the baby growing inside me. I couldn't feel it yet. Did it even exist? It seemed so unreal. I stirred the drink, then pushed it away and took a sip of water instead.

"I'm so sorry about what happened." I paused. "Are you going to try again?"

Her face puckered like an empty balloon.

"Oh no. I don't think so. It's too hard. I'm not cut out . . ."

"Ariel, I have to ask you something."

"What?" She picked up one of her proof sheets and held it against her as though to deflect unpleasant questions.

"When you adopted that little girl, how did it work?"

I heard a deep intake of breath. Lines appeared on either side of her mouth that I hadn't noticed before.

"I, um . . . look, I know this may be very sensitive, and feel free to tell me to shut up, but I'm working on a story about that little girl we saw at the airport and, well, I've just got this weird hunch . . . I was wondering if you could tell me about that adoption agency you used and how things went so terribly wrong."

It was all swirling in my brain now. Little girls from Asia. Weird, screwed-up adoptions that didn't take. Maxwell's horrifying comment about kids trafficked into child pornography. I thought of the paper that lay folded in my wallet. The solemn face. Had her mother taken the photo? Had she had second thoughts after it was too late? Or was it more sinister than that?

Ariel Delacorte downed her drink. Then she signaled the waitress to bring another, turning politely to ask if I'd like a refresher too. I declined.

When the waitress brought it, Ariel stirred her drink dreamily with the swizzle stick and then drank deeply, as if to fortify herself. When she put the glass down, it was half-empty. Ariel looked at me shrewdly.

"You're single too, right?"

"Yes," I said, startled. I thought about Silvio. I thought about Tim. Yes, I was definitely single.

"Ever think about babies?"

This conversation was not going the way I wanted. But it touched such a deep and melancholy part of me. In the last few days, I had thought about little else.

"Not really," I stammered.

"Well, it's not all it's cracked up to be."

I searched for an appropriate remark. After what she had been through, I could understand her sentiment, even consider it normal.

"I mean, here I was, a successful professional woman. I had a nice house, a nice car. A gratifying career. But there was a huge hole right here." She bunched her hand into a fist and held it somewhere near her heart. "It wasn't lack of a man. I had plenty of lovers. But one I could settle down with and raise a family? He was nowhere on the horizon. And meanwhile this ache was growing. It was utterly devastating."

She looked at me. "Have you felt it? The desire to hold a child in your arms? A tiny, powerless thing who depends totally on you, who you can shape and mold and watch grow up and infuse with all your wisdom and learning so she won't make the same mistakes you made growing up?"

"I don't know if it works quite that way, Ariel, but no, I don't think I have experienced that."

"Well, I have. I wanted a baby fiercely. And with adoption, I could save a child's life, give one a chance, and yet not have to go through pregnancy. I hear it can be awful. And my figure? Well."

"And you thought the agency could make it possible?"

"The agency did make it possible."

"But they were crooked. Or something," I said. "You lost the baby."

A look of grief and sorrow slowly suffused her features. She covered her face with her hands, leaning forward until her sleek, bobbed head lay on the table.

I had known it might be painful, but I didn't realize she was going to lose it right here at the Redwood. At the bar, several bodies twisted on their stools. I glared at them until they turned back, patting her shoulder all the while.

I shoved some cocktail napkins into her fist, and her fingers tightened around them and she dabbed at her face. Slowly, she straightened and her hands nervously found her hair and smoothed it back around her ears. Then she took another napkin, delicately blew her nose, balled it up, and placed it in the ashtray.

"It must be terrible each time you think about it," I said. "I mean, you had the child for what, months? You bonded with her. And then to have to let her go?"

This sent her into a renewed paroxysm of weeping.

"I'm sorry," I said when she finally came up for air. "That was thoughtless of me, dredging up all those horrible memories."

Ariel cast around the table but only ice cubes remained in her drink. I knew what she wanted. I pictured the waitress bringing another round, mine lining up like jets in a holding pattern at LAX. I pushed a glass of water toward her.

She took a big gulp, frowned, looked as though she wanted to say something, then changed her mind and kept drinking.

"Thanks, Eve," she said when she put the glass down. "Guess I don't need another drink right now."

"Believe me, I'd be in a lot worse shape if it happened to me. That dirty, cheating adoption agency. And how do you know she really went back to her mother? Did you report them? The *Times* could do a story. I'm sure you're not the only one who got rooked."

Her doe eyes widened in alarm. "Oh, no. That would not be a good thing at all." She took another sip. "You see, Eve, it's not what you think."

"You lost your baby," I said. "That's horrible."

"I gave up my baby," she said. "I willingly gave up my baby. And I can never forgive myself. Though it's not too late . . ." Her eyes got a faraway look and her voice trailed off.

"Perhaps you should—"

"I'm just not cut out to be a mother," she said sadly.

"Don't beat yourself up over it; why—"

But her voice had grown pensive. "Listen, I can sense something about you. You're not just asking me out of idle curiosity. There's something personal at stake for you."

"You've got it all wrong," I began.

"I don't care what you say, your eyes give you away. You're pregnant, aren't you?"

"Me?"

"No, that reporter over there in the corner."

I sat in silence, wondering how she had guessed. After a minute, I swallowed and realized I had waited too long to plausibly deny it. And what if she was right, that it was revealed in my eyes? A tiny embryo curled into the recess of each pupil, bobbing peacefully in the corneal fluids for anyone attuned to seeing such things.

"Barely," I whispered. "I, I don't know if I'm going to keep it," I said, my tongue thick and sluggish in my mouth.

"I knew it," Ariel crowed. But on the heels of her triumph came cautious sorrow. "I'm sorry," she said. "I take it this is not a blessed event."

"I'm not sure what it is."

"Is the father in the picture?"

"I don't know." I looked down at my nail-bitten hands. "I don't know anything anymore."

She patted my arm. Now she was the one comforting me.

"Listen to me," Ariel said, hunkering down so that we looked like two kindergarteners having quiet time at their desks. "Will you come to my house? You can follow me. I have some things to show and tell you. Please?"

CHAPTER 20

We walked back to the employee parking lot and I followed her to Hancock Park, a leafy, affluent community in midtown with some of the city's best-preserved architectural treasures. Ariel lived in a Spanish house painted a burnt reddish orange. Inside, the freshly waxed wood floors gave off an impeccable shine. I looked in vain for personal photos but found no sign that she had ever had a baby.

Instead, there was exotic plunder from her trips abroad, here a carved wooden elephant, there an Indonesian robe, spiky shells from the Bahamas, naif artworks from Haiti, Russian icons etched in gold, Afghan Buddhas smuggled out through Pakistan, and delicate vases in swirling colors blown from Venetian glass.

While I admired her treasures, Ariel put on Mozart's requiem and went into a sunny-yellow kitchen to fetch a container of hummus, some pita bread, mineral water, and a frosty blue vodka bottle, which she placed on a rough-hewn oak table in the dining room under a crystal chandelier. Then she sat down and busied herself serving food and pouring vodka. I joined her and helped myself to a glass of mineral water.

"I didn't lose my baby," Ariel said without preamble after I took the first sip. "That was a story I made up because the truth was too shameful."

She bit down hard on her pita. "I knew it would take a while for me to bond with Emma," Ariel continued. "Before she came, I vacillated between terror and euphoria. The books tell you that's normal so I didn't worry. And I did things right. I took three weeks off when she arrived. We were going to spend every moment together to become a real-life mommy and baby. She was eighteen months already, so I figured I'd take her to Disneyland. But it was sensory overload, after the orphanage. She was terrified of the big storybook characters."

And who could blame her? I thought.

"Oh, it was a disaster," Ariel said. "She woke up crying every night for months. She wasn't used to the food and it made her vomit. She hit me with her tiny fists. I could hardly wait to go back to work. Weekends were the worst. It was nonstop. I didn't have a moment to myself. I was in despair. I lived for Monday morning, when I could drop her off at the sitter's."

A chill went up my spine, but I tried for levity. "You mean you had a Guatemalan nanny raising your kid like half of Los Angeles?"

Ariel shook her head. "It was more complicated than that. And it happened so gradually that I don't know where to begin."

I waited, but she jumped up to rummage in the fridge. She returned with a jar of gherkins, fished one out with her fingers, took a drink, then popped it in her mouth.

"The Russians love pickled mushrooms with their vodka, but this was the closest I could find," she said. Her eyes grew unfocused, and I knew she was thinking back to one of her trips.

"So it was a tough landing for both of you," I said. "I've heard of worse. And a lot of people have nannies. The kids seem to do okay."

Ariel toyed with the ice in her glass. "But I work really long hours," she said. "I travel. I knew I'd have to cut back once Emma arrived, but I found I needed the trips more than ever. To maintain my sanity. Stay connected to the larger world. I found myself resenting her constant demands."

"That seems natural. Your whole identity had changed. Now you were a mother and a professional woman, and trying to juggle both."

"But I didn't, see. I had found a nice Salvadorean lady who looked after babies in her home. Conchita was loving and warm. Patient. Always with one child on her hip, another in her arm. I started working longer and longer hours because I couldn't face going home to Emma. I'd drop her off early in the morning, pick her up late. Conchita didn't mind, she had three of her own, so she'd just mix up one more bottle of formula, mash up another banana. Then one day it got so late I knew Emma would be asleep by the time I swung by. So I asked Conchita to keep her overnight. When I got home at ten, I put on Chopin's Nocturnes and made some dinner. I watched the news and went to bed and I felt almost giddy with freedom. It was the first time I had relaxed in months."

"You're allowed," I said stiffly.

"I promised myself that I'd see Emma before work the next morning. But I overslept. Then I felt so guilty that I left work early to pick her up by six. We got home and I made dinner. By eight o'clock, I felt I was going out of my mind. The next night I had a late assignment, so Emma stayed at the babysitter's again. Then I started doing it several nights a week. And here's the horrible thing: I liked having the house to myself again."

Ariel put her elbows on the table and propped up her chin. "Emma was growing, and changing. She got more teeth. She learned to run, then skip. She started drinking from a cup and eating beans and rice and chicken that Conchita would chop really fine. When she was sick, only Conchita could soothe her. Then one day, Emma fussed and cried when I came to pick her up. She didn't want to leave.

'*Mami, mami,*' she cried, holding her arms out to Conchita."

A dull thud was beginning somewhere in the pit of my stomach. I marveled at the way Ariel was able to deliver this story, so matter-of-fact, as if it had happened to someone else.

"How did that make you feel?" I asked, slipping almost unconsciously into reporter-speak. But she was oblivious.

"Of course, part of me was hurt," Ariel said. "But another part felt—I know it's odd to say, but, well, relieved. Like the burden of responsibility was shifting, somehow. And really, what did I expect? Emma pretty much lived there by then, even if I was the one supporting her. When I showed up, she'd run away and hide in the bed with Conchita's other kids. Often her hands were sticky and her nose was runny. She'd be munching on a fruit leather or a biscuit and I'd be in my work clothes. Those dry-cleaning bills can kill you. So I'd blow her a kiss and go home alone. I redecorated, put out a lot of things I had packed away when Emma came. Like those Italian vases. You might have seen them on the lacquered Japanese chest when you walked in."

"They're exquisite."

"They're also terribly fragile," Ariel said, "and Emma might have broken them. Children are so clumsy. But come, here's what I wanted to show you."

She pushed her chair back and stood up.

"That's okay," I mumbled.

"No," said Ariel, her eyes bright and her voice sharp. "I want you to see. I want you to see how much I love her."

She led me through the living room and down a hallway lit by painted glass sconces. She turned a silver doorknob and we stepped inside a frothy fantasy of a little girl's room, the air close and still but perfumed by lavender sachets, the walls papered with Laura Ashley prints.

"Look," she said. "I ordered this ruffled bedspread from a

catalog in Vermont. The bed is antique maple, hand-painted.
Of course, she was too little for that, she still slept in a crib. But
I figured once she passed that awkward toddler stage she'd
appreciate her things so much more."

Ariel walked to a wooden chest painted with forest animals. She sank to her knees on the plush white carpet and
threw open the lid. It was stuffed with toys and furry animals, dolls with uncanny glass eyes staring up at me.

"See," she said. She got up and went to the closet. As she
rolled open the sliding door, I saw racks of velvet dresses
and satin jackets, tiny coats and ruby slippers.

Ariel slid the door shut. It slammed and the sudden
motion made her drink slosh onto the virgin carpet. She sat
down heavily on the bed and fingered the dust ruffle, the
duvet with glossy pink buttons.

"The last time I visited, Emma wouldn't even hug me.
She just stood there clutching Conchita's leg. Babbling in
Spanish. Imagine, with that face, rolling her *r*'s with the
best of them. It was then I decided that it would be better
not to visit for now. It just upsets her."

Something in my face made Ariel want to reassure me.

"It's not like I've abandoned her," she said. "I pay
Conchita well. Someday Emma will be old enough to
appreciate what I've done. But in the meantime, I took
down all the photos I had here and at work. It's too painful.
This is the first time I've been in her room for ages."

She stopped and looked directly at me. "You can't tell
anyone, Eve. But I wanted you to know. To help with your
own decision." She smiled tentatively, but her face was taut
and sad. "We're a lot alike in many ways, I think."

It scared me that she thought so.

No, we're not, I wanted to scream.

"So there was no mix-up with the adoption agency?" I said
coldly. "That story about the birth mother wanting her back?"

"I couldn't exactly tell the truth, could I? That I wasn't

cut out for this motherhood thing and it was too late to back out. No thirty-day warranty, satisfaction guaranteed or your money back."

"Everyone at work thought you were in mourning."

"Well, I was. I had given up my dream. The only thing that gives me hope is that eventually Emma will outgrow Conchita's household; there's not much intellectual stimulation there. Perhaps I'll evolve into a favorite aunt, and we can go to the museum and, oh, I don't know, the ballet. It isn't really much different from the way children were raised a century ago, is it?" she asked. "Put out to wet nurse and such. Or boarding school. It's practically *de rigueur* in England. That's what Rebecca West did, you know? With her illegitimate son by H. G. Wells."

"He was two years old and never forgave her for it," I said. "He hated his mother and wrote the first of those *Mommie Dearest* books."

Ariel looked startled. "Emma won't hate me. She's in a loving family environment. And in the meantime, I'm clipping articles about interesting vacations to Southeast Asia. I think she might like that. Close to where she's from. We can explore her birth culture together. Oh, Eve," she said, and her voice was heavy and dull. "Who am I fooling? Do you despise me?"

I put my arm around her. Two weeks ago, I would have denounced her. Now, her confession just made me heartsick.

"Some people just shouldn't have children," Brenner had said. But how did you know until you did?

"What if you started going over to Conchita's once a week?" I said. "Establish a routine. Emma would get to know you again. Then slowly you could shift back over."

"I should think about that," Ariel said, nodding briskly.

The shock of hearing her story had thrown me off mine, but her talk about Southeast Asia had brought me round again.

"What is Emma's birth country?" I asked. "And what's the name of the agency where you got her?"

"Cambodia," Ariel said, barely skipping a beat. "And it was called Hands Across the Water. They have offices in Phnom Penh and an outpost here in Long Beach."

I sucked in my breath. Tried to focus on those marvelous Italian vases in the next room. HAW. Hands Across the Water. The agency I had tried to look up online. The agency the Klimts were using for their daughter, who looked so much like the abandoned toddler.

"It's very bare bones," Ariel went on, oblivious, "run by a fabulous woman named Lia Kalayan. She's a saint. I talked to a lot of people, but Lia's dignity and compassion impressed me the most. Especially after everything she's been through."

"Oh?" I took a careful sip of water. "What has she been through?"

"She was there under the Khmer Rouge. When Pol Pot emptied the cities and tried to turn the nation into one big agrarian commune. They killed all the intellectuals, anyone with glasses, and soft scholarly hands. She survived because one of the camp commandants took a fancy to her. But she lost her vision."

I swallowed. "You mean they gouged out her eyes?"

"No," Ariel said. "Her eyes are perfectly normal. But her husband and children were killed in front of her. It was too much. Her brain shut down her vision."

"Perhaps it was the only way to survive without going insane."

"It's like battle trauma," Ariel said. "The same thing happened to soldiers in World War One. Lia's lucky she's got the agency to focus on. A lot of these blind Cambodian women sit alone in shuttered rooms all day with nothing to do but relive the terror. I photographed some of them once. Very sad."

I pictured a woman rocking back and forth on a mat, her eyes white expanses of emptiness, her mouth open in a silent scream. And I wondered how you could ever really get over such a thing, and if you did, what scars it left on your soul.

"But Cambodia's coming out of that now?" I said weakly.

"In some ways. They learned about babies from their big northern brother, China. Chinese babies take one year, forty thousand dollars minimum. Cambodians'll deliver in three months for less than half that. Ah, those impatient Westerners. It's supply and demand. And Cambodia's got the highest birthrate in Asia—it goes along with poverty. Lia has these 'facilitators' combing the countryside for healthy babies. Families get a hundred fifty dollars for boys; girls fetch two hundred. Mostly they do it for food; some fathers have sold their daughters into prostitution to support drug habits. Perhaps that's what I saved Emma from."

She stopped, then looked to me, seeking affirmation that she had done the right thing.

"But I thought you said they were orphans?"

"Most of them are. But the others . . . Look, the families are starving, okay? They have nothing. And they want a better life for their kids. Is that so wrong? The first time I went there, months before her papers came through, I took Emma out shopping. People would stop us in the street and want to touch her. 'Lucky child,' they'd say wistfully, stroking her head as if it might rub off."

"So people thought it was a good thing?"

"Most did. But a few would avert their eyes when they saw us. They knew what it meant. I felt so bad when we said good-bye. But I had to wait for the paperwork to come through. Then, the week it finally happened, the paper sent me to Colombia to shoot the FARC guerrillas. I didn't want to go, but Lia offered to bring Emma to Los Angeles for a little more money. That way, she wouldn't have to wait one more day in the orphanage. And thank God I did," Ariel said, clutching her elbows, "because right after that, the U.S. government suspended adoptions from Cambodia. There were accusations of baby laundering. Forged documents. Families pressured into giving up newborns. It's left dozens of American families stuck in limbo, unable to bring over kids they've already bonded with."

"Ariel," I said, finding my voice and trying to keep it steady, "I need to talk to Hands Across the Water. Their local branch."

She nodded, understanding. Then she went to her desk and wrote down a number.

CHAPTER 21

I arrived home that night already planning my trip to Long Beach the following morning. There was a message on my machine from Samson Brenner.

"We've just learned that the INS is planning to send her back tomorrow afternoon," he said, "so I've gathered some people at my house and we're drawing up a temporary restraining order to keep her in the country. Sixteen-fifty-seven North Sierra Bonita Street in South Pasadena. You're welcome to drop by. And don't worry about the hour, we'll be here all night."

Samson Brenner had kept his word. I thrilled at this opportunity for fly-on-the-wall journalism, although some cynical part of me wondered why he was giving me such access. Perhaps to contrast starkly with the INS, who wouldn't tell me anything. It made Brenner look good, there was no doubt about that.

My exhaustion slowly ebbed as I thought about the dramatic night ahead. Still hungry despite Ariel's hummus, I grabbed some takeout from Sassoon Bakery, a tiny storefront in East Hollywood where a sweating Lebanese-Armenian baker slid cheese and spinach *boregs* and *lajmahjuns* in and out of pizza ovens with a wooden paddle. I got two *lajmahjuns*. As I drove, I bit into the flat Armenian pizzas smeared with tomato paste, herbs, and seasoned beef. They were still warm from the oven. Then I gulped down a carbonated yogurt beverage, tangy and salty. Reporters are the original dashboard diners.

When I got to South Pasadena, a quiet, tree-lined community at peace with itself in the warm night, the streets were dark. Checking the street numbers, I pulled up to an imposing two-story California Craftsman home. Warm light spilled out from the windows, casting a glow on the shrubbery. I walked slowly up the worn stone steps and knocked on the door, thick and broad enough to repel a battering ram.

The thumb lock depressed and the door opened into a haze of cigarette smoke and burned coffee. A young, attractive woman stood there, hair pulled back into a ponytail, wearing low-cut jeans, a hippie top, and tiny oval glasses. She had a look of quiet efficiency, her nails closely trimmed and without polish, no makeup on her face.

I introduced myself and she ushered me in. I followed her through a living room filled with Mission furniture and Tiffany-style lamps that were almost obscured by boxes of documents and file cabinets and four-foot stacks of legal papers and manila folders. In a couple of years, it would be a maze, and the house would be a bona fide public health hazard.

The young woman led me into a large den with recessed lighting. On the wall, I noticed a poster from World War II urging Americans to turn in suspected spies. A series of black-and-white photos of Japanese Americans being marched into desolate barracks. An emaciated, hollow-eyed Bosnian Muslim man staring out from a barbed-wire camp next to a photo of pajama-striped living skeletons at the liberation of Dachau. Those were Brenner's touchstones. This was his religion.

A young goatee-ed Latino sat cross-legged on an impressive Persian carpet, marking passages in a court document with a yellow Hi-Liter. A stern-looking black woman stood at a fax machine, yanking out pages as the machine burbled and hummed. A bespectacled Asian man was patiently feeding papers to another fax, squinting as he checked to make sure they went through.

Banking the far wall were three computer terminals, all of them in use. Two people sat at the first, hunched over the scrolling screen. At the second terminal, a man with a mustache and a knitted wool cap pulled low over his eyes slouched in his chair, typing. But the real action was at the third terminal, where three people argued while a fourth sat, shoulders sagging, fingers poised over the keys, ready to type.

"A priori," one said.

"Case law," another announced.

"*Reno* versus *Flores*, look it up," a third shouted.

"We don't have all day," the voice at the keyboard said.

Nobody looked up when I came in. There was an industrious hum, the air brimming with good intentions, the power of a civil society, and the unwavering, scrubbed belief that right makes might. From time to time, someone left the room and returned with another law book or legal document.

I looked around for Brenner but didn't see him anywhere. Just as I was about to ask, the big man himself strode in. He wore his sarong and a chunky Polynesian-looking necklace over a white shirt with rolled-up sleeves. His wavy mane looked unwashed and his eyes were rimmed in red and radiated exhaustion and grim purpose. In his hand, he held a beer stein filled with a steaming liquid that smelled like espresso. He took a sip, shuddered slightly, then put it down.

Seeing me, he gave a weary salute, then threw himself down into a leather club chair spiderwebbed with lacy cracks. Slinging his beefy legs over one side of the chair, Samson Brenner clanked his clogs together, looked at his watch, and said, "It's eleven P.M., troops, and I want a status report. But first, here are your deadlines. At one, I want a list of the main points. Three is the first-draft deadline. At five, I want it polished. I'll make the last changes at six. Then it's showtime. Leticia and Brad, I want you standing in front of the federal courthouse when it opens at eight. File the docs and wait there for my instructions. Let's see if we can't get it before a judge within the hour. This has to go off with military precision or that little girl will be on a plane with a one-way ticket to hell. Everybody got that?"

From across the room came murmured assents.

One by one, Brenner gazed at them, as if to personally infuse them with his fervor. Then he pulled a pencil from behind his ear and checked his notepad.

"All right, then. Clarence, you're up first."

A young black man on the phone nodded, hung up, and checked his yellow pad.

"We've got a similar case involving a minor in Florida in 1986. Adjudicated for the respondent on appeal. I'm gonna get Breanna to look it up right now," he said.

Brenner stroked his chin and nodded, and the young man sprinted to a woman at the first computer, pulled up a chair, and began dictating while she typed into a search engine.

"Camille?" Brenner rumbled.

"The amicus brief from Laura Thornberry's just arriving," the woman at the fax machine said. "Looking good."

"Jose?"

At another bank of machines, a man with a shaved head and an earring looked up.

"Two more pages to go," he said. "It's two A.M. in Washington but Krieder promises he'll review and reply within the hour."

And so it went, across the room, as they checked in and Brenner acknowledged their progress with grunts and nods. He seemed to have a special hold on the young women, who stammered and made cow eyes at him. They might have thought they were doing this for the cause, but I suspected they were really doing it for one man. It was Brenner's charisma that fired them, that drove them past all limits. They wanted his favor. A word, a nod, a smile. But he rumbled on, oblivious. When he was done, he turned to the stern young woman who had ushered me in and told her to brief me. Then he walked to a computer where several people huddled and pulled up a chair, the others moving aside so he could see the screen.

"Clarence and Camille, they're lawyers in Brenner's office," she told me. "He hires them right out of law school and works them like dogs. They'd do anything for him. As would I," she added quickly, blushing. "I'm the most recent hire. Just graduated from Boalt Hall in Berkeley. I'm waiting for my bar results, but I can still help out. He's such an inspiration to us all."

"Yes," I said, scribbling madly. "I can see that."

She beamed. "The guy with the red hair on the floor, he's with the Southeast Asian Refugee Center, the dude with the dreads is Fair Immigration Policy Network, the blond guy at the computer used to consult with the U.N. on unaccompanied minors, Red Cross out of Phnom Penh."

I realized that if a bomb exploded here tonight, the city's liberal brain trust would cease to exist.

"But what are all these outside-agency people doing here?" I asked, surprised that Brenner would want to share the limelight.

"This is a precedent-setting case that could affect immigration law nationwide when it comes to unaccompanied minors," she said. "This is not just about one little girl, it affects us all."

I wandered around and wrote down everything I overheard, aware that I was witnessing something being wrenched out of darkness and slapped into life. The night grew late. At around two, a gallows humor set in.

"Hard to believe the INS keeps the kid under armed guard at a hotel," the shaved-head youth with the earring said. He stood at the coffee urn, swaying perceptibly, his eyes bloodshot and sagging.

"So she won't stab them in the eye with a rubber nipple and make a run for it," a girl in pigtails said, yawning.

"You mean toddle for it," the guy said. "Shit," he added, as hot coffee spilled from his overfilled cup onto a court document. He shook the paper free of liquid, then wiped it against his shirtfront.

"Good as new." He looked around, then lowered his voice. "I heard they got explosives strapped to their diapers. INS got a memo. Top secret."

"Junior jihadis."

"Why wait till they're teenagers? Lose the element of surprise."

"People," said Brenner, turning his head from the computer screen. "You jest but this is exactly what we're fighting against. Little kids being locked up and treated like hardened criminals. Or being sent back to abuse and death. Remember: We cannot banish injustice from the world overnight. We must fight this war over many years, from battle to battle, person to person. In obtaining justice for even one individual, we win an enormous moral victory for the cause."

There was a murmur of assent. Recess was over.

Now Brenner seemed to remember my presence, the incessant scratchings of pen against page. He cocked an eye.

"And here is our very own Boswell, recording our work for posterity. A righteous work," he added, "and a crucial addition to the annals of human rights."

As he spoke, backs straightened and eyes grew brighter. Limbs moved with purpose once more and voices rang with urgency. The very air seemed to crackle, as though Brenner had pumped fresh oxygen into the room.

"Write what you will, scribe," he said in oracular tones, "but you must not interrupt them. They race against the clock. The time for questions will come later."

I bent over my notepad, making sure I got down every arch comment. The time for laughter would come later as well. Head bent, hands clasped behind his back, Brenner walked to the picture window that opened onto his backyard. There he stopped and stared into the darkness, unrelieved except for a small light burning in the window of what looked to be a guesthouse at the far end of the property. We felt the emptiness of the room now that his thoughts had left it, and no one dared to disturb him. Then he turned and his face was naked and painful to behold. He shook his head as if to shrug off his solitary thoughts, rubbed his face, and was back among us. And slowly, he grew animated again, seeming to feed off the energy that he had set into motion.

A young woman came in, teetering under huge aluminum cartons of take-away Thai food. The greasy, luscious smells of fried meats and noodles filled the air. When she set the cartons down on the table, I saw that it was Talina. Well, what do you know, she really is just the driver, I thought, playing back that intensely disturbing and yet erotic scene of Brenner pulling back her hair in Plummer Park. But now, he didn't give her a second glance.

By 3 A.M., I had crept into the living room for a nap. Unlike the others, I didn't have to stay up all night to write about their race against the clock. And as the initial thrill wore off, exhaustion kicked in.

Finding a couch, I sat down and arranged the pillows around me. From time to time, someone wandered in to search for a document or consult a law book. But soon I was too tired to care. Pulling my coat up to my chin, I curled up and slept.

I woke with a start, conscious of someone in the room. A young woman squatted by one of the cabinets, flipping through the hanging files with an intensity that grew as dawn approached. There wasn't much time left.

She pulled the cabinet out all the way, reached the back, and then slid it closed silently, so as not to disturb me. Then she straightened up, opened another cabinet, and looked through those files. From time to time, she pulled out a document, scrutinized it, then put it aside in a neat pile. I sat up on one elbow and yawned.

"How's it going?" I asked.

She turned, a look of consternation on her face.

"I'm sorry. Did I wake you?"

Like the others, she wore sensible, clunky shoes and low-slung pants. But unlike some of those I had met earlier that night, this one had a hard face, and looked like she had seen some things. Probably a refugee worker, not one of Brenner's starstruck ingenues.

"Don't worry. I appreciate your being quiet, but I need to get up anyway."

She murmured something and went back to her hunt. Then, with an exclamation, she pulled out a manila file, a look of quiet triumph on her face.

"It won't be long now," she said breezily over her shoulder as she strode out.

I lay there for several more minutes, marveling at the conviction that seemed to infuse all of Brenner's disciples. Perhaps by surrounding himself with young acolytes who worshiped him and taking on superhuman projects that required all his energy, he could blot out the parts of his life that hadn't gone so well.

Daybreak found me in the chill dawn air as Brenner sat at an ornamental iron table in his backyard, smoking and reading a final draft. The document was fifty pages long, including three amicus briefs mustered from around the world.

"Good morning," he said, looking up from the printout.

He glanced over at the little house at the edge of his property, where a figure stood silhouetted against the curtains. In the pink light of dawn, I saw that it was a carriage house. Perhaps once it had actually held a horse and carriage, but apparently had been converted into living quarters. Sneakily, I wondered if Talina lived there, crossing the lawn barefoot and wearing a thin shift on nights when Brenner didn't have to stay up working on globally significant cases. For some reason, I couldn't get it out of my head that whoever was behind the glass was watching us.

Brenner saw me looking and frowned, and I hoped he hadn't guessed my thoughts. He really wasn't a bad sort, I thought, feeling magnanimous now that he had given me such amazing access. But something in him seemed to deflate, or maybe it was just the night catching up with him.

"I've got a tenant in there right now," he said. "She's probably disturbed by all the activity in the main house. She's rather delicate."

Was Talina delicate? Or was it another one of his illegals? A prospective wife? Someone he was stashing until he could get her asylum petition approved? Brenner's clumsy attempt to answer my unasked question merely succeeded in raising more questions. He seemed to realize this and looked back down at his printout.

"I know I'm a geezer, but I like doing the final edit on hard copy," he said with forced heartiness. "I'm not like those young whippersnappers in there."

He inclined his head to the main house, then stretched and yawned and headed back inside. Out of the corner of my eye, I saw the curtain part, then drop back into position. Then the light went out.

CHAPTER 22

W e pulled up to the courthouse at 8 A.M. and walked to the clerk's office to file the documents. Within hours, they'd be in front of a federal judge and there would be a hearing. Meanwhile, I planned to get a little more sleep. I had called Thompson and told him not to expect me until late afternoon.

At home, I lowered the blinds and locked up the house. Climbing into bed, I pulled the creased paper out of my wallet. Smoothing it across the bed, I studied the girl's face. Who are you, little one, I silently asked, and what is to become of you? My little limbo girl. No mother, no father. Adrift without a home. Tell me your secrets. Guide me along the right path. Help me to find you, and find what I myself must do. For a long time, I stared at her. Then I folded the paper carefully, tucked it under my pillow, and put in earplugs.

They didn't keep out sound so much as muffle it. I still heard the white noise of my heart thudding, breath flowing, bones creaking, and the foam plugs themselves rubbing against my ear passages. But they kept out the worst distractions—lawn mowers and delivery trucks, the rattle of garbage cans and thump of a neighbor's bass-heavy stereo.

I was dreaming. Someone was calling my name with increasing urgency. They were trying to break down my door. I startled awake. The house was drenched in sunlight. I pulled out the earplugs and somewhere nearby, a jaybird scolded. It was two-thirty and I had overslept.

"Eve," Silvio's voice called from the front of the house.

I threw on a robe and ran to the front door. "Coming."

"They said you weren't at work. I was worried about you. I feel bad about the other night. Please let me in."

I stood there, leaning against the wall. The room spun. "Just give me a second to get dressed," I finally said.

I staggered into the bathroom and brushed my teeth, splashing cold water on my face. Then I rubbed my skin fiercely with the towel. I slid on jeans and a T-shirt and ran to the kitchen, where I grabbed a bagel, took a bite, and swallowed. Then I unlocked the door.

Silvio came in. He made as though to gather me up into an embrace, then stopped.

"Are you okay? You look terrible."

I gave him a rueful smile. He was so honest. Now perhaps it was time for me to return the favor.

"I was up most of the night on an assignment. That little girl," I said.

"I've been thinking that I was too angry and hasty the other night."

I looked away. He smelled so good. His skin was luscious. I wanted to crawl into his arms and stay there forever.

"I've been crazy busy. I'm strung out from not enough sleep and too much running around, chasing that little girl. It's such a terrible, mixed-up story."

"You look pretty focused to me."

"Tragedy becomes me," I said. "I'm great in a crisis. It's the in-between times that give me trouble. The other ninety-five percent of life."

Why didn't I ever say what I meant? I had to break the news to him, find out how he felt. As drained as I was, the scene at Brenner's house had inspired me, as had the photo under my pillow. I still didn't know how I was going to juggle work and a baby, but suddenly I didn't care.

I took a deep breath. "Silvio, I have something very important to tell you."

"Yes?" Grave, but not alarmed.

I walked over to the couch, grabbed the mohair throw, and pulled it up to my chin, as if it would afford me some protection. He was still on the other side of the room.

"Silvio, I think I'm pregnant."

He stood, not moving, striving to compose his features, but not before I saw a lightning bolt of alarm flash over his face.

"What do you mean you think you are? You either are or you're not."

So logical, always so goddamn logical it slayed me.

"Well, my period is late, and I took one of those home pregnancy tests, and it came up positive."

He walked over and sat down beside me, careful not to touch me.

"My God, Eve." He looked at me, and I could see him reassessing and reevaluating our entire relationship. "Was it from that night?"

I nodded, miserable. I thought about another night, when I might have made love with Tim in his car, and how easily things could have gotten even more tangled up. The optimism of two minutes ago evaporated. I was nuts even to consider having a baby with Silvio. I wasn't ready, and I didn't think he was either. But I was about to learn.

"I'm sorry. It's my fault. I told you it was okay . . ." I stopped. I scanned his features but didn't see what I was looking for.

"I just wanted to let you know. And I've decided to . . . aw, hell, Silvio. I can't have a baby. There's no way."

His eyes focused on the corner of the room, far from the couch. He pursed his lips and made a little susurrating sound.

"Are you sure, Eve?"

"What do you mean am I sure? Am I sure I'm going to get an abortion? Am I sure I'm going to have it and give it up for adoption?"

It. A depersonalization that grew stronger with each passing thought.

"I will support you in whatever decision you make."

"Great," I said bitterly.

What an evolved, enlightened feminist he was. It was up to me. He wouldn't force the issue. If he was being respectful of me, he was taking it a little too far. This was a time when I wanted him to read between the lines, to challenge me, to say what I had left unsaid, to interject his opinion. Because by not doing so, I knew Silvio didn't want this baby.

"What decision do you want me to make?" I asked softly.

A question was growing in his eyes. "Are you sure this child is mine?" he asked stiffly.

"Who else's could it be?"

I stopped, remembering the fight we had had at his *abuelita*'s house that night, me telling him about Tim, making a big fuss about how my involvement with Tim predated him, and how I needed time to resolve everything.

I groaned. Would he believe me if I told him that Tim and I hadn't slept together? Especially when it might have been fate, not my great self-control, that had kept us apart.

Cornered and feeling guilty, I jumped up and went on the defensive.

"If you think I would be that low, to claim the child is yours when it isn't, then that settles it for me. Get out."

He settled back against the couch. "But Eve—"

"But Eve what?"

"This clearly is not the time to talk about this. You've had a tough twenty-four hours and maybe you're traumatized by everything you've seen and done. You're not thinking rationally. It's understandable—"

"Don't patronize me."

"I'm not. I'm just suggesting . . ."

So calm. So rational. It made me seethe with irrational anger.

"Get out. Leave. Right now." I stood there, pointing at the door.

"Now I'm sure it's not the right time," he said.

"Out!"

"Eve, I love you. Listen to me." He leaned forward to embrace me. I shrugged him off.

"Out," I shrieked, and bounced up and down on the wood floor for emphasis. It was not my greatest moment.

He sighed. He stood up. I closed my eyes tight like an angry toddler, pretending he wasn't there, big and fumbling and unsure of what to say. I feared the sight of him would make me change my mind. I was terribly close to tears.

His footsteps retreated. A great aching emptiness filled the room, light and energy retreating with him. The front door closed with a sickening finality. Steps echoed off the porch. Then, from the window, Silvio's voice drifted back into the house.

"I locked you in. I'm sorry I butted in like this and woke you up. I'll call you tonight. Just promise me you won't do anything rash."

I didn't say anything.

"I'm not leaving until you promise."

"Okay," I said. "I promise."

"Bye, then."

I heard feet shuffling, then a truck door opening and slamming shut. The engine starting and pulling away from the curb.

Too late I jumped up, ran to the door, flung it open, and ran out into the street. I saw his truck rolling down the hill and ran after it, screaming his name and waving my arms. But he never saw me. Moments later, the truck reached the bottom, turned right, and zoomed off into traffic.

Desolate at my own stupidity, I stalked back inside and made a pot of licorice spice tea. I'd sit in my big brocaded chair facing downtown, where I'd lift up the cup of steaming tea and inhale the aromatic vapors, clearing my pores and sinuses.

The fight had left me wide-awake, nerves jangling again. As I lifted the tea to my mouth, the phone rang.

"I'm sorry if I woke you up," Thompson's voice said in my ear, "but there's been a double homicide in a hotel room near Chinatown."

I swallowed. I couldn't face anything else right now.

"It's messy," Thompson said. "Blood all over the walls. Cigarette burns. Looks like they were tortured." He paused. "Wires are identifying them as two INS agents on special assignment."

I sat up, splashing tea into my lap.

"Oh my God, Thompson, the ones who were guarding the girl. Did they find her too?"

"Two adults. That's all the information I've got, but I thought you'd want to know. Are you up for it? I can send Trevor—"

"I'm on my way," I told him and hung up. I changed into a skirt and blouse and low heels. Stuck in traffic on my way downtown, I called Thompson back because I couldn't stand the clamor of my own thoughts.

"They finally did it, Thompson. They got the kid."

"Now, Eve. We don't know that yet."

"They wanted her real bad. And they tortured the adults into giving her up."

Hands on the steering wheel, I shuddered, remembering the Hotel Variott. It could have been me.

"But the girl should have been right there with them," Thompson said.

"Maybe she was out with one of the INS folks, picking up lunch or something. And they tortured the other one 'cause they didn't believe her story. But then why would they torture the second one? It doesn't follow."

"Get off the phone and drive."

The hotel parking lot was a three-story chain place on the edge of downtown that had seen better days, though not much better. The massive freeway interchanges along the Harbor Freeway were two blocks away, a straight shot for someone who needed to get away in a hurry.

As I walked over to the thronged reporters, I saw three news helicopters circling overhead. They were urban bumblebees of doom, hovering above crime scenes within minutes of any tragedy.

In front of the hotel, an LAPD captain was giving an impromptu press briefing to a bristling bouquet of microphones. Next to him, silent but shaken, was a representative from the INS, and next to him was U.S. Customs Supervisor Scott Aiken. Maxwell's boss. From what they said, I gathered that the judge had granted the temporary restraining order, for all the good it did the little girl now. The briefing was drawing to an end, and as the LAPD honcho turned away, several newscasters scampered after him, shouting out more questions. I caught up with Aiken instead and set my pace to his, talking under my breath.

"Remember me from the LAX massacre? Eve Diamond with the *Times*. Who did this, Supervisor Aiken? And why is the girl so important to them?"

"Try showing up on time for a change, Diamond. I don't feel like repeating myself," Aiken said without breaking his stride.

"No insult intended, Supervisor Aiken. The city desk called me in from home."

"Nice hours you journalists work."

"I was up all night on a related story. As you well know, the INS wanted to deport the kid this afternoon and her lawyer was filing for a restraining order."

He looked at me for the first time, and his crew cut seemed to bristle. "I don't know where you're getting your information, Ms. Diamond, but I certainly cannot comment on that."

"And I'm not asking you to," I said. "But the girl. What's so important about her? There must be thousands just like her in Southeast Asia."

"No comment," Aiken said under his breath.

"Does this have anything to do with child pornography or fraudulent adoptions?"

His stride slowed, just for a moment, and I could tell he was wrestling with something. But then I saw him shove it aside. His steely blue eyes flickered onto mine.

"Why don't you ask your pal Maxwell? There he is, over by the emergency police tape. Because," Aiken said, shaking his head, "we've got a lot of theories, but at this point, your guess is as good as mine."

With Aiken's words stinging in my ears and half the LAPD watching, I made sure to steer clear of Maxwell, even though I was dying to speak to him. Why hadn't he tipped me off about the girl's deportation? Perhaps he didn't know. Instead, I got the details from an LAPD sergeant who held a formal news conference an hour later to update the press.

The cops felt pretty sure the INS agents had been murdered just hours earlier. They were beginning to interview hotel employees to see if anyone had seen or heard anything suspicious. According to the manager, the INS agents had checked into the hotel three days ago with a little girl, approximately two years of age. They were quiet and didn't leave the room except to fetch food. And yes, the hotel had a long-standing contract with the INS to house detainees at a weekly rate. There was now a statewide Amber Alert for Serey Rath, who was believed to have been kidnapped by the same people who had tortured and killed the federal agents. I only prayed she was still alive.

CHAPTER 23

W hen I called Brenner for a quote, it was obvious he had heard the news.

"This just reinforces our claim that this poor child needs political asylum, and you can bet your life I'll argue this very thing if, God hoping, she's found alive," he said.

I wrote it down, recognizing a sound bite when I heard it. "I just want to ask you one other thing," I said. "Did that little INS girl ever come up in conversation with Alexandra and Lothar Klimt? And did you by chance mention to them where the INS was keeping her?"

There was a momentary silence on the other end as Brenner absorbed the implications of what I was saying.

"Despite the fact that the Klimts are great and dear friends of mine," Brenner began, "I would never reveal such a thing, even if they asked, which they most certainly did not. The child's whereabouts were sealed by the judge for her own protection. Under the code of legal ethics that binds me, I cannot reveal those whereabouts to anyone."

"Okay, okay," I told him wearily, in no mood for a lecture. "I'm just trying to follow all the leads."

"But where on earth did you get the idea that the Klimts . . ." He stopped, apparently unable to envision a scenario in which his restaurateur pals would find such information useful.

"Forget it. It's just my paranoid mind."

I called in the story on deadline. After hanging up, I got out the piece of paper on which Ariel had written the Long

Beach address of Hands Across the Water. I called the number but it had been disconnected.

I wasn't naive. I knew that whoever had Serey Rath would kill anyone who tried to get her back. But this was an adoption agency. How dangerous could that be? And they might know something that would help us. I sat there in the hotel parking lot for a moment, then decided I owed it to myself to check out the address. See if they were even still there. A drive-by and nothing more, I told myself.

The traffic was fierce now, and I fought it out along the Harbor Freeway toward Long Beach, a port city just south of Los Angeles. Perhaps because of the harbor, it had also become home to 50,000 of the 200,000 Cambodian immigrants who had fled their native land for the U.S. in the aftermath of the Vietnam War and the obscenities Pol Pot inflicted upon his nation. Little Phnom Penh lay in North Long Beach, an ugly, gang-infested strip of land hit hard by poverty and crime.

Ariel's address led me to a depressed tract of wartime housing, clapboard bungalows off the main drag of Anaheim Street. It was a residential area dotted by the occasional tarot card reader and auto dismantling yard. I pulled up to the address and looked in vain for a sign in either English or Cambodian that would tell me I had come to the right place.

I checked the address. Yes, this was it. Perhaps this branch office of Hands Across the Water was unofficial or its proprietors wanted to keep a low profile. The politics of adoption vary from country to country but must be negotiated with excruciating delicacy when babies flow from the Third World to the First.

It was a warm, hazy spring day. As I sat in the car, wondering what to do next, two boys slipped out of the house, letting a screen door slam loudly behind them. Laughing and shouting, they ran down the steps to the yellowed patch of grass that made up the front yard and began dragging trash cans and old, broken-down toys onto the lawn to make barricades. Soon they were engaged in a lively game of war. Lacking toy guns, they used broomsticks to blow each other away and lobbed rocks into each other's fortress.

I mulled over their presence and what it might mean. It was hard to feel too scared with these kids around. I looked at the ramshackle bungalow, the front door standing open, as if in invitation. I looked for extra cars parked at the curb or in the driveway and saw none.

"Time out," the little one called. He was about five and wore a pair of overalls much too large for his thin frame. He ran back inside, emerging a moment later with two juice boxes and a bag of pretzels. He hunkered down with the older boy, who might have been ten. At that moment, the banality of the scene propelled me into a decision. These were not the accoutrements of kidnappers and murderers. Whatever went on in this house, it couldn't be as sinister as I feared. And my curiosity would not be assuaged until I spoke to whoever was inside.

I got out and walked up the concrete path, stopping in front of the boys.

"Hello, I'm looking for Lia Kalayan," I said, using the name Ariel had given me.

The older boy pointed the butt end of his broomstick toward the front door, then gave a war whoop and chased after the little one, shouting, "You're dead, you're dead," in accented English. I stopped.

"Is Lia your mother?"

"Not our real one," he said. The little one ran up and they regarded me with frank curiosity. Now that I saw them up close, I realized they had to be brothers.

"Any mean guys in there with a little girl?" I asked, nodding at the house and smiling.

"No," the little one piped up with somber eyes. "Just a couple of ladies with babies. My mama's making noodles for dinner. I hope she hurries up, because I'm hungry."

They ran back to their fortresses before I could untangle who these kids belonged to or ask what he meant by ladies with babies. They seemed at ease talking to me. I decided to keep going.

I knocked on the warped and rusting screen. The ocean air and the smoke that belched from dozens of nearby refineries must wreak havoc on metal, not to mention lungs.

Behind the screen, I heard a baby cry. I sniffed the air hungrily. The smell of meat and noodles mingled with curry leaves and fish paste. A woman came to the door and I saw a shadow, then the outline of her face as she pressed her nose against the screen.

"Yes?"

"My name is Eve Diamond and I'm a *Times* reporter investigating the disappearance of a little girl," I said, not wanting to mention the murders right away. "I understand that you're connected to a Cambodian adoption agency called Hands Across the Water. The missing child is also Cambodian. I'd like to talk to you if you can spare ten minutes."

The face withdrew. Standing there, I wondered whether the next thing I'd see would be the barrel of a gun. I stepped back from the door, envisioning how I'd run, taking the porch stairs with one leap. Then came a more pedestrian fear that she'd slam the door in my face. Then that fear died too. Not with two kids playing out front, I decided.

Soon she reappeared and the screen rattled as she invited me inside.

I cast my eyes around before entering but saw nobody else. The drapes were closed, and the house was shrouded in shadow. I stepped into the living room, realizing it was the time of day when light seeps so slowly from a room that you are surprised to find yourself standing suddenly in total blackness and fumbling for the lamp switch.

Except this wasn't my house. And I didn't know how to illuminate its dark recesses.

Before going any farther into the room's penumbra, I stopped and examined Lia by the fading porch light. She was about fifty, a tiny woman with delicate hands and long straight hair in a ponytail down her back. She wore a loose dress of crinkly Indian fabric and had bare feet. I looked into her eyes for signs of malice and saw none. Neither could I find any indication that she was blind. Her eyes were steady and brown in her oval face and seemed to regard me solemnly. Then she turned away and there was a spareness and grace to her movements as she bent to light a lamp. The room sprang from shadow and revealed itself: a shabby, sub-urban living room with no monsters crouched behind the sagging and worn furniture. Lia led me to a moss-green couch, holding her hands slightly out from her sides as she walked.

"I was finishing dinner," she said, standing quite still for a moment. Then the space she had just inhabited was empty, and she was halfway across the room, tucking her feet under her as she settled into an easy chair to await my questions.

"Are you Lia Kalayan?" I asked.

"Yes," she said politely.

As she spoke, my eye was drawn to the dining room, which held only a rickety card table loaded with foodstuffs, large economy containers of flour and sugar, baby formula and cereals. This is not the house of a murderer, I reassured myself.

In the gathering gloom of the room's corner, I made out a pile of sleeping bags and blankets, as though a bunch of fourth graders had just had a slumber party. I cranked my body around and peered through a slit in the curtain to look out the picture window. Outside on the lawn, the two boys still played their game, and several neighborhood kids had joined them.

"So I was wondering . . ." I continued, my heart beating

easier now, then seeming to stop altogether as something in the semiobscurity of the dining room wriggled and stirred, then reared up from the blankets, gurgling in a most unearthly fashion.

Jumping up, poised to run, I took one step, then stopped as I heard what was unmistakably an infant's whimper from the direction of the blankets. But this baby sounded new-born, or very young. This couldn't be Serey Rath. As these thoughts flashed through my head, the lumpy blankets resolved themselves into the shape of a woman. She pushed herself up on one elbow and pulled the infant toward her, fumbling at her breast.

"Do not be afraid in this house," Lia Kalayan said with a tranquil smile, as if she had seen my attempt at flight. She spoke excellent English tinged with the musical cadence of Southeast Asia.

"I'm sorry," I said, feeling foolish as I sat back down. "Could you please tell me what's going on here?"

The woman in the living room seemed to retreat inside herself. Then she spoke.

"We have offered her shelter," my hostess said in a soft, mellifluous voice. "Her husband beat her and threatened to kill the baby. She speaks no English and her papers may not be in order," she added delicately. "She had nowhere to turn. She came to us for help. How could I not take her in?"

I noticed that she started each sentence with a soft *mmmmm*, as if in benediction, or perhaps she was simply gathering her thoughts in this adopted language she navigated so well.

"Do you run some kind of halfway house for poor immigrants as well as an adoption agency?" I asked.

In the dining room, the new mother cooed to her baby and rearranged the pile of blankets. Then she rolled back onto her side, tucked her arms under her head to make a pillow, and grew immobile once more.

"No," Lia said, looking down. "Not in any kind of formal way. That's why my husband is very angry with me. We barely have enough for ourselves. But if I don't help these people, what will happen to them?"

"I understand that you suffered greatly in Cambodia and now you want to help others," I said.

She looked at me, and her head tilted almost imperceptibly, as if gauging what else I might want with her.

"But you have not come here to talk about history," she said finally, and a somber light suffused her face. She was smart, I could see it, but hers was not the type of intellect that flaunts itself.

"History is all around us," I said. "Without history, we wouldn't be sitting here. Because, see, about forty years ago, we came over to your part of the world and made one hell of a mess, and then we left, and now, well, there's this little girl, and I think she's from your country, and her name is Serey . . ."

I halted in confusion. In the back of the house, a piercing wail had started up, like a human car alarm gone awry. Lia leapt up, her lips pursed.

"If you will excuse me for just a moment," she said, bending her head and hurrying out, stumbling just once as the side of her foot caught on a toy fire truck that lay on its side. She put a hand against the wall to steady herself, then was gone.

I sat on the couch, watching the fire truck's wheels spin slowly in the air and feeling just as off-kilter. In the dining room, no one stirred, though I didn't understand how anyone could sleep through that racket. The unseen child's wails pealed through the house, overlaid by a singsongy lullaby crooned in some Asian language. It took a long time for the child's cries to subside. What am I doing here, I thought, and will I get out of here in one piece?

When Lia came back, she turned on a second lamp in the

living room, and in its illumination, I saw the dark circles under her eyes, the droop of her shoulders.

"Everyone wants a piece of me," she said. "Sometimes I fear they will nibble away until there is nothing left."

"I can only imagine," I said, envious for one tiny moment that so many people needed her. "The child you were soothing back to sleep?" I asked. "Is that one of those up for adoption?"

She smiled ruefully. "That is a tough case. The mother is fifteen, a child herself in need of adoption. Her chubby little baby girl will find many takers. Not so the mother. It will be hard to keep them together."

"Aren't there any relatives who could take them in?"

She looked at the floor. "Christy is Vietnamese. Her parents kicked her out when they learned she was pregnant. She is a high school dropout, illiterate in two languages. The child's father is in prison until the year 2017. It is a difficult situation."

"So tell me what made you start an adoption agency?"

She looked directly into my eyes, and I had to blink and look away before remembering that she was blind. I suppose she turned to the sound of my voice.

"Who told you about me?"

I explained about Alexandra and Lothar Klimt, and Ariel Delacorte, and how much they had praised her. It was hard to imagine any of those three sitting here on this sagging couch. I wanted to tell her about the murder of the INS agents but held back. I couldn't come on too strong. I sensed that approaching in a roundabout way would yield the straightest path.

"Perhaps I could do a story on you," I said, watching her reaction.

"I am not looking for publicity," Lia said. "We get all our business through word of mouth. It is . . ." She hesitated momentarily. ". . . better that way."

"Is that why you don't have a sign outside?"

"With our agency, every penny goes back to those who are most needy. If we keep operating costs low, we can serve more families."

Her head inclined to a thick photo album on the coffee table and I knew what I would find if I flipped it open—page after laminated page of baby pictures for prospective parents to choose from.

"But an article would help spread the word. You could place more needy babies."

She sat still, hands clasped in her lap. They were slender and chapped, slashed with rough red cracks.

"It is a delicate business," Lia said. "Too much publicity would upset the balance, as you say in English."

"Your English is excellent, by the way."

Her face creased in a painful smile. "My childhood was privileged," she said. "Cambodia was once rich in culture and learning, before . . . ah, well, nostalgia has died along with everything else. We must live in the present."

I thought of her, wearing a crisp schoolgirl uniform as she ran down the streets of Phnom Penh, sheltered from everything by high garden walls. And then, the extinguishing of that life, the desecration. I looked deep into her eyes and they were serene pools, as if all emotion had been washed away.

"I just can't imagine what you've been through."

"It's best not to. For several years afterward, I was barely human. I didn't care if I lived or died. Then, through a friend of my father's, I found sanctuary in a monastery. I studied with a great teacher who said blindness was irrelevant. I wrapped my nakedness in a saffron robe and went barefoot from village to village with my begging bowl. I would be there still. But I found I couldn't retreat from the world. My calling was an activist one."

"So what did you do?"

"I found work in one of the refugee camps. An American there fell in love with me. He thought I needed saving, but after we came here, I grew stronger. And then I didn't need a savior anymore."

She paused, and something dark flitted across her face.

"Instead, I knew I had to save others. In my country, you see, there are many orphans who die from hunger or disease. The ones who survive are doomed to poverty and exploitation. With my background and contacts, I can help rescue some of these unfortunates by finding them new homes."

I hardened my heart. It sounded too good to be true, and there was a slick and rehearsed quality to her answers, despite the halting speech.

"How do you find these orphans?"

"Some are left on the doorstep of our orphanage in Phnom Penh. Others we find in the villages. I employ people to travel the countryside. Often there are no birth records. All the Cambodian legal system requires is a document from the village chief, attesting that the child is orphaned."

"Who gets the money that the adoptive parents pay?"

"The bulk of the fees go toward running our orphanage. So that we can help more children," she said in a whispery voice.

"And babies fetch more?"

"Unfortunately." She hesitated. "The demand is greatest for photogenic, healthy ones."

It was an unspoken reproach, as though it was somehow my fault that shallow Westerners paid more for good-looking babies.

"But how can the adoptive parents be sure that the adoption will go through? I've heard there have been . . . problems recently."

Lia didn't respond immediately.

"It is unfortunate," she said at last, "and we hope it is only temporary. Our agency in Phnom Penh is working hard with the authorities to resolve these problems. It is only a matter of documentation."

"So who regulates you?" I asked.

She looked bewildered. "Regulates?"

"Yeah. Like Department of Children's Services, INS, the police."

"The police." She gave a little gasp. "Why would they get involved?"

I leaned in. "You tell me."

She straightened her spine. "We have very good relations with the INS."

"This baby you were getting for the Klimts. Where is she now?"

She met my eyes, a steady, empty gaze. Was it easier to lie if you couldn't see your victim's face? I got my wallet and unfolded the fraying photocopy.

"I don't suppose you can see it, but I have a photo here, and I think it's of the child the Klimts are adopting."

Tentatively, she reached out a hand and ran her fingers over the photo, as if reading the gradations of ink.

"I'm not completely blind," she said. "I can see shades of gray. Sometimes it's more blurry than others. When I'm tired . . . but no, I'm afraid I can't help you."

Frustrated, I refolded the photo. Then I paused, watching her face carefully.

"Well, it's all gone horribly wrong," I said. "This little girl has been kidnapped. The people who were taking care of her were slaughtered. We've got to find her."

I wondered now what lengths the Klimts would go to in order to ensure the adoption of their child. Not just any child, but the one they had picked out and christened Star Saffron, the ultimate accessory for their Asian-fusion life. They were gazillionaires, used to calling the shots, throwing their money around and getting their way. Would they let a little thing like INS regulations stop them?

"Her name is Serey Rath. She came in on a false passport and went into INS custody. Yesterday she was kidnapped out of the hotel where the INS was stashing her. She has disappeared without a trace, and the two agents who were watching her were found murdered in the hotel. I just wrote the story. But don't take my word for it, turn on the TV."

She blanched and put her hand to her mouth. "It is not possible."

"Yes, it is, Miss Lia, and I think you know more than you're saying."

Her face grew progressively paler as I spoke. A stubborn, defiant mien crept over her features and a hidden tension seemed to simmer below the surface of her skin.

"I have no idea what you're talking about."

"Don't you?" I sat and I waited. Behind the pious facade, something was very much not on the level.

She did not rise to the bait. A stillness enveloped her and I thought of her Buddhist training. This was not one who would be so easily rattled. So after an indecent interval, I went on.

"But what I don't understand is why these people have been chasing this child around Los Angeles for the last week, threatening and killing people, if she's only worth fifteen thousand. Why not just go back to Southeast Asia and get another baby?"

"I have no idea," Lia said.

"Is Serey Rath here with you now? Is she the child you just lulled back to sleep?"

Lia's cheeks flooded a dark angry red. She stood up.

"There is something you must see."

She walked down the dim hall and I followed, wondering what menace lurked in the poorly lit corridor. But then I considered all the children around me, the woman asleep in the dining room with her baby, the two older boys outside. Bad things couldn't happen around so many children.

She led me into a room where a fan whirred on the bureau to relieve some of the stifling air. Two mattresses lay on the floor, filled with sleeping children. One held a teenager clutching a teddy bear and a little girl in a pink dress, her mouth open in a snore. I caught my breath hopefully and squatted down, but it wasn't Serey Rath. The old tongue-and-groove floorboards creaked loudly under my weight as I straightened up and a little boy on the other mattress sat up, screaming something that might have been *Mama, Mama* in his birth tongue, staring blindly ahead, his arms flailing, starfishlike, in the air. Lia dropped to her knees and embraced him, whispering in his ear as she gently laid him back down and covered him with the sheet.

"He wakes up like that five times a night and it takes me so long to get him back to sleep," she said, her voice jagged with weariness. "I could just lie down on the mattress with him right now.

"But I have to finish dinner," she went on. "Those two outside, they're hungry. And my husband will be home soon. George loses his temper easily. He wants to go back to Cambodia and work in the camps. We argue about this. I say we can make more of a difference here. But he finds American life boring. He wants adventure."

"Lia," a man's voice called from the front of the house. The screen door slammed and I jumped. I followed Lia back out to the kitchen, where a man was bent over the fridge. I had a sudden stab of fear that I would recognize him as one of my attackers.

"Lia, how many times have I told you . . ." he said, then turned and saw me.

"Oh, hullo," he said in a not entirely pleasant voice. "George Savage. Nice to meet you. Lia getting you involved in one of her humanitarian projects, is she?"

He was short and wiry, with a receding hairline and a wide, dimpled face. His lips were thick and fleshy, his eyes bright blue, and he spoke with barely veiled sarcasm, scanning the kitchen counter. I had never seen him before.

"There it is," he said, twisting a beer out of a six-pack. "Warm again, as usual," he said. "Filthy as piss that way. I can't get her into the habit of putting it in the fridge. They drink it that way in Asia."

"George, you've got two hands. You can put it away yourself," Lia said in an even tone.

He ignored her.

"Well, what about some humanitarian aid for us, then," George said. "When's it our turn? Who wants to adopt us?"

He went and heaved himself onto a couch. The boys came in and headed for the cupboard. The older one reached up and opened a bag of chips and the smaller one hopped up and down, holding out cupped hands. After his brother poured out some chips, the younger one walked over to George Savage, who placed his hands under the boy's armpits and heaved him up onto his lap.

This simple gesture touched me. Much as I wanted to despise George Savage, I couldn't. I turned to Lia.

"Who else might want the girl? And why? These guys who most probably took her, one was Caucasian, one Asian."

She paused a moment too long. "I have no idea."

"What are you going to tell the Klimts? They're expecting her any day."

She looked at me wearily. "The Klimts are expecting a little girl named Star Saffron."

"Whose real name is Serey Rath?"

"Serey Rath is an old name from an old life. *Rath* means 'ward of the state' in Khmer. It is very common."

"But is it the same child?"

"Lia," came George's voice from the living room. "You shouldn't be talking about these things. I'm sorry, miss, but you'll have to go now."

He escorted me down the dark lawn and into my car in

silence and told me not to come back. As I pulled onto the freeway, I punched in Thompson's number. I wanted to tell him what I had learned. And to reassure him that I was still alive.

As I expected, he scolded me for my impulsive act, then immediately got down to business, ordering me to find out who regulated adoption agencies and what they had to say about Hands Across the Water. He said the kid hadn't turned up and there hadn't been any arrests on the INS murders. Metro had several reporters interviewing their families and writing obits for tomorrow's paper.

Forty minutes later, I reached my house. I killed the engine and thought about how close I had come to being murdered myself that day at the Hotel Variott. I'd have been dead too if those thugs hadn't mistaken me for a maid. A member of that vast and faceless army that toils in the shadows of every big city. I pulled down the car mirror to see what a maid looked like. The face that stared back was drained of blood. Beyond tired. All emotion burned away, leaving only an eggshell mask that would crumple if I touched it. Another pregnant maid, I thought nastily, not wanting to dwell on the decision that lay ahead.

But there was something I could do to help little Serey Rath. I could call the police and tell them about the thugs who had threatened us and ransacked the room at the Hotel Variott in their frenzied hunt for the child. Chances were good it was the same men.

I walked up the front steps, already envisioning how I would shuck off my clothes, don sheepskin slippers, and pad into the kitchen to scavenge dinner as I made my call. Then, something moved on the porch.

CHAPTER 24

G rabbing at a bush to steady myself, I saw a familiar figure sitting in the chair swing. I leaned over a hibiscus, casual now, deadheading the old flowers so he wouldn't know how badly he had startled me. The smell of mulch rose from the damp earth.

"Well, at least you used the front entrance this time."

"Hello, Eve," Tim said. "You look tired."

There was a concerned lilt to his voice, and suddenly I didn't want to joust anymore. The day's reporting had cracked my usually impervious shell, left me open, a soft sea creature beached by the ebbing tide.

I opened my hands and the shriveled petals scattered onto the walkway. "You want to come in?"

He pretended to mull it over. "Okay, for a little while. I was just passing through."

I didn't even dignify this with a response. I'd find out what he wanted soon enough.

He sat in the living room while I went to the kitchen and returned with two Mexican beers and a lime cut into quarters. "I think I've earned this tonight," I said, setting them on the coffee table and sprawling across the couch, hands clasped on my belly, before realizing with a start that I couldn't drink it. It still seemed so unreal.

Tim lifted a bottle to his mouth, the mouth I had always found as full and sensual as a girl's. He pressed his lips to the glass and I heard the liquid chug and slosh down his throat. His Adam's apple bobbed. I followed the flesh of his throat downward. Once I had traced this line with my fingertip, skating the contours of his body to the soft swelling of his clavicle where bone rose up to meet skin. My eyes halted at the top of his long-sleeved linen shirt. The land beyond was sealed off to me now, guarded by buttons carved from tawny bone. His shirt was the muted blue of veins throbbing through pale skin. He probably had one in every color, made by his personal tailor in Hong Kong. Well cut, finely stitched, and cheap. That's what happened when you perched at the edge of a poor continent, one billion people murmuring in your ear, vying for work.

A spark of resentment kindled deep inside me, low and unworthy but flickering nonetheless, for every sensation he had experienced and filed away in that nimble brain of his during our years apart—the gong of a temple drum, the sigh of a lover's voice, the heat of a charcoal brazier on a chilly morning, noodles slurped at an outdoor stall, the sharp salt tang of the sea on a slow-moving dhow—all of it washing over him and altering him in subtle and remote ways, spinning him farther down the road from me, loosening the molecules that had once bound us together.

"Is this the way they do it over there?" I said. "They just drop in on old girlfriends without calling?"

"The truth of the matter," said Tim, his eyes focused on the downtown skyline outside my window, "is that I need a place to stay."

I put my beer carefully on the table. "Where have you been staying until now?"

"With friends." He gave me a sideways glance. "They haven't exactly been a good influence."

"You know," I said, picking up my beer again because I needed a prop, "you're beginning to creep me out. You blow out of my life six years ago and then you come back without any warning, lying in wait on my back porch. Now you've done it again. You're like a vampire. I only see you at night. I have no idea where you live, what you're up to, why you keep coming here. Don't you think it's a little odd just to show up like this?"

"I didn't blow out of your life. You dumped me."

"You can't blame—"

"Betrayed me. You don't have the right to tell me what to do anymore. You lost that privilege when you left."

"That was ages—"

"And after that, what did you expect? That I'd stay in L.A.? When each time I opened the paper, there it was, your byline, reminding me, taunting me. Everywhere I went, I saw you. At a coffeehouse, hunched over your laptop. Dancing by yourself in a club at three A.M., eyes closed, arms twirling in bliss. At a department store, where I followed you up two flights of stairs because I caught the scent of your perfume. But when you turned, it was an auburn-haired girl with a stranger's face. It was always someone else. Never you."

"Get me off the pedestal. You know I came crawling back. You wouldn't even look at me."

As I spoke, very different thoughts sped through my brain: We have always been together, you and I. You were part of me, something inchoate and heavy-warm, like a half-remembered dream from childhood. Something that needed no words, a communion without voice. That's why this feels so wrong. With words, we batter the feelings we once shared. And bludgeon even the memory.

"You don't know how close I came to calling you. I'd pick up the phone and dial the *Times*. Then hang up when I heard your voice. My pride wouldn't let me."

And the damn thing was that I remembered those calls, little intern that I was then, trying to impress everyone with my professionalism, standing there, heart pounding, calling into the phone, "Hello, hello?" then shrugging for the benefit of my colleagues and carefully replacing the receiver. "Must have been a wrong number," I'd say nonchalantly, while inside, the silence on the phone rearranged itself into a scream.

But years had passed. I wondered how close we had come to sleeping together the other night, and was glad he had made the decision for both of us. Whatever had possessed me had certainly fled. Now I watched the man across from me with an increasing sense that something was not right.

"Well, now you're here." I sighed. "And it's late. You can sleep on the couch, but . . . I mean, you said you've been here several months, why haven't you gotten an apartment by now? Is it because you don't know if you're staying in the U.S.?"

I was trying to reassure myself. It couldn't be the money. Tim had always been frugal. And it wasn't about trying to woo me back. His behavior the other night had made that perfectly clear.

"Well . . ." he began.

I looked at him. "Well what? You were a dot-commer. You must have made obscene amounts of money."

"At one time, yes."

He bent over to pick at an invisible thread on his cuff, and a lock of golden hair fell into his face.

"You don't know what it was like. We worked eighteen hours a day. Constant traveling and meetings. All we ever saw of any city was the hotel and the office and the taxi in between. Shanghai. Bangkok. Beijing. Macao. Ho Chi Minh City. There was never any time off. Phnom Penh, Hanoi, Jakarta. I couldn't even cut loose long enough to cash the paychecks."

"The problem with that being . . . ?"

"Hear me out. When you work that hard, after a while, your energy flags. But you've got a project due in two days, three time zones away."

He looked at me with those steady blue eyes, daring me

to guess what came next. I wanted to put my hands over my ears, screw up my eyes, and hum loudly to drown out the creeping menace of his voice. Instead, I looked out the window and waited.

"And you just can't squeeze another drop of data from your wrung-out brain," Tim said. He crossed his legs and ran his hands through his hair. He looked behind him, some ingrained reflex, as if checking for eavesdroppers. Satisfied, he went on.

"So you do some coke to stay alert, bring the sucker in on time. And it's like you've plugged into the mainframe. Singing the body electric. Your brain pulsating with so many ideas, you can't write them down fast enough. The boss is stoked. You get a bonus, stash it away. But you're so wired you can't sleep. So you swallow a few downs. In the morning, you do a line to wake up. Which turns into two, then four. After a couple of months, you're burning from both ends like those swizzly Chinese firecrackers."

He always did have a high threshold for stimulus. It didn't feel real unless it was very fast. Very high. Very dangerous. The stakes were always escalating. I've read that criminals are like that. Something about serotonin levels. Like they're so deadened, it takes a lot for them to feel anything.

"Then a colleague introduced me to Lady H."

Years ago, he had flirted with it, late one night in Hollywood, at an after-hours club off a narrow alley where steam rose from the vents and swathed everything in strange blue light. I had gone for drinks and returned to find a girl with magenta tresses running black enamel fingernails along his forearm, tracing the blue highways that surged up against the skin, virgin skin it was, smooth and translucent.

"You have great veins," she had said, eyes already on the needle. Her voice was a soft lisp. Was he afraid? There was nothing to fear. Tim had hesitated then, imperceptibly, so he thought, except to me, who knew him. Then he had shrugged her off and we had left, driving home with dawn already a pale smudge on the horizon.

But something had been born that night, had passed between them in a way that excluded me. A chasm had opened at our feet. It would be a long time before the beginning, but I saw now that what happened in Asia was only the logical culmination of that Hollywood evening so long ago.

"At first it was just chasing the dragon," Tim said. "Chill out at night, but not so badly that I couldn't get up in the morning. They said you couldn't get hooked unless you shot up."

"Surely you knew they said wrong."

"I didn't *want* to know."

Tim stood up, a jerky set of motions. He strode to my bookcase, examining the volumes, his hand trailing along the spines. He stopped before a tchotchke, a Oaxacan turkey made of painted wood whose neck and tail bobbled when you touched them. Cupping it in his hands, he brought the bird back to the coffee table, setting it down next to his beer.

"I told myself I wasn't doing it for the high, just to soothe my nerves," Tim said. He leaned over the table, pushing the turkey's tail, then its head, making both ends bob and jiggle in unison. He seemed entranced by its kinetic powers and swayed along with it, a small child mimicking what he sees.

"But after a while, it wasn't about the calm anymore. I didn't even realize at first. I thought I had the flu. Achy all over. Runny nose. Nausea. I had a little left, and I was feeling so miserable already that I thought, what the hell, I'll just finish it. And it went away. My Singapore flu frigging went away. But next morning it was back, twice as bad. And then I knew it wasn't the flu."

We watched the turkey slow down, then stop. Tim frowned. He jabbed the tail hard, set it bobbing frantically, then did the same with the head.

"Hey, these are worth money, aren't they?" He looked up. "They're all the rage in Shanghai, you know. A shop just opened. It's run by a Chinese businesswoman who lived in Mexico for a while. I read about it in an in-flight magazine."

I wondered whether he thought he might be able to steal and pawn it to feed his habit, then felt guilty for such a thought. Each time the toy slowed, he punched it harder until I thought it would leave a permanent dent on his finger.

"Not really," I said. "They're pretty common here."

"Oh, too bad." Tim's finger slid off the wooden turkey and his eyes glanced elsewhere in the living room, scanning, appraising.

"So what happened with work?"

"Work? Oh, for a while it was no problem," he said. "Half the staff was on some kind of product. We used to joke that it was an occupational hazard of the job. And the foreign post. That we deserved hardship pay."

"Or at least monthly detox. But how could you keep it up?"

"I called in sick a lot. Started coming in late. I was useless when I was there. I tried crystal meth to crank me up but that just made me sicker. Then I switched to the needle. The damage done."

I realized then why I hadn't seen him in short sleeves, despite the heat. I had thought it some quaint carryover from living in Asia, how light fabric against skin would cool you on sultry nights, keep off mosquitoes. Now I knew the truth.

"Remember what you used to tell me, Tim? That our bodies were temples."

He smiled, a painful rictus. His gums were bleeding. Why hadn't I noticed that before?

"Ah, the temples I've seen. I've scored dope at Angkor Wat. On the beaches of Phuket. On the bourse, in Singapore."

"Didn't an American teenager get caned in Singapore a

few years back?" I said. "And for something minor like graffiti?"

"They catch you with drugs over there, it's *Midnight Express*, Asian style. Lock you up, throw away the key. The U.S. government doesn't like to protest. Makes it look like they're soft on drugs. I learned that the hard way."

"You mean you got arrested?" I couldn't believe how he had ruined his life.

"It was a setup. I was jonesing real bad so I took a chance. And my dealer turned out to be a government informant."

"Couldn't your job help get you out?"

"They had canned me already. It was a good excuse; the dot-com boom was going south and they were happy to throw me on the heap. I blew six months' severance pay in two weeks."

"Did you go to jail?"

Tim stared, bloodshot eyes, at my white carpet.

"I got a reprieve." He laughed, a hollow, mirthless sound.

"You mean you got off?"

"They had something else in mind."

"Who did?"

"Singapore's a pretty law-and-order place, but the syndicates are there, and they've turned some of the cops. They managed to 'lose' the evidence. But it cost me."

"What did it cost you?"

"Only my soul."

"What do you mean?"

"They needed a white guy, an errand boy. Go here, deliver this, fix that. A guy with an American passport and a briefcase, a clean-cut citizen who could move through Asia without suspicion. I became their man."

"What were they moving?"

"Arms. Drugs. They're not particular. Oh, and jade. You wouldn't believe what's going on in the jungles of northern

Burma. The junta, they've got alliances with these corrupt
warlords. I went there to pick up a package once.
Thousands of workers writhing naked in pits, covered in
mud, digging. Like a Sebastião Salgado photo on acid.

"'Work,' the warlord said to them, and cracked a whip.
'The foreigner wants to see you work.' And they did.
There's heroin on tap, and prostitutes in tents. When the
workers fall down, more take their place."

Sweat was beading his temples. His skin looked ashen,
under that tropical tan. He was shivering in the warm nighttime air, and he seemed to have shrunk, so that his fashion-
able clothes hung on a scarecrow frame.

"Eve, can't you get me fixed up?"

If I had been interviewing a junkie for a story, I would
have sidestepped the plea, told him thanks for the quotes
and referred him to a social service agency before driving
off. But this was my life. And I didn't have a damn idea
what came next.

I thought about Josh, my illustrious *L.A. Times* colleague, who had once left me in a downtown bistro to score
in the back alleys of downtown. What if I drove Tim there,
dropped him off, let him fend for himself? Quickly, I realized how impossible that was. We'd both get robbed.
Busted. Killed. And what was I, nuts? To risk throwing
away everything I had worked so hard for?

With the uncanny perception of the addict, Tim divined
my thoughts.

"Is downtown closer, or Hollywood? Either is fine. You
can put a junkie down anywhere in the world and he'll score
in ten minutes. I would have laid in more supplies last week
in Bangkok, but a little cash flow problem prevented me.
You'll loan me some money, won't you, Eve? I'll never ask
you for anything else again if you do this one thing for me."

It was the junk talking. So that's why he had come. But
I knew I hadn't seen anything yet. The night was young, and

his sickness just beginning. Then something else struck me.

"Last week?"

He had told me he'd been in the States for months, missing me, trying to work up the courage to come see me. Now, he saw that awareness dawning on my face.

"I lied to you," he said simply. "I just got here. They sent me to shepherd a package through."

"Who sent you?"

"You know," he said. "You knew the other night, when I asked you about the girl. I told them you'd know. But they sent me anyway."

"What do you mean they sent you anyway?"

He fingered something in his pocket, pulled it out, and regarded it sadly, shielding it from my sight. I thought he might cry.

"When I have some news, I can go back to them and claim my reward."

"Your reward?"

"They deal it, they've got the best stuff. But not even a taste unless I'm a good boy."

"What do they want?"

"They want to know where the girl is."

Outside my house and down the hill, a siren wailed. Somebody in trouble, an ambulance or fire truck pulling out of the station with lights ablaze, running the lights, dodging around cars and trucks like a big thrashing salmon swimming determinedly upstream. For one crazy moment, I wondered whether I had called the police.

"But I don't know where she is," I whispered.

He didn't seem to have heard. Or maybe he just didn't believe me.

"Why would they think I do?"

"I saw you at the airport that day, interviewing people. Some of them did too. They knew I used to date an *L.A. Times* reporter. So they called me in and asked my ex-girlfriend's name. I told them before I knew why they wanted it. And then it was too late."

He touched my knee, a weak caress, and I pulled away.

He opened his palm now. Nestled inside was a festive red and gold paper packet stamped with Thai lettering.

"I've done all the good stuff already," he said. "This is all that's left, and I'm afraid to do it. It killed a bunch of junkies in Thailand last week. But if things get bad," he said, holding up the pretty packet, "at least I've got a reserve. It's my insurance. So that I don't betray you, Eve."

"What do you mean?" I asked dully.

"I'd rather die than betray you. I love you."

"You love me? They sent you here to spy on me and you come and tell me you love me?"

"Even after all these years. That's why I wouldn't sleep with you."

I didn't want to sleep with him and I shuddered at the self-delusion that had ever sent me sprawling in that direction.

"I've got it, Eve."

He looked out the window. Down on Glendale Boulevard, the church bells of St. Teresa's pealed, grave and sonorous.

"What do you have, Tim?"

"I'm a plague dog."

In the far solar systems of my mind, a tiny white spirochete was slowly revolving, coming into view.

"Plague?" I said thickly.

"I couldn't risk infecting you."

"AIDS, Tim? Is that what you've got? From dirty needles?"

He grimaced at the window.

I couldn't look at him anymore. I noticed a rent in the fabric of the couch. Soon I'd have to buy a new one. And that rocking chair. The caning had torn. I should get it repaired. I went through the room, looking everywhere but in front of me, doing an orderly inventory. A mental list to focus my brain, to blot out what I was hearing. This was not my reality.

"Not yet. Not full-blown. I've been taking the pills."

His lips moved to attempt a smile. "And you would have slept with me the other night. I could feel it. Does that revolt you now?"

I couldn't look at him, much less speak.

He cocked his head. "You like asking questions," he said, "but I notice you're not so keen on answering them."

"You might have saved my life," I said wonderingly.

"So where's my thanks?"

"Wha . . . what do you mean?"

He sighed, as if explaining something for the third time to a slow-witted child. "I need to fix. On something that won't get me killed. Help me."

"You mean that . . ." I pointed at the packet between his thumb and forefinger.

"I don't know the purity. That's dangerous because—"

"How would you know the purity of anything you buy on the street?"

"The Mexican tar here, it's not nearly as potent as the Asian product."

"My black homegirl," I said weakly.

"Now how do you know that?" He shot me a penetrating stare. "Loan me the money, will you. Then I won't have to chance this." He held up the gaily wrapped smack like it was a prize in a game show. "And I won't have to go back to them," he went on.

"I just need to fix once more so I can think clearly. We could run away together. I don't want to ever see Asia again. But Europe . . . it could be just like last time. Remember, Eve? And I'll get straight. We'll lie on the beach and swim and watch the sun set. We can make our way through Italy and the Greek islands to . . . Turkey. We'll rent a room in Izmir, on the sea, and eat little fish fried in oil and drink arrack, and watch the old men play the bouzouki. Yeah, Turkey's the place."

And then I knew how delusional he was. His eyes took on a feverish cast and his voice lingered over the words. I knew why he had picked Turkey, an ancient crossroads between Europe and Asia, dotted with ports and trade routes. He figured he'd wait until I fell asleep to the sound of waves lapping the shore, then sneak out to score.

I thought of Silvio, standing ramrod straight and furious as he told me off. I wanted to call him and ask for help, but I knew this was a battle I'd have to fight without him. For all his savvy, Silvio was not wise to the ways of the drug world. But there was Josh. Josh, who owed me a big, fat clandestine favor, ever since I had kept my mouth shut about a secret of his I'd stumbled across.

"Tell me," I said urgently. "Why do they want the girl?"

He looked at me and laughed emptily. "You think they tell me? I'm just a foot soldier."

"But who are they?"

"I told you. The syndicate."

"What's their name?"

He ignored me. "United by common interests: open borders. But nine-eleven's put a crimp in their style. Everything's tighter. They need new allies."

"Why?"

He cocked his head at me. "For the natural flow of goods and services, of course. Don't you remember your Econ 101?"

"So how does this little girl fit in?"

"Especially goods."

"What kind of goods?"

"Rare, one-of-a-kind goods. More precious than gold."

"You mean jade?"

"I mean babies."

"They're smuggling in babies?"

"The Cambodians, Eve. They're involved in the baby trade. It's Hun Sen's people. They're ruthless. Stop at nothing."

I pictured mountains of grinning skulls lined up. "The Khmer Rouge," I said.

He was pacing, his arms and legs doing a herky-jerky dance across the room.

"Now can we please go?"

His voice rose in urgency and I flinched as a drop of his saliva hit my face. Surreptitiously, I wiped it off, wondering why I cared what he thought. He wasn't Tim anymore, he was a junkie who needed to fix.

He strode over to the table and scooped up my car keys. His eyes glowed with solicitous concern. "Where's your purse? I'll get it for you."

He spoke as though we were heading off on a Saturday morning to run errands. It was all the creepier because his voice had gone all modulated and soft. I tried to concentrate.

"So who's helping them?" I asked, not moving.

He decided to humor me. Get back in my good graces.

"They're looking for new friends," Tim said. "Especially Americans."

"You mean like U.S. Customs and the INS?" I said, thinking of Sandy Morse's fiery death and Bill Maxwell's supervisor, who had tried to set us up for a fall. The spookiness of that phone conversation with Maxwell still resonated within me.

"Sure. Plus lots more. My friends are patriots too. They're for peace. All this increased scrutiny has been terrible for business." He looked around. "Okay, all ready to go. Just waiting for you."

"Do you know a guy in U.S. Customs called Scott Aiken?"

Tim's eyes had gotten tricky and sly. "I might," he said. "I'll tell you everything. But first let's take a little spin. There's an ATM just two blocks away, I saw it on my way over. Unless you've started carrying cash?"

A stealthy, cajoling tone had crept into his voice.

I felt only pity for him, the assassin of love. Was I such a Judas that I'd trade him heroin for information?

Tim waited. I could see the hunger in his eyes.

I felt I was traversing a minefield on a moonless night. Everyone involved with this little girl was tainted. She was only a pawn, but they'd fight over her like hyenas until they tore her limb from limb. Even Samson Brenner was in it for the human rights glory, not for the flesh-and-blood child.

And where did that leave me, a journalist eager to ride this girl's story to prominence? How could I trust my emotional responses, especially when my own life had spun into such turmoil?

I swallowed and reached for the phone. And as Tim flung himself back down, cursing my inaction, I dialed the *Times* editorial switchboard and asked the operator to please connect me with Josh Brandywine at home. The phone rang for what seemed like a long time before a groggy voice came on the line.

"Thank you, operator," I said, then waited for the click that told me she had hung up. "It's Eve Diamond. I need to talk to you. It's kind of an emergency."

Josh's voice was thick with sleep. "Are you all right?"

"Yes, but I need to see you."

"I'm flattered. But can it wait until morning?"

"No. And I can't even talk about it on the phone. Remember that place downtown where we once had dinner. It's open late. I want you to meet me there as soon as possible."

I stole a look at Tim, who was curled up on the futon, trying to control a tremor that seemed to be running through his body. His effort to hustle me out the door had exhausted his last reserves. Sweat stains were bleeding down his shirt.

"Are you sure you're not in trouble? Wait a minute. Is this the first of April?"

"I'm fine," I said evenly. "And it's no joke. I'm dead serious."

Chapter 25

*T*wenty minutes later, I was at the ATM, withdrawing $200. It was breaking one of my cardinal safety rules—don't go to ATMs after sundown—but hell, I was in deep, and I wasn't about to sweat the small stuff.

I was alone. Tim had been furious at being left behind, but I told him it was that or nothing. I figured that Josh could think best on his own, without some glassy-eyed junkie quivering over his shoulder.

I drove to the Boyd Street Grill and took a seat where I could watch the door for Josh. The smell of cooking food reminded me I hadn't eaten. I ordered *calamari* and ate it as I waited, conflicting thoughts racing through my head. It was excruciating to see Tim curled up on the futon, shaking in such pain. But how could I buy him drugs? But if I did, he'd tell me who was after the girl and that might save the child's life—and mine. Round and round I went, getting nowhere.

Soon Josh walked in, fists shoved into a windbreaker, shoulders hunched. He slid into my side of the booth, and without preamble said, "Okay, spill. What's so urgent?"

I picked up a breadstick and traced a line on the table. "I have this friend who's in a bad way," I began, "and . . . aw, hell, Josh, he wants me to buy him some heroin."

Josh leaned in, disbelieving.

"It's not for me," I insisted. "Honest."

"Then who?"

"I told you. It's for an old boyfriend who's landed on my doorstep. And I distinctly recall sitting here with you, practically in the shadow of the Times Mirror building, discussing how to do this very thing.

"Don't worry," I went on, "I'm not going to go buy him drugs. But I need to know what to do. He's in my house, freaking out. Sick. Desperate. Do I take him to emergency? Call a rehab clinic and see if they can take him tonight? I have no experience with this and you do."

"I can't believe you're involved with a horsehead."

"He wasn't that way when we were together. He's a dot-bomber who's been living in Thailand."

"Whew," Josh said. "That market's been flooded with some heavy stuff out of Chiang Mai. People are OD'ing all over the place. Not that I would know, personally," he added, a smug tone creeping into his voice. "I was never a junkie, you understand. Just a recreational user. But I'm getting too old for that. I've got my career to consider."

As he spoke, I pulled ten $20 bills out of my wallet. "I have money," I said, fanning it under his nose.

"Put that away, for Christ's sake." Josh shook his head. "Did it ever occur to you that rehab places take credit cards? You act like you've lost your mind."

"That's exactly how I feel."

"So he's waiting at your house?"

"Yeah."

"That's what you think. He's probably halfway out the door with all your jewelry, your VCR, and your TV. You don't know the mind of a junkie, the soulless pit, the self-loathing, malevolent emptiness. . . ." Josh trailed off. "We're going to drive back to your house now. I'll follow you and help you deal with him. You can't have this guy staying with you. He will destroy you in his race to destroy himself."

"Okay," I said meekly, relieved to have him take charge. I had felt myself careening out of control all evening, making terrible decisions driven by fear and panic.

I took solace in seeing Josh's headlights behind me all the way up Second Street as it turned into Glendale Boulevard, then following me as I climbed Cove. He parked behind me and sprang out, pushing up the sleeves of his windbreaker as if ready to tackle something particularly unpleasant.

"Thanks for doing this. It's above and beyond."

I had thought about it a lot in the car. We'd confront Tim, then drive him to a hospital somewhere, convince him to check himself in. Actually, I was surprised when Tim didn't rush out immediately as the cars pulled up. Perhaps he was too sick from withdrawal.

I opened the front door and stepped into the hallway, flicking on the light. There was no sign of him.

"Tim," I called. "I brought someone back with me. A guy I work with," I babbled stupidly. "His name's Josh, and, uh, he understands what you're going through because . . ."

I walked into the living room and fumbled for the lamp. To make it cozy for the three of us. I'd make tea and bring out Mint Milanos and we'd discuss this like civilized adults. I looked around. Still no Tim. My stomach felt queasier than usual. Maybe Josh was right. Had he taken off, too impatient to wait, grabbing whatever he could sell? But no, the stereo was still there, the CDs.

"Tim?"

"He split," Josh said, throwing up his hands. "Typical junkie bullshit. You think I don't know. I've spent enough time around those scuzzballs. They'd pimp their own daughters for a hit."

I stood outside my bedroom. The door was ajar. It was dim inside, with only the flickering light of a red candle I hadn't recalled lighting. I pushed the door open. The candle cast a ghostly light over the room, illuminating the figure crumpled facedown on the bed, arms thrown out, as if to stop his cartwheeling into the void. His expensive shirt was rolled high above his elbow, a plastic hose unfurled near his upper arm, a fix kit next to him. Cotton ball. Lighter. Alcohol. The smell of something acrid that had bubbled and cooked on a tiny tarnished spoon. And on my hand mirror, an unfolded and creased square of red and gold paper, stamped with Thai characters. It was empty.

"Oh God," Josh yelled. "Oh . . . my . . . God."

I ran to the bed, grabbed one shoulder and flipped him over, scanning for signs of life in the dim light. Tim's eyes rolled back in his head. He was clammy and cold. His limbs were heavy and inert, but not stiff. The floor felt oddly slick. I squatted to look more closely and saw a syringe puddled in dark liquid. The same dark liquid had sprayed like a fountain across my olive comforter.

"Pulse," screamed Josh. "Check his pulse. Call nine-one-one. He's ODed. I'm not going to touch him. I think he's dead. Oh Lord. I . . . I've never seen a dead body before."

I suppressed my own hysteria and fixed with fascination instead on Josh. All his reportorial cool had left him, as had his druggie insouciance. Joshua Brandywine, star Metro reporter, son of a famous foreign correspondent, was a quivering ectoplasm of fumbling and fear. Maybe grace under pressure wasn't bred in the genes after all.

"I'm not so sure he's dead." I pushed myself off the bed and reached for the phone. I dialed 911 and got a recording, telling me to stay on the line. For some reason, Josh's frenzy had summoned up in me a glacial calm. I knew his was the more appropriate emotional response, but I couldn't let us both go to pieces. Later, I will mourn, I thought. And then I may never stop.

Suddenly, a miracle happened.

The body on the bed groaned and the head rolled.

"Tim," I said, shaking him. "Hang on. Just a little longer. It'll be okay."

"Planning," Tim said, his breath coming in ragged gasps.

". . . if I'm not back . . . They think you . . . h-h-hiding her.
Be . . . careful."

I stared at him, my thoughts spinning madly.

"Who? Where? We'll have the police round them up."

His lips moved, but no sound came.

I turned to Josh.

"Dot . . ." Tim sputtered. "Her."

"This has something to do with the dot-com? Are they
the ones after her? What was it called?"

Tim tried to raise himself up, struggled to speak, then fell
back. I leaned over him, desperate to catch his next words,
but there was only a rasping whisper and it seemed to me
that I heard the word *love.*

Then he slackened in my arms. A tremor shook his body,
and his weight was such that I had to lower him onto the bed.

I unbuttoned his shirt, feeling the impersonality of the
gesture. I put my hand over his heart but felt no thumping.
I checked his pulse. Nothing. Should I attempt mouth-to-
mouth resuscitation? But there was the HIV. At the very
least, I should hold up a mirror to his mouth to see if it
fogged, but the only mirror I had was sitting on the bed,
loaded with evidence, and I didn't want to move it. So I did
nothing.

Time had slowed to a crawl. I was still on hold with 911.
I didn't know if thirty seconds had passed, or thirty minutes.
In the dimness, a spider lowered itself on a gossamer strand,
indifferent to our chaos. I never killed them and I forbade
the landlady to spray with insecticide. They didn't bother
anyone. In some cultures they were even good luck. I was
able to focus with clarity on the spider precisely because of
the body lying on my bed. I felt strangely disconnected
from it. Finally, the operator came on and I told her what
had happened. She said an ambulance was on the way.

"He's dead," mumbled Josh. "Oh God, they'll think we
killed him. They'll find the dope. We've got to get rid of it."

His hand went to the mirror, and I grabbed his wrist, restraining him.

"Leave it," I said. "The cops are coming and your prints shouldn't be on it. Besides, we don't know if he's dead."

I figured there was no sense in hiding anything. I could see the headline already: "Smacked-out dot-commer returns to ex-girlfriend's place to OD." That was the problem with being a reporter. You imagined your life as a series of lurid headlines.

I jumped up and flipped on the light but found I couldn't look at Tim quite yet. Instead, I focused on the puddle of blood on the floor, the red spin-art designs on my comforter. I hadn't known that shooting up involved so much blood. Josh stood there, shivering, arms wrapped around his chest.

"My father will kill me if this gets out," he moaned. His eyes were huge with fear as he wept, and I pitied a man for the second time that night and was glad I had no parental legend to live up to.

"You don't need to be here," I said. "This has nothing to do with you. You were doing me a favor, though neither of us realized how huge it would turn out to be."

"I'll stay with you," he said, though I could tell that he'd much rather not.

"No," I said. "Go home. Really. I'm a big girl. Just do me a favor and leave a message with Thompson. Tell him I won't be in due to the death of a . . . a close friend."

He didn't move.

"Eve, I'm sorry," he said. "You two, at one time, you must have been—"

"Yeah," I said, cutting him off. "We were."

He stood there a minute.

"Now go," I said. "Before the ambulance and the police get here. Maybe you'll cover it for the paper tomorrow morning. Nothing more than a digest, let's hope. But leave. Shoo. Scat."

After the door closed behind him, I walked back to the bedroom. I blew out the candle and watched the smoke curl into the air and disappear. Much as the spirit might have left Tim. I inhaled the smoke, felt its bite in my lungs. Then I pushed a lock of hair off Tim's forehead, as I had done so many times before. My hand lingered at his temple. I lowered myself beside him and waited for the ambulance.

The two policemen who arrived to interview me were solicitous and polite as they confirmed that Tim was dead. Soon a forensics van arrived and began setting up. They left with the body as dawn crested, saying a detective would contact me later in the day. That reminded me to turn the ringer off my phone. Unwilling to sleep on the bed where Tim had died, I got blankets from the closet and tugged the futon to the carpet, crawling onto its thin batting and placing a pillow over me to hide the daylight.

Perhaps I should have wept or pulled out my hair or gouged at my face with my nails, but I was too numb. The Tim I knew had died years ago. I didn't want to remember him as he had been last night. Exhaustion was dragging me under, and I gave in and slept for a long time. The next thing I knew, the last rays of sunlight were streaming in through my curtainless living room windows and someone was knocking at my front door.

It was a female detective. She made a sour comment about me not answering my phone. Then, seeing my sorry state, she asked if I wanted to take a shower while she looked around. I would give permission, wouldn't I?

I told her yes, thinking only of blessed hot water pummeling my body. In that sanctuary, I bowed my head and finally cried and my tears mingled with the water and rolled off.

When I got out, feeling newly invigorated, I saw the policewoman had been busy. She had upturned chairs and removed nearly all of my paintings from the walls. I saw my treasured samizdat poster of Andrei Sakharov sitting face-down on the coffee table, but before I could protest, she called me over with a look of triumph on her face.

"What's that?" she asked accusingly, pointing to a familiar-looking red and gold packet taped with precise neatness onto the back of the frame.

I knew she was expecting a vociferous denial, but I could only shake my head and marvel at Tim. Even as he had pleaded with me, he'd also been lying and scheming with an addict's furtive cunning when he swore he'd only had one hit left. In the desperation of his withdrawal, Tim had still thought ahead, figured he'd better lay in supplies in case I relented and let him stay longer than one night or came back empty-handed.

Did I want to tell her what that packet was doing hidden behind *my* poster? the detective asked solicitously. She seemed determined to trip me up and suggested that Tim and I might have been druggies together. I scoffed, pointing out that I wouldn't have been able to function at work if I were a junkie.

She rolled her eyes.

"Check for prints and you'll see," I told her, annoyed at her presumption. I began to wonder if I would need to hire an attorney.

The detective took me through the previous night's events one more time, frowning as she wrote and asking the same questions several times to see if my answers varied. After she left, an unshakable gloom descended and I decided I'd better eat something before checking in with work. Ten minutes later, armed with a plate of scrambled eggs and toast, I walked to the answering machine.

It was blinking with eight messages. The first was from Tom Thompson, saying Josh had called him with the news and not to worry about coming in; he'd give my messages

to another reporter to sort out. Three calls were from the
LAPD, wanting to interview me. The other four were
increasingly urgent messages from Silvio, the last saying he
was coming over if I didn't call him back within the hour. I
looked at my watch and realized the last call had come in
forty-five minutes ago.

CHAPTER 26

I called him back at once.

"Where have you been?" said Silvio. "You haven't done anything rash, have you?"

"No, Silvio, I—"

"Good. We need to talk. But before I forget, let me just tell you that this woman has called me several times at work, saying she's a friend of yours and needs to see you urgently. I gave her your work number. She sounds completely unhinged."

Now what? My brain raced.

"Did she give you a name?"

"She's called you a bunch of times but you haven't returned her calls. She met you last week and says you gave her two press passes to the Arena La Puente. You told her about us; that's how she knew to call me. She sounded desperate to talk to you."

I cast back in time. The pregnant maid. Why had she called Silvio? Why did I have to deal with this right now?

"Eve, are you still there?"

"Yes," I said. "Silvio, we have to talk."

"Yes, absolutely. Just let me finish, because I promised her. This woman's English isn't too good. And I don't think she's legal. She's afraid—"

"What does she want?"

"She wouldn't say. Does this have something to do with a story you're working on?"

"Perhaps. I don't think she'd call me unless . . . yes, Silvio, you did the right thing. This could be very important. What's her number?"

"Well, that's just it. Her phone's been disconnected. She lives in Echo Park, though. She gave me the address."

I was beginning to think I knew why the maid needed to speak to me so urgently.

"What is it? I'll go there," I said.

"Then I'm going with you. I'll pick you up."

"No," I said. "You live in La Puente and it will take you an hour to get here. Meet me there. It will be faster. What's her address?"

He hesitated.

"C'mon, you'll be right behind me," I said.

He sighed and gave it to me. She lived at 1950 Castlemar, off Echo Park Avenue.

"I don't even know her name," I said.

"Lupe Monterosso," he told me.

"I'll see you there."

There was coffee left in the pot, and I didn't remember how old it was. It might be bad for the baby growing inside me, but I also needed to be at my most alert.

I poured the sludge, inspected it for mold, and found none. Then I added half a cup of milk and microwaved it. Grimacing, I gulped it down, the warm liquid triggering a deep shuddering that started in my stomach and radiated upward through my shoulders.

Echo Park was Silverlake's poorer, more funky relation, and while the hills had gentrified years ago, the flats were a mix of multigenerational Latino families, thrift-store-clad artists, intrepid yuppies, and struggling renters of every color. Here, yards landscaped with poppies and drought-resistant rosemary sat next to scorched lawns with dead palms. Some backyards held elaborate kiddie jungle gyms crafted in rustic pine while others hid chicken coops, illegal day-care centers, and sullen pit bulls with swollen teats.

Lupe Monterosso lived at the end of a hillside cul-de-sac in an old apartment building festooned with turrets and balconies. LE CHATEAU ECHO, read a sign in ornamental iron script, but the metal was rusted and the building's paint was scabbing off.

I saw the unmistakable signs of too many people crammed into too few square feet—overflowing Dumpsters filled the air with the putrefying sweetness of death and beat-up cars double-parked along the curb and even on the sidewalk. The street signs and trees were defaced by graffiti, though someone with civic pride had tried to whitewash the trunks, making the trees look even more diseased. The hillside was littered with broken toys and bicycles long ago scavenged for spare parts. A gibbous moon hung high, casting a pale, watery light on a handful of boys at the end of the street who watched my approach.

There was no lobby, just a long, dimly lit hallway. From behind closed doors, I heard a child crying and someone clanking pots. There was no Monterosso listed on the mail slots, so I knocked on the first door, figuring I'd have to ask until I found her.

A filigreed-iron grate in the door swung open and a woman in curlers peered out, her mouth a downturned arc of distrust. I asked if Lupe Monterosso lived there. A baby gurgled and grabbed at the pink plastic tubes in the woman's hair. Patiently, the woman disentangled the tiny hand and brought her face closer to the grate to examine me.

What she saw must have reassured her.

"Numero seis," she said. Number six. Then the grate shut and I heard her footsteps recede and a lullaby start up in Spanish.

I walked down the hallway, found number six, and knocked. There was no answer. I put my ear to the door and thought I heard a muffled cough. I knocked again, straining my ears for any sound. Something told me she was standing on the other side, willing herself to keep still.

"Lupe," I called softly. "Lupe Monte—"

"Quién es?" a tight voice cut me off. Who is it?

I cleared my throat. *"Estoy buscando a Lupe. Soy una periodista. Me llamo Eve Diamond."* My name is Eve Diamond. I'm a journalist looking for Lupe.

This door had no little grate.

"Momentito," the voice called.

As the deadbolt snapped open and the doorknob jiggled, I considered whether I might be walking into a trap. What if she was in league with the traffickers? Or they had kidnapped her as bait to lure me here? I had learned a lot of things in my years on the job, things I hoped might one day save my life. Now I ticked them off.

Never park next to vans. With rope and duct tape and ruffled curtains blocking the view, a person could do a lot of damage in a van. Never pull over at night for a car with flashing lights until you're in a well-lit area with people around; any psycho can get hold of sirens and police lights and badges. Never get in a car with someone you don't trust. Then there were the preparedness rules: Use ATMs before dark. Make sure your car has plenty of gas and runs well. Keep your mobile phone charged. Make sure someone knows where you're going and when you're due back.

But Silvio knew where I was headed. He was on his way to join me. And I didn't have any specific rules about knocking on the doors of people who needed help.

The jangle of a chain brought me back to reality. The door opened two inches, then jerked tight, still leashed to the wall. A woman's face appeared at the slit, just below the tarnished gold paint of the metal chain. It was the maid from the Hotel Variott.

I stood motionless while she checked me out, standing

on tiptoe to look past me and make sure no one was hiding in the shadows. She had steeled her face to show no emotion, but the effort came out as grim fear.

"*Está sola?*" she asked. Are you alone?

"*Sí,*" I replied.

"*Seguro?*" Are you sure?

"*Sí,*" I said, adding that Silvio was also on his way.

The door closed with a tight slap. I heard the rattle of the chain as she unlatched it, then the door opened again. Lupe Monterosso grabbed my wrist, yanked me inside, then quickly shut the door, leaning against it with her shoulder while she did up the various locks as if she were hooking up a corset.

Lupe fluttered her eyes closed and made a shaky sign of the cross, kissing her thumb as she finished. Then she opened her eyes and gave me a sober look. Cradling her huge belly, she whispered for me to follow. She led me through a small but immaculate living room with a threadbare sofa where the aroma of stewed meat with onions had long ago settled into the fibers. The living room carpet was stained but clean. We walked into a wood hallway that smelled of lemon furniture polish. She put her finger over her mouth and led me into a darkened room. I heard soft snoring. The room was hot and stifling and I wondered, for one fleeting moment before I banished the thought, whether someone would step out from behind a door and train a gun to my head. Lupe walked across the wooden floor, her rubber soles squeaking, and turned on a lamp.

The light illuminated a bed where two children lay sleeping. They were about the same age. One was a black-haired boy who had Lupe's strong jaw and mouth. The other was the little girl I had last seen in the arms of the security guard at LAX. Serey Rath. Her fist was bunched up tight against her mouth. She whimpered in her sleep, sucked rhythmically on her thumb, then was still.

I grabbed the door molding to steady myself. A feeling of vertigo swept over me, as if I were in free fall. Through it surged a fierce joy. The child was safe. At least for now. Here in this Latino barrio, where no one would dream to look for her. I looked at Lupe Monterosso, who was watching the child, a look of furrowed concentration across her brow. Bless you, I thought.

"You told me she was in danger," Lupe whispered in Spanish. "I had to save her from those bad people."

She spoke sternly, staring at the little girl. A strand of hair came loose from her ponytail and drifted over her lips.

I tightened my grip on the door. "How . . ." I asked in wonderment, my voice trailing off.

"When those men with guns came, I was sure they would kill us," Lupe said. "And then what would happen to my child? I was frightened, so I quit."

"I know you did. I came looking for you."

"My sister, she's a maid at another hotel. She called me yesterday, saying she had sprained her arm and asking if I would help her make up beds and scrub. Of course I said yes. At one of the rooms, a man opened the door a crack when we knocked and said to come back in an hour. He looked familiar but I couldn't place him. Then a lady came up, carrying a little girl who was crying.

"The lady was trying to shush her but she didn't know how to comfort children. You get a feel for these things when you're a mother. They walked in and shut the door. A few minutes later, they all came out and the man told us it was okay to clean because they were going down to lunch.

"I got a good look at the girl that time and saw she was Asian. The woman was white and the man was black. An unusual family. Then I remembered where I had seen them. In the stairwell of the Hotel Variott. God forgive me but when we got inside that room, I looked through their belongings. After what you said, about how you had to rescue that little girl, I was afraid for her. I saw a paper on the desk that said Deportation Order. I don't speak English, but I know that word. In one of the drawers was a pouch with the girl's passport and airline tickets to Asia. The flight was one-way. Someone had laid out clean clothes on the bureau—a frilly dress trimmed with lace—and I touched it and felt something break in my heart. I wanted a little girl so much. And here was a little girl in trouble. She looked so sick and unhappy in that lady's arms. And me with my boy and another on the way. I thought about it the whole time my sister and I stripped the beds. And I decided that it wasn't right for them to deport her. I told my sister everything you had said. Then the people came back, carrying their food in a bag.

"They put the little girl in bed and turned on cartoons. She was coughing a lot, but then she fell asleep. The grown-ups were on the phone. Then the lady left. The man looked at some documents on the bureau and asked if I'd thrown anything away. No, I told him. Then he walked over to the window. We finished and got ready to leave. The man looked over at us, really staring, and I was afraid he might ask us for our papers.

"Then to my surprise he asked us in bad Spanish if we'd stay with the girl for two minutes while he went to the car to look for something he had misplaced. He said he couldn't leave her alone and didn't want to disturb her because she was asleep.

"'*Sí, señor,*' we said. I went onto the balcony and watched him walk to his car and then I saw another car pull up and two men get out. I almost fainted. It was *them*. The *malditos* from the Hotel Variott."

"Oh no," I said, feeling her fear.

"I ran back in and told my sister. I knew they'd go from room to room and they'd find me with the girl and think I had lied to them at the Hotel Variott. Then they really would kill me. I was so frightened I couldn't think right. I picked up the girl, blankets and all. My sister grabbed her bag and we put the girl and her bag into my cleaning cart. Then I rolled the cart to the door. When Magdalena told me it was clear, we hurried through the hall and down the service elevator. We knew the La Migra man's car was parked in front and the *malditos* were somewhere in the building.

"We pushed the cart as fast as we could to the parking lot out back and nobody even looked at us, two maids doing their work. Lucky for her."

Lupe ran her hand along the sleeping girl's brow, moist with perspiration, and smoothed back her hair.

"When we got to my car, I realized with horror I had left my purse with my car keys in the room. Never mind, we'll catch a bus, I said, but my sister offered to run back and get the purse."

"But what if the La Migra man came back?" I said.

"My sister said she'd explain that we took the girl so the *malditos* wouldn't find her. 'We have to stop hiding behind our fear,' Magdalena said. I was so proud of her then. But she was always the brave one. At home, she joined a peasant cooperative working for the rights of indigenous peoples. That's why we had to leave Guatemala."

"Yes," I said. "But what happened at the hotel?"

"Magdalena ran back inside. She was in the stairwell when she heard a noise. Like the grunts of an animal. Peeking out, she saw two men struggling with the lady from La Migra. It was the *malditos*. One had his hand over her mouth. The other bent down to pick up the hotel key on the floor, next to her briefcase. They unlocked the door, went in with the lady, and shut the door behind them."

"Oh my God," I said. "You got the kid just in time."

Lupe shuddered and bent over them again, touching their cheeks. They slept the heavy, zombielike slumber of children.

"Then what happened?" I said.

"Magdalena ran back to the car. And meanwhile, I had found my purse. It was in the cart, under some towels, but I was so shaken up I didn't remember. I had the engine running when she jumped in.

"'Drive,' my sister said. 'Hurry.' Her face was white and she was shaking. I prayed our car wouldn't break down; it's a piece of junk but it's all we can afford.

"We drove to my house and unloaded the little girl. Then she told me what she had seen. Magdalena wanted to go back to work and find out what had happened. I begged her not to, but she said that when the police came, she would have to explain why we had taken the girl. Meanwhile, she'd be safe at my apartment."

"The two of you were so brave," I said.

"Crazy is more like it. When Magdalena got back, there were police and ambulances everywhere and they were sealing the hotel off. The manager says the police are interviewing all the workers. Magdalena's supposed to go there tomorrow to give a statement. And we're scared and don't know what to do. You'll help us, won't you, Ms. Diamond?"

"Lupe, you know what happened to those INS agents, don't you?"

Lupe bit her lip and stared at the floor. "We heard it on the radio. That's when I called your friend Señor Aguilar and then tried calling you at work. We are afraid. If the *malditos* find us, they'll kill us. If the police find us, they'll deport us. But it's not safe in our home country either. My family is on a list. Because of my sister's activism. The paramilitaries were looking for us when we left. Two months riding freight trains. You can't imagine. At night the gangs came. They demanded money. They beat the men. The women, they . . ."

Something caught hold of her face. With a great effort, she shook it free.

"Lupe, it's okay, you don't have to—"

"I am not ashamed, Ms. Diamond. They will burn in hell for what they did to me."

"And you got pregnant and you . . . kept the baby?" I swallowed hard.

"That baby was Pedrito. I have forgiven his father. I am a Christian, and I prayed for him. And God rewarded my prayers. Pedrito has brought me more joy than I could have imagined. And he is a U.S. citizen. He was born here, with rights that I can only dream of."

Yeah, if he doesn't turn to gangs and drugs and father his own illegitimate son at fifteen, I thought. The statistics were against both him and Lupe.

"Then who is . . . ?"

"The father of this baby?" Lupe patted her stomach. "My fiancé, Rogelio. We will be married next month, when he returns from Guatemala. His mother died unexpectedly and he had to go back."

I stared at her. Scratch the surface of so many lives here and you'll find suffering of biblical proportions and very little redemption.

"When is Señor Aguilar coming?" Lupe said, echoing my own thoughts. "Oh, Ms. Diamond," she said, "it was my fault those people died."

"No," I said. "You did the only right thing."

"They are killers," she whispered. "What if they find out that I have the girl?"

Stung by a thousand needles of apprehension, I realized that we couldn't wait for Silvio any longer.

"I'm going to call the police right now."

She seized my hand, her eyes dancing with fear.

"No. They'll deport us."

"But we've got to get this child some protection."

"And what protection for me and my children and my sister?"

My thoughts flashed to Samson Brenner. He could file

asylum petitions for both of them. If Lupe and Magdalena's story panned out, it seemed to me they had a pretty good case as political refugees.

"I know a man, *un abogado*, a lawyer. He can help. I'll write a story about how you saved this little girl's life. And what you fled from back home. We'll get the Latino community behind you. The INS won't dare to deport you. Or the little girl."

"You don't know how La Migra works," she said bitterly.

"Lupe," I said, "those INS agents were tortured, then shot in the back of the head. Their killers are still out there. Do you want them to come for you? What about Pedrito? And this one?"

I touched her belly and automatically, her hand went there and cradled the beach ball under her clothes. Silvio would be here any minute, and then we could drive the little girl to the police station together.

I called Brenner and left a message about Lupe. There was no time to waste if the cops would soon be interviewing her.

Lupe got the Disneyland-Tokyo bag she had spirited out of the hotel along with the little girl and filled it with frilly dresses and overalls, dolls and stuffed animals, holding everything to her cheek first.

"I washed all her clothes," Lupe said. "They smell nice and clean, like fabric softener."

She handed me the bag, then sat back down and smoothed her skirt over her thighs. But every few minutes, she found something else she had forgotten. A bib. Another toy. A pair of white socks trimmed with ruffly lace. It wouldn't all fit, so she got a grocery bag and began filling that up with baby things too.

I heard a car approach and peeked through the curtains. False alarm. When I turned back, she held the bags out to me.

"Put them in your car."

Another car rumbled outside. We saw the headlights pull into a nearby driveway and idle. Still holding the bags, I let myself out of the apartment and stood on the porch, watching the car. Soon a girl climbed out, wearing a sleeveless top with her bra strap hanging out. Oval bruises marched along her collarbone and up her neck. But the girl seemed unperturbed by the angry purple welts.

"Are you all right?" I asked. Her eyes were lined in black and her brows plucked into thin arches.

She saw me staring and her fingers glided up to her neck. Then she giggled and I realized my error. The torture death of the INS agents had blotted out the possibility of a more benign instrument, the human mouth. Now a word from my teenaged years popped unbidden to my lips. "Hickey."

Embarrassed, I walked slowly toward my car. I threw the bags into the backseat. Serey Rath's worldly belongings.

Another car whizzed up Echo Park Avenue, and I had a bad premonition. Running back into the house, I told Lupe to wake up the child. Silvio would have to follow me to the police station.

I walked back out and scanned the street. I felt trapped and exposed here. In the buzzing light, two moths collided and one fell to the ground, its wings batting weakly.

The girl twitched but didn't wake as Lupe brought her out. We stood at my car and I opened the passenger door and stopped. Weren't kids supposed to ride in car seats or something? But then I realized she was in much more danger of getting killed by those *malditos* than in a crash.

"There are blankets in the brown bag," Lupe said. "Take them and make a nest down there."

She pointed to the passenger foot well, all the while holding the sleeping child and doing that swaying dance all mothers do with babies, some kind of tidal motion involving the hips. I hauled the brown paper bag out of the car, plopped it on the curb, and pulled out some baby blankets.

Then I wadded them around the foot well, padding it so we could lay her down.

As Lupe settled Serey Rath, I hopped up and down with nervousness. Oh hurry, please hurry. My ears strained for car noises. It was a sound I both dreaded and longed for. I wanted the car to be Silvio's, not the killers'. Finally I ran around to the driver's side, slid in, and started the car.

Lupe stepped back onto the sidewalk to take one last look at her little girl. Just then, another car came up Echo Park Avenue and I panicked, jerking my car into gear. Lupe jumped backward, and the passenger door slammed shut of its own accord.

I drove to the end of the cul-de-sac and turned around. The other car had gone past and disappeared. Where was Silvio? It was too late to worry about that now. A right turn onto Echo Park Avenue and then a left onto Sunset and I'd be only a short glide from downtown and Parker Center, the LAPD's central nervous system. Once I'd delivered the girl, I'd demand to know the full story. There was no way they could cut me out now.

Waving good-bye to Lupe, I saw headlights looming at the intersection. With a sickening screech, a BMW tore into the cul-de-sac where I waited to turn, almost hitting me. In the split second as we passed, I saw a face that made me shudder. Remembering the cold metal pressed against my temple, I pressed on the gas and shot forward, only to see a second car bearing down on me from the right. So instead of turning that way, and down the hill and toward Parker Center and safety, I wrenched the steering wheel to the left and I shot up Echo Park Avenue, barreling through the narrowing street as it rose up into the hills. Behind me, I heard the screech of wheels. Someone was gaining on me.

CHAPTER 27

B ehind me, I heard honking and the grinding of gears. He must have recognized me as we passed and pulled a U. But what about the second car? Was Silvio in that one? I thought of calling 911 but my phone was in my purse on the backseat and I had to lose my pursuers, not waste precious seconds fumbling with buttons on a tiny keypad.

Miraculously, the child still slept. *Think, think*, I urged myself. This was my turf, not theirs, and that was my only advantage right now. The terrain was hilly and winding here in the Echo Park hills, an encrypted landscape that repelled outsiders. Where streets started out flat, then morphed into asphalt K-2s, rising and plunging in vertigo-inducing night-mares. Wasn't Baxter coming up on my left? An eighty-year-old roller coaster of a road whose descent evoked free fall. Yes, here it came. Willing my panicked heart to still, I gripped the steering wheel at ten and two o'clock, as my father had taught me years ago. Clouds covered the moon. But they couldn't extinguish the streetlights that illuminated the small clapboard houses and their patches of scruffy lawn. Lights were my enemy, I thought, turning off mine. Behind me came my pursuers, close enough for me to see the glint of their headlights. But ahead was Baxter. I floored it, then spun the wheel savagely to the left. The road climbed steeply. I downshifted into second. Gravity threw me against the seat and pinned the back of my skull to the headrest.

The car crawled its way up, tires gripping like surefooted

ponies. To the right, something rolled and shifted and my right arm shot out, an ingrained reflex to block my little passenger from toppling forward and slamming into the windshield. Then I remembered she was in the foot well.

"Keep both hands on the wheel," my long-dead father's voice echoed in my head, and it soothed me to think of him guiding me through this, even as I realized I was hopelessly alone.

I risked a quick glance at the child and saw the bundle stir. From it came whimpers. I prayed she would lie still and not try to climb into the seat.

"Hang on," I told her, in a soothing tone I did not feel.

From the rearview, I saw a car shoot through the intersection in a blaze of light and disappear up Echo Park Avenue. But my momentary exultation evaporated when I heard the screech of brakes and the whining of a car reversing. My own car was slowing as the engine labored up the steep grade. "C'mon, baby," I cried, sweet-talking the chugging car. "You can do it."

Below me, an engine coughed and began its climb. I was almost at the top now. *Please.* From behind, I heard the grinding of gears, a high revving like a sack of agitated bumblebees that sang to me an insect song of hope. So they had manual transmission too. Easier to stall. I hoped they weren't used to hills. At least not jagged Himalayan mountains like these.

My car's nose was now pointed straight up, nearly vertical, and I was pushing second gear for all I was worth. *C'mon, baby, c'mon, baby.* And then I was at the top, perfectly balanced like the Grinch's sleigh at the top of Mount Crumpet, teetering before plunging down, with a gathering speed that sent my heart plummeting. Despite myself, I covered the brakes. Nearing the bottom, I looked in the rearview and saw a flickering headlight crest the hill. They were still on my tail.

I fed that puppy gas as I leveled out, honking and plow-

ing right through the stop sign. God help any possum or
skunk that decided to cross these pastoral roads tonight, I
thought, not to mention humans. But I didn't think anyone
would be out right now if they valued their lives. From
behind me, I heard whistling sounds and a muffled *pop pop
pop*. They were shooting at me.

I hit the next incline at forty miles per hour, rising again
like a crazy roller coaster and downshifting to get more
power as the slope stiffened. As we rose, I leaned forward
as a jockey leans into a horse, as if angling my weight
would get us there faster. This hill was even steeper than
the first, and I thanked the Lord I drove them regularly, so
that I could almost do it in my sleep, though I knew plenty
of people who wouldn't even dare them in broad daylight.

And then I heard it, the magical sound my ears had been
straining for. Behind me, the pursuing car choked and splut-
tered as the engine died halfway up the hill. Next came a
discordant metallic howl as the driver tried to start the
stalled car. The engine's gears ground mercilessly, and from
the open window I smelled their clutch burning. It was the
sweetest smell I had ever known.

A high-pitched scream of human frustration rose from
below as I crested the hill and teetered again, balanced like
a seesaw at the top of the world. Just before the car plunged
down the other side, I heard the scream deepen to a roar of
alarm and watched in the rearview mirror as the car below
me began to slide backward, the gears zooming menacingly
as it careened drunkenly and jumped the curb. And then I
was over the hump and flying down, sweet freedom, and
behind me I heard metal crumpling as the car crashed
against something hard, then bounced off and crashed again,
continuing its crazy pinball descent to level ground.

I didn't know if the crash would stop them cold or merely
cost them a few minutes, and I didn't intend to stick around
and find out. I wondered where the second car had gone.

Now I could call for help. I reached into the back and groped for my cell phone, and as I did so, I noticed for the first time that my car was listing and bouncing, a steady *clippety-clop* as the wheels turned. I knew what a flat felt like. This was more than that. Those thugs must have shot out my tires. I tried to correct the steering and the car skidded. I slowed down, felt the sleek curves of the phone, pulled it into my lap, and called 911. It was busy. With a sinking feeling, I recalled a *Times* story bemoaning the long wait that people sometimes faced on the city's overburdened emergency line.

On my dashboard, a red light was flashing. The car was whining in an alarming way. I looked through my windshield, into the night, and thought I saw steam rising from the hood. Or was it smoke? If they had shot and punctured something in the engine, the car could explode.

I was on Allesandro now, still heading north. Could I make it to a police station? But that smoke. I couldn't risk it. I looked for a passing car to flag down, but the road was dead still and empty. Pulling over by the freeway, I gathered the girl in her blanket cocoon, feeling the sweet awkwardness of holding a child. She couldn't have been more than twenty-five pounds, I thought, thankful for the weights I lifted at the gym. Yes, that was definitely smoke coming from under the hood.

Then, with the girl in my arms, I ran. There was a purity to the air. Usually safe in bed at this hour, I would hear the yip of coyotes. The hoot of a distant owl. The white whir of traffic. But my ears rang with their own noise now in this silent, screaming expanse of night. I had to get off the road; that's where they'd look for me. I cut across a field. One of my shoes caught and slipped off and I wasted precious seconds backtracking and looking for it in the dark before giving up and running barefoot. I felt my skin bruise and prick as I ran, my soles soft and uncalloused, and wished for the

days of my youth, when I'd practiced walking barefoot on
the sizzling Valley sidewalks to toughen up my soles for the
superhero adventures I would have when I grew up. It was
often hot enough to fry an egg. We had tried when the mer-
cury hit 114. The whites had bubbled up nicely, but the yolk
stayed a bit runny. I had been a tomboy, hair cut so short I
was mistaken for a boy. The grit, the pebbles, the cut glass,
I had endured it all. I was a ninja in training, before we
knew what ninjas were. Then I had grown soft and pliant,
and now when I needed it, I was useless.

My unshod feet throbbed. Hearing a noise, I froze. From
somewhere, a car door slammed. I was back on the road
now. Against my skin, I felt the cold breeze that ushers in
deepest night. It skated across my shoulder blades and I
shivered, the fuzz on my nape rising as if electrified. The
shrubbery on my left side parted and several figures
emerged and crawled along the balcony railing of a half-
built house.

They had masked faces, snouts long and sharp.
"Raccoons," I said, my body going limp. Four of the biggest
raccoons I had ever seen. They set to work daintily nibbling
from the cat food bowls that someone had thoughtfully left
filled.

My legs quivered. From inside her bundle, the little girl
had stopped snuffling, as entranced by the sight of these
strange nocturnal creatures as I was.

I crossed someone's front yard, hobbling on the gravel
that dug into my pale arches. I felt the sharp edges of a hundred granite pebbles pressing into the soft flesh, breaking
through, and knew I had to banish the pain from my head.
At the door I knocked. "Help," I screamed. I waited, ears
alert for any sound, but heard only the silence. I couldn't
wait. I jogged along a walkway, up a set of stairs, and onto
the next street, my breath coming in wheezes. All the houses
here were perched at the top of the hill. I'd have to climb up

steep driveways and stairs to get to the front door. What if the next person I tried wasn't home either? Then I'd be forced back to the exposed road. Instead I cut through the hills, ankles wobbling in the uneven earth as I ran, the tops of my feet scraped by thorny weeds. Crossing an abandoned lot, I scanned the shadowy ground to avoid sharp rocks. My instincts were to put as much space between myself and my pursuers as possible. All the time I clutched the child to me, synchronizing my breathing to her small mewlings, her strange faerie cries, and as I ran, I began to sing softly. I didn't really know any nursery rhymes or bedtime songs, so I sang the first thing that popped into my head.

"High hopes, we've got high hopes, we've got—"

Suddenly, overcome by the black absurdity of it all, I laughed hysterically. Of all the songs in the world, I had to pick this one. But the lyrics wouldn't come. So I clutched her to me and I huffed up the hill, making them up as I went along.

"High hopes, we've got high hopes, we've got hang-me-by-a-very-high-rope hopes . . ."

Halfway up the hill, I remembered I was still on hold with 911. I fished the phone out of a pocket and held it to my ear, wondering what the 911 operator would think if she heard a drunken female sailor crashing through the underbrush, massacring the words to a classic chestnut. Forgetting to scan the ground, I stepped on something sharp and treacherous and almost toppled. Instead, I held tight to the girl and hopped on one foot, lifting up the other. I crooked the cell phone against my ear and shoulder and probed my dirt-encrusted foot. My hand came away bloody. The recording was still playing, telling me to hold on and not to hang up and that the first available operator would help me.

Gingerly, I put my foot down, found it would support my weight, and took a step. Then another. Soon I was doing a crippled lope, dragging my injured foot. Tetanus, I thought as I ran. Rusty nails and infections. I shook my head free of such thoughts. If I didn't get out of here, I wouldn't live long enough to die of tetanus.

Then my house came into view and I realized my homing instinct had brought me here without even thinking. But home wasn't so sweet right now. If the thugs got their car started, would they head here? Or would they see my car abandoned down the street and look for me on Allesandro or Glendale Boulevard? Out in the open, they could pick me off. I decided to wait here. At my house. But just to be safe, I'd enter through the back door. I didn't want to be standing at my front steps, fumbling for the key while a car's headlights pulled up and caught me like a frozen deer.

I unlatched the backyard gate, ran to the stairs, and hiked up to my kitchen door. The child was still whimpering, staring at me, her brow furrowed. I cupped the tiny face, smoothed back hair soft as corn silk. For the first time, I noticed thin loops of hammered gold in her ears. Her charcoal eyes were large and luminous, above a bas-relief nose and delicate mouth. Features barely indented on her face, like half-baked bread that hasn't finished rising. No wonder Americans wanted these children; they were beautiful.

"It's going to be okay," I said.

I knew she didn't understand, but perhaps she caught my soothing tone.

Inside my darkened apartment, I laid the little girl on the couch and she huddled there, clutching the blanket and staring around her. Perhaps she sensed that I wouldn't hurt her, because she didn't try to run away, but looked down with morbid fascination. I followed her eyes and saw that my feet were encrusted with mud and blood. Just then I became aware that they were throbbing violently. I put the still-engaged cell phone on the table and heard the recording telling me to stay on hold. Then, with a drunken gait meant to minimize the weight I put on my mangled soles, I walked over to fetch my house phone and dial 911. Again I got the recording. Now I had two lines going. Who the hell was calling emergency at this hour? Could there be anyone out there who needed help more desperately than me?

Suddenly twin headlights bathed the house in light. Keep driving, I prayed, grabbing the child more tightly and putting my forefinger across my lips in what I hoped was a universal gesture of "Shhh." I heard the engine die.

CHAPTER 28

With one last desperate look at the phones, I wobbled over to the darkest corner of the living room and waited, holding one of the curtains open a slit. They couldn't see in; the house was dark.

I saw with relief that it wasn't the BMW the thugs had been driving. This one was older, American-built. But then who was it? Silvio drove a truck.

I heard the crunch of gravel as someone walked up the path. The tread was heavy and measured, nothing furtive about it, as if fine, upstanding people regularly showed up at my door at 2 A.M. It couldn't be Silvio, even in a borrowed car. He'd be frantic and shouting my name, after arriving at Lupe's house and learning what had happened.

Then came the doorbell. Assassins didn't ring doorbells, they just broke down the door. Somehow this knowledge didn't give me much succor.

"Eve Diamond," a man's voice rang out. Official, as if he had every right to be there. The voice sounded familiar but I couldn't place it.

"Open up if you're there, Ms. Diamond. This is U.S. Customs Supervisor Scott Aiken."

Maxwell's boss, the man he had warned me about. For several moments, all I heard was the thudding of my heart. Then shoes scuffling on the stoop.

"Eve Diamond? Are you there? Please open up. I'm sorry to disturb you so late, but it's important."

I bet it is, I thought. I didn't dare look at the little girl in case I broke into tears. To have escaped the other two men, only to be caught by Scott Aiken. Had he been in the second car? I cursed the instincts that had brought me back home.

"Ms. Diamond?" The voice rose in urgency. "Please open up if you're there. We've been trying to reach you all evening. There's been an investigation and, uh . . . some concerns were raised. We just want to make sure you're okay."

Again there was that unnatural silence. Yeah, right, an investigation, I thought. Whoever heard of a customs official showing up at a reporter's door at 2 A.M.? I'm still not sure why I didn't flee again immediately. Maybe I held out hope that he was legit. Or that a live 911 operator would come on any minute. That Silvio would show up. Maybe I was just too exhausted and my feet hurt too much to carry the girl into the wilds of the night again.

I heard a muttered oath, more shuffling of shoes, then the footsteps started up again, growing fainter. The car door opened. Then it shut. Please, I thought, pushing him into the car and down the hill with every fiber in my brain. But instead the footsteps came back my way. This time they didn't stop at the front door. They scuffed alongside the house to my living room window, then paused, as if to consider something. I realized with a jolt that in my haste to get out the door earlier this evening, I had left the window unlocked. Well, not exactly unlocked, but the house was old and had settled and it took a tremendous effort to make the casement window lock slide into the groove on the sill.

Now I heard a grunted expulsion of breath as Scott Aiken squatted by the window. I could see his shadow against the gauzy curtains. I saw hands reach out and fit themselves against the screen. He gave a tug and it came off, clattering to the wooden porch. Then the hands came up and gripped the glass. With a practiced movement, he shook the panes,

hoping to jiggle loose the clasp. Twice he did it and twice
the metal chattered. When he did it a third time, the latch
suddenly flew free of the clasp and the casement window
creaked and rose. By now I had gathered up the girl and
retreated clumsily to the kitchen to get the biggest knife I
could find and then to the back door, where I huddled
against the dimness of the porch and waited, still not believing that he was about to break into my home. At least I was
armed. Not that I intended to fight him. I'd run away again,
but I had to wait until he got into the house. Then I could
run along the side of the house, back up to the front, and let
myself out the side gate.

This time I resolved to run down to Glendale Boulevard,
flag a car, and beg a ride to the nearest police station. They
would see my disheveled state and the whimpering, terrified
child and know that something had gone horribly wrong.

Now a disembodied leg appeared through the open window and braced itself. Then came his lowered head and
torso, then the other leg. He had a gun in his hand, pointed
straight ahead, and it pivoted with him as he scanned the
room, legs spread apart in a parody of an old gunslinger.

"Ms. Diamond, it's Scott Aiken. If you're here, please
come out. I have to talk to you. You're in danger."

No shit, I thought. I had seen enough. Stealthily, I began
easing down the back stairs, leaning against the railing to
spare my feet. The little girl had twined her arms around me
and buried her head in my neck. So this is what it feels like
to hold a small, powerless child who is totally dependent on
you, I thought, remembering what Ariel had said. It wasn't
just about saving myself, I had to save her. I was consecrated
to a higher purpose. Samson Brenner's words about fighting
injustice person by person came echoing back, infusing me
with determination.

And so I crept down the stairs. The air had turned cold and
the descent seemed endless. Just two more and I would be at

the bottom. Then I'd run. But one of the blankets came loose and unfurled, tripping me, and I went clattering to the ground, knife, baby, and all.

Above me in the house, I heard a sharp intake of breath.

"Ms. Diamond," Scott Aiken yelled out. "Don't run."

And before I knew it he was on the porch and had spotted me and was leaping down the stairs, four at a time, his breath coming in jagged rasps.

I lunged for the knife and shoved the girl behind me, scrambling into a crouch as he froze on the steps and saw me waiting for him, knife gleaming in the porch light.

He put his hands on his hips and laughed.

"Well, I'll be damned," he said. "You found her. You did our job for us."

"Don't come a step closer," I said, brandishing the knife.

"Whoa, whoa, whoa. It's okay, Ms. Diamond. You've got it all wrong. I'm here to protect you. There's some bad folks out there who are after that little girl, and it appears that some of them may know where you live. I'm sorry if I scared you, pounding on your door like that."

We regarded each other with suspicion. He splayed his hands out in front of him like a TV preacher.

"Why don't you put that down," he said, in the wheedling voice you'd use on a child or a lunatic. "And what happened to your . . ."

"No." I tightened my grip. "Stay right there. I called nine-one-one. They'll be here soon. So don't try anything."

He smiled. "Well, I'm glad to hear that. There's been quite enough excitement for one day."

"Stay away," I screamed. I felt a rope of spittle settle back on my chin, but didn't dare wipe it away. All my powers were concentrated on thwarting Scott Aiken.

He took a step forward. His face changed and his voice grew more menacing.

"Let me see her."

"I'm warning you," I screamed.

"Shut up," he hissed. "Stupid little girl. You don't under-stand. They're here, all around us. You'll lead them to her. My car's out front. You two have got to come with me. Now."

He made a move to grab my free arm, but I stabbed at his hand, connecting with tissue and bone. He cursed and trained his gun on my arm. I was screaming hysterically. Wake up, you fucking neighbors, and call the police. But Violetta was off visiting her sister and the houses on either side were empty and for lease. If he was going to kill me, then he'd have to do it now. I wasn't going to let him take me and the child anywhere. I knew what happened to girls who got into cars with bad guys. It was one of my rules. At all costs I had to stay out of his car.

Then we heard the thudding of feet through my apart-ment. We looked at each other, and to my surprise, his face registered as much fear as mine did.

A broad body was silhouetted against the kitchen door.

"Eve, where are you? What the fuck is going on?"

It was William Maxwell. What was he doing here? Unless he had been tailing Aiken . . .

Suddenly, all that mattered was that I was no longer alone with Scott Aiken. Maxwell stepped onto the porch and looked down. At the same time, Aiken ducked under the porch and into the darkness, concealing himself from Maxwell.

Panting heavily and still holding the bloody knife, I stared up at Maxwell, the words jamming up in my throat so I was unable to speak. I wondered what I must look like to him.

"Eve," he cried. "You're all right. Where's the little girl?"

His voice rose in urgency. Before I could answer, we had to deal with Aiken. I searched the darkness so I could point him out to Maxwell.

At that moment, Aiken stepped into the porch light. I heard someone say, "Don't move," and several shots rang out. Without even thinking, I flew through the air toward the child, shoving her into the bushes and falling on top of her. I'm dying, I thought. This is it. The earth was cold and the plants were slick with dew and I wanted so badly to be warm. To at least die without this terrible cold seeping through my veins. Beneath me, a high keening started as the child's hands clutched at my front, writhing and tugging. I arched my back so as not to squash her. They'd have to shoot through me to kill her. I heard a clatter as someone moved down the stairs.

"Get up," a voice said hoarsely.

An arm jerked me upright and to my surprise, my limbs seemed to work, though I stumbled against this new body, my feet no longer able to support me. Was that mud smeared across my face, or blood?

I looked up and saw Maxwell towering over me. Five feet away slumped Aiken. He was on the ground, his pistol still clenched in his hand. From his head, a widening pool of red flowed onto the brown earth.

"Oh, thank God. You were right about him, Maxwell."

But Maxwell was looking at the sprawled figure of his boss. I was glad Aiken was lying facedown and I couldn't see his eyes.

"That was close. Oh God, that was close," I said.

Maxwell looked at me. I thought I might be sick.

"Put that away," I said, pointing nervously to the gun. But he didn't.

"Are you okay?" he asked. "How about the girl?"

He squatted on the ground and made to touch her, but she shrieked and shrank away from him, burrowing toward me.

Maxwell appeared alarmed by the way her voice carried on the still night air. He looked around, then seemed to come to a decision.

"We've got to get you two out of here. Somewhere safe."

"Two guys chased me. They shot at my car. I think they're the same ones who killed the INS people. I was going to drive straight to the police station, but they were following me so I led them on a chase. I lost my shoes and . . ." I held up one bloody foot, but Maxwell seemed not to register it. "I ended up here. I didn't know where else to go."

He looked at me now, as if for the first time.

"You did the right thing. But now we've got to go. Quickly. You're still not safe."

"You were right," I said. "Aiken was after the girl."

Maxwell just cleared his throat.

"We all want the child, Eve. C'mon now." I was listing again, so he pulled me roughly to my feet, and though it hurt like hell, I stayed upright like a good soldier. He moved to pick up the girl, but she wailed and darted toward me.

"Let me. She seems to trust me," I said.

"Fine. Just so long as we hurry."

We climbed the stairs back to my house. Maxwell stopped and looked into each room, as if searching for something.

"Where are her things?"

"Her things?"

"Her bags, clothes, toys, whatnot," he said. "Shrinks say these little tokens of familiarity can help a child feel more secure."

"Oh," I said stupidly.

"Well, where are they?"

I thought for a moment. "They're in my car. Which is on Allesandro. But isn't it dangerous to go back there? What if those thugs have found it and are crawling around?"

I shivered at the thought. I did not want to go back there right now; I had a bad feeling about it.

Maxwell patted the revolver he had stuck back into his holster. "Don't you worry about that." He grabbed my arm, steering me toward the car.

"Maxwell, really, I know what the shrinks say, but I don't think—"

"There may be papers or documents in that bag we'll need as evidence," he said, cutting me off. "We can't risk leaving it there overnight for some little homey to rip off. It will just take a minute."

We got in the car and I held Serey Rath in my arms as he drove, crooning to her and smoothing back her hair, which was wet with perspiration. She snuffled and I took my sleeve and wiped her face with it.

CHAPTER 29

*A*s we approached my car, the hair on the back of my neck prickled. Maxwell drove past slowly, flicking his brights, but the street looked deserted, with the car just as I had left it, one door still gaping open.

He left the engine running and with his gun drawn, ran out and grabbed the bag from the backseat. Miraculously, it was still there. So much for L.A. petty crime.

"There," he grunted, carefully lifting it into the backseat. "Safe and sound."

He spun the car around and we headed back down to Glendale Boulevard and toward downtown. But when Alvarado came up, he took the right fork instead of continuing straight on Glendale Boulevard, the car hurtling south and west down the dark streets, farther away with each revolution of the engine from LAPD headquarters.

"I thought we were going to Parker Center."

"There's one closer."

Some tingle of apprehension went off in my brain.

"Where?"

"Near Koreatown. Rampart. You've heard of that, haven't you?"

He sniggered, and I laughed uneasily with him. Rampart was the name of a scandal-plagued police station in midtown.

His cell phone rang. "What?" he exploded. "Get another car and get over there." A pause. "Right."

He jogged west on Beverly and then left on Western

Avenue. Then he pulled into an alleyway and gave me an oddly somber look.

"Well, here we are."

"What do you mean . . ." I shifted the silent bundle in my arms, clutching her tightly to me.

I didn't get to finish. From the shadows cast by the red-brick buildings, two figures glided out and pulled open the door. Arms jerked me out of the car and into an open doorway. Still barefoot, still holding the child, I stumbled and fell to my knees. The girl gave a soft cry and clung to my neck. They hauled me up and shoved me inside.

"You assholes," Maxwell said. "I give you her address and tell you to follow her, and you manage to lose her."

I didn't look at him. I couldn't. I had bet on the wrong horse and lost. I recalled what Scott Aiken had said in my house, the urgency in his voice. In those first seconds, I had misjudged things terribly.

Without the girl, I might have tried to bolt. I could have thrust her at them and used the ensuing seconds of surprise to run. Even with my cut-up feet, I'd be able to sprint into the boulevard for help. They wanted her, not me. I pictured it but knew I couldn't do it. Our fates were intertwined, rooted in what was growing inside me. The events of the last weeks had led us to this dim room in the shadows, the three ghouls closing in around us. In my arms, the small child whimpered.

"Fire in the hole, fire in the hole," said a nearby voice. The ringing sound of bullets and mortar fire punctuated my beating heart and I flinched, shielding the girl and myself. Now what? Then slowly I straightened, realizing at last where we were. It was the place I had gone looking for the mysterious Frank. We were in the back room of the twenty-four-hour CyberNation cafe. And then I knew I was saved. Opening my mouth, I screamed as loud as I could, a loud and bloodcurdling cry for help. There were probably a dozen young guys not twenty feet away who could rescue me.

Without warning, a fist hit my mouth so hard that I staggered back, my head ringing, suspended in seconds of disbelief during which I had time to consider the discrete hairs of those knuckles slamming against my lips, to feel how thick and wiry they were, before I choked on my own scream and went down, the girl still in my arms. Somehow I remembered to fall sideways. Almost unconsciously, my hand went up and cradled the back of her head.

I heard a gun cock and felt it snuggle up under my jaw, intimate and cold. The little girl's head was buried in the side of my neck and it felt like she was trying to crawl down my shirt. She slid against my flesh, slick now with her own tears and mucus, rubbing her body deeper into me. I prayed she wouldn't look up and see the gun.

"Try that again, bitch, and you're dead."

Not Maxwell's voice. Someone else's. The thug from the Hotel Variott. I didn't move. Someone out there must have heard me scream. Help would soon be on the way.

"Got it?" The gun rotated under my jaw.

"Yes," I managed to whisper.

"Gag her, Jimbo," Maxwell said, throwing the other guy a dishrag.

As he walked toward me I saw it was the Asian guy from the airport, the Crypto-Dad who had arrived at LAX with Serey Rath, then disappeared in the melee. Only to pop up again at the Hotel Variott with his Caucasian friend. The *malditos*.

"Hey," the one gripping me called out. "What if someone out there gets curious and comes to investigate?"

"Those kids?" Maxwell said. "You could explode a bomb in here and no one would look up, much less move. They're hard-wired into their game. Those zombie brains don't have no room for anything else."

I despaired. To be so close to help, and yet so far. But I had seen the glazed look in their eyes. I knew Maxwell was right. How could real-life groans and thuds of boots against flesh compete with simulated ones?

"But then again, it never hurts to be safe." Maxwell strode over and slid the bolt across the door to the front room. "I knew my little investment would come in handy one day."

I watched him with hatred, remembering how he had told me that La Eme laundered their drug profits through legitimate businesses. I guess they weren't the only ones.

With the white guy still holding the gun under my jaw, Jimbo gagged me.

"Tie up her legs and I'll do her arms," Maxwell said, throwing some rope to the thugs I had spent most of the night trying to escape.

They did as they were told. Maxwell checked my leg bonds and retied them much tighter. Then he pried the little girl off me, clapping his hand over her mouth as he did so, and tied her up too, making sure to gag her first. Her tiny body stiffened, then went limp in surrender, and all I could see in her face was those beseeching eyes. He lay her next to me and she wriggled her body like an inchworm, trying to get closer to me. Stealthily, I slid my legs over. She squirmed into me, then lay still.

I figured they would take off with her now, but instead they gathered at the other end of the room and recounted to Maxwell how I had given them the slip. After getting their car started, they had gone back to Lupe's apartment but found it empty, they told Maxwell with a significant look.

Merciful God, I thought. At least Lupe and Pedrito had escaped.

"I think it will be okay," Maxwell said cryptically. He left and returned a moment later with the Disneyland-Tokyo bag, depositing it on a table with much more care than he had used for me and the girl. The three of them began sifting through its contents, pulling out, then flinging aside the clothes, the diapers, the shoes, until they came to the dolls and stuffed animals.

These came in for special scrutiny as the men, with their big, pudgy fingers like grown babies, turned them in the light and shook them. Then the white one laughingly pulled out a switchblade, threw a toy rabbit into the air, and speared it as it came down.

"Easy with that knife, Frank," Maxwell said, and then I knew what I already suspected, that this was the man who had come looking for Serey Rath that first night in the Chinatown hotel. The man whom I had traced to this very cybercafe.

With a practiced tug, Frank eviscerated the toy animal. Batting spilled out. The three of them pounced on the soft innards, tearing them apart, cursing as the thin strips tore into ever smaller pieces, then sticking their hands deep inside the toy to grope for something.

Out in the cafe, a series of explosions detonated. "Fucked him up bad," an exuberant male voice said.

The thugs moved on to a toy cat, with the same result. Next they examined the dolls, pulling them apart limb by limb. Then they reexamined the tiny dresses, tearing out hems and linings. They slashed open the girl's sippy cup. As they worked, their movements grew jerkier, their faces angrier.

Maxwell walked over to me. "Where's the rest of her stuff?"

I looked at him, wondering how he thought I was going to answer him with a dishrag in my mouth. He asked again, nastier this time, and I rolled my eyes together and down. With an angry curse, he started forward and yanked the gag off my mouth.

"What stuff?" I said. "You've got it."

This time his arm swung up and plunged down, hitting me in the stomach. Pain seared across my organs. Before I could recover, he lifted me up, then hit me again, and the furniture tilted as the rubber floor slammed up to meet me. Next to me, the girl groveled and bleated as she tried to squirm under a tarp. I couldn't think about her anymore. I lay, limbs crumpled under me, cheek against the mat, feeling each distinct groove in the rubber pressing roughly against my cheek. Pain was spreading in ever-widening circles from some fundamental point deep inside my belly, and I knew I had to protect myself. I curled into an apostrophe, my bound arms over my stomach, my face averted from them.

"We're not fooling around. Where are the rest of her things?"

"What do you mean?"

"Her fucking stuff. There must be another bag."

"Another bag?" I said stupidly. They had her bag. I couldn't concentrate. Pain radiated out from my lower body, cleaving me like a split piece of kindling. I closed my eyes, but all that beamed across my brain was the girl's passport photo, somber and unhelpful. Somewhere far away, I heard the buzz of a june bug. I opened my eyes and saw a brown carapace moving toward me, but it might have been a hallucination, feedback from my misfiring brain.

"Hey, Frank, you hear an echo in this room?"

He kicked me in the side. I curled like a worm at his feet, trying to scrunch into a fetal position. Just so he wouldn't hit my stomach again. I felt something sticky start to drip, a warm trickle through my underwear. With it came another whooshing pain, slamming into me like a freight train.

Think, I beseeched my brain. What could they want? Anything so as not to concentrate on the pain.

"Kill him," someone screamed in the next room, and I heard the machine gun *rat-tat-tat* of an AK-47. "Man down, man down," a recorded voice said urgently.

The ground seemed slick and warm and slippery, as though I had soiled myself. I clamped my thighs together and felt them stick.

"I'm bleeding," I whispered.

"You ain't seen nothing yet," someone snickered.

"Her bag," Maxwell said again. "Where the fuck are her things?"

Light was slowly beginning to dawn, at the same time that it was beginning to dim.

"What about the bag?"

"The stuffed animals. There's a bear. Where's the fucking teddy bear?"

He sounded like an insane adult regressing through childhood. But I knew now that it wasn't the child they wanted. It was what she carried.

The one called Frank stepped up, bristling the way a dog growls behind its master. "Where is it?"

Maxwell squatted down beside me and I couldn't even focus on the depth of his betrayal. My entire world had shrunk down to the need for him not to hit me again.

"What bear?" I said. "You mean her teddy or her Winnie the Pooh bear? I think she had two."

Vague, flickering images went through my head of Lupe packing various stuffed animals into the little girl's bag. I thought about how ludicrous it was to be conversing with these murderers about children's toys as though we were having a perfectly logical playground conversation.

"That is her stuff," I mumbled. Blood trickled from the side of my mouth and pooled on the floor. I raised my head. "Maybe there's a hidden compartment," I slurred.

"Hand that bag over," Maxwell said to Frank, his voice coiled and sinister as a snake. But Frank must not have moved fast enough because suddenly Maxwell was across the room and reaching for it.

"Let go," Frank objected, as a tussle ensued.

Suddenly both men were pointing guns at each other.

Yes, I thought. Kill each other. A fitting end. Then finally someone will find me and the little one here, tied up and beaten, in the morning.

"Drop it," Maxwell said, and I saw the gun hold steady on Frank, who erupted in petulant whines. Finally the bag thudded to the floor. Whatever contraband they were after, it was worth dying for.

I wished I could give them what they wanted so they would go away. But I also knew that once they found whatever they were looking for, they would kill me. The only reason I was still alive was because they thought I knew something and they intended to beat it out of me. I had to keep them going.

"I'm going to double-check the car and make sure nothing fell out," Maxwell said.

As he left, the other two shifted uneasily. I summoned the last of my energy and raised my head.

"Maybe Maxwell already has what you're looking for," I said. "Ever think of that? Maybe he's hidden it and he's going to go retrieve it once this is all over."

"He wouldn't do that," Frank snapped, but I could see that I had planted something that would bloom a fetid flower.

"Look," he said, "we're going to ask you one more time. Where's the bear?"

"He hid it."

"Where?"

Frank lifted up my head and looked into my eyes with his dead ones.

I lay on the floor, a memory gelling in my brain. Of Lupe packing the girl's things. That wouldn't all fit. So she had brought out a brown bag. That in my desperate hurry, I had left on the curb near her house, next to the giant Dumpsters overflowing with refuse. Today was trash day in Echo Park.

"Maxwell stashed it," I said, knowing I had to hurry before he returned. "He plans to take you on a wild goose chase that you won't survive. Then he'll come back for it. I know where he put it. I was there."

They looked at each other, their eyes crafty pinpricks.

"Tell us. Quick."

I smelled the black rubber mats on the floor. I heard the firing of missiles, felt the reverb as they hit and exploded. Maxwell would be back soon.

"It wouldn't all fit in one bag. So we put her stuff in another bag. There were two. The second one's at . . . at my house," I gasped.

I felt like I might pass out. But I needed to hold on. The seconds stretched, then snapped like rubber bands, one colliding into the other; sixty of them made a minute; string enough minutes together and you'd get an hour. It had to be daylight soon. Silvio would have gotten the police looking for me by now. But how would they find me, here in the back room of an obscure cybercafe? I smelled the warm metallic funk of blood, which mingled with my own rank sweat. My sphincter twitched and I felt boiling lava, clenched to hold it back.

"She's lying," Jimbo said, quiet and deadly, and I knew he was the one I had to convince.

"No, I'm not. There's an attic. It's hidden, inside the closet, and I have a poster covering the ceiling. He put it there. He made me show him the hiding spot."

"If you're lying, we kill you."

"We kill her anyway," Jimbo said. "But we have to find it first. Congratulations! You just bought yourself another hour of life."

Maxwell glided back in silently and stood behind Frank.

"What's this all about?"

Startled, Frank spun around.

"Son of a bitch to sneak up on me like that," he screamed, pointing his gun at Maxwell.

Off in the corner, Jimbo was pulling something out of his waist. The little girl had given up trying to get under the tarp and was lying still.

"What the fuck's wrong with you?" Maxwell said.

"William," Jimbo said softly. "Why didn't you level with us?"

Maxwell whirled. He saw Jimbo covering him. "Why you lousy . . ." he said, and reached for his own gun. There was a shot, and he fell, hand still at his waist, landing with a thud. The girl whimpered and moaned. Over in the corner, William Maxwell made wet, gurgling sounds from deep inside his throat.

Now someone will surely come, I thought, but just then, we heard the echo of synthetic fire from the other room. You could massacre a hundred people in here and no one would be any the wiser.

I saw Frank and Jimbo exchange glances. Now Frank came up to the body, prodded it with his foot. There was a deep groan. "This is for you, buddy boy," he said, and put the gun to the base of Maxwell's neck and fired again, once. The body jerked forward, then was still.

Now he straightened up, looked at Jimbo. "You stay here with her, I'll go check if she's telling the truth."

"No," Jimbo said with the authority I had heard that day in the hotel. "You think I'm going to let you go find it? We go together, or nobody goes."

"What about them?" Frank pointed the gun at me and the girl.

"They look like they're going anywhere?"

Frank walked over and trained the gun on my head. It didn't get any easier, each time he did it. My fists clenched and my temple throbbed.

"You lying, you'll be very, very sorry," he said.

I prayed they would leave, but they sat on canisters of compressed gas they used for the soda machines and actually lit up cigarettes. I wondered if the whole place might blow but was too sick to care. Blood trickled from between my legs, pooling beneath me.

"All right," I heard Frank say. "We drive past and if it's still quiet, we go in. We have to hurry before it gets light."

I lay there, trying to figure it out. Cautiously hopeful for the first time in hours.

"It's there," I said. "Don't you worry."

"Mayday, Mayday," came an urgent recorded voice from the other room.

There was an evil laugh. "Gag her again."

They did, and then they walked out. The door slammed and I heard a key turn in the lock.

CHAPTER 30

I didn't have much time. I had to get free, get the child free. I looked around to see if there was anything sharp I could use to cut my bonds. Maybe I could writhe a few feet. Against the far wall, I saw a sprinkler valve. In case of fire, you turned it on. It had sharp, serrated edges. If I could hobble over there and rub the rope against it, would it weaken and fray?

Before I could move, I heard the key in the lock again. My heart sank. It couldn't be them, back so soon.

Huddled against the floor, I saw a huge and familiar foot encased in a sandal. I looked up, already knowing what I'd see, and still disbelieving it. He stood there, taking in Maxwell's dead body, me bloodied, the floor slick with it, the child trussed up next to me. His foot nudged what remained of a princess doll. Her clothes had been stripped and her limbs torn from her body in the lunatic scavenger hunt that had just ended, leaving doll parts scattered around a naked torso with pink plastic breasts. The doll's porcelain head was cracked and hung from her neck at an unnatural angle, but her trusting eyes looked up at the man and her red mouth curved in a forgiving smile.

The man didn't say anything. His eyes, which had radiated alarm when he first walked in, grew opaque.

"I'm sorry," Samson Brenner said.

As if it had been a big mistake. Gently, he undid my gag. I waited to see if he would undo the other bonds, rush to comfort the child and release her, restore my faith in him, but he just sighed as though it had been a terribly long day and said, "What happened in here?"

And that told me all I needed to know.

"Why, Brenner?" I said. "You of all people."

His eyes glanced away from me, fixing on a crack in the plaster, yellow and peeling where damp had settled. I thought he looked pained, somehow. He didn't answer.

"It just doesn't make sense. You're supposed to be defending her human rights, not destroying them."

Shame bloomed on his cheeks. But something in his face hardened.

"I wouldn't be the first to . . ."

I knew it was crazy to be talking to him like this, with my limbs bound, my body bloody. But I had to appeal to some higher purpose in him. To make him see that we could still have a rational discussion. It was the only gambit left.

"It's obscene," I said. "You, of all people."

"Stop saying that," he snapped. He turned on his heel and stepped away. "You can't imagine how weary I am of living up to what people expect of me. I'm only . . ."

"Human, Brenner? Is this how one human being treats another? It's not too late. You can put a stop to all this. Take my phone and call the police. I need medical attention. I think I'm . . . I was pregnant, Brenner, and they kicked me, they beat me up, and, well, I'm afraid something's ruptured. And this little girl, your poster child for political asylum, after what she's seen today, she's like that shattered doll over there. It will take her years to recover. If ever. But it's better than what's coming down the pike for me and her unless you do something. Save us, Brenner. And redeem your soul."

He listened, his mouth set in a grim purse, and shook his head.

"You don't know the half of it. The only way I can redeem myself is to go through with this to the bitter end."

In him I saw a man who had somehow become twisted beyond his blackest nightmares.

"Sometimes a man just has to take a stand. And this is mine."

I spoke with the deepest disdain I could muster. "You stand for murder? For torture? For the destruction of innocent lives? Oh, that's gonna buy you some real great karma in that Buddhist afterlife of yours."

I wanted to goad him, to shock him into some realization of how wrong he was. But he only grimaced sadly. Then he leaned down to gag me again.

"They've gone back to your house, to try to find the bear," Brenner said. "And if you've misled us, I fear it will go badly for you."

And then he walked out.

I lay there, feeling weaker by the moment, knowing I was losing a lot of blood. It had to be close to dawn. Soon they would be back. I had to get out of here. But how? Did I even have the strength? Then I heard the noise of a window being raised and my heart went to my throat. But the *malditos* wouldn't come through the window, they'd use the door. I watched in disbelief as a small body emerged from the opening.

It was Lorenzo, the gamer-boy from the cybercafe. I saw him in the predawn darkness; my eyes adjusted to the gloom while he, coming from outside, with its streetlights and cars and neon signs, was temporarily blinded. He carried two large canisters, and I caught the oily, overpowering smell of an auto garage. Lorenzo crept closer, trying to make out the three bundles on the floor. He put down his burden and lit a match, his thin, pinched little face suddenly appearing in the light, flooded with surprise.

"Ms. Diamond," he said, coming closer, a look of shocked surprise on his face. "What are you doing here? Who did this to you?" He stopped in front of me and regarded me thoughtfully. Then he saw Maxwell's corpse.

"Is that guy really dead?" His voice was more impressed than scared.

I gestured to the gag, then looked at the little girl. Lorenzo's eyes widened. I stared at him beseechingly now, my eyes flickering to let him know he had to help me and could start with this damn gag. Lorenzo looked around. The match went out.

"Just a minute," he muttered. He walked toward the window and I hoped he would flag a passing car or call the police. But he merely bent down and began lugging over what I now saw were two large jerricans of gasoline. An expression of stealth had come over him.

"I'll untie you both very soon," Lorenzo said, as if he were making me a business proposition. "I've got to do something first but don't worry, it will only take a minute."

Then he heaved up one of the jerricans and to my utter horror, carefully upturned it, dragging the spout along the wall as the stuff gurgled out and the sickly metallic vapors of gasoline filled the room. He hummed as he worked, trickling a trail of gasoline around the room, making sure to douse the computers as he passed by and to saturate the stacked cardboard boxes.

"Why are you doing this?" I screamed, but only a muffled growl came out.

He looked at me thoughtfully, then came and sat down cross-legged next to me. His eyes went to the gag.

"I'm sorry, Ms. Diamond. I can't take that off until I finish. I know you'd just try to stop me, and I can't allow that." His face looked grim. "They've had their chance. Now it's too late. If I can't play here, no one can."

Lorenzo stood up and picked up the canister again. He moved slowly through the room, like he was watering a flower garden. The can was heavy and full. Once he tripped on the rubbery floor and gasoline sloshed against his T-shirt before he could catch his balance.

"Oops, better be careful," he muttered. "I promise I'll untie you and the baby before I light it," he said solemnly. "Don't worry, I would never do anything to harm you, Ms. Diamond. It's just these bastards here."

"No," I screamed, but the cry strangled in my throat.

The oily fumes rose up in waves. The little girl tried to cough, but choked on her gag. I was terrified the whole place would go up before he could make it back to untie us. Now he unlocked the door into the front room of the cyber-cafe and disappeared, hauling a gasoline canister.

The sound of explosions and gunfire grew louder. "Sniper on the right, sniper on the right," a robot voice intoned.

Lorenzo had left an empty canister of gasoline two feet away. I saw it had a rough edge, and slowly I wormed my way over to it. Then I took my bound hands and ran them along the canister. The rope burned and seared the skin on my wrists, but I kept going, breathing through the pain, gag-ging on the fumes, motivated by the knowledge that I had to hurry. Finally, it started to fray.

At the same time, I heard a buzzing sound that seemed to be coming from inside the dim room. Something crackled behind Maxwell's dead body. I saw a single red spark, then a shower as something thin dislodged itself from the wall and swung around. Too late, I realized that when Frank had shot Maxwell, one of the bullets must have hit some kind of elec-trical wiring, and it had smoldered for a while and finally caught. Again I screamed but no sound came out. In seconds, the sparks would catch on the gasoline and the room would become an inferno.

The door opened and I heard Lorenzo's high, clear voice:

"Hold on, Ms. Diamond. I'm just about done, then I'll run back and release you both."

"Mayday, Mayday," a mechanical voice called. Explo-sions rocked the front room, and for once I did not know if they were real or simulated. "We need backup now," the voice said.

With one last frantic effort I dragged my bonds across the can and they rippled and came free. Then I fumbled for the knots at my feet. Lorenzo came through the door, skipping gleefully. I tried to motion to the sparking wire but he began to walk over and at that moment, there was an almost instantaneous explosion. I heard a scream as the boy turned, his hair and chest on fire, arms outstretched like a lit scarecrow's.

There was no more time. Pushing painfully to my feet, the gag still in my mouth, my legs still bound, I hopped over to the girl, scooped her up, and hobbled toward the door, feeling the heat from the flames singeing my eyelashes as they licked higher and closer. Behind me rose a wave of flame and smoke and I coughed and buried my face in the girl's hair, crouching down as low as I could without losing my balance. My eyes stung and I fought to keep them open. Amazingly, my feet didn't hurt anymore but each step jarred my insides painfully. I could see into the front room now. Unbelievably, kids were still at the computer terminals, too engrossed in the game to notice. Or maybe they thought the explosions came from someone else's game. Then came the heat as flames rushed in, following the gasoline trail, and began leaping from terminal to terminal like an incendiary game of tic-tac-toe.

As I reached the front room, I saw kids finally wrenching themselves away, throwing off their headsets and pushing back their chairs with stupefied stares that dawned into terror as they looked around. The fire was raging all around as they staggered out the front door, still dazed and unbelieving.

Now the entire cybercafe was ablaze, walls of fire rearing up around me, flames licking greedily at the terminals as the plastic bubbled and machines melted in the heat. I inched my way forward, willing my body to move faster but terrified I would fall and doom us both. Behind me, something exploded.

Lorenzo ran screaming past me, his arms flailing, swathed in fire, a creature of the flames. Sheltering the girl against my chest, I hopped, my entire being focused on the front door. I had to make it. Just ten more hops. My breath came fast; then I couldn't breathe. I feared I would choke on toxic smoke and lose consciousness. Black stars danced in my eyes. Out of the corner of my vision, I saw a timber come crashing down, heard another explosion, and a surge of adrenaline coursed through me, propelling me forward. Then I was through the door and on the outside, falling into the arms of a slickered fireman holding an ax.

CHAPTER 31

M uch later, I lay in a hospital bed with crisp white sheets. Opening my eyes for a split second before my head burst and I had to close them, I saw I was hooked up to an IV drip.

Silvio sat beside me, pale and worried. Head bent, he held my hand in his and stroked it gently.

"What a fool I was," he whispered. "Let her and the child live and I will . . . I swear to you by all that is holy."

"Silvio," I said groggily.

"*Querida*, you're awake!"

I tried to lift my head from the pillow. Silvio bent over me, cradling my head.

The little girl. Lorenzo. I wanted to ask if they were okay. But the words swirled around in my head, the letters elongating into thin black columns of smoke that rose into the night and were gone. I slept. I dreamed of flames licking at my body. I screamed, waking with a start, only to realize no sound had left my lips. I felt the hospital bed shake as Silvio leaned against it, then his head dipped and stopped somewhere near mine. I tried to focus but everything went black.

From far away, I heard noises and felt movement. Slowly, light ebbed from the room. I felt my hand lifted by two large, cool hands. I heard Silvio whisper to someone that I was still asleep. Slowly, the footsteps swished away. Then Silvio murmured, "When you wake up, *querida*, I'll take your hand in mine, just like I'm doing now, and I'll kneel at the bed, see, just like I'm doing now, and I'll say, 'Eve, will you ma . . . ?'"

Sensing the gravity of his words, I struggled to lift my head, to see him. But the effort was too much. I fell back and swam through dizzying depths.

Time passed. Men and women in white coats came. They prodded me and changed my bandages. A woman with warm, antiseptic breath bent over my IV, changing bags. Once when I woke, the bag had turned red, catching the light of the sun that rose on the horizon. I drifted, bobbing on waves, then submerging, deep bubbles of exhaled air rising to the surface.

When I woke again, the bedside light was on. Silvio sat there watching me. A look of tenderness stole over his features.

"How do you feel?"

I struggled to raise myself onto one elbow. No dizziness. "Better," I said. "I think I'll make it."

"It's been two days. You lost a lot of blood. A hemorrhage," he said.

I put my hands up to my face and felt bandages. My lip was cracked and swollen and my jaw was throbbing. I flexed my feet and felt bandages. Pinpricks of pain. I felt like I was lying in a pool of stickiness. I groped at my backside and my hand came away red.

"Oh, Jesus Christ, you've bled through again." He pressed a button and called for a nurse.

"You're losing the baby. For a while we thought that . . . but they beat you up too badly. . . . The artery above your cervix ruptured. The placenta detached."

"I don't even know if they call it a miscarriage at this stage," I said dully. All this talk about babies didn't seem real. But then an image of a flesh-and-blood child swam before my eyes.

"Silvio, is the little girl okay? And the boy Lorenzo?"

Silvio took my hand.

"That boy had burns over ninety-five percent of his body. He died on the way to the hospital."

He paused to let it sink in, but the right image wouldn't come. All I could think of was Lorenzo swirling into infinity with his beloved numbers.

"And the little girl?" I asked, tasting metal in my mouth. An alloy of fear and hope.

"Good news to report there, *querida*. She's safe; they have her in the pediatrics ward and they're running tests. The nurses love her, they've adopted her, and there's someone in the room with her all day, singing songs and playing games. She's doing much better."

"Have you been here this whole time?"

He smiled wanly. "How could I leave you?"

"Every time I came to, I saw you. I thought I was hallucinating. I dreamed you were about to ask me something very important."

"You've lost the baby."

"Yes," I said. I remembered the blows, the trickle of blood quickening to a torrent. My insides pulsed with pain. My heart felt hollow, scraped out. I hadn't ever really let myself believe it, but now that it was gone, I felt a desolation that threatened to overwhelm me.

"It was growing inside of you and they killed it. They killed our baby."

I turned onto my side to face the wall. My hand slid out of his grasp. "I think it was for the best."

Silvio's voice went on, filled with wonder. "Within forty-eight hours, I find that you are bearing our child and that our child is dead. If only I had gotten to Lupe's house ten minutes earlier. There was an overturned truck on the freeway and—"

"It wasn't a child, it was a fetus."

He made an exasperated sound. "It would have grown into a child. Our child."

We were silent for a moment. I stared stonily at the wall.

"That's not the way you were talking the other day."

"Eve, I . . . I'll be sorry for that the rest of my life. You caught me off guard. I was in shock. But I stand by what I said earlier. What I started to say, before we knew for sure you'd lose it," he amended. "Will you marry me, Eve?"

I rolled over. I looked at him, standing over my bed, his face naked with emotion. A very rare sight. But behind that was a solidity I could reach out and hang on to. I had always known that about him. He was not a man given to grand or frivolous gestures. This was for real.

I thought about Tim, and everything I had gained and lost in several brief weeks, all I had been through, and I knew that I wasn't yet ready to be anyone's wife.

"I love you, Silvio," I said. "But I can't accept your proposal like this. It was noble and honorable when you thought the doctors might be able to somehow save our baby. But they couldn't," I said hollowly. "So I won't hold you to it."

"I don't care if you're not pregnant. You'll get pregnant again. We'll have loads of babies."

I faced him full-on now. "But I don't know if I want loads of babies," I said. "I'm barely used to the idea of having a boyfriend."

"But I'm asking you to marry me," he said with bewilderment.

"I know. And I love you for it."

"It's that other guy, isn't it?" Silvio said suddenly. "Your old boyfriend."

It brought home anew the pain and shock of Tim's death.

"He's dead, Silvio. He died at my house of a heroin overdose. I didn't love him anymore. We weren't together. I was just in love with what we once had. I finally realized that."

"My God, Eve, what hasn't happened to you in the last two weeks?"

I smiled crookedly.

"Well, I still haven't gotten the okay from the *Times* lawyers to see you."

"Fuck them," he said expansively.

"Yes," I said slowly. "It's time to live my life. Our life."

Just then, a familiar face loomed on the TV screen above my bed. Some kindly nurse had turned the volume off but left the picture. It was Samson Brenner. Then he disappeared and the screen showed Brenner's house in South Pasadena. Then that was gone too and a perky Latina anchor with a grave face mouthed words I couldn't get.

"Silvio, turn that up, will you?"

He looked with annoyance at the screen.

"I'm trying to talk to you about our future," he said with exasperation. "Can you stop being a journalist for just one minute in your life?"

"Oh, never mind," I said, realizing that the remote was tethered to the bed. I fumbled for it, found the volume button and punched it. But now a commercial filled the screen. "I have to find out what happened. That was Samson Brenner. He's the one behind all this. Oh my God, I've got to tell the police."

I flipped through all the channels, pausing for a moment at one that showed me and the little girl being led from the burning Koreatown cybercafe by uniformed firemen, the blinking, sleep-deprived gamers clustered in the background, severed by violent force from their electronic umbilical cords. Then I clicked until I found more local news.

"And when we return," said a pert black anchor, "we'll have news of the grisly discovery on North Sierra Bonita Street in South Pasadena. Stay tuned."

After sitting through what seemed like interminable commercials, the anchor came back on. With an old clip of Brenner giving a speech next to his Statue of Liberty replica she announced: "In the latest development to the sensational story that KABC has been bringing you for the past forty-eight hours, police responding to neighbors' complaints about gunshots in this quiet suburban neighborhood found prominent immigration attorney Samson Brenner dead in his home office of a single bullet wound to the head. Brenner, a lifelong humanitarian, social activist, and self-proclaimed Red Diaper baby, was best known for winning a $122 million class-action lawsuit against the Immigration and Naturalization Bureau in 1989 that forced reforms in how the federal agency investigates asylum claims.

"Police say the gun found near Brenner's body was legally registered to him and had never been used before. Authorities are looking into whether this death is connected to his representation of an abducted two-year-old Cambodian girl named Serey Rath who was rescued early Thursday from a burning building in Koreatown along with *L.A. Times* reporter Eve Diamond, who had been investigating the case.

"As we told you yesterday in a KABC exclusive, the body of ten-year-old Lorenzo Valdez and a missing U.S. Customs official named William Maxwell were unearthed from that wreckage, and another U.S. Customs official, Scott Aiken, was discovered dead of gunshot wounds at reporter Eve Diamond's house early yesterday. Police are hoping that Diamond, who has been lying heavily sedated in a local hospital due to injuries sustained in the burning building, will be able to provide crucial information about these deaths. Already in custody in connection with the case are Frank Stassio, a former LAX airport employee, and James "Jimbo" Dong, a known affiliate of the Bamboo triad with a criminal record for heroin trafficking, who were discovered breaking into Diamond's house early on the morning of the killing and are now being held on suspicion of murder. Authorities say they'll be looking for any links between this latest death and the trail of carnage involving the abducted girl that has led from LAX to Chinatown to Silverlake to Koreatown and now South Pasadena. Police, who decline to say whether a suicide note was found near the body, say they have launched an investigation into whether Brenner, known for his abrasive manners and extravagant lifestyle, had enemies or money problems. The immigration attorney was forty-eight and leaves no known survivors."

"Oh my God," I said, my head spinning.

I was relieved to hear that the two remaining thugs were in custody, but something still troubled me. It was hard to think of Samson Brenner taking his own life. He was too narcissistic for that, too in love with life and its many pleasures. Maybe someone just wanted to make it look like a suicide. Maybe I should be asking for an armed guard. I turned to Silvio.

"The police have been here three, four times a day, trying to interview you," he said. "Each time the doctor tells them to come back later."

Suddenly we saw an image of a grim-faced Alexandra Dubrovna and a bewildered Lothar Klimt, giving a press conference in front of Tong.

"They've been all over the news, saying that kid you saved was theirs, that they were going to adopt her next week," Silvio said. "They were in Cabo for two days and had no idea. They demand that the kid be released to their custody from the hospital. Star Saffron, they call her."

Just then, a knock came at the door and Silvio jumped up to answer it. When he came back, he said, "It's the police again. I told them to check with the doctor. I'm sure he'll say no. You're in no condition—"

"I am too," I said. "And I think I'd better tell them everything I know for my own safety."

The phone rang. Silvio picked it up and I saw him nodding. He put his hand over the receiver and mouthed *"L.A. Times."*

"Give it here," I said, struggling up in bed.

"Hello, Eve. Boris Johannsen. Glad you're finally up and at 'em. We're, uh, running a story about the kid and those

dead Customs folks and want to jack up the drama with
your eyewitness account. Then we've got an obit running on
Samson Brenner, which I'm sure you can add to. But first,
tell me how you found that little girl. Wait one sec. I'm
pulling the story up now."

Boris Johannsen was an assistant editor who liked to stand
close to female reporters as they typed, angling his crotch to
their eye level and then jiggling the coins in his pocket. He
had once asked me out, suggesting in the same breath that he
would be happy to put in a good word about me to his old
friend Jane Sims. Ever since then, I had avoided him. Now, I
tried to forget that and focus on work.

As Johannsen typed, I started with the phone call from
Lupe Monterosso and took him through the Echo Park
apartment, how I had found the girl asleep on the futon, the
wild hillside chase, the death of Aiken, the double-crossing
of Maxwell, the abduction to the cybercafe, and how I broke
free as the fire engulfed us. I left out Brenner, figuring I'd
save him for the other story.

"Jay-sus," Johannsen said as I stopped for breath. He
asked me to hold on and I heard him yelling that he needed
twenty-five more inches and for someone to go fetch the
Page One editor.

"And so you carried her out in your arms?" Johannsen
said.

"That's right."

"And when you stepped outside, on the curb, what did
you see?"

"I told you, the firemen with the axes. In those silly yellow slickers. Then I must have fainted."

"And the weather?"

"The weather?" I stopped, wondering what relevance
that had to anything. "It was overcast."

"You sure about that?" He sounded disappointed.

"Yes, I remember clearly. You know how it is when time

slows to a crawl and your perception is heightened almost unbearably."

"Not really." Johannsen's voice had an unpleasant nasal whine. "But then the sun came out."

I thought about it. "Nope."

"Not even for a minute?"

"It was overcast. I already told you. The sun didn't come out."

"Yes, it did." I heard him typing.

"No. It. Didn't."

"You were suffering from smoke inhalation," Boris Johannsen said. "The sun did come out. Only for a brief moment. But its rays shone down on the child you held in your arms, like some modern-day Pietà. And it was an omen. You realized that from now on, everything would be all right for this kid. Then you collapsed."

I heard him tapping his florid lies at the keyboard.

"You can't write that. It's not true."

The typing stopped.

"Sometimes a story has a higher truth that isn't immediately apparent, even to a seasoned reporter like you. The single ray of sunlight. That's our kicker. It will be beautiful."

"But it didn't happen that way." I was frantic to make him see that.

"You just don't remember," he said. "Yeah," he called to someone in the newsroom. "I'm sending it right now. Just tweaking the ending.

"You're traumatized by what you've been through," Boris Johannsen went on. "It's normal. Now tell me all about that Samson Brenner. We'll give him his own story, alongside the obit. This is great; you have the inside track and we're gonna scoop the pants off the *Daily News*. Eve? Eve, are you there?"

I hung up.

CHAPTER 32

I told it all to the cops later that day, though. Every single last bit of it. I hope I gave them enough to put the *malditos* away forever, because I sure don't want them getting out and looking for me. The next day, who should show up in my room but Alexandra and Lothar Klimt, holding Serey Rath and bearing fragrant food in boxes marked TONG. Alexandra fed her bits of noodle and pork with a pair of ivory chopsticks and for the first time, I thought she might make a fine mother after all. As for the little girl, she was laughing and clapping her hands. I couldn't believe the change and marveled at her resiliency.

It was two more days before I was able to get out of the hospital, so I had a lot of time to think about things and to reflect on what had gone down.

I was beginning to feel safe again. I was also starting to mourn. For a bright, misguided little boy who had perished in a fiery inferno of his own making. For my ex-lover. And for the life that had been growing inside me. It came upon me at odd, unbidden times, reducing me to tears. For what had been lost. For the enormity of it. Something I hadn't even begun to acknowledge. And I knew that I was forever changed, would never look at children the same way without calculating the years, wondering if that boy or girl could have been mine.

If anything, it had drawn Silvio and me closer. When he picked me up from the hospital, I made him drive us right to Lupe's apartment. We sat in the tiny kitchen and held hands under the table while Lupe made Nescafé. Silvio had hooked her up with his lawyer, and things were beginning to look good on her asylum claim.

"Why do so many Latinos drink instant coffee?" I asked when Lupe served up three steaming cups. "Doesn't Guatemala produce great coffee beans? Or is that Mexico?"

"Both," Silvio said. "But the coffee companies have convinced the Latino public that it's more posh to drink the powdered stuff. So they harvest all those uncouth beans and send them north. And what do they get in return? Overpriced Nescafé."

"Thank you, NAFTA," I said, sipping my sludge. "Now, Lupe, we have an important question for you."

"I'll do my best," she said. She too had spent a lot of time answering questions lately. To police, INS officials, and reporters. The Spanish media had declared her a hero and editorials all over the city were urging that she be given asylum in return for her brave deed.

"What happened to that brown paper bag you packed that night for the little girl? Remember how it wouldn't all fit in her tote? Did the trash truck pick it up the next morning along with everything else?"

"No, of course not," Lupe said. "I took it with me when I fled to my sister's house with Pedrito that night."

Silvio and I looked at each other. I had told him everything.

"Do you still have it? Can we see it?"

"Sure." She went into the bedroom and returned with a brown bag. I dumped the contents out onto the table, looking in vain for a teddy bear.

"Lupe, didn't she have a teddy bear with her?"

Lupe looked startled for a moment, then thought back. "No, I don't think so. Why?"

"Well, apparently that's what those guys were after all along. Not the kid. There were drugs inside. That's how they transported them. In the stuffed animals of these kids they brought into the country."

We sat and sipped our Nescafé, digesting this.

"Maybe the toy got left behind at one of the hotels where they stayed," Lupe said. "I never saw it."

Then I remembered something, and I flashed back to Berta Rodriguez at the Clínica Los Niños, touching a bear on the shelf in her examining room. A teddy bear.

"Oh my God, I think I know where it is."

With trembling hands, I called the clinic and asked to be transferred to Dr. Rodriguez. She came on and I introduced myself, and of course she remembered me. I had been on TV nonstop the last week. Now I explained about the bear.

"Why, yes, it's funny you should mention it," Dr. Rodriguez said. "She did leave a bear behind. I kept it for a few days, then I put it out in the waiting room. Our little patients have to wait so long to be seen. We try to keep games and books and stuffed animals out there for them, but they never last long. I suppose someone took it home and is now giving that bear a lot of love."

My heart almost leaped out of my chest at the incongruity of it. A poor toddler somewhere in L.A., sleeping on $10 million worth of heroin.

"Any idea who might have taken it home? I mean, could you check your records?"

"Well, like I told you, we get hundreds of families here each day. We're the only game for miles around; it's terribly overcrowded. And I have no idea when this might have happened. I think it would take a court order for us to nail down such a thing."

"Don't be surprised if you get one, Dr. Rodriguez," I said.

CHAPTER 33

The next day, the *Times* carried a story with the coroner's conclusion that Samson Brenner had died of a self-inflicted gunshot wound. The cops theorized that he wouldn't have been able to live with the shame once his role in the drug-trafficking gang became public.

But the question that nobody seemed to be asking was why he had gone bad. Brenner's feelings toward the huddled masses had seemed genuine, and even necessary. His personal life might have been a disaster, but he'd still had this noble abstraction to cling to, and it was his lifeline. And as I turned this thought around in my brain, I began to understand that the answer I sought lay in that deep chasm between the two halves of his life.

I thought about Brenner that night at Tong and his impassioned speech about the little girl. I thought of Tim's dying words. And I thought about the TV, panning over the California Craftsman house in the nicest part of South Pasadena. The house where I had spent a full night, watching Brenner work his magic on an exhausted cadre of civil rights disciples, keeping them fired up into the predawn hours, long after I had fallen asleep on the leather couch, only to wake and find a bright-eyed underling pulling out yet another file.

The more I thought about it, the more I knew I had to be right. Alone in my house that afternoon, I embarked on the biggest round of spring cleaning I had ever undertaken.

That night, I drove to South Pasadena. A FOR SALE sign was planted on Brenner's lawn, and it creaked back and forth in the wind. One of those mild Santa Anas that blow down from the canyons and through the arroyo, ruffling everything in its path like the careless hand of God.

The big house exuded an emptiness that said no one would be coming home anytime soon. I sat in my car for two hours but didn't see anything out of the ordinary. Finally, I got out and walked along the driveway into the backyard. The carriage house was dark and deserted-looking.

I got back in my car and thought some more. What if I was wrong? I decided to give it another twenty minutes.

About fifteen minutes into my wait, headlights approached. A motor slowed and gears growled as someone downshifted. The car turned slowly into the driveway and pulled all the way in and out of sight. It was a cherry-red Karmann Ghia.

I waited while the ornamental iron gates creaked open, then clanged shut. After ten more minutes, I walked to the gate, making sure not to slam it behind me as I let myself through. I saw warm lamplight spilling out through the closed curtains in the carriage house. The front door was closed.

She would have been in a hurry. She might not have remembered to lock it. I reached for the knob and turned it slowly, careful not to make a sound. It gave and I pushed the door in. For a moment, I stood there, looking over the living room. Two bulging suitcases stood in the entryway, a coat and umbrella slung over them. Farther in, Brenner's Aibos sat on the coffee table, their heads cocked as if to detect intruders. I tensed, then relaxed as I realized they were turned off and would not be baying any alarms tonight. Next to them lay a hammer and what looked like the door to a small safe. Taking one last look around to make sure no ambush awaited me, I stepped inside. The house was silent as a catacomb.

Crossing the living room, I came to a hallway and was glad it was carpeted, glad for the sneakers I had worn to sprint away fast if the need arose. I came to the bedroom and looked in on an unmade bed, clothes scattered on the floor, half-eaten plates of food. I kept walking. The room at the end of the hall must be the bathroom. It was closed so I turned the glass knob silently and the old iron hardware slipped free with a metallic sigh. I stepped over the threshold, still gripping the knob, ready to slam the door in her face.

She was slumped on the toilet, head against the wall, naked except for lacy bikini underwear. I remember that detail, because it's why I didn't notice the blood at first. I thought it was part of the rose petal design.

Her eyes had rolled back in her head, leaving a wide and startling expanse of yellowish white. Her skin was sallow, her small breasts withered, ribs pushing through so savagely and distinctly you could have plucked them like a harp. She moved her arm slowly, as if to push me away, and I saw old scars. Blood from a fresh puncture dripped from elbow to wrist like red tears, then onto the tile floor. It was the girl who had woken me up, rooting through the file cabinets the night I had fallen asleep in Brenner's living room.

"I know you," she said groggily.

She struggled to bring her eyes into focus. Her affect was flat, her manner unperturbed. We had all been wrong about Brenner. He had the biggest Achilles' heel of anyone I had ever met, and I was staring at her.

"He loved you," I said. "He ruined his life for you."

She blinked and didn't answer.

"I know all about you," I said. "I know who you are."

"You don't know shit."

"For you, he gave up everything he found holy. In the hopes it would save you. And this is how you thank him?"

I kicked the syringe at her feet and it spun on the floor, hit the sideboard and ricocheted across the room.

My words had roused her. She raised her head.

"He never gave a shit for anything except himself."

I wanted to keep her talking. There was so much I still didn't understand.

"He was a complicated and flawed man," I said. "I know it doesn't give you any solace to hear this, but he thought it was as important to save the world as to save one person. And he had faith that you'd come out all right. That's why he let you back into his life."

She took a strand of hair and put it in her mouth. Sitting there on the toilet seat, her thin shoulders curved, her face puckered in a defiant scowl, she looked like a perverse toddler.

"He let me in because I asked," she said. She didn't seem to mind that she was mostly naked in front of a stranger, blood dripping down her arm. I guess if you have enough heroin in you, it's hard to get worked up about these things.

"Tell me," I said.

I heaved myself up onto the tile counter and swung my legs like we were two schoolgirls gossiping in the lavatory.

She leaned her head back against the wall.

"Why should I?"

"I'm not going to try to convince you," I said amiably.

She regarded me with surprise. But I had reached into my purse. I fumbled past the compact, the lipstick, the checkbook. And pulled out a yellow and red packet with Thai lettering. The cops had overlooked something. I figured that if Tim had hidden one hit, he might have hidden more. And after several hours of searching this afternoon, I had found it, stuck inside a plastic sandwich bag and taped to the inside of my toilet tank. Just above the waterline.

Now I held it up.

"No sir, there's nothing I can say that will make you talk to me. Not one word."

She licked her cracked lips. She was high now. But junkies are like squirrels, always thinking ahead to the scarcity of winter. There was never enough.

"So?" I asked. "Do we have a deal?"

She gave me the look of disgust I deserved.

"Where do you want me to begin?"

"How about with how and when you came back into his life."

Now she pushed herself off the toilet, went to the door, and pulled a bathrobe off a hook. The heroin seemed to have revived her. It's a myth that junkies always lie there slack-jawed after shooting up. Lots of addicts are perfectly functional, so long as they get their fix. I had learned that much from Tim.

She walked shakily out to the living room, sat on the couch, lit a cigarette, and tucked her feet under her like she was about to file her nails. Always making sure she had that red and gold packet in her sights.

"We had a terrible falling-out five years ago. I don't know if he told you," she said, dropping the spent match into the ashtray.

"You tell me."

She took another puff.

"I had already started using and I was always broke and asking him for money. One month the car broke down. Then my rent went up. In winter I needed new ski equipment. In summer it was a trip to Hawaii. He kept sending checks, but he's not stupid. Finally he flew up to Berkeley to check up on me. My roommates told him I had dropped out of school months earlier. That they had kicked me out when I got behind on the rent. Somehow he tracked me down to the Tenderloin. Discovered I was on the needle. He tried to force me onto a plane back to L.A. but I screamed so much he nearly got arrested for kidnapping. After that he'd still send checks occasionally when I'd call up crying, begging him, promising to get straight, but finally even that dried up. He never knew I had moved back here."

"So how'd you support yourself?"

She twirled a strand of hair around her finger.

"I met a guy. He worked security at LAX. Had access to

stuff coming in from Asia. They'd confiscate it and no one knew the bag was a little lighter when it got to the evidence locker."

"I can see why you'd like such a guy."

She just looked at me with those empty eyes.

"But one day he took too much, and someone noticed. They were getting a grand jury together. So he and his friends had to take care of the problem."

Sandy Morse, I thought, flashing to the four motherless children, the overwhelmed grandmother now stuck raising a new generation. How wrong I had been to think that she and Maxwell were having an affair. It was the residue of murder I had seen in his eyes that afternoon, not love. To these people, Sandy Morse was just a "problem" to be gotten rid of.

"And your boyfriend's name was?"

"Frank," she said. "He's in jail."

"I've met him," I said, shuddering at the memory of steel against my temple. "Prince of a fellow. So you were in L.A. this whole time and you never tried to look up Samson? Until now?"

She stared at the ground. "It's a big city. And I was busy. We were moving dope and other stuff regularly with one of Frank's pals from Customs. That's how we got involved with the kid."

"I'm missing something."

"It's a twofer, see. Actually, a three-fer. "The 'wife' is being trafficked in to work as a prostitute. The 'husband' is with the organization, escorting her in. The kid's the decoy. And the courier. Feed 'em codeine to knock 'em out on the trip over."

"Lovely," I said, but again the sarcasm was lost on her.

"So everything's working like clockwork; this kid's made a dozen or so trips and they're getting ready to switch papers on her, farm her out for adoption. That's the third part. We work with an agency here."

"Hands Across the Water?"

She pinned me with her eyes.

"Well, if you know that, you know that Lia helps find them good homes. Often their passport's been flagged and it's too risky to fly them back."

"So Lia's in on this too?"

Nothing surprised me anymore. Still, I felt let down. I had needed to believe that her motives were pure.

The girl shrugged. "Lia's happy with the thought of rescuing one more kid. She's one of life's true innocents, poor thing. Living in squalor with her flock. You won't find me doing that. Anyway, this was Serey Rath's last trip. But then that shoot-out happened."

"What caused the shoot-out?"

She gave me an odd look, sensing that suddenly she was holding a valuable card.

"Can I see that dope for a minute?" she asked coyly.

I rubbed the packet between my fingers. "Sure."

She made to grab it and I snatched it away.

"Just as soon as you answer my questions."

I dangled it in front of her again, just out of reach. She seemed mesmerized, her mouth slightly open.

"What happened at the airport?"

She jerked her head back several inches and blinked.

"The sooner you tell me the sooner you get your reward."

She seemed to consider this for a moment. She lit another cigarette.

"The Russians were tailing our people," she said. "Frank figured they planned to follow them out of the airport and fake an accident to get the dope. But something was wrong with their papers. They panicked and grabbed for it right there at the airport."

"But Customs was already onto you. That's what Maxwell told me."

She gave a snort. "Yeah, he warned us too. Don't worry,

we would have gotten rid of the goods long before they
busted us. If only it had worked according to plan. Instead,
the Russkies jumped us and Jimbo shot them. He managed
to get away in the confusion that followed. But he left the
dope behind."

"He left three people dead and a small child stranded," I
said.

"That's what started this whole mess. She had the stuff
with her and we had to get it back."

Her voice was muffled, and I strove to make out what she
said.

"Frank was on her trail right away, but L.A.'s a big place.
Then I read that Samson was representing the girl."

I recalled how Samson had implored me to wait a few
days before printing his name, and how I had laughed at
him and arrogantly claimed journalistic privilege. So I had
played an unwitting role in this debacle too.

"I wrote that story," I said. "But how did you get him to
go along?"

She smiled, and her pinched face lit up like that of a
wicked, clever child.

"We didn't need to. That was the beauty of it. We just
needed to find out where they were keeping the girl.
Something only her lawyer would know."

"And so Rachel Brenner, prodigal daughter, came back
into her daddy's life?" I said softly.

She turned away. I crackled the packet between my fingers
and almost despite herself, she turned toward it. Her lower lip
trembled.

"I called him, all tearful, and told him I'd just finished a
ninety-day rehab stint in Arizona and needed a place to live.
He was so eager, it was pathetic. He cried on the phone.
When he picked me up at Burbank airport, he called me his
baby and hugged me. He said I looked so thin and
unhealthy. I told him he looked fat."

"What a way with words. And he had no idea?"

"Why should he? That first night, he made macaroni and cheese even though I always hated it as a kid. And he told me about his newest case. He was so excited. He said it was going to be big."

"But he didn't tell you where the INS was keeping her, did he?"

She leaned forward and ground out her butt. A concerned expression flitted across her eyes. "You gonna give me that dope soon, right?"

I shook the package. "It's here, safe and sound. Got your name on it."

She nodded, then settled back on her haunches.

"Of course not. I snuck into the house at night and went through his court documents. I used to work for him after school so I know some law. And he does a lot of work at home. It took a few days but finally I found it. In a cabinet in the living room. He hadn't locked it because they were working through the night."

"I saw you," I said. "You woke me up. We had a conversation."

I thought about the father working around the clock to save the kid while the daughter worked equally hard to undermine him. That very morning, she'd sicced her boyfriend and Jimbo on the right hotel.

"It was because of you that those INS agents got murdered."

She shrugged. "They had what was ours," she said. "Or so we thought. If only that little shit at the cybercafe hadn't lit the place on fire, we would have gotten the stuff back. Now it's gone, up in smoke along with everything else."

I didn't tell her any different.

Instead I said, "But you still haven't told me how Samson got involved."

"After those INS agents got murdered, he began to suspect.

He checked the file and found that the document with the hotel name was missing. He confronted me before I could put it back. He was a wreck. 'I trusted you,' he said. 'I opened my heart and my life to you.'"

She took a hit off a new cigarette, then lifted her head and blew the smoke out thoughtfully.

"But then I made him an offer he couldn't refuse."

"I wouldn't have thought you could buy him off so easily."

She gave a cold, shrill laugh. "Not with money. I had a more valuable currency."

"What was that?"

"Myself," she said, tipping the ash from her cigarette. "I confessed everything, then threw myself at his feet and said they were going to kill me if I didn't come up with the dope. I promised that as soon as I got it back, I'd get clean. He could check me in himself. I told him he had never been there for me as a kid but now he had another chance to prove that he really did love me. I told him no one else would get hurt so long as we got the stuff back."

I recalled Brenner that night at Tong, the animation in his eyes as he talked about redemption and making things right. I had assumed he was referring to Serey Rath. But Samson Brenner had been thinking about an entirely different little girl. His own. Why hadn't he seen that she was just using him? Manipulating the bond between parents and children by subjecting it to this fake litmus test of love.

"Two wrongs never make a right," I said.

She moved on the couch to get a better look at me.

"Are you so sure?" she asked. "Wouldn't you go to the mat for your child?"

I felt her words reverberate inside me. I thought about Serey Rath, whose mother had sold her, of Lorenzo dancing in the flames while his mother worked two jobs to support them, of Ariel and the child she gave up, of Dorothea Wainright, who would now have to raise four grandchildren alone, of Samson Brenner making the ultimate perverted sacrifice. And of course, of Silvio's and my child, lost before it had barely begun. Of all our failed efforts to connect, of the way the deck is sometimes stacked, and of how well-meaning parents can destroy their children.

I'll never know, I wanted to tell her. *My child died because of me*.

"I'm not a mother," I said.

"Then who are you to judge?"

"You used him," I told her. "You had no intention of getting clean."

Her fingers moved across her leg, pinching the stubbled material of the bathrobe.

"We used each other. He wanted absolution. I wanted my dope back."

"So he agreed?"

"It was the last thing he could do for me."

She leaned over to light another cigarette.

"Rachel," I said. "Your father made the ultimate sacrifice. He took your fall. Then, unable to live with what he had done, he killed himself. You're the only one who can clear his name."

"His name?" Rachel said. "What did I ever care about that? I just wanted him to be home for dinner. Do you know what a burden it was, growing up with a saint? I felt selfish for wanting him to come to my piano recital. Not that he ever did. But how did he think I'd turn out, when I've felt guilty since the day I was born for wanting his love? For taking him away from his important job of saving the world? He didn't leave me a penny, you know. Luckily, he never bothered to change the combination on the home safe."

She threw her cigarette into the ashtray and looked around wildly. Her gaze settled on the hammer lying at a jaunty angle on the coffee table. She jumped up, her fingers closing around the handle. Alarmed by the grim purpose on her face, I shoved my hand into my jacket pocket and groped for my own weapon. I raised my other arm, ready to block and trip her if she came at me with the ball peen, but she lifted it above her head and brought it down with a grunt of satisfaction on the closest metallic dog. The Aibo skittered to the floor. To my horror, it began to rear up on its iridescent legs, growling and lunging, its switch somehow activated by the force of impact as it hit the ground.

"Horrid thing," Rachel screamed, hitting it again. The growl turned into a squeal, and the robot dog ducked its head and scrabbled away. Rachel cut off its escape and brought the hammer down again. The Aibo yelped once, then went still. She crouched over it now, smashing it again and again, a wild cry rising from her throat each time the hammer connected with metal. Soon it lay shattered and broken, springs and coils jiggling from its innards, this hated creature upon which her father had lavished his love. Then, careful not to activate the other one, she put it on the floor, shivering as her hands touched the cold metal. With methodical concentration she pulverized the second Aibo. When it lay in pieces, she straightened up. She was panting, her eyes flecked with rage and hatred. Then, as I watched in stunned silence, Rachel let the hammer drop and sank back on the couch, rubbing her eyes with balled fists like a small, hurt child.

"He loved those robot dogs more than he loved me, his flesh and blood daughter," she sobbed.

"That's not true," I said. "You should have heard his voice soften when he talked about you."

"No," she screamed. "It's a lie. And now he's abandoned me again. The only thing I own is that car out there. I'll be driving it into the sunset now. You just caught me, you know. Couple more hours and I'll be on a plane."

I nudged a shard of metal with my toe. The Aibo's doomed attempt at escape had shaken me. Nothing in its programming could have prepared it for such an assault, and yet it had reached back into some deep pool of canine consciousness and tried to fight, then run away.

"Tell me one thing," I said. "The red Ghia. Do you know someone named Tim?"

She sniffed and looked up, her face streaked with tears. "And then you'll give me the dope?"

"And then I'll give you the dope."

"Jimbo sent him to find out about the girl. He said he used to know you."

"I did know him, but that was a long time ago and . . ." I trailed off, unable to continue. A dull ache was starting up in my chest.

"Can I have that stuff now?" Rachel's voice rose in a petulant whine. "I thought we had a deal."

"Here," I said, tossing it onto the coffee table. "You've earned it. Frankly, I think you've earned a lot more, but that will be for others to decide."

She made a greedy lunge for the packet and didn't see the door close behind me. Once outside, I reached into my jacket and turned off the tape recorder. I removed the kitchen knife I had brought. Squatting by the Ghia, I stuck it into the back tires until I heard the sucking whine of air escaping.

Then I let myself out the iron gates, sprinted for my car, started the engine, and pulled away, dialing 911 as I headed downtown to write my story. This time, I didn't care how long it took the operator to answer. Rachel wasn't going anywhere. And I had long ago flushed Tim's heroin down the toilet and replaced it with baking soda. I had my own good name to worry about.

ACKNOWLEDGMENTS

I would like to thank the members of the Silverlake Fiction Workshop, who encouraged this work from the beginning, and Ellen Slezak, Leslie Schwartz, and Donna Rifkind for their careful reading and suggestions for an unruly manuscript.

Thanks go to the late, great *New Times Los Angeles*, especially Rick Barrs, Jack Cheevers, Susan Goldsmith, Tony Ortega, Jill Stewart, Suzanne Mantell, and Meredith Brody. A special thanks to tragically departed "Bite Me" columnist Maryne Oppenheim, whose kind heart and sparkling prose will long have a place in my heart. R.I.P., *chica*.

Thanks to the journo grrrls, especially Cathy Siepp, Amy Alkon, Emmanuelle Richard, and Hillary Johnson.

Thanks to Anne Borchardt and Susanne Kirk for being my literary shepherds, and to Susan Moldow, Louise Burke, and Maggie Crawford for support and enthusiasm.

For technical advice, I am indebted to Dr. Alice Frausto, Douglas Ingraham, Marissa Roth, Marlene Aguilar, and Jose Ramos. Any mistakes are solely mine.

I couldn't have done it without the S & S team of Sarah Knight, Kelly Kervick, Sanyu Dillon, Angella Baker, John Fulbrook, and Henry Sene Yee.

To Barbara Seranella, thanks for your eleventh-hour help with the title.

And most unabashedly, thank you to David, Adrian, and Alexander.

Scribner proudly presents

Denise Hamilton's

new Eve Diamond novel

SAVAGE GARDEN

Available in May 2005
in hardcover from Scribner

Turn the page for a preview of *Savage Garden*. . . .

All day the sun had baked the concrete, sending waves of heat shimmering skyward. Now a breeze blew through the canyons of downtown and people crept from buildings and sniffed the air like desert animals at the approach of night.

Perched at the edge of a fountain outside the Dorothy Chandler Pavilion, I felt my mood lift along with the crowd's. It was opening night at the city's premier theater, and soon we'd file inside and leave the pavilion empty, save for the saxophonist nestling his instrument in its blue velvet case, the bums sifting the trash for crusts of panini, and the cashier savoring a cigarette before closing up for the night.

I sipped my Pinot Blanc and watched the café grill send up wisps of woodsy smoke. It felt delicious to be anonymous and alone, the crowd swirling around me in a way that suggested New York or Budapest or Paris. This was as good as L.A. street life got, even though it wasn't a street at all, but a concrete slab ringed by theaters and concert halls.

My city had been wrenched from the desert, willed into being by brute force and circus barkers who sold people on a mass hallucination that became a reality. And for generations, the loudest of those barkers had been my newspaper, the *Los Angeles Times,* and its onetime owners, the Chandler family. Their name graced this square, with its reflecting pools and shimmering fountains. It was sheer hubris to send water cascading skyward in the heat of an L.A. summer, but then, water had been the original currency of this land. Without it, the city would sink back to chaparral and sagging clapboard, a provincial outpost doomed to fitful dreams.

Then a man was walking toward me. He wore a *guayabera,* the accordion-pleated shirt of Mexico. His black, wavy hair cascaded over his collar. As always when I saw him from afar, before recognition hit, a wave of impersonal pleasure passed through me at his beauty. Then the pleasure grew personal and my heart quickened as I realized it was Silvio Aguilar, the man who occupied an increasingly large part of my heart.

We had met the previous year when I profiled the music-promotion business that his family had built from a swap-meet stand into a multimillion-dollar empire. The attraction had been instantaneous and mutual, but Silvio was grieving over the death of his brother and I wasn't supposed to date sources, so we tried to control ourselves, which only made things more explosive when we finally did get together.

I loved his complexity, his Old World chivalry, the masterful control with which he ran the family business and the utter abandon I saw in his eyes when he made love to me.

Straddling the formal Mexican culture of his parents and the easygoing American ways of his home, Silvio grappled daily with the duality of his existence and wondered where he belonged. Sometimes he turned inward, retreating into pride and moody secrecy, and then I wondered how well I really knew him.

But tonight promised to be perfect. One of Silvio's childhood friends had written *Our Lady of the Barrio,* the play that would premiere in less than an hour, and we had front-row tickets. It was a triumph the entire city could celebrate, because Alfonso Reventon was a gangbanger who had been saved by the arts, a playwright whose tales of streetwise magical realism brought him growing acclaim and commissions. *Our Lady of the Barrio* was poised to be a smash hit. As Silvio drew closer, though, I saw a harried look on his face.

Striding up, Silvio looked at his watch, frowned, then took my hand and caressed it absently.

"Hullo, Eve."

"Is something wrong?" I asked. My lover's mind was clearly elsewhere.

"I was just backstage, dropping off flowers for

Alfonso. The stage manager says he's hysterical. It's forty-five minutes to curtain on opening night and Catarina hasn't shown up."

"Who's Catarina?"

"Only the leading lady." A hint of incredulity in his voice.

"She's probably running late. You know those temperamental actresses." I was determined not to let his words shatter my good mood, the Old World theater aura, the air like crushed velvet against my skin.

Silvio's cell phone rang and he answered sharply. "Yeah?"

On the other end, a man spoke quickly. I could not make out his garbled words.

Silvio listened, then said, "Absolutely. You can count on me."

He hung up and scuffed his feet against the concrete, refusing to meet my eye.

"Look, uh, Alfonso says Catarina's not answering her phone. It's a fool's errand, but he's asked me to go by her house. It's only ten minutes away."

My vision of a romantic evening, a shared drink at the fountain, holding hands in the darkened theater, vanished.

I looked at my watch: 7:20. Curtain was at 8:00 P.M. There was no way I'd be able to sit still, knowing Silvio was out there, hunting down the star.

"I'm coming," I said.

By the time we wheeled his truck out of the underground lot, seven more minutes had elapsed.

"At this point, it would take a Medivac helicopter landing on the roof to get her there on time," I said.

Silvio grunted and kept driving. Tense and focused, he swerved in and out of traffic, his eyes on the road.

"So what's Catarina's story?"

Silvio explained that Catarina Velosi was a fiery Latina. For years she had been Alfonso's muse and his lover. But she was capricious. Unstable. The final straw came when she took off to Berlin mid-run with a composer who had scored one of Alfonso's plays. An understudy took over the part, and Alfonso had no choice but to get over the actress, too. He married, fathered a child, and grew increasingly prominent. His gangbanger past, when it was mentioned at all, lent him a greater nobility for having escaped it. His plays received critical raves and he won a MacArthur "genius" grant. Eventually the artistic director of the Mark Taper Forum commissioned a play. In Los Angeles, it was theater's Holy Grail, and Alfonso yearned to be its Latino Lancelot and Arthur combined.

"He wrote *Our Lady of the Barrio* for her, you know," Silvio said. "Every woman he creates is based on Catarina."

"What a burden."

Silvio shot me an insulted look. "It's an honor," he said. "But the director didn't want to cast her. He had heard the diva stories. So Alfonso got on his knees and begged. Then he had to beg Catarina to audition. She thought it was beneath her." Silvio exhaled through clenched teeth. "Oh, he ought to kill her for this."

The truck shot out over Glendale Boulevard and up around Echo Park Lake. Silvio turned right, making his way along a hillside street above the water.

Catarina Velosi lived in a freshly whitewashed duplex draped with bougainvillea and banana plants that was set back from the street. We trudged up a short flight of stairs to the entrance. From the house next door came the loud thumping of Spanish rap, the faint smoky scent of something sweet. Pot?

Silvio knocked, then stepped back. He knocked harder, calling her name. He swore in Spanish and yelled something at the rapper's window. A young man with a shaved head and a scraggly goatee stuck his head through the yellow curtain.

"Can you turn that down for a second, I'm trying to reach the lady in there," Silvio said.

The man scowled and withdrew his head. A moment later, the volume was lowered.

Silvio knocked again and tapped his foot. He tried the knob. It wouldn't turn.

"Poor Alfonso," he said. "Every critic in town is there tonight."

"How do you know she hasn't turned up by now?"

"He promised he'd call." Silvio tapped the mute cell phone in his pocket.

He stood there, undecided, for a moment. Then he said, "Do me a favor. In my glove compartment, there is a screwdriver. Could you please get it while I check the window?"

Eager to help, I walked down to the truck, somewhat encumbered by my outfit, a 1940s cocktail dress of raw silk with a scoop-neck that curved nicely around my hips before ending just above the knee. It was a frock made for sipping Cosmopolitans and clapping for encores, not hiking down a stone staircase. The high-heeled black leather pumps didn't help, either.

Inside the truck, the glove compartment held only papers. I looked on the floor and groped under the seats to no avail. Then I ran up to tell Silvio the bad news. He was standing at the front door, now ajar, and shoving something into his pocket. I heard a faint jingle.

"I thought it was locked."

"I jimmied it."

"Well that's good because I couldn't find the screwdriver."

He gave me an odd look. "Well, never mind."

And with that, he stepped into the house. From somewhere inside, we heard a low, guttural growl. Silvio stumbled backward. At the same time, something soft brushed against my bare legs. I shrieked. Craning my head over my shoulder, I saw a fluffed orange tail disappear into the shrubbery.

The cat's eerie *rrowwwlll* reverberated up my spine.

Silvio straightened, pulled a tissue from his pocket and sneezed several times, his allergies distracting him momentarily from the task at hand. Then he grasped the door with renewed determination.

Inside, the windows were closed and the curtains drawn against the heat. Silvio flipped on the light. When my eyes adjusted, I saw the room was empty. An overhead fan chugged at high volume, its blades whipping the hot, tired air.

From the recesses of the house came faint music, male voices singing plaintively in Spanish, their voices twining in the style of long ago.

"Someone's home," I said.

Silvio ignored me and moved into the living room. Mexican serapes were slung over a leather chair. There was a rattan couch upholstered with toucans and tropical flowers. A low coffee table scattered with Hollywood trade publications. I saw a purse tipped on its side, spilling out coins, a brush, and a leather wallet.

"Catarina?" Silvio called.

I followed him, sniffing the air. The sickly odor of gas from a tidy, two-burner stove in the kitchenette mingled with the overflowing contents of an ashtray, each butt kissed by bright red lipstick. Two mugs of half-drunk tea sat on a 1950s chrome table. Above the sink, colorful Fiestaware cups perched along the windowsill. A bleeding Jesus crowned in thorns gazed out from a dispenser of "Wash Your Sins Away" hand soap. An avocado seed stuck with toothpicks sprouted in a cloudy glass, its vines tumbling to the floor.

"Catarina, are you here?"

The tiny house seemed to absorb and muffle his words. Silvio walked into the hallway, floorboards squeaking under his weight. The singing was louder now, voices naked and anguished. He pushed the bathroom door open and called again, but the only answer was the slow gurgle of a toilet tank. He headed for the bedroom and I followed.

The music seeped out, crooning a silvery ballad from long ago. I could make out the lyrics now and they seemed sinister, at odds with the soaring melody and sweet harmony.

> *Eres una flor carnivora*
> *En un jardin salvaje.*
> *Bonita pero fatal*
> *Devorando mi corazon.*

I went back over the words in English to make sure I had it right:

> *You are like a carnivorous flower*
> *In a savage garden*
> *Beautiful but deadly*
> *As you devour my heart.*

As the strings died away, I heard a scratchy whir, the pop of a record ending. Then the click of a phonograph arm rising, moving then dropping, the needle nestling back into the vinyl groove in a blur of white noise. The song started up again. It was plaintive and mournful, like the cry of a heron at dusk when the river holds no more fish.

But Silvio wasn't listening. At the bedroom arch, I heard his sudden exhale.

"Maybe you should wait here."

His voice was unsteady. He turned to block the doorway, but I was already looking beyond him.

The bed was empty, its white eyelet sheets pulled back and tousled. A torn screen balanced precariously against the pillow. The sash window above the bed, which looked out onto an alley, gaped open. I craned over Silvio's shoulder to see more.

"Is she there? Let me see. For God's sake, I'm a reporter."

"Catarina?" Silvio said.

You are like a carnivorous plant

Silvio stepped into the room. He strode to the closet and threw it open, pushing aside clothes and meeting only empty space. With a cry of exasperation, he strode to the linen hamper and lifted the lid. Nothing. His eyes roved, considering where else a woman might hide.

In a savage garden

He brushed past me and soon I heard him outside, calling hoarsely for Catarina.

I walked over to examine the bedsheets. There was no blood as far as I could see. Maybe the screen was old and warped and had fallen in. Maybe it had been torn for years.

Beautiful but deadly

My gaze went to the window and I thought I saw a faint smear of red on the sill. I bent closer. It was rusty, already dry and slightly ridged, like a furrow in a field.

As you devour my heart

Why was this song playing over and over? It was as though someone was trying to tell us something.

"Silvio," I called, but he didn't answer.

I moved to Catarina's bedside table, filled with framed photos. All held the same pale-skinned woman with long black hair, an oval face, and dark eyes. She had a disquieting way of staring directly into the camera, the force of her will radiating through the photo and into the room. My eyes flittered over more frames. There she was, clad in a negligee and cradling a cocktail in her *The Thin Man* phase. Defiant with a group of zoot-suited men, arms filled with flowers. Dressed in a T-shirt and boxers, her thin, sculpted arms flung around a boyfriend. One of the photos had fallen to the sisal carpet. It lay face down. I squatted to pick it up, then thought better of disturbing a potential crime scene. Slowly, I stood up.

"Don't touch anything," I called to Silvio. "You

already have to explain to the police why your prints are all over the knobs."

I considered Catarina Velosi. A single woman who lived alone. I pictured her putting on her favorite album and twirling around the room in the arms of an imaginary lover. Sliding between those sheets for an afternoon nap before her *Taper* debut tonight. Then someone raising the window left unlocked in the heat, slashing the screen and climbing in. Every woman's nightmare. Did he have a gun or a knife? Had he put it to her head? Had a struggle ensued as she tried to fight him off, a struggle in which some-one's blood spilled on the windowsill?

Or had she put on the record for a lover before they headed to bed, then left in such a hurry that she forgot to take it off? What if Catarina Velosi was striding onto the *Taper* boards to mass applause right now, her biggest concern a case of pre-show butterflies? And Alfonso so relieved he'd forgotten to call?

I pictured us two hours from now, gathered back-stage. We'd make toasts and drink champagne, and Silvio and I would turn this into a funny little anec-dote. Remember that night Catarina gave us such a scare . . . ? But what if that wasn't it?

There are pivotal moments in everyone's life, when they see the future laid out clear as a seer's vision, and there's both a hallucinatory and a hyper-real quality about it. *Can this really be happening? Is it what my gut tells me it is? Should I go on my instinct, even though I'll be roundly embarrassed if I'm wrong?*

As you devour my heart, the man crooned.

Slowly, I pulled my cell phone out of my purse.

"There's something that looks like blood on the windowsill," I yelled to Silvio. "I'm calling 911."

"No," he said, his footsteps echoing back into the house. "Wait."

Amazingly for L.A., an operator came on immediately. I took a deep breath.

"I'd like to report a break-in," I said. "A woman is missing. There's a dried substance that looks like blood. Echo Park, above the lake. The address is . . ."

"Don't," Silvio said. He ran up, a queer look on his face as he realized I was already talking.

"I'm waiting, miss," the operator said.

"What's the address here?" I asked.

Silvio stared at me for a long moment.

"862 Lakeshore," he finally said.

It was only after I hung up that I considered the apprehension I had seen on Silvio's face.

"Why did you tell me to wait?" I asked.

The corner of Silvio's mouth twitched.

"Because there's got to be some logical explanation," he said. "Catarina's pulled these stunts before. And frankly, I'm worried that bad publicity could kill Alfonso's play."

His answer seemed anything but frank.

"What if Alfonso's not the one getting killed," I said, leading him to the rusty red mark on the sill. "What do you think that is, nail polish?"

He looked at it and repeated that there must be an

explanation. I thought he might be trying to convince himself. But then I thought of something else. Again, I heard the jingle in his pocket.

As the sirens drew closer and the singers wound up again with their beautiful and disturbing song, I asked my lover: "You have a key to her apartment, don't you?"

**Purchase a hardcover copy of
Denise Hamilton's newest novel**

SAVAGE
GARDEN

available May 2005, and receive a $2.00 rebate by mail!

Mail the original store receipt for *Savage Garden*
(ISBN 0-7432-6192-5) dated on or before June 30, 2005
along with your name, address, and zip code to:

**Simon & Schuster
Marketing Department/Denise Hamilton
1230 Avenue of the Americas, 12th floor, New York, NY 10020**

Not sure what to read next?

Visit Pocket Books online at
www.SimonSays.com

Reading suggestions for
you and your reading group
New release news
Author appearances
Online chats with your favorite writers
Special offers
And much, much more!